LISA HELEN GRAY
MAX
A CARTERS BROTHER NOVEL BOOK 4

©Copy rights reserved
2016
Lisa Helen Gray
All rights reserved
No part of this publication may be reproduced or transmitted in any form or by any means, electronic or mechanical, including photocopy, recording, or any information storage and retrieval system without the prior written consent from the publisher, except in the instance of quotes for reviews. No part of this book may be scanned, uploaded, or distrusted via the internet without the publishers permission and is a violation of the international copyright law, which subjects the violator to severe fines and imprisonment.

This book is licensed for your enjoyment. EBook copies may not be resold or given away to other people. If you would like to share with a friend, please buy an extra copy, and thank you for respecting the authors work.

This is a work of fiction. Any names, characters, places and events are all product of the author's imagination. Any resemblance to actual persons, living or dead, business or establishments is purely coincidental.

DEDICATION

To my Readers, this one is for you.

LISA HELEN GRAY
MAX
A CARTERS BROTHER NOVEL BOOK 4

PROLOGUE

MAX

Fuck! My head hurts.

Why did I agree to have a drink tonight? Oh yeah, because it was the only thing getting me through the poxy prom my twin brother dragged me to.

After everything he's been through the past few months, I owed it to him to go. He's been banging on about it for a while, wanting his girl to have something special.

Throwing the bloodied tissue in the bin next to me, I glare at the copper who arrested me when he walks past. I can't believe I'm taking the entire rap for this shit.

My story is that I was attacked, picked up a spray can to *hit* said attacker, and accidentally got spray paint on the church.

I'm also lying through my teeth.

I *was* spray painting the wall *but*, in my defence, I didn't know it was attached to the church building. I also didn't know the kid I started fighting with was a community support officer until it was too fucking late. I thought he was some graffiti artist, pissed that I had tagged his spot.

I'd been dead fucking wrong.

I chuckle just thinking about it. The lads I went with to the church all pegged it out of there when they heard the sirens, leaving me to fight with the officer. If I hadn't been so drunk I would have gotten away, but shit happens. Plus, I really needed the drink tonight. How else would my twin brother get me to go to the fucking school prom?

The minute I hear the door to the station slam open, I begin to wish they had locked me up in a cell for the night. At least then I'd be protected.

My granddad is mates with someone who works here so he made a call and got them to keep me out of a cell for the night. I'm pretty fucking lucky, but you won't hear me voicing *that* out loud. It also helped that it's a Friday night and the cells are filled up with other drunken idiots.

I know for a fact my granddad is going to be pissed, but I'm more concerned about Maverick, my eldest brother. He's been riding my ass more and more lately about getting my act together. Another reason I wished they'd put me up in a cell, the other is because I could really do with getting some shuteye.

Speaking of Maverick, I hate letting him down. I hate letting all my brothers and Granddad down, but this shit isn't done intentionally. I just get roped into shit that sounds freaking awesome at the time. Like the time I ate a goldfish as a dare. It was all fun and games until I had nightmares thinking he was still alive, swimming around in my stomach. We had to go to the hospital in the end just to make sure.

R.I.P. Goldy.

Sad times.

"What were you thinking, son? A church? A Goddamn church, Max," my granddad roars and I jump, wincing when I notice how pissed off his expression is. I'd normally laugh right about now, making a pun about using God's name in vein, but his red faced, angry expression and the veins in his neck that are pulsing angry is a sure sign that he's deadly serious and not to be messed with.

"Would it better if I told you it was only the community hall *and not* the actual church?" I ask sheepishly, not knowing when to keep it shut.

"Don't be smart with me, boy. You're in a world of trouble," he starts, but he's cut short by the other prick that arrested me.

"Are you Mr. Williams, Max Carter's guardian?"

"Yes, sir."

Sir? Fucking sir? Does he think we're at school? Jesus! Words are gonna happen between the two of us when we get back; he needs to take a walk. Bloody Sir! Pfttt.

"Can we talk?" the officer asks my granddad who replies with a stern nod. He follows him to the door but stops before entering. He turns my way, glaring holes into my head. I blow him a kiss and sink back down into my chair, hoping like hell this hangover is gone by tomorrow morning, or later today for that matter. I've got early practice and our coach will be pissed if I miss one more game. The season is almost out so I don't want to spend the last three games sitting on the sidelines watching my team lose.

Eyes on the side of my head start making me feel uncomfortable, so I turn my attention to the community support officer who I got into it with, and grin. He's been sitting in the chair in the far corner with a couple of icepacks since we arrived. Poor fucker is gonna hurt in the morning.

"I'm not one to let people down, mate, but I'm just not into you."

"Pardon?" he snaps, looking at me like I just asked him to suck my dick.

"Sorry, I must have done something to your hearing when I clipped ya. What I said was, I'm...not...in...to...you."

"Max, I'd shut it if I was you," Maverick warns, walking in with Malik behind him.

Great! A family outing.

"Well, unlucky for you; you're not me, so the point's mute. Also, did you call the whole family tree? And did you bring any food?" I smirk. I'm starving. I haven't eaten since I arrived at prom and even then it was freaking party food which I hate. I don't get why they have those small sausages and sausage rolls. They wouldn't fill a baby up, let alone a bunch of growing teenagers. I even told the principal that, reminding her that we're all growing lads. It didn't go over well that's for sure. I guess I'm lucky she loves my sorry ass.

"Shut the fuck up, Max. Do you realise the trouble you're in? Do you even fucking care? What is wrong with you?" Maverick shouts, pacing in front of me with his hands pulling at the ends of his hair.

Ladies and gentlemen, I represent to you my brother, Maverick Carter, the worry wart. I swear no one can worry like he does. He's gotten worse in his old age but I don't want to be the one to tell him that. I wish he'd get laid more, he'd probably relax somewhat. The bloke is twenty-four yet acts like he's eighty.

"I just feel like I don't get enough attention," I tell him, pretending to sniffle. I groan when a hand smacks the back of my head. I should have known that shit wouldn't work. I get enough attention. Fuck, I'm centre of mostly everyone's.

"You need to tone it the fuck down, Max. Granddad and Maverick have bent over backwards for you and this is how you repay them? What is wrong with you lately?" Malik butts in when Maverick walks off.

I shrug, not wanting to answer. He wouldn't understand anyway. None of them would. The door opens but I don't bother looking up to see who it is.

"Is that our nan's great-aunt's, daughter's, daughter?" I ask sarcastically, closing my eyes.

"Joan? Is everything okay?" Malik asks and my head turns to watch Joan storm in. Next Myles walks in with Kayla behind them, his eyes scanning the rest of us before settling on me. He looks disappointed but I don't care. Kayla looks worried; clinging to Myles' arm. She's a good girl, one I approve of and she's cool. When I take in her appearance I notice how flushed she looks and I burst out laughing gaining everyone's attention.

"Looks like Myles got himself some," I laugh and everyone in the room stares me down with a glare.

Shit! Wrong thing to say. I forget about Kayla sometimes and all the shit she has been through. How that girl manages to get up every morning is amazing. Another reason I love the girl. She's one of the strongest girls I know.

"Shut the fuck up, asshole," Myles growls, stepping towards me. Kayla stops him, but I just ignore it and instead give a bright red Kayla a wink. That's when I see her. A girl my age or younger, I don't fucking know, stands next to Joan shivering. She's looking between us with wide eyes, her hands twisting together.

Who the hell is she?

"Who the hell are you?" I ask, making her jump.

Fuck, she's beautiful. Her hair is piled up in a bun at the top of her head. And fuck me there's a lot of hair there. Her sharp blue eyes cut to me and I feel myself harden beneath my trousers. Just looking at her makes me want to strip her down and have my wicked way with her. Maybe if I ask the coppers nicely they'll let me have a room in the back there for five minutes.

'Or not,' I think, looking at the bulldog sitting behind the counter at the desk. The guy looks miserable about being stuck on desk duty, but then, to be fair, it doesn't look like the guy knows what exercise means.

The girl looks to Joan shyly before glimpsing at Kayla with recognition. Do they know each other?

"None of your business, Max Carter," Joan snaps, looking annoyed with me.

Shit! She's the one person I hate getting on the wrong side of. It doesn't help she's been looking at me a lot lately like she's got something cooked up her sleeve.

"Sorry," I grumble, meaning it for the first time tonight.

"Malik, I need a favour, sweetie. Can you call Harlow and see if she has some warm clothes she could bring over to the house?"

"Sure, but why?" he asks warily. He's grabbing for his phone, still looking between Joan and the new kid.

"This is Lake, Lake Miller. She volunteers at the church food bank and will be staying with us," she tells him, not elaborating further.

Malik nods his head whilst texting away on his phone. Maverick is eyeing the girl too, with a look of suspicion. What is up with everyone tonight? The girl is smoking hot. I'd definitely bang her. But they're acting like she's invading their personal space and smelling like dead fish.

"You don't need to do this; I can stay at a friend's place," Lake says quietly, not looking at anyone but Joan.

"If you had a friend's house to sleep at then you wouldn't have been sleeping in the church shed," Joan snaps before gentling her tone. Kayla gasps and takes a step toward Lake, ready to reach out, but the girl just pulls away looking ashamed. Joan's face saddens and she steps forward towards Lake. "I'm sorry, sweetie. I just can't have you staying out in this weather. We have a spare room we don't mind you sleeping in. You're welcome to stay with us for as long as you like."

Lake nods her head, looking to the floor, and I watch as Joan's body sags with defeat. I can tell straight away Joan cares for the girl and wants to help her but is struggling on how to.

I stand up and walk over to Lake. Fuck, even her name is hot. I remove the jacket Myles made me wear to prom and hand it over. Everyone's being quiet and I know they're all looking at me, at her. I've never handed my jacket to any chick before. In fact, I don't usually care if a chick's cold or not.

When she doesn't take the jacket, I sigh, wrapping it around her shoulders anyway, and step away before she can refuse it.

Then I ruin it.

"You can sleep in my bed if you don't like bunking it at Joan's," I tell her and everyone groans. "What?" I'm looking around the room and everyone is shaking their heads, but a kid who was here when I arrived grins at me, his yellow teeth rotting and glowing in the dimly lit room. He gives me the thumbs up but I ignore him, not wanting to get into it with him about dental hygiene.

"Shut up, Max," Myles snaps.

"What? She needs a place to stay; my bed is as good as any," I blink, offended.

"Cut it out, Max. When I'm through with you tonight you will wish you never left the house, let alone vandalise a church," Joan snaps angrily, shocking me.

"Joan, my granddad won't appreciate you talking dirty to me," I tease, winking. She just shakes her head looking disappointed with me. I get that a lot.

Another door opens and I turn to see Granddad walking out of the back with the officer from earlier. I move forward hoping like hell I'm going to be let off with a fine or a warning, but with the look on Granddad's face I'm thinking I should just give up.

"What did they say?" Maverick jumps in before I do.

"He's lucky..." he starts. I begin to grin but it's soon wiped off when I hear his next words. "They're only giving him community service. He'll be working at the church donation centre; cleaning the graffiti off the walls and helping out with the food bank until December."

Wait, what? That's four months away, no way.

"No way, that's in four months."

"You're lucky you didn't get longer or get arrested, Max. The church decided not to press charges. We also know there were others involved tonight. Now let's go, you've got a long day ahead of you tomorrow."

I look down at my phone, groaning when I notice the time. It's nearing on half five in the morning. "Shit, I've got to be at practice in a few hours."

"No, son, you don't. I'll call coach when we get back and leave him a message."

"You can't do that," I yell. He can't. I need football, I love it.

"You've left me no choice, Max. You've been warned more than once about your juvenile behaviour."

"If you haven't noticed I am a kid. *We* make mistakes."

"Yes, and you should also take responsibility for them too. So, as from tomorrow there will be no football, no going out to parties, and no hanging out with any of your mates."

"Why don't you concentrate on the new girl? She needs your attention more than me," I snap.

He looks at me confused, before his eyes reach Lake's and they soften. Fuck's sake, does she have to have everyone wrapped around her little finger? They should be focusing on the fact she's been illegally staying on the church's property, rather than on me.

"This is so unfair," I groan, moving to leave.

"Life's unfair, son, you have to live with it. Now move. We've got a lot of talking to do," he snaps and I ignore him, walking out. When I get to the door, the kid with the yellow teeth holds his hand up for a high five.

"Dude?" I ask, shaking my head. He looks up at me confused. "I wouldn't touch your hand if you had just sanitised it."

He goes to stand up but the officer guarding him puts a hand on his shoulder, shoving him back down.

"Go, before they arrest you," Maverick snaps, grabbing my arm. I try to shove him off but it doesn't work.

Then I turn, noticing Joan helping Lake into her car. She's bent over getting into the back seat and I have to bite back a moan.

I vouch here and now, I'll bang her before the four months are up. Maybe up the church's wall, the very one I vandalised and being punished for.

When she's in and has her belt on, her head turns, her sharp blue eyes snapping to mine. Neither of us looks away and for a second my heart does this crazy thing - beating wildly - but then Maverick cuts my view off, shoving me into the car.

LAKE
TWO HOURS EARLIER...

What on earth is that noise? It's making the pounding in my head ten times worse and, believe me, it was already painful to begin with.

With sore limbs, a blocked nose, and a throbbing head, I drag myself up off the dusty blankets I accumulated from a box stored at the back of the shed I'm currently living in. It's not home but at least it's keeping a roof over my head. I just wish it kept the cold at bay. Especially now I'm suffering with a horrible flu.

Loud voices bellow from the outside; not sounding near yet not sounding very far either. My feet stand and, wrapping around another blanket I found - this one thinner, I look through the clouded, blurry, plastic window. It's hard to see but when my eyes finally manage to focus on something I notice a group of lads laughing - one is drinking from a glass bottle and another two are sitting on the ground laughing while they watch another lad spray painting the wall. I gasp in shock and disgust. Who would vandalise a church? Really? That's just... I have no words; it's sickening is what it is. I move towards the door, wanting to get a closer look, and when I look through the crack, my breath hitches when I see its Kayla's boyfriend, Myles. Kayla works at the food bank with me - the building next to the one he's spray painting. I can't see Kayla being onboard with this, she doesn't seem like the type of person who could let this go on unpunished. And judging by his attire he's obviously been to prom. She's been talking about it all week; worrying over dresses, makeup, shoes and what have you. From the way she talked about tonight, I could tell she had something more planned and seeing him here and not with her isn't good.

To me, Prom is the night I destroyed everybody's lives. Not intentionally but I still did it all the same. Now their lives and mine will never be the same.

Hence the reason I'm sleeping in a shed. It's not by choice, it's just what I had coming. Including the damn fucking flu I'm suffering with.

Staring at Myles, I take him in; he looks a little different to when I first met him. Not that I met him to talk to but I still took in his appearance when Kayla introduced us. He seemed less rugged, slimmer built, whereas in his suit he looks bulkier, more muscled, and from this angle and from what I'm seeing, more dangerous.

Another man walks out from the shadows before blinding everyone with his torch. Finally someone has arrived to stop them and get rid of them. I slump down onto the floor in relief. I keep my eyes focused through the small gap in the shed but lean against the side, my body tired from exhaustion. This cold is really kicking my ass.

Shouting begins and my back straightens. Crap, they're moving towards me. They start fighting, rolling around on the floor, and I bite back a scream when another tries to jump the man holding the torch. Just as he's about to jump, Myles tells him to fuck off and to not get involved. The whole thing shocks me.

That's when police siren blares in the background, flashing blue lights clear to see. The lads with Myles turn to look at each other before hightailing it out of the churchyard. What a bunch of dickheads, leaving their friend to defend himself. Speaking of dickheads, my head turns to find Myles on the floor, his movements jerky and wobbly. Has the man actually hurt him? That's when they stumble towards my direction and I sink back a little, hiding myself in the shadows. They crash into the shed, the wood creaking, and I cover my mouth with my hand. My heart is pounding. The thought of being caught has adrenaline racing through my system. I can't get caught. I have nowhere else to go. The police will call my parents, or worse, make me go home to where I'm hated.

Just remembering the last time I saw my mother and the look on her face as pure devastation washed over her facial expression makes me shudder. The dead look in her eyes as she looked at me. I knew then and there I had to go, to get out of there. She hated me. And I knew back then that my dad would too when he found out what I had done.

Reality comes slamming back when they crash through the shed door; two police men running in our direction. I move quickly on my ass, scooting as far back as I can into the shadows towards the back end of the shed. Not that the shed's big but it's the part that I never had chance to clean or get tidy. I didn't want someone coming in and finding clues of me staying here.

The policemen bark orders at Myles and, surprisingly, he doesn't resist arrest. He just sways on his feet as they handcuff him; giving the other man he was fighting a toothy grin.

"You fight like a girl," Myles smirks. God, even his voice isn't as I remembered, it's deeper, cockier. I'm also freaked out at how his voice sends shivers down my spine.

They take him away just as another police officer arrives, shining his torch into the shed. The light blinds me and I wince at the pain it causes behind my eyes.

"You alright, mate? Holy fuck," he gasps. I can't see him yet I know he's spotted me cowering in the corner. I've tucked my knees to my chest to try to block out the chill seeping into my bones, but to also shield myself from the light currently shining on me.

"Shit," another voice says.

"The owner has arrived with one of his supervisors. I'll go get her. We don't have a female police officer on site," I hear murmured.

I don't take in what they say. I'm too scared to move, to look. It's over. It's all over. I'm going to have to live every day knowing the two people I love the most in the world hate me. And be reminded everyday of... I cough hard. I can't think of him right now. It hurts too much.

"Hello, sweetie. Are you okay?" I hear said close to me and I jerk in response.

I know that voice. I'd know that kind voice anywhere.

"Joan?" I cough, looking up and wincing at the blinding light. The officer must notice because he lowers his torch. I look up into Joan's kind, soft eyes and immediately feel ashamed. I never wanted her to see me like this. Will she fire me? I don't get paid much but its worth much more to me than any of them will ever realise.

"It's me, sweetie. It's okay now. You're coming home with me," she demands and my eyes widen in shock.

"No! No! I can…"

"I don't want to hear a word of it. Let me make a call then we will get out of here. You need to get into the warmth," she tells me softly and I nod, not wanting to argue.

The police officer from earlier steps forward and I flinch. Is he going to arrest me? I'm shaking and not just from the cold; Joan notices and takes my hand.

"It's okay. He's got a clean blanket. Do you need to go to the hospital?" she asks me gently and I look around the other people who are watching me with curious expressions.

I shake my head. "No. I'm…" I cough painfully and pause before continuing. "I've just caught a bug. I'll be fine." I cough again, following it with a sneeze.

Joan looks around the room, her face hardening before her gaze cuts back to me.

"You've been sleeping in here a while haven't you?" I can't tell by her tone if she's mad, curious, or just sad, and it breaks my heart. Joan is one of the kindest people I've met since I ran away from home, she's a part of the reason I've stayed working at the food bank instead of moving on somewhere else.

I nod my head, not able to look at her. I'm embarrassed, scared of what's going to happen. Then she shocks me by pulling me in for a hug. I'm not much of a hugger and when my body stiffens she either doesn't notice or she doesn't care.

Her phones rings and she looks up at me. "Let's get you in the car. My man is waiting in his car. That's who's calling," she tells me, helping me to my feet. I sway, feeling shit, but lean on her a little till I get my balance. She answers her phone with a 'hello'. "That boy! I'll wring his bloody neck. Is he? Okay. Well, we have another situation, baby. It's one of my girls from the food bank. It looks like she's been here for a while. I've already told her. I'll call home for someone to get some clothes ready for her. Okay. We're walking up the path now," she tells him, ending the call and pocketing her phone. "Come on, sweetie, we'll get you warm."

The blanket around me is actually helping, the thickness doing more than the flimsy blankets I had plus the shed combined.

"Thank you," I whisper.

"No need to thank me. I just wish you would have let me help you sooner. No girl your age should be living on the streets," she tells me. "We'll talk more when we get you home."

Home.

I want to tell her I don't have one but she's doing so much for me already.

Meeting Mark, Joan's man, was more embarrassing than I thought it would be. I don't know what I expected, but when I saw the good-looking, old man sitting in the driver's side, he was not it. I don't know why but I pictured her with someone else. I don't know who, I just did.

"What is taking them so long?" she mutters, cursing. "He said five minutes, it's been fifteen, and I swear Malik and Maverick walked in not five minutes ago."

It seems Joan isn't a patient person. It turns out Myles is Mark's grandson and lives with them. That shocked me more.

"Right, that's it, I can't take no more," she curses again and turns around in her seat. "You're coming with me because I don't trust you not to run away," she tells me and I nod my head, exhaustion consuming me.

She doesn't have to worry about me running; I know a lost cause when I see one. I'm too exhausted and knowing Joan as well as I do, she'd hunt me down.

Walking into the station I feel someone walking in behind us. I don't turn around to look. Not with the way I look. My hair is scraped up in a messy bun since I lost my brush the day before. My clothes are ratty from crawling around in the shed and from trying to keep warm. But without a coat and an actual fireplace I was shit out of luck with that too.

"Who the hell is she?" is boomed across the station; the same deep voice that sent shivers down my spine earlier. My eyes cut to his and I take in a short breath. Holy fucking Christ he is sex on a stick. His eyes rake my body up and down and chills follow in their wake. How is he doing this, controlling my body's reactions like this? Especially when he's the fucker who got me caught and has a girlfriend.

A girlfriend I happen to really like and am friends with.

Joan makes a noise at the back of her throat and I turn my head towards her, feeling shy and embarrassed and not knowing what to do or if I should answer him.

"None of your business, Max Carter," Joan snaps and I watch Myles' eyes turn fearful. Is he scared of Joan? She's tiny, adorable and the kindest person I've ever actually met. There's no hidden agenda beneath the surface. She's the sort of woman who'd give her right arm. But then, from the sound of her sharp voice, it does sound like he has something to worry about.

And why is she calling him Max?

"Sorry," he grumbles, looking genuine. But I don't know him to make that call.

"Malik, I need a favour, sweetie. Can you call Harlow and see if she has some warm clothes she could bring over to the house?"

"Sure, but why?" he asks warily. He's grabbing for his phone but his eyes dart between me and Joan like he wants to say something. And to be honest he looks kind of intense. It makes me want to take a step back but I don't want to draw attention to myself.

"This is Lake, Lake Miller. She volunteers at the church food bank and will be staying with us," she tells him, introducing me. I'm thankful then that she doesn't explain why I'm with her or where I've been staying.

The lad, Malik, nods his head not questioning her and texts away on his phone. I feel another set of eyes on me and I turn to find another lad, one older than the others, staring at me. It makes me feel uncomfortable and I wring my fingers together, fidgeting. He looks like he'd eat me alive. He also looks upset that I'll be staying with them.

"You don't need to do this; I can stay at a friend's place," I tell Joan, not able to look at her. I don't want her to see how scared I am right at this moment. I don't know any of these people save for Joan.

"If you had a friend's house to sleep at then you wouldn't have been sleeping in the church's shed," Joan snaps, clearly upset. I flinch when I hear a gasp. My head turns and I notice Kayla from the food bank and... Oh my God, there's fucking two of them. Two of them! That's why Joan has been calling the lad who caused all of this Max and not Myles.

Kayla steps forward, reaching out for my hand, but I pull it away at the last second looking away. I can't believe she heard all of that. That she knows. She doesn't seem like any of the other girls at the food bank who are serious bitches, but still, you can never know and I'm worried she might tell them.

My eyes catch Joan's and her face saddens. I feel guilty immediately for upsetting her. She steps forward towards me, "I'm sorry, sweetie. I just can't have you staying out in this weather. We have a spare room we don't mind you sleeping in. You're welcome to stay with us for as long as you like."

I relax a little and nod my head looking to the floor. Joan breathes out a sad sigh from next to me and I feel bad for acting like this. I'm just not used to all this attention. Maybe once, yeah, but not now. I'm used to being on my own and looking after myself.

The lad, Max, stands up, walking towards us and my eyes bug out of my head. Fuck, he's huge. Like seriously huge. From the corner of my eye I watch him remove his jacket and I have to bite my tongue from sighing. His white shirt clings to all that is him. He looks even hotter and for the first time, my body starts to heat.

Everyone's turned quiet and I worry my bottom lip, feeling their eyes on me. When Max holds the jacket towards me I blink in confusion. Why is he giving me - a girl who probably smells like dust, has greasy hair and tatty clothes - his jacket? Does he not realise I'd probably ruin it?

When I don't take the jacket, he sighs and moves forward, startling me when he wraps it around me anyway. I don't even have chance to refuse him, to hand it back to him before he takes a step back, his eyes still on me.

This is so bizarre. He's nothing like the lad I witnessed graffiti the church wall or start a fight.

But that soon changes when he opens his mouth.

"You can sleep in my bed if you don't like bunking it at Joan's," he tells me seductively, and everyone around us groans, including Joan. What on earth? "What?" he asks innocently, looking around the room. Everyone is shaking their heads, including the monster of a bloke who was staring at me like he disliked me earlier.

"Shut up, Max," the real Myles snaps.

"What? She needs a place to stay; my bed is as good as any," he declares, sounding offended.

"Cut it out, Max. When I'm through with you tonight you will wish you never left the house, let alone vandalised a church," Joan snaps angrily, shocking me. I've never heard her speak like that, not even to those bitches who give her a hard time at the food bank. Yeah, it's not just me they're bitches to.

"Joan, my granddad won't appreciate you talking dirty to me," Max flirts, winking. She just shakes her head looking disappointed with him.

A door opens and Mark, Joan's man, walks out of the back with an officer. He looks furious, pissed, and his eyes are glued to Max.

"What did they say?" the lad who had been eyeing me with dislike asks Mark.

"He's lucky..." he starts, pausing before taking a deep breath. It seems this isn't the first time Max has gotten into trouble. "They're only giving him community service. He'll be working at the church's donation centre, cleaning the graffiti off the walls and helping out with the food bank until December."

No. No. No.

He cannot work at the food bank. No way! He can't. Surely they won't let him? I mean, he did just vandalise the church wall.

"No way, that's in four months," Max argues, looking pissed. Glad I'm not the only one. Maybe he'll talk his way out of it. I find myself praying he does. There's no way I can be around him. Just... No way.

"You're lucky you didn't get longer or get arrested, Max. The church decided not to press charges. We also know there were others involved tonight. Now let's go, you've got a long day ahead of you tomorrow."

Max looks down at the phone he's holding before speaking, "Shit, I've got to be at practice in a few hours."

"No, son, you don't. I'll call coach when we get back and leave him a message."

"You can't do that," Max yells at his granddad.

"You've left me no choice, Max. You've been warned more than once about your juvenile behaviour."

"If you haven't noticed I am a kid. *We* make mistakes."

"Yes, and you should take responsibility for them too. So, as from tomorrow, there will be no football, no going out to parties, and no hanging out with any of your mates."

"Why don't you concentrate on the new girl? She needs your attention more than me," he snaps, and my eyebrows draw together. Could he read my mind and now he's getting back at me? Surely not! My face heats and when I feel Mark's eyes on me, I look up to find them soft and thoughtful. Max scoffs and my gaze turns back to him.

What the fuck is his problem? I didn't get him arrested or into fucking trouble. I sure as hell didn't get myself involved. If he hasn't forgotten, he was the one that got me in this fucking situation.

I don't voice any of that, I just bite my tongue and narrow my eyes, concentrating on not lashing out at him.

"This is so unfair," he groans, ready to leave when no one says anything, to which I'm thankful for.

"Life is unfair, son; you have to live with it. Now move. We've got a lot of talking to do," Mark snaps, but Max ignores him and carries on. We all turn to follow but a kid sitting at the door stops Max by putting his hand up. Was he one of the kids that was with him? But I'm sure I heard Mark say they didn't catch the others.

When I feel Kayla looking at me, I turn, giving her a sad smile before looking back in front.

"Dude?" Max snaps at the kid and the kid looks up at him shocked, or confused? I don't know. "I wouldn't touch your hand if you had just sanitised it."

Oh my God, he did not just say that. There are officers everywhere. The kid goes to stand up but the officer sitting next to him clamps a hand on his shoulder, pushing him back down.

"Go, before they arrest you," the angry eyed lad from earlier snaps, grabbing Max. I'm not sure what to think about him. He seems scary. He's got tattoos but you wouldn't know unless you looked close enough like I did. He's obviously the oldest which is probably why he feels like he's responsible for the others. Most brothers wouldn't get involved and would stay at home, but this family, they all came together, even if it was to ream Max's ass.

Joan helps me back into the car; my body protesting and aching all over. I cough, followed by a sneeze as she shuts the door. She looks through the window sadly before moving out of the way, giving me a clear view of Max. He's staring at me with such intensity that I have to hold myself back from squirming in my seat. Tingles shoot up my spine and my belly flips over causing a shocked gasp out of me. It's quiet, but still, I'm thankful no one has yet to get in the car.

His eyes don't leave mine and the more he stares the more I start to believe he can read me. See inside me. I can't let that happen.

It's then that I vouch I won't let him get to me and to stay away from him. How hard can it be?

ONE

LAKE

MY BELLY FLUTTERS WITH NERVES as I lean against the kitchen sink. Today, after being sick with a bad case of the flu for the past two weeks, I'm finally allowed to go back to work. Everyone is going to know I was the squatter by now and I'm unsure how everyone will react. Not that I care what they say to me, it will be nothing that isn't true. I just want to lead a peaceful life and not one where I'll be constantly judged.

The door to Joan's house knocks and I freeze looking at it. In the two weeks I've been here everyone has been real nice to me, but it's not my home. I hardly know these people and, yet, they've welcomed me with open arms. I've spoken to the girl that lives here, Harlow. She seems pretty cool and so does her boyfriend, who is fine to look at, but so freaking intense. He's also broody a lot too. But we've not gotten to a stage where we're comfortable around each other. I think we're just walking around on eggshells, not knowing what to say to each other.

It's another reason why I'm not getting up to answer the door. It just doesn't feel right making myself at home. Footsteps thump coming down the stairs and I know its Malik coming down. Harlow left this morning to meet up with some girl from her class to study and Mark and Joan left a few hours ago.

"Good morning, where is she? Has she come out of her room?" a voice that sends tingles down my back. I know who it is without peeping around the door. It's the boy, Max, who got arrested and the dickhead who got me caught sleeping in the shed. I've not seen him, his twin, or anyone really since that night. I've stayed in the room Joan gave me to sleep in and haven't left it. I'd been so ill that she came in to take care of me which I'll be forever thankful to her for.

I knew I was feeling worse for wear before I'd even been found, and I'm glad in a way that I was. I'd never been that ill from a cold before. It was horrible. And I honestly believe if I had still been in that freezing cold shed it would have been a lot worse.

"Shut the fuck up, she's in there," Malik hisses on a whisper.

"Well, shit! Let's go give her a Max welcome."

"Let's not," I hear grumbled, right before their footsteps sound closer. I sit down - not feeling comfortable - and then stand back up. It makes me feel like I own the place and that I'm taking advantage. I don't want to come across like that to any of them. It just doesn't feel right.

I turn, putting my mug into the sink, when all of a sudden hands wrap around my waist and swing me around, keeping me tightly held against a hard body. I squeal, surprised at the sudden intrusion, and when I realise it's Max that has gotten me, I start kicking out.

"Put me down, now!" I snap.

He does as I asked; setting me down before turning me to face him. As soon as the dizziness subsides I push against his hard chest.

"You fucking asshole," I growl before shoving past him.

"What? I'm a hugger," he shouts after me. I grab my coat before heading out the door, pulling my hood up as I go. Trust it to still be raining. I'm lucky Harlow had a spare coat she didn't mind giving to me. She said it hadn't been worn in years. Not one to cut my nose off, I'd happily taken it. It's only what I was doing before. Taking hand-me-down's to get me by. It was also nice having something to wrap up warm in. The weather was only going to get colder.

ARRIVING AT THE FOOD bank my heart sinks. Coming back here is worse than I originally thought it was going to be. Everyone's eyes are glued either to me or to

Max as we walk in. Joan is already in full boss mode when I finish hanging my coat up.

"You look so much better, sweetie," she coos. She reminds me a lot of my own grandma before she died. She was kind, caring, loving, and always hovering; making sure everyone was okay and got what they wanted. She also acted like a teenager, not caring she was inside a seventy-five year old body.

"I feel it. Thank you."

She gives me the eye, the one I've noticed her do a lot during the two weeks I've stayed with her, the one that says she doesn't quite believe me. Her eyes then flick to Max and soon turn to annoyance. When I move to see what he's doing I find his eyes fixated on my ass.

Typical.

Though, I won't lie, it feels good to have the attention, especially his. If that's not a sign telling me it's been too long, I don't know what is. It also doesn't hurt that the boy is fucking gorgeous.

"I've been told you finished painting over the vandalism," Joan states annoyed at Max.

"Yeah, it turns out spray paint is harder to scrub off than I originally thought," he shrugs. "I also bought the paint myself."

"Don't make it make sound like you're being noble, Max Xavier Carter. The church isn't going to pay for your mistakes so stop looking like you've been put out or should be thanked."

Max doesn't say anything for a minute. He just eyes up Joan curiously like he's mulling over what he wants to say.

"You still love me, though? I'm still your favourite, Carter, right?"

"No, Myles has bumped you off that position."

"Sly fucking dog," Max mutters, genuinely looking pissed. "Now, where do you want me?"

"You'll be shadowing Lake today. Everything she tells you to do, you do. No questions asked."

"I can handle that," Max winks at me, his eyes appraising my body up and down. I roll my eyes at him, wishing the job was harder so I could run him ragged.

"I'll leave you to it, then. Oh, and Lake, Max is paying for your lunch today so no paying," she warns me. Yeah, like I'm going to take another hand out, especially one from *him*.

25   MAX

We leave Joan to it and head into the back where we'll be labelling dates on the foods. I don't bother talking to Max, I just grab everything we need and pull up a chair.

"You don't like me much, huh?" Max asks after a few minutes of silence.

"You seem surprised," I answer, sounding bored.

"Well, yeah," he says giving me a duh look. "I'm a fucking loveable person."

"You also got me caught you fucking dickhead," I snap.

"Bit of a good job I did, wouldn't you say?" he snaps back, shocking me. "Sorry, that was harsh. I just don't think it's safe for you to be sleeping out in a shed in this weather and on your own, Lake."

"Well, it was safer than other places I've stayed at," I mutter, getting back up to get a few more bags of food.

Sitting back down, Max gives me another curious look before sighing loudly.

"What?" I snap, knowing he's got something to say.

"Look, I'm going to come right out and say this. Do you have parent issues? Is your mom a crazy psycho that's going to run you over? Get you kidnapped? Disown you?"

"Huh?" I ask him open-mouthed. What on earth...

"It happens a lot around here, you'll be surprised."

"Am I supposed to answer that?" I ask him, still wondering if he's being serious. From his deadpan expression I'll say that he is, but from what I heard, you can never know with Max.

"Um, yeah. Have you not heard about the moms that run in this circle?" he tells me, and then shudders like someone just walked over his grave.

"I guess not," I tell him slowly.

"So?" he says, shaking his head at the same time as he rolls his eyes.

"Oh, no, no parent issues," I half lie. My parents aren't psychos, they're wonderful parents; it's me that's the disappointment. I'm the one that ruined our lives, who ruined theirs. But I'm not telling him that. I can never tell a soul what I did.

"I'm going to have to take your word for it, but, just so you know, I think my brothers and I have got psycho moms down to a T. We got this shit, so if you need us we've got your back," he winks.

"What are you doing?" I ask quickly, not admitting what that wink did to me. My stomach is still doing summersaults from his touch this morning. He picked me up so easily, like I weighed nothing.

"Writing on the labels you just handed me," he tells me slowly.

"Um, no, Max. You have to write the expiry date on them."

"Why? They're already on them."

"Just do it. It's important," I snap.

"Jesus, you really are bossy," he grins, picking up fresh labels.

We've been working non-stop for the past few hours. Max has been huffing and puffing for half of that and it's grating on my last nerve.

A few of the other younger volunteers walk in, stopping me from yelling at Max to shut up. When they start sniggering I look over to find them looking over at us. It's hard to tell whether it's aimed towards me or towards Max. He's had a lot of female attention since arriving, even from the older generation.

It's sickening really; to most of them he's basically jailbait, but none of them seem to be bothered about that.

I shiver, remembering one of the cougars who full on flirted with him – I threw up in my mouth.

My eyes catch one of the girls nod to her friend in a way that has my back straightening. These girls have been getting on my tits since they first started volunteering. You ever watched *Mean Girls*? Well, they define *Regina George*.

"Did you hear about the tramp they found squatting in the shed?" the girl known as Liv says, her voice screeching across the room. Max's head turns a little in my direction but not enough to draw attention to me. I like that, though, it doesn't matter since we all know they're on about me. My hopes of them coming to flirt with Max and leave me alone for once evaporate.

"Yeah, I heard about that. Disgusting if you ask me. Apparently the person had been sleeping in her own piss for weeks," Jessica sniggers. I really despise that girl. She's always got an opinion about everything and everyone around her. If only she concentrated on her own life like she did everyone else's. The bitch probably has more enemies than Voldemort.

"Yeah, I heard she's been robbing from the church, too," the other girl, Sarah, sniggers. Like stealing from a church is something to snigger about. Stupid idiot! None of what they're saying is true so it doesn't bother me so much. Their lies and stories do nothing to me; I let it wash over my head because nothing can hurt me bar one word. One word, six letters, and that word is enough to destroy me because, unlike what they're saying, *that* word is the truth.

"Wouldn't put it past her if she's on the run from something," Jessica says loudly. That comment pisses me off. It's too close to the truth it's untrue. If she knows something, I'm gone.

Max stands up, his chair scraping against the floor loudly. It makes us all turn our heads but I soon look away when I find Jessica looking at me with a smug expression, her eyes gleaming.

Evil bitch.

"Hey, Max," she coos sweetly, her chest sticking out, her hip cocked to the side and her eyelashes flapping like she's got fluff stuck in them.

I just vomited in my mouth. Literally.

"You know what I heard?" Max answers his voice deep. It's deadly and it makes the hair on the back of my neck stand on end.

"What did you hear?" they ask, sounding amused and glad he's playing along. I swear, if he says anything about me I'm going to grab the closest thing to me and wrap it around that bloody fat head of his. I might just do that anyway, but if he does then at least my actions are justified.

"I heard she was a famous actress that needed somewhere to hide out. But she wanted to know how girls like you live," he tells them cheerfully.

"Excuse me?" Jessica coughs, amusement leaving her voice and confusion written all over her.

"Oh, and I've got some paint stripper left if you want it."

"I... I don't understand. Why would I want that?" Jessica says, sounding more confused and slightly pissed. Her eyes drift towards me and narrow and I just give her a deadpan look in return.

"To get all that shit you've painted on, off your face. Don't know about you, but I like a girl that's all natural. Look at Lake for example, that girl is all natural," he says suggestively, his eyes twinkling as he looks me up and down.

"Like you care what girls look like," Liv snarls.

"You're a prick, you know that?" Jessica snaps, stepping forwards towards him.

"Oh, baby, you have no idea. And it's a fucking big prick," he grins and I watch in fascination as Jessica's face goes bright red in anger. Now I don't think I'll be wrapping something around his head. After that he deserves a freaking hug.

"Whatever," she snaps before storming out, her little gang of cronies following behind her.

"Unbelievable," he shouts before turning to face me like I have the answers.

"What is?" I ask sheepishly, ignoring the way my heart beats like crazy from him sticking up for me.

"I just gave her the best advice she'll ever get in life and the bitch has the nerve to call *me* the prick," he heatedly answers, shaking his head.

I can't stop the laugh that erupts from my mouth. I try to cover it up but all I do is muffle the sound, looking like a complete dork. He really is something.

"I'm sorry," I tell him, holding my hand up. He looks hurt and amused over my outburst, his expression… it's so ridiculous. "That was just…"

"Obviously funny," he laughs, but then looks at me, suddenly serious. "I need feeding and your skinny ass *definitely* needs feeding."

"I do not have a skinny ass," I snap, outraged, but then palm slap my forehead. I walked right into that one.

"No, you do not," he answers, emphasising each word; his eyes on my ass.

"Shut up. And didn't you eat like ten minutes ago?" I ask. I could swear he was eating a BLT from the kitchen, but whatever.

"No, it was fifteen minutes ago and I'm a growing boy," he states. I look him over, the way his t-shirt hugs his muscled arms and the way his trousers hug his strong toned legs, I'd certainly say he's done growing. "Are you checking me out, Lakey?"

"Never, and I mean *never*, call me Lakey. Are we clear?" I warn him, looking at him with a deathly glare.

"Okay," he says, drawing out the word. "But seriously, can we go get some food?"

"No one is stopping you from going out for food. Although, I'd probably go check with Joan first; you seem to be in her bad books," I smirk.

"I know, yeah. You'd think having 'Max woz ere' written on the wall of a church would make the woman proud. She's been dying to get me to church since she and my granddad got together."

"You really have a weird way of looking at things," I tell him dryly.

"No, I'm just fucking awesome," he winks. "Food. Now!"

"Like I said, there is nothing stopping you from going out and getting yourself some food."

"Right, hold that thought," he tells me, then turns and disappears. I'm actually disappointed it didn't take much to get him to clear off. I sigh. Feeling lonely is something that I've become accustomed to, but in the past two weeks, and this morning, that loneliness seemed to fade. I know being on my own, feeling lonely, down, and disconnected from everyone and everything is something I deserve.

"Lake?" Joan's soft voice interrupts my thoughts. I look up to find her walking in with Max tailing behind her, a smug grin on his face. My eyes narrow on him but then soften when I turn to Joan.

"Oh, hi, Joan, is everything okay?"

"Yes, but Max here just said you didn't want to eat. You need to eat. He's going to take you to the pub down the road. They do a lovely soup that will help you with your cold," she tells me softly. I look to Max who I didn't see before and send him a glare.

"I'm good," I tell her, hoping my voice stays firm. Then my stomach betrays me and rumbles loudly. Max chuckles and Joan just sends me a pointed look. Damn freaking stomach. I've hardly eaten over the past two weeks but now my appetite is back and I'm starving. There's no hiding it. Thanks to my traitorous stomach. And to make it worse, the pub they're on about serves food that is orgasmic. I'm friends with the owner and chef. He's brilliant.

"Of course you are. Max, take her to lunch, and before you say anything, missy, you will be going. If Max here tells me you haven't eaten with him *and* let him pay, you will be on washing up duty at home for a month," she warns me before walking out.

My eyes water.

Home.

For a month.

She actually sees me with her for a month. I've not had this. Not had someone care for me in such a long time. Although I don't deserve her kindness, a part of me wants to relish in it. Enjoy it while I can because I know a time will come when I need to move on, to run, to hide, and to start from the bottom.

I'll never settle down, make a home, or even rent a flat. I'm where I should be. Down in the gutter living day to day being miserable, unhappy, and scraping by.

"Come on then, grab ya coat, Lakey," Max tells me excitedly.

I send him a glare. "I told you not to call me that," I snap and huff as I walk down the hall to grab my coat.

When I grab it and put it on something smells funny. My hand reaches into my pocket and I cringe.

Ewe, what the hell is that?

Pulling out the offending object a mouldy banana comes into view and I quickly throw it into the trash can.

"You really should put shit in the bin," Max comments, scrunching his nose up.

"Hmmm," I comment, and when I reach into my other pocket and find a bunch of notes shoved into it my eyes widen.

"I thought you were homeless," Max gasps. "Dinner's on you."

"This isn't mine. The fucking banana wasn't mine," I cry, wondering what is going on. Joan walks past the door and before she can get too far away I shout her name.

"Good, you're going," she smiles as she walks in, her eyes find the cash in my hand.

"Yeah, yeah. Look, Joan, I found this in my pocket," I tell her, handing her the notes. There has to be over eighty quid there.

"Don't forget the banana," Max adds and I elbow him in the gut.

"Fuck, that hurt," he wheezes but I just shrug looking at Joan.

"Say something," I tell her, my back straightening. Something is off, I can tell by her posture.

"This is Miss Robins' money."

"So what's it doing in my pocket?"

"She came to me about twenty minutes ago telling me she needed to go home to get the raffle money. She said she swore she brought it with her, but when she went to get it out her bag it was gone," she says quietly.

"I didn't steal this," I shout, feeling my eyes well-up. I can't get fired from here. I get paid pennies compared to what I'd get working a minimum wage job but I love it here. It's the only place around here that pays in cash.

"She didn't," Max agrees, looking serious. "We arrived together; we've been sitting in that dusty storage room all morning, together. She hasn't left and the only time I left was to get you and when I got my BLT," he tells her and I hope she believes him. I know they are all close and pretty much family but he did just spray paint the church wall so he might not be the best person to get an alibi from.

"Oh, honey, I believe you. I never doubted you for a second; what has me shocked is the fact someone has done this and put the blame on you. We would have had to have called the police in if Miss Robins couldn't find the money. Your bags and pockets would have been searched..." she says, trailing off. I know what she's not saying, though. They would have arrested me. I don't need her to tell me this, I just need her to know I didn't do this. I'd never steal. I've gone a week, probably longer, without food and I never sunk low enough to steal money from someone. Food? Yeah, but never money.

"I promise you, Joan, I didn't do this. I wouldn't do this."

"Calm down. Why don't you take the rest of the day off-" she starts. I interrupt feeling panicked.

"Am I fired?" I croak out.

"What?" she asks, shocked. "Of course you're not. I just want to see what people say. So far it's only us in this room that know I have the money. I want to see who points the finger first," she shrugs mischievously.

"You sly little dog," Max chuckles. "This is awesome. We can go get something to eat and go meet up with Myles and Kayla. She isn't in today either."

"I didn't say you could have the day off, Max," Joan tells him, wiping the smile off his smug face.

"Oh, come on, she needs company. She's been holed up in her room like a hermit for two weeks," Max argues.

"I had the flu," I defend, then realise I shouldn't have reacted. He winks but turns back to Joan with a puppy dog look. She can't really be buying this crap.

"You're right, Max. It will be nice for Lake to get to know all of you. Maybe you can join Denny and Harlow? They said they were watching a movie later."

"I'm right here," I speak up, waving my arms around.

"That's a great idea. She needs to get used to us and used to socialising," Max agrees.

"Are we going?" I snap, turning around to face Max. His body is closer than I first thought and it has me taking a step back. Tingles of awareness shoot up my spine and I hate how his closeness affects me.

"Yes, come on. I think I can shout out for a coke, too," he smiles. I ignore him; looking to Joan worried about this money crap.

"Go on, I'll sort all this out," she tells me, her hand touching my cheek lightly. Her hand is cold but the soft touch has my heart clenching and again I have to fight back tears.

TWO

MAX DRAGS ME DOWN THE STREET towards the local pub I used to scrounge food from. The chef, Antonio, saw me one night hanging around in the alleyway - hungry, cold and wet from the rain. He invited me into the kitchen and fed me after much persuading. It was Antonio that introduced me to Joan and got me the job at the church. It wasn't for much money but every penny counts when you're homeless, hungry and freezing cold. We've been close friends ever since. I really like him. And it doesn't hurt his food is dee-lish-ous.

My face immediately warms up when we walk into the warm pub and see Antonio standing at the end of the bar chatting up one of the newer waitresses. She's around the same age as him - short hair, dyed purple, and an hourglass figure. From what I remember she's divorced and has three kids. She seems nice and Antonio seems pretty smitten with her.

When the door shuts behind Max, Antonio looks our way. When he sees it's me, a huge grin spreads across his face. He's a handsome man, middle aged, tanned skin and is quite lean for a dude his age. His hair is cropped short and he's always sporting a five o'clock shadow.

"I think he wants me," Max whispers close to my ear, sounding frightened. The sensation of his breath on my neck has me breaking out in a sweat and a delicious shiver runs down my spine.

"Lake, my girl," Antonio shouts across the pub, his arms open wide.

"Or not," Max mutters and I fight the urge to giggle. He actually sounds disappointed that Antonio didn't want him.

"Hey, Antonio," I greet coolly.

"You're too skinny, piccola ragazza. You need fattening up," he scolds, shaking his head. I can feel Max's eyes on me and I can only wonder what is going through his depraved head. "Who is this young man?"

"Max. I'm a friend," Max says shocking me. His easy banter and cocky attitude has disappeared. He's all serious and straight-faced. I'm also surprised he knows how to be polite, especially to an elder.

"She needs a friend," Antonio agrees, nodding his head. I just shake mine and roll my eyes. What the hell is it with people talking about me like I'm not here today?

"I said that too," Max nods and grabs a menu off the bar. "What's the best thing to eat?"

"Everything, but for you I'll make my famous pizza, pasta casserole. It melts in your mouth." Smiling, I hold back a giggle from how animated he is over his food. Antonio can talk for hours over food and not get bored or out of breath for a second. He's that passionate about it. He told me once that where he lived was a poorer town and food was a luxury that people didn't have over there. I think it's another reason he took me in. He knows what it's like to be hungry.

"People say they starving, all day, every day, when, piccola ragazza, they do not know meaning of the word starving. We do."

It wasn't until that day when he said those words that I realised he was right. Even stupid comments like, 'Starving Marvin,' 'I could eat a horse I'm that hungry,' when in reality you don't know the meaning of hungry until you've actually starved, gone weeks without food. It explained why he knew everyone from the food bank. It turns out he donated a lot of food and even offers full cooked meals every Sunday for the homeless. Granted, they need a ticket that the food bank gives them; otherwise anyone could walk in and have a free meal, even people who can afford it.

I look to Max to find him licking his lips and nodding his head. I roll my eyes and I mentally slap myself. I seem to be rolling them a lot around him. I've only been with him five hours and already the little twerp has gotten under my skin.

I'm putting it down to the fact he stuck up for me. He doesn't seem to judge me and, in all honesty, I kind of like him.

"Lake, you too?" Antonio asks with hopeful eyes.

"I've..."

"She's had the flu for the past two weeks, so something light for this one," Max interrupts and I punch him in the side.

"I have a mouth, I can talk," I snap.

"Yeah, you do," he coughs, his eyes staring lustfully at my lips.

"Oh, we have only a chicken and mushroom homemade soup on for today. This is not good for my piccola ragazza."

"I love homemade chicken and mushroom soup," I jump in before anyone can say anything else.

"Good, good, it's good," Antonio tells me and then disappears into the back where the kitchen is.

"Go take a seat at the table over by the window and I'll bring it over. Would you like any drinks?" the waitress, Cam, asks and I give her a smile. She returns it with a giggle, her eyes flickering to Max before looking towards me with appreciation.

"Yeah, can I have two glasses of orange juice, please?" Max answers. She nods her head and before I can open my mouth and ask for water he pulls me over to the table by the window. It has the nicest view and I wonder if he knows that or if he just sat here randomly.

The view overlooks the river and, with all the boats that float by it's the most relaxing place to be. The water ripples, the trees rustle and in today's case, the rain splatters on the window. You can't beat the sound of rain to relax your mood. But for the first time, it doesn't work for me and I turn my attention to Max.

"Can you stop talking for me?" I hiss when we sit down.

"I haven't," he dismisses and I look at him open mouthed. He can't be serious. He's been doing it all morning. God, he infuriates me. First he gets me caught hiding out in the church shed and now this.

"Whatever! Just stop doing it."

"You're really feisty," he winks. "I like it."

I sigh, looking up to the ceiling. I can see this being a long lunch. Deep down, though, I kind of like his full-on behaviour. It's refreshing and different.

Lunch was entertaining to say the least. Max not only dominated all of the conversation – not taking a breath – but he also asked inappropriate questions.

Worst one was what size tits did I have. I could have smacked him across the face but I'd been too stuffed from the wonderful food Antonio had fed me that I kept myself planted in my chair.

"So, where did you live before the church shed?" he asks me as we walk back to Joan's. I thought I had gotten out of all the questions when we left the pub. Obviously I was wrong.

"You decide to ask a reasonable question now? You're not going to ask me how many people I've slept with or if I've ever been given an S.T.D?"

"That's a bit personal, Lake," he tells me sheepishly.

"Are you serious? You asked me my bra size and if I liked giving head," I snap.

"Yeah, those are reasonable questions. I like to know what I'm working with and if I'll be getting head," he tells me straight-faced; not an ounce of amusement evident in his expression.

"You're a jerk," I snap.

"So..." he trails off then sighs when I don't speak. "Come on, where did you come from?"

"My mother's womb."

"Fuck you're hot, but seriously, answer the question or I'll get a mate of mine to do a background check on you," he teases. My back straightens and I hurry a few steps ahead before turning and stopping in front of him. I push him back a step and he looks at me wide-eyed.

"If you ever, and I mean ever, get someone to look into me, I'll have your balls for breakfast. And if that isn't enough to stop you, then I'll cut your dick off and make sure it hurts."

"I think the balls did it," he winces. "Why all the privacy and avoiding my questions?"

"I lived in Endington," I half lie. It's not where I'm from but it is where I stayed before I moved here. Running farther and farther from my life back home took time. I'm currently five hours away from my hometown and with each town I got to, my heart broke a little bit more and in replace was a void I had built.

"See, was that so bad?" The teasing in his voice lightens the mood again and I turn to carry on walking.

We arrive just at the Carter's house when Max stops me, grabbing hold of my arm. I growl wanting to get out of the rain – it's been bad for a few days, but today the storm seems to be getting worse.

"What?" I ask, looking at his hand holding my arm.

"Where are you going?"

"Um, Joan's?"

"Nuh huh, we're going to Denny and Mason's."

"Hey, let go," I yell when he doesn't let go of my arm and instead drags me towards Denny and Mason's.

"No, I know what you're going to say and what you'll do if I let go and I'm not listening to your bullshit excuses. Plus, everyone wants to meet you."

I pull with all my might, finally getting free. I stumble for a second but catch myself from falling and as I turn to run, strong arms wrap around my waist, stopping me. He lifts me up, throwing me over his shoulder and I scream at him to put me down. I threaten bodily harm but he ignores me *and* my fists that are currently pounding on his back.

I hear a door open and the chatter of voices, but as soon as we get closer all conversation comes to a halt. All the blood has rushed to my face but even if I wasn't hanging upside down, I'd still be bright red right now.

"Is there a reason you've kidnapped Lake?" a deep voice asks.

"She needs to socialise. Some fucker at the church planted money in her pocket. Joan's sorting it out," Max answers and I cringe. Now they'll all going to think I'm a thief. It's only right. I'm homeless for fuck's sake. Who else would they blame? Everyone at the church is going to think the same too.

"Well, that explains why you're here and not there," another deep voice rumbles, walking in behind us. I lift my head, but all I manage to get a look at is black boots and a pair of strong legs.

"Who would do that?" Harlow gasps. I've spoken to her a few times so her voice is one I recognise. She's pretty freaking cool if you ask me and, shit, she's fucking pretty too.

"My guess? The bitches who were giving her shit this morning," Max shrugs and my body bounces from the movement. I stay silent, too embarrassed to speak, and silently I curse him to put me the fuck down.

"Let me guess, Jessica and her little dolls?" Kayla speaks, her voice soft. If anyone knows what they're like it's Kayla. She's had to listen to their shit for nearly as long as me.

She hasn't been working a lot, though, since she lost her best friend. Joan filled me in, but even if she hadn't, everyone at the food bank had been gossiping about it. You can still hear the sadness in her voice from losing her. I've spoken to her a few times about her, wanting to support her, but mostly, with a hidden agenda. She'd been coping extremely well, all things considered, and I wanted to know her secret, but alas, there is none.

"Yeah those," Max says.

"Sounds like something they'd do," Kayla agrees, her voice laced with venom which shouldn't shock me; she's spoken out for me a few times. Still, being even a little hard-toned doesn't suit Kayla in the slightest.

"Is there a reason you're still holding Lake?" the deep voice from behind speaks again and I silently thank him. I'm starting to feel sick and I'm about to warn Max but he interrupts, his voice causing me to shiver.

"Shit, forgot you were there, sweet cheeks," Max chuckles then slaps me hard on the ass and I squeal in pain. When he slides me down his hard body, I'm in two minds, but I go with the most hostile because I think the alternative, which is rubbing myself all over him, would cause mixed signals. I push him back, giving him a glare and narrowing my eyes. He gives me a wink, but I carry on glaring. I'm about to storm out of the door but I'm stopped short by running into a hard body. I look up and the older brother, Maverick, looks down at me with a kind smile. I have to say it's a much better greeting then the hostile one I received at the station a few weeks back. But still, the older brother still unnerves me.

"You joining us?" he asks and I shake my head. He's really good looking. Not Max good looking but he has this bad boy, mysterious vibe going on that you can't help but be drawn towards. I've seen him a few times over the past few weeks, but now I realise I had seen him before but hadn't been paying much attention. He would help with the deliveries at the food bank sometimes for Joan.

"I...I..." I stammer.

"Of course she is," Max interrupts.

"Yay! I'm so happy you're feeling better. Joan said to give you time to settle in and get back on your feet before we could come and see you. Plus, she didn't want us all catching the flu," Kayla smiles when I turn back around.

"This here is Mason; that goof is the ugly twin, Myles; that grumpy fucker is Malik and you've met Maverick, the one behind you. The hot blonde one is Denny, this hot one is Harlow, and you already know Kayla. Oh, and she's hot too. The only one you need to know is this little princess, Hope, she's beautiful," Max tells me, introducing me to everyone.

I watch in fascination as Max picks up the most beautiful little girl in the world. She gives him a toothy smile and smacks the building block on his mouth. He just laughs and nuzzles his face into her neck, blowing raspberries. This is not the Max I've come to know. This is... this is just puzzling. Never, and I mean never, would I have pictured Max to be like this with children. He seems like the type to run away and hide from a kid.

"Hey," I wave shyly at everyone, yet my eyes can't leave the sight of Max holding the cute little girl. She's giggling uncontrollably and I find myself smiling with her. It's infectious.

"Lake," Kayla's loud voice makes me jump and I look to her and shake my head. I have to fight the urge to look back at Max. It's bizarre seeing him with that baby. As if the good looking git needs to be more attractive, but seeing him with her just makes him so much more attractive.

"I said; is watching, *'The Longest Ride'* okay with you?"

Scott Eastwood shirtless? Hell, yeah. I don't mind one single bit. I've not seen it. In fact, I can't remember the last movie I watched. Even at Joan's the past two weeks I've not really watched one. I watched some tele, but I'd been too ill to concentrate. Even so, I'm still not out of touch with the world of hot men. I've even seen pictures of him and Taylor Swift in her new music video. Hot, damn, that boy is all kinds of hot and you would have to be dead not to agree. Even his dad, Clint, was a looker back in his day. If my nan was still around today she would tell me he still is a looker, but hey, I'm not into the whole older men scene.

"I don't mind at all," I answer quickly and all the girls giggle like they know what I'm thinking. None of the boys seem to care. In fact, Malik looks more interested in watching Harlow, Myles looks like he'd do anything Kayla wanted him to, and Mason is too busy kissing Denny to even care.

How...fun!

Half way through the movie I start to feel awkward. There's a hot sex, shower scene and it's making me feel uncomfortable. Not the actual act itself but because I'm in a room full of, basically, strangers. It just feels awkward, but then it could just be me making it that way.

"You okay?" Max whisper yells, gaining everyone's attention.

I could kill him right now. What a jerk! I don't even bother to acknowledge him; if I do, I might end up strangling the lad.

"Yes," I hiss back, staring at the tele.

"You turned on?"

"What the fuck?" I snap, turning to glare at him. Harlow and Denny chuckle, but Kayla gasps in shock. For all I know she could have gasped thinking I was turned on. This is just pissing brilliant.

"I am, want to feel? I'm big," he winks and I turn my head looking back at the screen, not even wanting to answer him. I'm too stunned and... honestly? A part of me wants to find out how big he really is; then an idea occurs and I grin.

"Dude, cut it the fuck out," Mason snaps and I'm thankful in that moment.

"What? It's an innocent question," he shrugs.

"Why the hell not?" I grin and lean in closer. His chest rises quickly, his eyes wide with shock. I reach down, grabbing his package and tut looking disappointed. "Nope... Not very big at all," I state, causing everyone to giggle. I let go and give him a smug smile. "The only thing big about you is the size of you're..." I pause for effect, boldly looking his body up and down. As a girl I can appreciate what a fine specimen Max is, but as a person with feelings, I can also tell he's a huge player. His eyes are still narrowed from calling him small but I can see a shimmer of hope in his eyes. "Yep, the only thing big on you is your head," I deadpan.

"I'm not fucking small," he yells but then he smugly smirks and my breath hitches. "But...I do have a big head. You should see it when I'm about to come," he breathes out, leaning in closer. I try to move back but I'm already at the edge of the sofa.

"Fuck you," I snap and try to look away; fed up of playing this game with him.

"Guys, cool it," I hear Maverick, the eldest of the brothers, tell us. We both ignore him, staring each other down. I'm not one to back down from anything; well, I never used to be anyway.

Groaning, he looks at me with a smile that would melt any woman's panties. "Say that again, I love it when you talk dirty and make promises," he winks, a smirk playing on his lips.

"You're a pig."

"Oh baby, I can be whatever you want me to be," he tells me, his body scooting over so he's nearly sat in my lap.

"Will you give it up already," I snap at him, feeling my face flame when I notice everyone's attention is on us and the movie has now been paused.

This is just bloody brilliant! Insert sarcasm right here.

"I'm more than ready to give it up for you, baby," he teases.

I lean in close so that our lips are a near breath away and stare at him in his eyes. It's the first mistake I make. His eyes are mesmerising and behind the lust and desire I notice he has a hidden pain in there. The second is that being this close to him has me fighting the urge to move the rest of the way to kiss him, it's overpowering.

"*Baby*," I start, mimicking his words. "I don't do easy and you, Max Carter, are easy," I tell him and then move back, giving myself some breathing room.

He opens his mouth to reply, looking a little shocked and if I'm not mistaken, aroused.

When a phone starts ringing in the room we break apart, and everyone shuffles, checking their phones. It's not mine – I don't own one – but it at least takes some of the attention off me and Max.

"Hey, Lexi, you okay?" Denny answers cheerfully. "What?" she replies, sounding on the verge of crying. I look around Max and find Denny with her phone tucked into her ear and shoulder, handing Hope over to Mason before standing up. "What? When? Is she okay? Oh my God, no, please no," she cries and I sit back in the chair feeling a little awkward, but it's mostly because I have to fight the urge to get up and comfort her. The phone is taken from her hands when Mason takes the phone off her. He talks to whoever Lexi is, barking questions before ending the call.

"I should go," I whisper to Max, not wanting to be in the way. This is obviously bad news and she'll need her family around her, not some stranger looking on while she breaks down.

He puts his hand on my leg to stop me and tingles shoot all up leg, up my body and down my back. His touch is like a flame; my skin burning from a simple touch.

"Is everything okay?" Max asks first and I notice everyone is now sitting on the edge of their seats. Mason walks over, ready to hand Hope to Max, but all of a sudden I find her being placed in my arms.

"What the hell, brother?" Max asks, looking at Mason like he just gave away the last cookie. I smile down at Hope, my body stiff as a board. I've never held a baby before. Well, she's not exactly small, but still, she's a baby.

"Not now," Mason snaps before kneeling down in front of Denny.

"Baby, we should go be with Kennedy. Lexi said she doesn't have any family with her," Mason whispers and I wonder who they're on about. I can't help but hurt for Denny. The broken look on her face is gut wrenching.

"Yes, she does, she has us," she tells him fiercely. He looks taken aback for a second then nods his head in agreement.

"Bro, what's going on? Is there anything we can do?"

"Evan, Denny's brother, found out he had a baby not long ago."

"What?" they all shout, before the brothers burst into laughter.

"That dick. Told you he didn't wrap it before tapping it," Max laughs but soon loses it when he sees the glare Mason's sending his way.

"Chill. I'm joking. What's happened?"

"Their little girl, Imogen, was taken earlier today," he tells us and I feel my blood run cold. Who would take a baby? I look down at the little girl in my arms and even though I've just met her, I can't picture someone wanting to harm a baby. It's not right.

"She's just a tiny baby. She was so small. I argued with him. I didn't even get to hold her," Denny cries and Harlow moves to sit down next to her.

"Hey, it's not your fault. You weren't angry at Imogen, babe, you were angry with your brother and he understood. But it's worse, baby," he says and Denny's head snaps up, looking at him.

"Oh my God, is Evan okay? Did he get hurt when they took her? I bet Kennedy is losing her mind. I couldn't cope if anything were to happen to Hope," she sniffles, looking over at the baby in my arms.

"He's fine, but Kennedy, she was in an accident and is critical in the hospital. Lexi is on her way, so we should go."

"Oh no!" she panics, but Mason whispers a few soothing words we can't hear. "Okay," she says, then it's like mayhem in the room. The brothers all stand at once, arguing about who's going and who's not. Maverick ends up offering to drive them as the storm outside is getting worse. It's not stopped raining all day. It's been dark and gloomy with thunder and lightning coming and going.

"We'll stay here with Hope. Call us if you need anything," Max says as he gives Denny a hug. Harlow rushes in the room with some bags and everyone looks at her in confusion.

"Going somewhere without me, babe?" Malik, the quietest of the brothers, asks as he stands tall by the door with his arms folded across his large chest. He's a scary motherfucker but I can tell with the softness and the love he shows his girlfriend that all that hardness is just on the outside.

"What? No! I just got a change of clothes and stuff for Mason and Denny," she tells him, smiling.

"How come?" Mason asks, walking back in the room, pulling Denny under his shoulder.

"In case you're there all night. I don't know what's going on, but you need to be there. Plus, I just looked at the weather forecast and the weather is getting worse. You need to hurry if you want to get there safely."

Mason gives her a gentle smile before taking the bags off her. He bends down giving her a gentle kiss on the forehead, earning a growl from Malik.

"Thank you," he tells her, then quietly they all walk out leaving me sitting alone with baby Hope. None of them know me so it has kind of shocked me that they would leave their daughter with me. They all seem like a tight bunch who take care of each other. I never had that with my brother. Thinking of him hurts and tears sting my eyes.

A few minutes later the front door flies open and everyone, minus Mason, Maverick and Denny, walks back in. They're all shaking the rain from their hair and coats and I have to be thankful it was me who was handed Hope and got to stay inside. It makes me sound selfish but to be fair, I'm kind of a baby when it comes to rain or snow. I hate being cold. It's been a nightmare since I left home, living under any shelter I could find and not having a warm, cosy, safe home to stay in. I guess that's another reason I don't want to get used to the luxury that living at Joan's brings. It took me months to get used to fighting the cold. Not that I ever really got used to it.

"Hey, want to play spin the bottle?" Max winks as he jumps on the sofa next to me, nearly waking a sleeping Hope up.

"How about you go outside and play by yourself?" I tell him dryly.

Not knowing where to look, I look back up at the paused movie, and find it paused on the part the girl is pinned to the shower wall. Jesus, Scott Eastwood is so hot. I look away, quickly feeling embarrassed for ogling.

"Aww, don't be like that, babe. You could always spin on something else," he winks and the gesture awakens my body. Why he affects me so much is beyond me. One minute I want to strangle the dickhead; the next I want to kiss his face off.

"How about you spin on this?" I tell him, giving him the middle finger.

"Now you're just turning me on," he tells me, then shocks the fuck out of me when he takes my hand, sucking my finger into his mouth. His full lips wrap around it sending tingles all the way to my toes. God, how can something so frivolous turn my body to liquid? I snatch my hand away quickly. A cocky grin spreads across his face making me want to smack the smile off it.

"Hey guys, Malik and I have um... We have..."

"To go and fuck each other's brains out?" Max finishes unashamedly.

"What? Of course not," Harlow glares, her face going bright red and I giggle into my hand watching her.

"Yes, we are, talk to you later," Malik says shortly, grabbing Harlow around the waist and picking her up.

"My coat," she shouts just as I hear Malik reply, "I love you wet."

I burst out laughing. It feels good. It's not something I've done a lot of; in fact, I can't think of the last time I laughed like this which is just plain sad.

"You have a beautiful laugh," Max tells me and I turn to look at him shocked. Had he been watching me the whole time?

"You really do have a way with words," I tell him seriously, wondering if his charm works on everyone. Who am I kidding? His looks alone would have women queuing the block to be with him.

"I have a way with a lot of things," he teases quietly.

"You really are something," I deadpan, looking away. It's hard to look at him for more than a few minutes. He's so goddamn good looking.

"I know, right," he says cheerfully and I have to fight back a smile at the playfulness he's forever portraying.

"Hey guys, I have to get Kayla back before the rain gets any worse. I might just stop the night there, so call and let me know if you hear anything from Mase," Myles calls from the door. I look up to find Kayla grabbing her coat and umbrella.

"Alright, bro, you walking?" Max asks shocked.

"Yeah, Kayla's dad doesn't want to risk her being out in a car in this weather. It seems there have been a few crashes today," he informs us sadly.

"Shit," Max says, running his hands through his still wet hair.

"Let us know when you get there."

"Will do."

Kayla waves goodbye and tells me to look after Scott Eastwood for her. I laugh, looking back at the paused movie.

"I'm just going to get changed into something of Mason's. The rain soaked through my hoody," Max says, getting up.

"Will his clothes fit? You're big," I tell him, then groan when I realise what the fuck just came out of my mouth. Why did I bother speaking? Oh, I know, because I'm an idiot.

"Oh, baby, trust me, I'm well aware," he smirks, grabbing his junk. I send him a glare before looking away. I grab the remote that Denny had left on the end of the sofa and press play. Not realising how loud it was I jump in fright and end up waking Hope up from her nap. She starts fussing which has me panicking. Standing up, I place her over my shoulder and tap her back. I've watched moms do this with their kids all the time, but when it doesn't work, I start rocking her from side to side. Well, okay, *I* start rocking from side to side, but you get the drift.

Max rushes in with his top barely over his head. Frozen to the spot, I stare at his rippling muscles as he pulls his top on with one hand.

Fuck me!

He has a body of a goddamn model. Jesus! How the hell has a lad his age got that kind of muscle? He's fit. I mean, you could trace each line of his six pack - well, eight pack - and dip your finger down his V line. I've never seen one of those on anyone in the flesh, only in pictures. I started to believe they were a fantasy and were just airbrushed, or whatever photographers do, but looking at Max I can see they are very, *very* real.

"You've got a bit of drool there," Max says, touching my mouth with his index finger.

Humiliated, I jump back, slapping his hand out of the way. I can't believe I just lost myself in his body. A loud burp next to my ear reminds me of Hope.

"Oh shit," Max says, stepping closer.

"What?" I ask, wondering if I'm holding her wrong.

"She's been sick," he says looking grossed out, his face scrunched up in revulsion.

"And? It's just a bit of sick," I dismiss.

"Um... It's in your hair," he says and it's then I notice he's not grossed out, but worried I'm going to start having a hissy fit over Hope's sick being in my hair.

I roll my eyes. "Here, let me go wash it out with some water. Do you think Denny will mind if I use a towel?" I ask unsure.

"Nah, go ahead, they're in the bathroom cabinet."

I give him a smile and watch him tend to Hope for a second. He's so gentle with her. He wipes her mouth with a wet wipe and with that I leave them to it and rush up to the bathroom.

The house looks so tiny from the outside but it's a decent size inside. The walls up the stairs are covered in photos of Hope, Mason and Denny. Some are of the brothers together and some with their girlfriends, they all look happy. I smile looking at them and when I get to the top one, one of a girl I've not met yet, holding Hope, I'm confused. She's pretty. Really pretty, but she doesn't seem to be anyone I've seen with any of the brothers or the girls.

Shaking it off I open the first door to the left and find myself in Hope's room. It's beautiful. So beautiful in fact that I feel a little envious of Hope.

Shutting the door behind me, I try the one across from it. Thankfully it's the bathroom and I make quick work of washing the sick from my hair and back of my top.

THREE

LAKE

IT TURNED OUT MY HAIR NEEDED more than a bit of water. Even after rinsing it out, I could still smell the sick in my hair. Hoping they wouldn't mind, I quickly washed my hair and towel dried it. I'm just brushing my fingers through the knots when I hear Joan's voice from downstairs.

Walking down, I'm greeted to her sitting down already with a cup of tea and watching a now sleeping Hope.

"Hey," I wave, walking in and hoping everything from earlier has been cleared up. I'm nervous as hell and honestly? My hands are shaking and worry ignites me. I don't want her to dislike me.

"Oh my, what's happened to you," Joan giggles, eyeing my wet hair.

"Hope was sick in my hair. I hope Denny won't mind but I quickly washed it. I couldn't get the smell out with just rinsing." Embarrassed, I can only stand there and twiddle my thumbs. It felt rude washing it upstairs, but now standing and telling someone, I feel intrusive.

"Nonsense, of course she wouldn't mind. You're actually in luck; I brought some clothes over for you. I went into town after the food bank closed and got you some new things. A new hairbrush and stuff is in there too."

The first thought in my head is that she's buying me stuff so I can move on, find somewhere else to go. I've become accustomed to not being wanted. I don't deserve to be after what I did. Sadness pervades me. I actually like it here. I said I'd never settle in a place where I started to like it. My life should be miserable, cold, lonely and unloved. After what I did it's the least that should have happened to me. But having Joan take care of me, Mark making me laugh and actually having warm food and a bed to sleep in has made me feel something other than dead. I don't want to lose that feeling.

"What's wrong?" Joan asks, breaking through my thoughts.

"You didn't need to get me new stuff. It's very kind of you but you don't need to do that," I tell her honestly. She shouldn't be wasting her money on someone like me.

"Stop talking nonsense, sweetie, I don't mind. I love treating my girls. You and Harlow should be spoilt," she smiles and I feel my eyes water. She's not even known me that long and already she's stationed me inside her family. *Her girls*. My heart shouldn't like her saying that but it does; it also brings a new wave of sadness to my heart. My mom used to call me her girl. I was always her girl. With it only being my brother and I, I seemed to get spoilt more with clothes, girly stuff and what have you. It'd been great until it hadn't. I don't know what my mom would call me now but I know *my girl* won't be it.

"You want me to stay?" I breathe out, not meaning to say it out loud.

"Who wanted you to go? Fuck me," Max says, walking in from behind me and making me jump. I turn around, my hand over my heart, and give him a glare.

"You scared me half to death. And what are you looking at?" I ask, taken aback by the intensity of his stare.

"Fuck me," he breathes again, and I notice his eyes on my hair, following it all the way down to my ass where his eyes stayed glued.

"Max, pick your jaw up and wipe that mouth," Joan teases and I snap my head back around to hers.

"Um, yeah, what were you saying?" he asks, but his attention is still on my hair by my ass.

"Did you order the food with Mark or not?" Joan asks and Max snaps out of whatever he's in when she mentions food, his eyes lighting up.

"Yeah," he grins then sits down at the other end of the sofa. "You gonna stand there all day?" he asks, looking at me, his eyes raking up and down my body.

"Sit here, let me put your hair in a French braid before you catch pneumonia," Joan says and my heart rate picks up. My mom used to love playing with my hair. It wasn't as long as it is now but it was still long enough for anyone who would see it to comment on it. I get it a lot. People wishing they had my hair or asking if it's my real hair.

Not trusting my voice, I sit on the floor in front of Joan with my back to her. I hear her rummage through the bags next to me and hear her triumphant 'whoop' when she finds what she's looking for. Then I feel the brush running through my hair.

It's not long after she gets all the knots out that the motion of the brush running through my hair brings tears to my eyes. I loved it when my mom would sit and brush it for no reason other than to brush it. It would send me to sleep, relax me after I had a bad day. Having Joan doing the exact same thing forms a lump in my throat and tears threaten to spill over my cheeks.

"I spoke with everyone at the food bank," Joan starts. Max grunts, causing a small smile to twitch at my lips.

"Who said I did it?" I ask quietly, knowing full well one of them blamed me, if not all of them. It had been their intentions all along.

"Liv and Jessica. Sarah didn't say much but then I don't think they got her involved. Put a little pressure on that girl and her mouth has verbal diarrhoea," Joan tells us, making me choke back a laugh. Oh Lord, this woman really has no filter. Max laughs out right, agreeing with her. It turns out the two went to school together or something.

"What did Miss Robins say?" I ask, hoping she didn't blame me. She's a lot like Joan: fun, easy going, but if you get on the wrong side of her you'd better watch out.

"Honestly, I never gave anyone a chance to say anything, but Miss Robins and Mr Dickens spoke up before I could say anything. They both disagreed and were outraged that the girls could accuse such an innocent girl," she tells me and I hear the smile in her voice.

If only she knew I wasn't an innocent girl. What I am is far from innocent.

"So what's happened?"

"Well, I've told them they can't volunteer anymore and that the church won't condone a hostile environment, but Jessica seems to think her father won't allow it. He's one of the big donors for the church. We will just have to see what happens, although, if I know her father, he won't tolerate her behaviour either."

At least she's honest. Most people would avoid telling you the truth just so they didn't have to deal with the aftermath.

"That's good," I smile, leaning forward as she finishes the French braid.

The doorbell rings and I look up, shocked. Who the hell would be out in this storm? They're crazy. Joan was crazy for going shopping, so whoever this is must be an adrenaline junkie like her.

Max gets up the same time as Joan and I do. When Mark walks in carrying two bags of takeout food, my belly rumbles. I should have guessed it was Mark when I mentioned adrenaline. I laugh inside thinking about how perfect the two are together.

"Right, I best be going. I've got some pyjamas in that bag so make sure you try them all on," Joan says and I look between her and Max, who is leaving the room with the food bags, in confusion.

"Let me get my coat, I'll walk over with you," I tell her, ready to get out of here. Anymore alone time with Max and I'll shoot myself, or jump him. The jury is still out on which one.

"Oh, didn't I tell you? Denny will be staying over at the hotel by the hospital. It seems the weather is much worse that end, blocking the main bridge. You and Max are on Hope duty. I've gotten you some food, a few movies and spoke to Denny to let her know you'll be okay. She said to stay in her bed and let Max sleep on the floor," she winks and grabs her coat.

"Wait!" I shout and she turns to me, waiting for me to speak. My mouth opens but nothing comes out. "Nothing," I grumble, not wanting to be one to complain, not after everything they've done for me. This is the least I can do for them.

I nearly change my mind when Max comes in with two plates of food. He gives me a wink and I inwardly groan. This is going to be a long night.

"LADIES SHOULD GO FIRST," I shout at Max outraged. So far, he's eaten my food once he devoured his, then finished my can of Pepsi and now the sod wants to choose the movie. It's only fair that I get to choose.

"No, I put Hope to bed," he smirks, skipping through the movies Joan had brought over.

"She's your niece," I deadpan. "Now, let me choose."

"I'm not watching that," he tells me outraged.

"Yes, you are. It's really good."

"It's a bunch of overgrown apes stripping," he tells me and I roll my eyes.

"It's not the bloody *Planet Of The Apes*, Max," I tell him, punching him in the arm.

"Ouch," he wheezes, rubbing his arm. "No, it's worse because they have actual man parts," he grumbles, looking at the DVD like it's an offending object.

"Oh my God, Max, just watch it, please," I beg, giving him the puppy dog eyes that always worked with my dad. I can see his resolve melting. It's working like a charm.

"Argh, don't do that," he tells me groaning.

"Come on, I promise we can watch whatever you want after. Even if it's the scary horror movie Joan put in. What's it called? Insidious Three?"

He shudders which has me leaning back a little. Is he turned on by the thought of watching a horror movie or is he scared? Nah, he can't be scared. He looks too tough to be scared of anything.

"I'll do you a deal," he says, looking at me mischievously. "I'll watch Magic Mike if you watch that strip show with Christina Aguilera in it." He's looking at me with a smirk, looking much too pleased like he thinks I'll say no.

No one says no when it involves having to watch Channing Tatum. EVER!

And huh? What strip show with her in it? I look through the DVDs and grin when I come to Burlesque. I used to watch this film on a continuous loop when I was back at home. I'd sing along, dance, and then do it all over again when the movie restarted. Christina Aguilera has an amazing voice. Watching this movie is no hardship.

"Deal," I shout, a big grin covering my face as I hold my hand out.

He takes it, looking at me sceptically. "Why do I feel like I just got played?"

"Watch and learn, my friend, watch and learn," I tease, walking over to put the movie in. I walk back over sitting on the other side of the sofa. Before I have chance to curl up, Max is pulling me to the other side of the sofa. I squeal, surprised.

"What are you doing?" I ask shocked, and a little pissed. How dare he man handle me like that?

"Easy, tiger, we've got one spare blanket. Whatever Denny did with her sleepover ones I haven't a clue. It's freezing and you're only wearing a thin pyjama set," he tells me, eyeing my body like it's not covered in said pyjama set.

Pervert!

"Oh, okay," I give in. I am cold and I've been pressed against Max for all of two seconds and already my body is heating up.

He nods his head and throws the blanket over the both of us. I snuggle in and watch the movie.

"I cannot believe we watched all that and not even any nudity. I'm disappointed."

"You were complaining before about seeing men parts, Max," I say, fighting back a grin. He's right, though, the movie wasn't all that good, but to be honest, I never really noticed anything past Channing Tatum.

"Come on, you have to agree. We sat through all that bullshit for two minutes of them prancing around at the end. I might have to become a stripper, though."

"You that hard up for cash?" I splutter, bug eyed. Why is the thought of him stripping actually pretty goddamn hot?

"Nah, but think of the women that would ride my dick each night," he grins and my bug eyed expression turns flat.

"You seriously are a pig."

Hope's cry comes from upstairs and Max looks at me. "What?" I snap.

"Your turn. I'll put the next movie on," he grins, showing off all his pearly whites.

Smacking his leg I throw the cover off us and jump up. Hope's cries get louder the farther up the stairs I get. Joan promised earlier she was a good baby, but if this is what they call a good baby then I'd hate to see what they call unsettled.

Walking into her room and over to her cot, I find her wailing her lungs out, her face bright red with her hands and feet everywhere. I lift her up under the arms and hold her against my chest.

"Come on, little cookie, everything's not that bad. You've got a home, a mommy and daddy who love and adore you, and you pretty much eat and sleep. Life's good," I tell her, trying to console her. Nothing works and I find myself sitting down – after ten minutes of pacing – in the rocking chair. Hope's room is pretty freaking cool. If I had a kid I'd want their room to look like this. Her name is beautifully written above her cot. In fact, the whole design spread around the room is pretty amazing.

"Come on, baby. Your mommy doesn't even know me and if she finds out that you've been crying for more than five seconds because I couldn't calm you down, she'd probably string me up. You don't want that. No one does," I coo quietly.

Forgetting my hair is in the braid, Hope tugs at it like its rope. I giggle down at her when she stops crying and she keeps tugging. She tries to chew and suck on the end, but I pull it away before she can get her slobber all over my hair.

"You'll get a fur-ball," I laugh. "How about you go to sleep for me and I'll think about us being best friends, huh? Yeah?"

A laugh at the door startles the shit into me. I'm flying up from the chair thinking its Denny or her bloke, but instead I find Max looking comfortable, perched against the doorframe.

"How long have you been there listening?" I blink in surprise.

"Long enough to hear you blackmail my niece," he grins blissfully.

"Pfft," I wave him off. "We have an understanding," is all I add quietly, noticing Hope settling down.

"Come on, I've made some popcorn and got some snacks."

"You're going to eat, again?" I add for good measure. Since we left for the food bank this morning, he has to have eaten every fifteen, maybe twenty, minutes. Where the fuck he puts it all is anyone's guess. Most girls would kill to be able to eat what they want and not put any weight on. Max having that ability is just plain mean. He's already got the looks, the body, he doesn't deserve to be able to eat everything his belly desires. It's just unfair. It's like God decided, when he was giving out people's genes, to dose Max with everything.

Selfish.

Greedy.

Unfair.

Yeah I'm jealous. When I had a healthy appetite I only had to look at something and I'd put ten stone on.

"Well, yeah. I've not eaten since we began the movie," he shrugs, watching as I put Hope back down in her cot.

"Whatever," I mutter under my breath as I follow him back down the stairs.

AFTER TRICKING MAX INTO watching a horror movie, we finally call it a night. Hope has been waking up every so often, screaming. A part of me thinks she knows something's going on: that her mom is upset. It has to be, right? Because even Max said she's not normally like this. The storm brewing outside comes to mind too because the wind howling and branches hitting the windows is pretty scary.

Speaking of scary, the door to the bedroom Joan said I could sleep in creaks open and in a moment of panic my heart stops. That is until I hear his voice whisper across the room, my body relaxing somewhat. But then it tenses for another reason entirely. Why is he walking into the room this late?

"Lake," he whisper yells, and I choose to ignore him. I don't know if I'll be strong enough to turn him down if he starts something with me. Every time he's around me I turn to mush or he opens his mouth and I want to strangle him.

I'm facing the other way so he can't see my face but, still, I shut my eyes tightly. He steps into the room, his feet moving closer towards the bed.

"Lake?" he calls a little louder but then silence fills the room.

Just when I think he's given up, his hand touches my shoulder and he violently shakes me. If I wasn't already awake he'd have a black eye and sore nuts for a week right now. Doesn't he know not to sneak up on girls when they're sleeping?

I've always had to be on guard, even in my sleep. Once, while staying at a refuge, someone tried to pinch the money that was tucked into my bra. It didn't turn out so well. They had scared me awake, frightening the life out of me, and my instincts had me attacking first. Ever since that night I've been worse. I've become a light sleeper and a part of me misses the deep sleeper I used to be. A full goodnight's sleep is something I really bloody miss.

"Jesus fucking Christ, Max. What are you trying to do? Give me a fucking heart attack?"

"I thought I saw a spider on you," he tells me. I feel him shifting on the bed, getting himself comfortable, which just gets my back up.

"So, you snuck into the bedroom to watch me sleep and you were paying that much attention you happened to see a spider? In the dark? You do realise spiders are black, right?" I snap, turning to look at him.

"Look, I keep hearing noises and it's freaking me out," he tells me honestly, scrubbing a hand down his face.

Seeing he's deadly serious, I roll over into my pillow and burst into laughter. Oh, my God, I thought he was exaggerating over the movie. He doesn't seem like the kind to be scared of a little blood and gore. I laugh even harder when I think back on the time I shouted at him for touching my leg in a tight grip. I thought he was copping a feel, but it turns out he was telling the truth and that the movie made him jump.

"Stop laughing," he groans, shoving my shoulder.

I turn sideways to look at him, not able to hold back my laughter. "I'm sorry," I laugh. "But, you're you…and you're scared… of dolls," I cry harder, laughing.

"There's no need to be fucking mean. I'm never going to look at Hope the same. One of them looked a little like her, didn't you see?"

"No," I choke out laughing, my ribs and stomach hurting.

"Oh, come on, the one could turn its head all the way around. It was fucking scary, Lake. I'm glad Granddad let us chuck the porcelain dolls out that my nan used to collect," he curses right before I hear the bed shake from his shudder.

"It's a movie, it's not real and it still doesn't explain you becoming a creeper coming into my room," I scold playfully, still not able to hide the grin from my face. My cheeks are hurting so bad from smiling and laughing but it feels good.

"I wasn't being creepy. I just wanted to know if you were awake."

"And when I didn't answer the first time you didn't clue in?"

"I thought you were ignoring me," he shrugs looking away and I know he's lying which makes me smile. "Plus, I told you, I keep hearing noises."

"What kind of noises?"

"Creepy ones," he shudders, lying back down on the pillow and shoving his hands behind his head. The movements cause his top to ride up a little and what I wouldn't give for a little light right now.

Just get comfy, I think sardonically when he starts shifting pillows.

"And how do creepy noises sound?"

"Like, I don't know, creepy. The floorboards kept creaking and, I swear, the walls were talking to me, with a tick-tock sound clicking in the background."

"One: it's because we've all come to bed. My mom used to tell me it was the floorboards relaxing having so many people walking on them all day. Two: you do realise the tick-tock sound could actually be the clock above the fire place making the noise?"

"What is your mom like?" he asks, catching me off guard. My body tenses and I find myself unable to answer for a few seconds.

"Don't change the topic," I snap a little too heatedly.

"Look, I'm scared as fucking shit. In fact, I've checked my fucking boxers twice just to make sure I've not shit me self. All I'm asking is for you to reach into your heart and let me have the right side of the bed."

"I'm not sleeping with you," I shout, then wince and listen out for Hope, the grouchy little cookie.

"Babe, I'm not going to touch you. I'm too fucking scared. In fact, touching you reminds me of that clip you showed me of Piranha 3D where the fish eats his dick. Inside the fucking woman," he shudders, holding his crotch.

I laugh; I can't help it. I told him he could watch that or this movie about dolls. When I showed him that clip from Piranha my plan couldn't have gone any better. That was until he started cursing me for putting on the new doll movie.

"Okay, Okay, but you've got the next Hope duty," I add, holding my hand out.

He takes my hand with a scoff before shaking it. "You're going to be the death of me. You're a cunning woman and so tiny too."

"Goodnight," I smile and roll over onto my side.

I'm drifting into the place between dreams and reality when Max speaks.

"Are you awake still?"

Maybe if I ignore him now we've already spoken he will let me sleep. My eyes are stinging and I can't see Hope staying asleep much longer.

"Max, go to fucking sleep."

"Okay, but can I ask a question, a serious one?"

"Yeah, but it doesn't mean I'll answer," I answer him, my eyes now wide open, wondering what he's going to ask me.

"Why were you sleeping on the streets? You could have gotten a job and rented a place, or hell, even gone to the council and gotten the help you need to get a place."

His question is so innocent but so personal at the same time. However, unlike any other time someone asks me a personal question; I find myself answering honestly as I can instead of avoiding it.

"Some people don't deserve the luxury of a home, the fullness of a decent meal and fresh, hot water to bathe in. Don't kid yourself by thinking I've been given a shitty hand; where I am, Max, is where I deserve to be. Never mistake that for one second," I breathe out quietly. Neither of us says anything else but I can hear him thinking from all the way over here. I tune out his heavy breathing and the thick tension now between us and fall to sleep.

FOUR

MAX

I'M LAGGING AND DRAGGING MY feet the next morning. Not only did I do the next wake up duty with Hope but I also did every one after that. It seems I pissed off Lake more than I realised last night by asking questions because, after I came back from the first shift, I walked back into the bedroom to find her gone.

I'm still unsure if it was because I woke up spooning her or if it was what she revealed last night. How she thinks she deserves the life she's been given is fucking stupid. No one deserves that. No one.

Her words still echo inside my head. She seemed so sad, her words so dark and for someone so beautiful with so much light inside of her, I find it hard to believe she truly believes that about herself. If she does, I'll have fun showing her differently. She should be bathed in love, given everything she ever needed and... fuck, I sound like a fucking pussy.

Shit, I'm turning into Myles.

That shit needs to end right now.

Its mid morning by the time I get Hope settled again and I'm on my tenth cup of coffee. The front door opens and in walks a tired looking Denny and Mason, both looking worse for wear. If I wasn't so tired I'd say something witty but I just want my bed.

"How's your brother's girlfriend and kid?" is all I manage to get out.

"Good, they're all good," she smiles sadly.

"Good," I yawn.

"Dude, you look like shit. You get any sleep?" Mason asks and then I notice Denny looking around for Lake.

"She's not here," I tell her, then look over to my brother with a deadpan expression. "I slept like a baby, Mason. Up every few fucking hours. I'm knackered. I need a break. You're going to have to watch her for a bit. I'm going to bed," I shout out and then groan when I hear Hope start crying.

"Nice one, dickhead, you scared her awake."

"I'm going. I can't even argue," I yawn again. "I'll be back in a bit to go over the stag party," I wave off. I get up, walk up to Denny and give her a hug and kiss. Mason growling is something I'm used to whenever I'm near Denny, so I make him sweat by hugging her harder.

Chuckling when Mason pulls me away, I walk back into the front room to Hope. She fell asleep in her bouncer not even twenty minutes ago. Leaning down, I kiss her head.

"Princess, I love you, but I'm popping home to do that thing you couldn't seem to do all night... Sleep."

"Wait till you have kids of your own," Denny giggles.

I turn, giving her a small smile. "Some lucky fucker would be thrilled to have kids with me," I tell her before leaving.

No one knows that I don't want kids. I mean, how could they? They've never even asked. They look at me, see a player and that's as far as it goes. Then they see me with Hope and believe it's what I want.

Looking at Hope everyday makes me believe I could but then I remember where I came from, what blood runs through my veins, and the thought disappears within a second.

It's no secret my parents were shitty ones that never loved us but at some point they had to have loved each other. That's why I'll never fall in love. I'll never let anyone turn me into what my parents turned each other into. Somewhere along the line they broke each other, or maybe they were always like that.

I'm still unclear why my mom even had us. She cleared off the second she could, leaving us with that monster. A part of me prays that I'll never end up like them but as they say, 'an apple never falls far from the tree'.

"Hey, do you know where my iPod is? I want to go for a run," Maverick asks when I walk in a few seconds later.

I look around the spotless room before turning to him tiredly and saying, "Ask Joan." I don't stick around and choose to ignore his cursing as I make my way upstairs to bed. I fall down face first and fall to sleep.

———

"We're not having a joint stag party," I yell at Harlow.

"Why? It would be so cool. We could…"

"What? Sit around and paint each other's nails?"

"Bro, you wanna back off?" Malik growls, coming to stand behind Harlow in a protective stance. I roll my eyes at him. Pussy whipped. Harlow has had him by the balls since she moved in next door. I can't even dislike her either because I love her like a sister. But still, Malik was badass before.

"Look, all I'm saying is a stag party is a rite of passage. For centuries grooms have been given a night of freedom, a night to reflect on what is and what will be. It's a night for a group of close friends and family to give the groom a night to remember without the constraints of their fiancée there."

"You make it sound like I'm chaining him down," Denny snaps. I give her a sheepish look. Isn't that what a wedding ring is? A chain that holds them down?

"Henry Vlll had a stag party, Spartans even had a stag party, so, goddamn it, Mason will have a stag party," I boom, slamming my fist down at the table.

"Hey, um, Joan said could you keep it down," Lake whispers, walking in.

"No! Not until Mason agrees that I'm right," I all but yell, standing up. My eyes glue to Lake's body. She's wearing skin tight leggings with a hoody that looks extra large on her. Her hair is pulled up into a messy bun and she's not wearing any makeup, not that I've ever seen her with any on. She looks hot as fuck.

"On second thoughts, we can have a joint stag party. Lake here can be the stripper. Bagsy having the first lap dance," I grin, giving a wink to Lake. Her face turns stormy and before I know it she's in front of me, pointing at my chest. I'm shoved back in my chair completely shocked. She's actually going to give me a lap dance. I smirk up at her, placing my hands at my side. But instead, I get a slap around the face.

"What the fuck was that for?" I cry, holding a hand to my stinging cheek. My eyes start watering and I curse loudly.

"Oh, he's gonna cry," Malik teases from behind me.

I ignore his comment and the others as I race out of the room after Lake. She's in her room by the time I catch up to her. When I slam the door shut behind me she looks up from the bed wide eyed. I'm about to lay into her about hitting me but then I see her tear streaked face and I keep my mouth shut.

I've never been good with tears: men or women. But seeing Lake cry, a crippling pain etches inside my chest.

"Hey, I'm sorry," I tell her softly, sitting on the edge of the bed. I don't know what I'm actually apologising for but it seems like the right thing to do. I've watched Mason do it a thousand times with Denny when she's upset. Malik just carries Harlow off to their room and somehow I can't see Lake being okay if I did that.

"Just because I don't have a home, or any family, or a well paid job, doesn't mean I'd do that for money. Don't treat me like a piece of meat," she sniffles into the pillow.

"Lake. Fuck. What I said downstairs was a joke. Not that I wouldn't want a lap dance off you, I fucking would, but I didn't mean it like you heard it. Harlow is trying to convince Mason and Denny to have a joint hen and stag party. I was just trying to get her to see the error of her ways," I rush out, hoping she believes me. It's not like she has any reason to; I come out with stupid shit all the time and I've never had to explain myself.

"It was degrading, Max. You made me feel a fool in front of them all."

"I didn't mean to. I really am sorry," I heatedly tell her, knowing this time I mean it one hundred percent. "Why did you leave last night? Did I try to feel you up? I've been told a time or three that I have a tendency to do that."

"What? No, you didn't," she tells me, her lips twitching while she wipes her eyes.

"You sure? I can get really touchy feely. You only had to wake me up," I wink.

She scoffs. "I'm sure I did. Now go away, I'm tired."

"Me too," I grin, waggling my eyebrows.

"Do you ever give up?"

"Do you ever give in?"

"Do you always answer a question with a question?"

"Why? Is it bothering you?"

"Oh God, just go," she whines, throwing herself on the pillow.

"Nah, I'm bored."

She turns a little to the side as I lay back on her bed next to her. She looks annoyed but I can see by the way her lips twitch that she's dying to smile.

"So, go out," she tells me, trying to push my large frame off the bed. I grab her wrist, stopping her, and turn to face her.

"I'd rather keep you company. I don't want you to get bored. You know what it means when a girl gets bored right?"

"No, do tell," she says dryly, not pulling her hand away from my grasp.

"It means they want sex. So, if you ever get bored just call me, I'd hate to know that you're bored," I tease, but, in all seriousness, if she ever did get bored she could actually call me. I'd bang her in a second. I'd probably last that long too; she's that fucking hot.

"Oh my God! You're such a dick," she laughs. The door to her room knocks before it opens. Joan walks in with a smile on her face.

"Mark and I are popping out, honey, I'm bored," Joan tells Lake. "I'll be back in about a few hours."

"No, darling, make that four," Mark shouts from another room and Joan grins excitedly.

I look to Lake to find a blush has risen to her cheeks and I have to bite my lip to stop myself from laughing.

"Okay," Lake whispers wide-eyed.

"Oh, Max, while you're here can you make Lake dinner. I'm not sure if we'll be back in time," she winks.

I nod my head while answering, "Yes, I'll do her some dinner."

"Good boy."

Joan waves goodbye before leaving the room. The second the door clicks, Lake and I turn to each other and burst into laughter.

"Oh my God," she laughs hard.

"I told you," I laugh, holding my ribs. If only she knew half the shit Joan and Granddad do. Hell, I shouldn't know half the shit they do, but they have a tendency to fill you in on shit.

"That means nothing. Oh my God, I can't breathe," Lake wheezes out, making me laugh harder.

I lean over so I'm half lying on her. "Want me to give you mouth to mouth? I'm told my kiss could bring back the dead."

"I'm sure you could," she insists, pausing. "With breath like that," she adds giggling.

My mouth hangs open in shock and I think I just fell in lust with Lake. She's seriously fucking hot when she gives it back. I growl loudly making her laugh harder, but before she can take another lung full of breath, I start tickling her, making her scream and shout for me stop.

"I love it when you scream my name. Now beg," I declare, roaring with laughter. I have to dodge her hands when they come flying out of nowhere, but I miss her elbow a second too late and it rears back hitting me square in the jaw.

"O.M.G. I am so sorry. I didn't mean to. I just hate being tickled," she panics looking at my jaw wide-eyed.

"I got that when the elbow hit my jaw. Just for that, I'm picking the first movie," I wink then playfully slap her thigh before jumping off the bed.

"Just don't pick a cartoon," she moans, flopping back down on the bed. Jesus, two days with this chick and I can't leave her the fuck alone. In all fairness, I've wanted to get in her pants since the first time I saw her, but now, knowing how cool she actually is for a chick, I want to get to know her.

Get to know her? Fuck, I'm turning into my brother. Speaking of...

"Hey, want to help me think up a prank to get Myles back?" I ask, flopping back down on the bed. I chose Avengers. It seemed to be the only thing Joan had put in here that was up to date. The rest look like old black and white movies.

"Why do you need to prank your brother?" she asks warily.

Shit. How do I explain this? It wasn't so much him sending the messages announcing I was batting for the other team but more about the fact I got asked out by Tim Scott. It seemed word got around after my brother sent those messages, and let's not forget little miss smarty pants, Kayla. She sent fucking Poppy a message making me look like a dick. The chick stalked me for weeks. I threatened her with a restraining order. It took me to dial 999 in front of her for her to leave me the fuck alone.

"It's a long story but trust me when I tell you it's been a long time coming," I shrug.

"Okay, what did you have in mind?"

I love that she doesn't question me any further and readily agrees with me not even knowing the true cause.

"I'm the looks, not the brains, this is where you come in," I tell her pointedly. I don't want to get my hopes up but I see good things in the near future for this prank. "I'm thinking something big, something that involves Kayla."

"Ha, like what? Tell Kayla that Myles is enrolling in the army?" she laughs and my ears perk up.

"YES! That could actually work. I could forge a form, okay, maybe ask Liam to forge it for me and then show it to her. Make a big deal out of it. They argued about what university they were going to go to after college. I think they've made up their minds now, but this, this is great," I laugh evilly.

"Are you trying to break them up?" she asks horrified.

"Nothing could break those two up. Trust me, they're super-glued together, or melded."

"That's good and all but it's kind of boring."

"True, but it can be a start. Let me think. Okay, I'll let you think, but you get the drift."

I sit thinking it over and look to find Lake engrossed in the movie. "Hey, you're supposed to be thinking," I snap.

"Um...Chris Hemsworth is on the television, that's the most concentration you'll get out me."

"I'll turn it off," I warn.

"You wouldn't," she gasps and I give her a pointed look that tells her I would.

"Okay," she snaps with a huff. "What about...?" She pauses before laughing. "What about tying his shoe laces together? That way, when Kayla finds out about the whole army stuff, he falls flat on his face when she storms off."

"You do know he's not going in the army?" I ask her carefully.

She sits up quickly looking at me. "Better yet, why don't you start a prank war between them? You start it, but make them think it was the other? Then ta-dah," she sings, throwing her arms in the air. "You step forward, give a bow, and tell them it was all your doing."

I'm wondering now if she doesn't live at home because she's crazy, but the more I think over her idea, the more I begin to like it. I could work with this.

"I'm a genius," I grin.

She gives me a dark facial expression. "Don't you mean me? I *was* the one who came up with it."

"Yeah, yeah," I wave her off. "But I'm the one that come up with asking you, therefore, I'm the genius."

"I'm struggling on whether to slap you or laugh," she deadpans, lying back down.

"Don't. It would ruin my pretty face and after that elbow to the jaw, I think you've done enough damage."

FIVE

LAKE

BANGING ON MY BEDROOM DOOR wakes me up. I groan into my pillow, ready to tell my mom to go away when I realise that I'm not at home. I can never go home again. Not after what I did. Tears burn the back of my eyes but the continuous knocking on the door stops them from falling.

"Mav, go away," a deep rumble barks out and I jump up with a squeal. Max is lying down next to me on the bed, his sleepy eyes looking up at me with a lazy grin. The person at the door decides that's the time to barge in and I have to bite my lip from whimpering. They're going to think we did something together. Oh no! Joan will think we did something together.

"It's not what it looks like," I blurt out worriedly. I relax when Denny and Hope walk in, Denny wearing a grin.

"Of course it is," Max yells outraged, looking at me. I turn giving him a grave expression. He just grins in return, lazily folding his arms under his head and lying back down on my pillow. "How's my girl?" he coos and for a minute I think he's talking to me, but when I turn again to look at him he's looking all soft faced at Hope.

She mumbles something; her baby vocabulary limited.

"Did she just say Max?" Max shouts, flying off the bed and rushing over to Hope. Denny stares wide-eyed between the two of us before turning to give Max a death glare.

"No, she didn't, Max," Denny deadpans.

Hope says something else and, yet again, it doesn't make any sense whatsoever. "Listen, she said it again," Max yells and I can't stop the giggle that escapes my mouth. He looks like a little boy who's woken up at Christmas and has received the toy he's been wishing for for months. It's adorable. "Don't look at me like that, Lake. She did. She said it clear as day."

"Of course she did," I snicker, rolling my eyes. Denny laughs, shaking her head.

"Max, let it go," Denny breaks in, interrupting Max before he has a chance to argue. His shoulders sag in defeat. I chuckle. He looks like Denny just kicked his puppy.

"She said it," he boasts, clearly not letting it go.

"Max, shut it. We've ordered in a chippy next door. I weren't sure if you had eaten. In fact, I didn't know you were here at all," Denny smirks, looking at Max and then over to me. I feel my face heat but, thankfully, it takes more than this to make my face go red. "But luckily you're both here."

"Starving," Max adds, rubbing his belly.

"Lake?" Denny asks. Not having any money to contribute, my expression turns grim.

"I'm not hungry, but thank you," I smile, hoping it comes off as genuine.

"Bollox, you've not fucking eaten all day. Ants have eaten more than you," Max barks out.

"I'm fine," I bite out, giving him a warning look.

"We've already ordered now. When we couldn't find you..." she says to Max and then turns back to me. "And *you* weren't answering the front door, we decided to just order for you. Harlow only came back ten minutes ago with the key to let me in. Hope you don't mind. It's only sausage and chips," she shrugs. "Honestly, it will just go to waste."

Looking at Denny I can tell she's telling the truth, about them ordering that is. No doubt the others won't have trouble eating what they ordered for me but I am actually hungry, and my stomach chooses the worst time to grumble, so I agree.

"Take that as a yes," Denny grins.

Max laughs and I elbow him in the stomach. I can't believe the guy is growing on me. As annoying as he is, he's the first friend I've had in a year. At least a friend that's my age anyway.

"Will you stop hitting me," he wheezes. "I'm going to need mouth to mouth if you keep on."

"I bite," I grin before grabbing my jacket. I don't bother with my hair; I'll shove it up in a bun when I get over there. Denny laughs and as we're walking down the stairs she speaks up.

"You know what they say, if the opposite sex hits you it means they like you."

"No, Denny, that's called domestic violence," Max says slowly, sounding disgusted. I laugh, not able to help it, and watch as Denny stops at the bottom of the stairs and turns to Max rolling her eyes.

"It's a saying. You know when a boy teases you at school, it means he likes you."

"No, that's what parents told little girls to make them feel better about themselves. They clearly don't have the heart to tell them how it really is," Max tells her not caring. We both look at him open mouthed, then to each other shaking our heads.

I'M STILL UNSURE HOW IT happened. First I was eating sausage and chips, then I got roped into playing Monopoly where Max continued to cheat, and then it turned into watching a movie.

Before I know it, I'm waking up to Max whisper yelling at me. "Will you get up?" he hisses.

"Fucking hell, Max," I curse, pushing him away and, in turn, pushing him on his ass. Looking around I realise I must have fallen asleep watching the movie because everyone has gone and its pitch black outside.

"Come on," he whispers at me, grabbing my hand. I shove him off still feeling a little out of it and tired as hell.

"Where are we going?" I groan, standing up and stretching my back. It clicks and it feels so good I let out a moan. Max starts coughing and I look at him wondering what the fuss is all over. "What?"

"Fuck! I really want to shove your knickers down to your ankles and sink right into you so hard that you make that noise you just made over and over," he confesses, shocking the hell out of me and, if I'm a little honest, it's turned me on.

"You're such a lad," I chide him, smacking his arm whilst trying to act like his words didn't bother me, when really they've made wetness pool between my legs.

"Hey, hey, none of that, you heard what Denny said; it means you like me," he winks then grabs something from his back pocket.

"What on earth is that?" I ask, ignoring his earlier statement.

"Permanent markers," he grins, holding up black and red permanent markers.

Why on earth does he have those? Then it clicks and I giggle. "Myles is so going to kill you. I thought he was at Kayla's tonight?"

"Nah, Kayla's dad is out of town with his missus so Kayla's staying here. It was too late for them to go back after the movie anyway," he tells me and a thought occurs to me.

"Hey, you haven't drawn on me while I was asleep have you?" I ask, looking for a mirror to check my reflection.

"As much as I was tempted to draw a dick on your face, I'd rather stick mine in your mouth," he grins winking.

I smack him upside the head. *Max and his dirty mouth*, I muse.

I shake my head. The thought of him in my mouth kind of makes me cringe. I've only ever done it once and spent the whole time gagging for air. Plus, my boyfriend at the time kind of smelled funny down there. Like sweat, or musk, I don't know. I just know the smell alone was enough to make me gag, let alone his dick shoved to my tonsils. Just thinking about my ex has me wanting to throw something across the room. That fucker has a lot of blame leading up to the events that changed my whole life, my parent's whole world.

"Hey, you look like you want to take my dick and sink your teeth into it. Please stop having those thoughts; my dick can sense it," Max whispers, stopping on the stairs. My eyes reach his, forgetting about my ex, and I nearly laugh at the pure fear that has washed across his features. When I don't speak, he grins before turning and carrying on up the stairs.

I look at his retreating form and shake my head. I've never met anyone like him. How he managed to make me smile after having thoughts of my ex is proof he's one of a kind. That and he's fucking nuts.

We come to a door that must be Myles' bedroom and Max wastes no time in opening it; careful to make little noise. He seems to know where to stand so the floorboards don't creak and I have to say that's clever as fuck.

I think about all the times my brother got caught sneaking out to go to a party because of some creaky floorboard. My parents would go mad at him every single time, but it never stopped him trying again and again.

I shake my thoughts away once I step a little into the room. I try to adjust my eyes to the darkness of the room but it doesn't come. The hallway is lit up from the moon shining through the windows, but with the curtains in the room closed, I can hardly make out a thing. Max must know where he's going because I notice his large form bending over the bed before I hear the lid from the pen pop off, echoing in the silent room.

One of them stirs and Max crouches down low, hiding from view. When the body turns away from us I notice Max relax before kneeling back up and carrying on. My eyes adjust a bit to notice the body that turned away from us is larger than the other one. I gasp when I realise it's Kayla he's drawing on. I'm sure she said she had early lessons tomorrow and a job interview for a local supermarket.

Ten minutes later Max is walking out of the room wearing a silly grin on his face.

"Did you draw on Kayla?" I whisper yell, ready to walk back down the stairs. Max's hand reaches out stopping me.

"Yes, and where are you going?" he whispers back.

"Um, home?" I tell him, wondering where he thinks I'll be going at this time of the morning. Then I realise I've left my keys in my room. "Shit, I don't have a key. You don't suppose Malik and Harlow would be up do ya?"

"Nah, it's half three in the morning. I'm surprised I woke up when I did. We fell asleep again on the sofa."

"Seems we keep doing that," I add on a grumble. Max grins and I hate it when he gives me that grin. He's hot and he knows it. Usually this type of lad would have me turning the other way, but something about Max's confidence and arrogance is appealing. I think it's because I see something hidden behind those eyes of his. Behind all that fun, outgoing exterior there's a broken boy somewhere; he's just afraid to show it.

"Come on, we can sleep in my room," he declares, and my steps falter.

"I don't think so," I hiss.

"Oh come on, it's not like we haven't slept together before. Plus, I promise if you touch me inappropriately I'll let you," he smirks, eyeing me up and down. The look sends chills up and down my spine and I have to fight back the shudder my body desperately wants to deliver under his penetrating gaze.

I don't know what I was expecting when he opened the door to his room, but walking in, this wasn't it. It was spotless.

"Holy shit, you clean your shit?" I ask, completely shocked.

He looks at me sheepishly, his cheeks turning a tinge of pink and I narrow my eyes.

"Technically, Joan keeps my *shit* cleaned. I'm a busy man," he cringes and I burst into laughter.

"Don't worry about it. My mom cleaned my brother's room for him but never mine. I think it's a boy thing," I laugh, but then stop short when I realise what came out of my mouth. I've not spoken to anyone about my brother, Cowen. My vision begins to blur as memories start to surface. My body starts shivering from the cold rain, however, when the feel of two warm hands land on my shoulders, it brings me back to the present, my mind is back in the room with Max.

"Sorry," I croak out, images of my brother filtering through my mind.

"It's okay. So, a brother, huh? You the youngest or the eldest?"

It's then that it occurs to me that Max and I have one more thing in common. A small smile gifts my lips but it's soon gone when I think of everything my brother and I shared.

"Younger," I tell him, avoiding his eyes, not really wanting to talk about Cowen or my life back home. It only hurts me more.

"What about you? Who's the eldest between you and Myles?"

"Me," he boasts, pushing his chest out. I giggle and sit on the edge of the bed.

"You don't talk about your family," he states, and I look up at him shrugging my shoulders. His shoulders sag a little, yet, it's enough for me to notice. I watch him sit down next to me on the bed and hear him take in a deep breath before speaking. "My brothers think I don't remember much from our childhood, but I do. I remember most of it and all of it was bad. My dad wasn't a good person, neither of my parents were. But somehow we managed," he sighs, running his hands down his face. I'm completely stunned by his admission. I'm not sure what I expected him to say, but that wasn't it. "I don't even know why I'm telling you this. I guess I just want you to know I understand. I know I've asked you before, but who spills all their secrets when just meeting someone? Plus, I wasn't lying when I told you we all have experience in this shit."

"Max," I start, wanting to assure him, but he holds his hand up stopping me.

"Don't lie, please, just don't lie. No one can hurt you here."

I look at him with a sad smile. "That's not true. What if the person you're running from is yourself? What if the person that can hurt you is no one other than yourself? Not everything is black and white, Max. My parents are great people. The best parents a child could wish for."

"No need to rub it in," he teases, lightening the mood.

I chuckle, not taking my eyes from him. "Seriously, though, my parents are great. The only mistake they've ever made was ever having me," I tell him, not meaning for the truth to slip out. As soon as the words leave my mouth I know there's no way to take them back.

This is the first moment since running away that I've desired to tell someone. But I know as soon as the truth about what I did leaves my mouth, I'll have no one. And as much as I promised myself I'd make myself suffer for what I did, I still yearn for that warm touch, for that love blanketing me. And I know in an instant of telling the Carters and their family, I'll lose every single one of them.

"I don't believe that for a second. How could you be anyone's mistake?"

Tell that to my brother who is now 6ft under, I whisper to myself. I shrug not knowing what to say or wanting to answer him, scared I'll reveal more than I intend to.

"Enough of the depressing anyway, I could just go listen to Myles talk about college for that shit. Tell me, you ever had an orgasm?" he teases, lying back on the bed with a cocky grin on his face. I follow, lying down next to him and just laugh at him, the earlier tension easing from my body.

"By myself or someone else?" I ask teasing him back.

That's how we fall asleep, talking about nothing important and getting to know each other. It turns out the arrogant boy has more to him than just his muscles and looks.

SIX

LAKE

THE SOUND OF SOMEONE LETTING one rip jolts me awake. I roll over, glaring at a sleeping Max. He's lying flat on his back again, although, this time he's got one hand down his boxers and one on his bare chest.

That's when the smell catches up with me and I begin to gag, pushing Max off the bed. He falls with a loud thump before jumping to his feet in fright.

"What? Where did he go?" he shouts, looking around the room with an alarmed expression. I cover my mouth to smother the giggle. He's shirtless, standing in Bart Simpson boxer shorts, hair looking like he's been electrocuted and wearing the most adorable facial expression I've ever seen on him.

I'm about to fake waking up when a loud scream comes from down the hall, scaring me half to death.

"Myles, how could you?" Kayla screams, her voice full of sadness and anger. Her raised voice is followed by heavy footsteps stomping down the stairs.

Max and I look to each other before jumping off the bed and running down the hall and down the stairs to where they've stormed off to.

"How could you do this? I've got an interview later on and I can't go looking like The Bride of Chucky," Kayla cries.

I turn the corner just in time to see Max's handy work. Laughter erupts from my mouth before I have a chance to cover it. Max has drawn raindrop shapes around her eyes in black and somehow he's managed to colour them in. How he did that in the darkness is incredible, it's a little smudged but that's most likely from moving around in her sleep. It's the mouth that is the funniest. He's drawn a full blown smile across her mouth in red and even in a temper she looks as happy as Larry.

Max starts laughing like a hyena and Kayla and Myles turn to glare at him. My laughing soon stops, not wanting to be on the receiving end of their glares.

"I'm going to get a drink and then I'm leaving," Kayla snaps at us all before storming off into the kitchen.

"What did you do?" Myles grits out the second Kayla is hidden from view. His eyes are hard and completely focused on Max, his look deadly and ready to strike.

"Me? Nothing. What did *you* do?"

Myles sighs looking at his brother for any indication that he's lying. When he can't figure him out he turns to me, but I just hold my hands up, palms facing him, and back away without saying a word.

Kayla walks in still looking as happy as can be, her eyes narrowing on Myles. "I'm going home; I don't think I'll be back later," she tells him shortly, storming off. Myles follows her, but she turns back around quickly, stopping him and giving him a sad expression. "Myles, I'm supposed to be storming off, I can't do that if you're following me," she sighs.

He nods, his head letting her go and once again she turns around squaring her shoulders before storming out of the house. Myles looks confused once again as he watches the now closed door.

"Is it bad I'm wondering if she still made me lunch?" Myles asks before shaking his head. "Never mind. Oh and Max, if I find out you had anything to do with this I'll pay you back."

Max grins. "Now, now, Myles, you don't want to go playing around with Karma now do you? You know how much of a bitch she can be," he winks before heading into the kitchen. I follow a few seconds later, wondering why there isn't a full blown punch out.

This family is so freaking weird.

If I had done something like that to my brother he'd go ape shit right there and then and cause a massive riot.

Then again, with the strength and love this family have for each other, nothing should surprise me.

Walking into the kitchen I'm surprised by the mess. Chippy wrappers are littering the sides along with other bits and bobs, the sink is piled up with dishes and I'm pretty sure the bin needed emptying last week.

"I take it Joan didn't get around to the kitchen?" I ask, peeling a wrapper away from the stool.

"Yeah, she did it yesterday morning. This is from last night," he says, absentmindedly looking into the fridge. He starts shoving things around before grabbing the loaf of bread out of the bread bin and I watch disgusted as he makes a jam sandwich. No one should be forced to eat jam, especially on a sandwich. I used to hate it when the school dinner ladies made us eat them.

Opening my mouth to give him shit, I watch as he shoves the sandwich into a container before throwing it into the fridge. He then continues to throw a foiled – what looks like a baguette – under the sink. I'm stunned to silence then watch as Myles rushes in freshly showered and dressed.

"You could have told me it was half ten, dickhead. I'm late," Myles snaps at Max.

"You're pregnant?" Max gasps wide-eyed but an unamused Myles ignores him, heading over to the fridge.

"Shit. Max, I'm going to make you pay for doing what you did. I know it was you. Call it twin intuition or just common fucking sense but I know you did that to Kayla and now I'm the one paying for it. She switched my sandwich to jam," he moans, slamming his head against the closed fridge door.

"Your girlfriend makes you sandwiches?" I ask shocked. They're like a married couple. Jesus! They're barely out of nappies.

Ignoring me, Myles walks over to Max, shoving him against the sink. "I'm going to get you back," he yells, right before he slams the jam sandwich at Max's chest.

"Well then, that went well," I mutter, jumping off the stool.

"Where are you going? You want to lick the jam off me?" Max winks and I look to him in disgust.

"There is nothing powerful enough on this earth to get me to put jam in my mouth."

"Oh, but the licking me part is still in? That's cool," he nods, grinning.

I groan, walking towards the front door, listening to his bare feet paddling after me. "See you later, alligator."

"In a while, crocodile," he shouts back, making me smile.

"In an hour, sunflower," I chuckle, carrying on the rhyme my mother would always say.

"Fuck, I got nothing after the crocodile," he shouts when I reach Joan's. He's still standing on his front porch and I turn around laughing. "But an hour it is."

"Go away," I laugh. My fist rises to knock the door when I'm pulled in by a frantic looking Harlow.

"Um, morning," I wave, feeling uncomfortable. As much as I've gotten close to Max in a couple of days, the others, not so much. Jesus, a couple of days? It feels like I've known him longer. It's weird. Then again, an hour in Max's presence and it will feel like a month.

Snapping back to reality, Harlow's mouth is moving but she's talking so fast I don't understand a word coming out. She's pale and looking frantic, her eyes moving everywhere in the room, but at me.

"Slow down," I break in.

"Sorry."

"Okay, now tell me what you said, but remember, slowly," I coax her. She looks around warily before grabbing my hand and leading me up the stairs. A snarky remark about '*this is too soon in our relationship*' wants to escape, but I hold it in. Judging by Harlow's spooked, pale expression, I can tell whatever it is that she needs to get out is serious. I'm just wondering out of all people she has around her, why it's me she's chosen to talk to. I'm actually feeling pretty privileged.

It could be because you're outside the circle, my thoughts tell me, but I tell them to fuck off and go away.

She leads me to my room and starts pacing the tiny space. Sitting down on the edge of the bed, I wait patiently for her to get her shit together. She's takes a few more minutes before taking another deep breath.

"Okay, so a few months ago, a month before you arrived, I'd been really ill with the flu. You know, the normal flu."

Cause there's a deranged flu, I think as I watch her start pacing around again. It's starting to make me feel dizzy, though, I don't voice that.

"I thought I'd just gotten that back again. You know with you being ill and all that. I didn't think much of it, but then this morning, Malik asked me when I needed to get my birth control prescription. Everything started to hit me, but now I'm panicking. I did some onlineresearchanditsaidthat..." she rushes out without taking a breath.

"Wow, wow, wow, slow down there," I warn her, grabbing her shoulders and sitting her down next to me. The door flies open and Denny rushes in out of breath. She looks between us and her shoulders relax.

"There you are. When you texted saying it was an emergency I rushed over as quickly as I could."

"I called you two hours ago," Harlow shouts, standing up. Denny pauses, taking a step back. She looks to me for answers but I shrug my shoulders not having any clue as to what's going on. All I've managed to get so far is the flu.

"I had to do my makeup..." she pauses seeing Harlow's stormy expression and back peddles. "I mean I had to feed and change Hope."

"Whatever."

"So? What's the big emergency?"

"As I was saying, Malik asked me this morning about my birth control pill prescription. You remember when I was ill a few months back and had to go on antibiotics?" she asks Denny.

"Yeah," Denny urges, nodding her head.

"Well, Malik and I had unprotected sex," she blurts out, covering her eyes.

My eyes shoot to Harlow and then down to her small, flat stomach.

Holy fucking shit on eggs.

"And? You always have unprotected sex," Denny deadpans and I feel like I'm getting in the way. They don't need me, a complete stranger, here while they talk about unprotected sex. More to the point, I don't need to be here to listen to them talk about unprotected sex.

"My God, will you listen, I WAS ON ANTIBIOTICS," Harlow shouts, her face bright red. "I did some research and antibiotics mess with the pill, so they don't work. I haven't had a period now in two months. I was due on yesterday."

"Holy crap," Denny grins and then begins to jump up and down like a lunatic squealing. I watch, feeling out of my element, and decide to move around them to my clothes and grab some clean ones before discretely get changed behind the wardrobe door.

"This is not a time to be happy. I can't be a mom. I'm not old enough to be a mom. I can't even look after myself, let alone a baby for Christ's sake. What the hell am I going to do? I've got my whole life ahead of me," she cries, tears begin falling down her face.

I rush to get ready, not wanting them to notice me dressing when Denny smacks Harlow in the arm.

"I'm a mom and we're the same age. What are you trying to say?" Denny asks offended.

Oh no! Please don't let there be a cat fight, please don't let there be a cat fight, I chant as I put on a clean pair of socks. There's one thing I can't stand and it's girls fighting. They don't fight fair and they pull fucking hair. With someone who has a lot of it you can see why I hate girls getting into fights. That shit hurts.

"I don't mean you, I mean me. You're mature and it's different."

"How is it different? We're the same age, we both have boyfriends and, may I add, you've been with Malik a lot longer than Mason and I have," Denny starts, counting them off her fingers.

"Because it just is," Harlow cries. "How can I bring a child into this world when the mothers in my family leave their child in one way or another? Gram's basically let mom walk out of her life and then my mom left me; she died and she's never coming back. She's not here for me to cry to, to ask advice to and I need her. I need my mom," Harlow sobs, falling to her knees on the floor. "She'd know what to do. She'd help me."

"Hey," Denny speaks softly, bending down to kneel on the floor. I sit on the floor next to Harlow, needing to show her my support. I didn't know her mom had died and it saddens me, but it's mostly seeing Harlow looking distraught. She's always so well put together. Seeing her like this is heartbreaking.

When Max said they had crazy parents running in the family I presumed that's why Harlow lived here with Joan, not that her parents were dead. My eyes water, filling with unleashed tears as I listen to her sob into her hands, wishing I could do something to make it better. But I've got both of my parents. Not in a way I can go and see them, but they're alive so I have no idea how Harlow must be feeling right now.

"It's going to be okay," I assure her but she doesn't hear me over her own tears.

"Harlow, you have all of us. I know we will never replace your mom but you're not alone. Do you really think your grams wanted your mother to go? No. And do you really think you'd leave a baby? Your mom died tragically, Harlow; it wasn't her fault or your own. I promise everything will be okay."

"How? How can you promise that? I couldn't bear to let a child feel the emptiness I feel everyday from not having my parents in my life. And then knowing I was the reason for that pain? I don't think I can do it."

"Yes, you can," Denny says sternly, looking pissed. "Don't you dare do this, Harlow. I know you're scared and you have every right to be, but think of all the love and life you'd be giving another human being. Isn't that worth it? Isn't it worth knowing yours and Malik's love made something so beautiful?"

"Trust me, I remember the day clearly and there was nothing beautiful about how I got pregnant. I was still feeling ill, but we'd gone a week without touching each other and by the end of the week it built up, ya know. So everything happened quickly and ha-"

"I'm going to cut you off right there," I jump in, covering my ears. "How about you calm down, and then tell Malik the news so you can both talk about it together? If it was me, I'd pretend to be furious and throw the pregnancy test at him," I laugh, but neither Denny nor Harlow laugh with me. "What?"

"I haven't done a test," Harlow admits sheepishly. When Denny and I give her a look she holds her hands up in defeat. "Hey, I was scared. I'd read all this shit on the internet and when I realised I missed two periods I began to panic. You can't blame a girl for that."

"So you may not even be pregnant," Denny breathes, shaking her head and if I'm not mistaken she looks kinda disappointed.

"Well, there's only one way to find out," I tell her, jumping to my feet. I help her up and shove her towards the door. "Go buy a test."

"Okay, come on."

"Oh, I'm going to watch a movie or something," I wave her off, not used to hanging around with girls. Not that I hang around with boys but I've always found it easier to get along more with lads than girls. Girls can be bitches and fuckin' ruthless when it comes to getting what they want and, oh my God, the lies they tell each other just to make themselves look good. It's laughable and now I'm just babbling on.

"Oh no, you're coming with us. You're one of us now," Denny grins, grabbing my arm.

"Brilliant," I smile sourly, wondering what the hell I've gotten myself into.

Half an hour later I'm sitting outside Harlow's bathroom door with Denny. We've been waiting now for a good five minutes, long enough for her to have peed on a stick and gotten the results.

"Come on, Harlow. The suspense is killing me. Do I need to break down the door?" Denny shouts through the door. I stand up, my ass dead from the hard carpet. I'm not even fully standing when the door flies open, scaring the shit out of me. Harlow rushes out, tears streaming down her cheeks and makes her way down the stairs.

"Oh no," I whisper and run after her along with Denny.

We call her name but it isn't until she leaves the house and runs next door to Max's house that I realise she must be looking for Malik.

Harlow slams open the door, rushing in and leaving it wide open. We follow seconds after, Denny shutting the door behind us.

Max and Myles are both sitting on the sofa playing Call Of Duty. It seems Max does a lot of that since he hasn't decided if he wants to go to college or not. From what I've heard Mark say, Max doesn't know what to do with his life. It sounded like he had been worried about it for a while too.

"Wow, where's the fire?" Malik asks, looking at a panting Harlow. When he realises she's crying he throws the remote control to the sofa, but before he can stand up, Harlow throws the pregnancy test at his chest.

She went with my idea, I'm so proud, I grin.

"You asshole. You got me pregnant," she cries.

"What? How? When?" he shouts, standing up, his face turning a shade lighter than pale.

"Now that is a mystery," Max shouts out, interrupting. Denny and I turn giving him a warning glare to shut up. Harlow and Malik ignore us like we're not even in the room and carry on having a domestic.

I watch behind the sofa as Max leaves the room, walking into the kitchen. I wonder if we should follow to give these two some space but the death grip Denny has on me isn't letting me leave any time soon. When I shake her off, in the end doing it roughly, she winces and mouths, 'sorry'.

"How? How? You stuck your penis in my vagina," Harlow yells.

"But we, you... You're on the pill. How could this have happened? What are we going to do? How can you have a baby with *me*?"

"What?" Harlow asks, her voice calmer, but no less deadly. I freeze, wondering why the air in the room has shifted. The two stare at each other, the silence in the room choking.

Max walks in with what looks like a fruit bowl full of popcorn. "Really?" I mutter, narrowing my eyes.

He shrugs, sitting down on the sofa, already digging into the popcorn. Shrugging my shoulders I follow suit and sit down next to him. Digging into the pop corn, I watch in time for Malik to get his shit together. Somewhat, anyway.

"You know where I come from, what blood runs through my veins, Harlow. What if I end up like my parents?" he whispers, looking pained. My heart actually beats harder for him and I wonder if this has anything to do with what Max was trying to say last night about his parents not being good people.

Denny sits down, following suit and digging into the popcorn on Max's lap; watching everything unfold in front of us. I'm still wondering if we should leave, give them some privacy, but I'm actually curious to know what's going on.

"I give it ten seconds before Harlow cries her undying love for Malik," Max whispers, taking another handful of popcorn.

"I give it fifteen," Denny puts in.

"You two are just," I start but the sharp look they both give me has my shoulders sagging. "I give it a few seconds; she's on the verge of an emotional breakdown."

"And what if I end up like mine?" Harlow answers breathlessly.

"Huh? I thought your parents were golden?" Malik asks, a hard edge to his voice.

"My parents were the best but, Malik, they still left me."

"Babe," he says like that answers everything. I look dumbfounded over it all. It's like a live reality TV show.

"This baby, it's a part of you, a part of me, and our love made her. I love her so much already and I've known about her for all of ten minutes. The thought of leaving her... It hurts, Malik, really fucking hurts. But knowing I've got you to share that with..."

"Well, they do say, a baby isn't just for Christmas, it's for life," Max butts in and we all look at him confused.

"Shut up," I grumble under my breath.

"Jesus! I was just saying."

"Well, don't," Malik snaps before turning back to Harlow, his expression softening. "I don't know what to say. Half of me is scared I'll turn out like my parents, but the other half is over the fucking moon that we've been given this gift."

"But we're so young," she murmurs, moving closer to him.

"This is so romantic," I whisper, grabbing another handful of popcorn.

"Jesus! Please! Do not cry on me," Max says horrified.

"Well, my job here is done. Congratulations, yada yada yada, oh and Harlow, if you dare put on an ounce of weight before my wedding, I will kill you," Denny warns, getting up.

Harlow nods, waving her off, but her eyes never leave Malik's. It's quite sickening really. In a loveable and adoring way.

Malik grins at Harlow, leaning down to whisper something in her ear, before he sweeps her off her feet, throwing her over his shoulder and carrying her out of the door.

"You're welcome," I shout after them, but the door has already slammed shut and her giggling begins to fade off.

"Want to play Call Of Duty?"

"You got anything else?" I ask Max as I take my shoes off and tuck them under me.

"Grand Theft Auto?"

"Oh my God, I *love* this game," I tell him enthusiastically.

"We're getting married," he winks and my stomach does a summersault.

SEVEN

LAKE

A FEW WEEKS LATER I'M WALKING round to Max's house so we can walk to the food bank together. We usually carpool with Joan but she had to go in early due to an emergency, so it's just us today.

Over the past few weeks everything has been hectic. Joan and Mark have been going bat-shit crazy over a newly expected arrival in the family and everyone has been arguing over the stag and hen parties for Mason and Denny. Mostly it's been about the baby, about Harlow and what will happen when the baby is born. Joan is freaked out, saying she can't build a house on her garden like Mark did. Harlow groaned, telling her they'll find somewhere else to live, though, I'm positive Joan hates the idea.

Letting myself in I find Max playing Grand Theft Auto and I squeal with glee. "Ohhh, can I have a go before we leave?" I love this game. Since the first time we started playing it's become more addictive.

"NO!" he shouts, getting up and turning the game off.

"Why not?" I demand, narrowing my eyes at him.

"Because."

"Because...?"

"Because you stop at every bloody traffic light, even when the police are fucking chasing you. You have to find a parking spot before you leave the car and don't even get me started on you running over prostitutes," he barks out, looking pissed.

"Hey, it's sexiest and really disgusting," I shout back, outraged he'd bring it up. It's completely demeaning, even if it is just a video game. "And you're just jealous I got skills and will pass my actual driving test before you."

"Lake, don't knock a man down. Even computer characters need to get a little nookie nookie, you should try it," he barks and I rear back in shock. What an asshole! I wonder what's gotten up his ass this morning.

"This isn't about sex or my lack of it. This is about you dissin' my driving skills."

"I can't even argue about this right now, I just need to go," he says, walking off. I follow, fuming, behind him and all the while wondering what the hell just happened.

"You're an ass," I snap, shoving past him.

"I'm surprised you have a problem with my ass with the amount of time you spend staring at it," he snaps back.

I turn around and give him my middle finger before stomping off to the food bank, trying to ignore him following behind me.

We arrive at the food bank ten minutes early. I'm pissed at Max so when I push open the staffroom door I use more force than necessary. It bangs into the wall behind it with a loud crash and I wince at the sound.

"Well, good morning to you too," Joan greets, not looking at me. She's too busy staring inside a cardboard box.

"Please don't tell me someone left something gruesome in a box again?" I stress, ignoring her earlier comment. Max slams into the back of me and I hiss at him; he ignores me, walking to the other side of the room to hang his coat up.

Moving out of the way of the door I make my way over to Joan and nearly squeal when I hear a cute little meow coming from inside the box. I'm jumping up and down like crazy when I reach the box, scaring the cute little kitten curled up in the corner. Its fluffy fur is pure grey all over, parts looking frazzled like he's been electrocuted. It's adorable.

"Where did you find him?" I whisper, not wanting to scare him again. My eyes light up with glee when he starts to get up, moving towards me with caution.

Seeing the little guy is another reminder of home. My cat, Tabatha, was everything to me; I loved her. I'd had her on my fourteenth birthday and she was still going strong the day I walked out on my life. I nearly took her with me but I knew I'd struggle to find places to sleep myself, let alone bringing an old aged cat along for the ride. I couldn't put her through it. And I was certain I would stick out more. I mean, who can go unnoticed when they have a cat with them?

"She was outside. I'm certain now we need that sign put up, stating only food and clothes to be donated," Joan mutters then looks up at me. Her doleful expression changes once she looks up in what has to my dreamy eyed expression. I don't dwell on her sudden change, my mind is too occupied on the cute little things the kitten is doing. He's purring, rubbing himself up my arm and rolling onto his back: loving the belly rub I'm giving him.

"I wish we could keep him? Do you think the vicar would mind?" I chirp, thinking how ace it would be to have a cat around the place.

"The vicar would; he's allergic."

"To one of God's creatures?" I gasp, mocking outrage.

"Oh my God, is that a rat?" Max yells, cringing at the kitten inside the box. I punch his arm, pissed off that he'd call the kitten that.

"No, he's a kitten you dipshit," I snap and from the corner of my eye I notice Joan glancing curiously between us.

"Well, that's settled then," Joan declares, clapping her hands once, loudly.

"What is?" I ask, turning my back on Max.

"The kitten; he can stay with you," she tells me and I stand with an open mouth, utterly shocked. No way? No fucking way? I want to squeal, jump up and down, but I don't want to get my hopes up. This is just so fucking cool.

"Me?" I mutter, my index finger pointing at my chest.

"Yes, you," she cackles.

"But... But, I don't have a home," I whisper, looking down at the cute little kitten. Even before Joan opens her mouth I already know I'm taking him home. Just looking down at him I know I'll take good care of him. I'll call him Thor.

"Yes, you do," she tells me sharply, my attention focusing on her again in shock. "You have a home with me, with Mark, Harlow, Malik and the rest of them."

"I... Thank you." I'm completely gobsmacked, speechless. She's been so kind to bring me into her home and for her to call it my home as well, it's overwhelming.

I'd been treating the place like it was temporary and a part of me knows that's all it can be. But then, looking back down at Thor, I don't think I could leave another cat. Leaving Tabatha behind was nearly as hard as leaving everything else. She depended on me. She was always at my side.

"No need. But I do not clean out cat poop so make sure you are sure before taking on such a big responsibility."

"It's a fucking rat not a dog," Max barks and I turn to him sharply.

"What exactly do you have against Thor, Max? Is it because he's sleeping in the corner and not sprawled out like a starfish? Or is this just another way for you to have a dig at me?" I demand and with each poke to his chest Max takes a step back looking taken back.

"Who the fuck is Thor?" he cries, throwing his hands up in the air like he's the one that's confused by *my* behaviour.

"I'll leave you two to it. Oh, before I leave, we don't need either of you today. The vicar needs the building for a function. I forgot all about it until this morning."

I give Joan a glance, nodding my head to let her know that I heard her. I watch her pick up the box Thor is in and make her way to the door, her lips twitching. What she has to be so happy about I don't know.

"I'll just take Thor home so he can get settled in his new surroundings. I'll get Mark to pick up some bits for him on his way home. We have enough to last us until then."

"Thank you," I tell her smiling, giddy about having him. I can't wait to get home, play with him and watch him do adorable things.

"You called that thing, Thor?" Max asks distastefully.

"Yes, you got a problem with that?"

"Fuck, yes. You might as well have called it Splinter," he growls, stepping in my space.

"He's not a fucking rat, it's a cat," I growl taking a step towards him, our bodies nearly colliding.

"Rat. Cat... Who the fuck cares? I'm calling it Splinter." His eyes are focused completely on my mouth, distracting me a little.

"Don't you dare call him..." I start, but then Max's hot lips crash down to mine. Surprised by the sudden attack I'm unsure of what to do. It all happens so quickly, yet, the second I register what is going on and I remember his attitude towards me all morning, my hands move to his chest, ready to push him away.

His hands tighten on my hips as if he can predict my next move and his tongue licks the seam of my lips, demanding access, and my whole body melts against his. Any thoughts I had about pushing him away have been buried to the back of my mind, the only focus is getting him to kiss me harder.

Max, it seems, isn't shy when it comes to kissing. The kiss started out hard, demanding, yet unhurried, his tongue coaxing mine, but after a few minutes he slowed it down, like he feels the need to savour every second.

His hands roam my body shamelessly. Even through the coat I still have on I can feel his touch burning me alive from the inside, my body igniting in a way it's never done before. The sensation has my body doing things it's never done before. I'm touching him, my hands roaming up his hard body, around his neck and into his dark, thick hair. I can't get enough of him. The feel of his soft fuller lips against mine, the way he holds me against his body tightly like he's scared I'll pull away, feels good. All of it, good.

Voices down the hall have Max pulling away and I feel the loss of his lips instantly. Both of our breathing is heavy, both of us panting. I lift my head up when I feel his gaze; his dark eyes capture mine, sending me a look that promises more, which causes a shiver to tingle down my spine, all the way to my toes.

I'm frozen to the spot. My mind racing over what happened, how good it felt and how I wish we weren't interrupted. Neither of us says a word to each other. I wish I knew what he was thinking. Is he regretting what happened? Do I regret what happened? I don't think so. I don't know. I groan inwardly at everything swirling around in my brain.

Just when I'm about to open my mouth to tell him that it's okay and that what happened was just a silly mistake, he moves, making me pause. He lifts his hand to cup my cheek before gently gliding his fingers across my jaw and down my neck in a deliberate slow stroke before coming to a stop at my pulse. His eyes watch the movement of his hand like it's the most fascinating thing in the world. It has my heart racing, making me feel things I know I shouldn't be feeling. Things I don't deserve to be feeling. Not with him; not with Max. He needs someone worthy of him, not me, not after what I've done.

His head begins to descend again and I panic knowing that if I let his lips touch mine again, I'll be in trouble. Taking a quick step back I watch the heat in his eyes change, another emotion I don't get chance to read before I bow my head, hating that I've hurt him. I want to tell him it's for the best but with an ego like

Max's, he won't listen to reason.

"We should go," I mumble under my breath.

He coughs, his feet shifting from side to side and for the first time since meeting him I feel awkward.

"Yeah, we should um, go get breakfast at Antonio's. He's expecting us today, remember?" His voice is husky, the sound flowing through my body. Maybe it wasn't hurt I thought I registered in his eyes but something else.

'Or maybe it was just a kiss to him, Lake?' my inner thoughts scream at me.

Not wanting to keep contradicting myself about how he does or doesn't feel I shut myself off from it all, needing to move on so we can get to Antonio's and eat. After that I'll go back to Joan's and let my brain run wild.

"Um... Yeah, okay," I agree, remembering Antonio and Max becoming fast friends and organising us to do a breakfast food taste every other Sunday.

Antonio wants to start opening the bar up earlier to see if a breakfast menu will bring in more clients. But first he wants us to try out some recipes he has. After all, Antonio can't serve 'crap food'. His words, not mine.

"MY TWO FAVOURITE PEOPLE," Antonio shouts, walking over to us with his arms wide open. I greet him with a smile, my face still flushed from my earlier encounter with Max. When Antonio takes a closer look at me, his facial expression changes and a huge grin spreads across his face. "You two make love? No?"

My eyes pop out of their sockets as I stare at him completely shocked and utterly embarrassed. "What? No! God, no?" I shout defensively.

"Oh, I see two people in love," Antonio disagrees, looking far too happy with himself. "It's my food, no?"

"No, it's not. Now are you cooking us breakfast or not?" I snap none too harshly.

Max laughs, clapping Antonio on the shoulder. "She's just feeling uptight after I told her she had to wait until we had your fabulous breakfast and got married before we had sex."

I rear back, blown away by his words, but then his words fully register and before I can stop myself my hand pulls back before flying forward and smacking Max across the face.

My mouth hangs open, completely surprised by my horrific actions. The palm of my hand is stinging from the slap, but although it was a tad harsh and a little on the hard side, it was totally justified.

Max looks traumatised; his face completely void of emotion. I know he's going to hate me after this and I prepare myself for the verbal ass whooping. A huge grin spreads across his face and I'm more stunned over that than I am that I actually used physical violence.

"Knew you'd like it rough," he winks. He leaves me there to follow Antonio into the kitchen.

If Antonio is shocked by my behaviour or by Max, neither of them show it. I'm still stunned I even raised my hand to another person, let alone followed through with it. I've never hit anyone in my life, or started a fight, and I blame Max entirely for the whole incident. Something about him sets me in every possible way imaginable. It's not just the violent reaction and the snappy comebacks but the desire, the lust, the way he makes me happy and helps me forget everything that's ever happened in my life. It's been that way since the dickhead got me caught sleeping in the shed at the food bank. Maybe that's it, maybe it's hate I'm constantly feeling towards him and those other things are just karma's way of confusing me.

That doesn't answer why you can't stop being around him or why you are always thinking about him, Lake.

I'm such a plebhead. I need to get a grip and lose the fascination or whatever the hell it is with Max. I know all too well not to trust lads, especially ones like Max. They will shit on you the second another vagina gives them attention. And by attention I mean walking into a room.

It doesn't help the only boyfriend I've ever had not only cheated on me but is part of the reason I'm here. If it had not been for his involvement I wouldn't have been in that car, I wouldn't have lost what I did and I wouldn't wish I could take my brother's place every second of every day. That's where trusting a lad got me: homeless with no family, no friends, and feeling like an outsider. So, trusting Max? Who, by the way, has the power to take everything away from me once again? Not going to happen.

Ever!

And something tells me letting him in will cost me a lot more. My heart is already broken but Max has the power to mend it, but having it break again? The aftermath will kill me.

"Are you going to stand there all day staring at the ground or are you going to come try this breakfast? It's fucking awesome," Max grins and my heart pounds faster just hearing his voice. How can he be so calm and collected? Why isn't he freaking out about all of this right now?

Staying away from him and not trusting him is going to be harder than I imagined. Just his cheeky handsome face has me melting towards him.

I just need to remind myself he called my cat a rat. That should do it.

I shrug my shoulders and follow Max behind the bar and into the kitchen. When I enter, the aroma of food has my belly rumbling.

It smells like heaven in here. It reminds me of walking inside my house on a Sunday and instantly smelling the roast dinner my mom would always have cooking. It was the best smell in the world. But smelling this right now, I have to admit, is much better.

"Max tell me you call your rat Splinter? Why you buy a rat, piccola ragazza? My good friend Roberto has dogs. I get you a good deal on dog," Antonio emphasises and I shake my head before turning to roll my eyes at Max.

"Joan found a kitten, we're keeping him. He's not a rat and he's called *Thor*, not Splinter," I growl out, kicking Max in the shin.

I really do need to stop hitting him. One day I may permanently damage the poor sod.

"I'm going to press charges the next time you hit me. It's called freaking child abuse," Max hisses out, glaring at me. His jaw is hard but it makes the outline of his dimples more profound. I can't help but feel the look makes him look hotter.

"Bite me," I snap, trying not to let the look he gives affect me.

"Your wish is my command," he winks, his eyebrows wiggling up and down.

"Of course it is," I answer dryly.

"You two, so young, so much in love. It's so powerful. I feel it in the room," Antonio announces, gushing. I'm stuck on a comeback to say as he places a plate of food in front of me, making my mouth water. I don't even bother asking what it is; I just start shovelling food into my mouth and it tastes better than it smells.

"Nah," Max says, waving him off with a serious expression and my body relaxes. He's done teasing, I think, but then he finishes chewing to continue to speak and again, I'm back to hating him. "It's all the sexual tension between us that you're feelin', my man. Isn't it, my sugar plum?"

"If you say so, *my little pea*," I growl sweetly.

"I do, princess," he replies, moving a strand of hair from off my cheek.

I scoff, hating it when a lad calls a girl princess. It's just another way of informing them they're high maintenance, to me anyway.

"What do you think, piccolo ragazza?" Antonio asks eagerly, motioning to the food.

I'd been so annoyed with Max that I totally missed what I was supposed to do. I look down to my plate and notice that it's already empty. I give Antonio a wide grin ready to tell him I love it when Max leans over me, his aftershave making me lean in closer.

Has he always smelled this good?

Of course he has, I mutter to myself.

"You look like you're about to become a serial killer, tone down the smile," Max whispers and my face falls.

"It was yummy, now tell me, what was it?"

"Mushroom and sausage omelette," he tells me, looking at me like I'm crazy.

I look at Antonio, surprised, then back down to my plate. Max and his damn kiss have my mind jumbled. Nothing is registering.

"What did you think it would be? Snails and frogs?" Max laughs and I snap my head to him.

"Um, not to piss on your cornflakes and all, but it's the French that eat snails and frogs," I laugh and glance gratefully at Antonio when he places two cappuccinos in front of me and Max.

"Oh yeah, well, shit," he laughs back, not caring he just sounded like a complete dork. It just makes me smile wider at him.

"Next week I make you dinner, my favourite meatballs," Antonio suggests. "You come here about five, I have table ready for you and wine," he winks at Max and Max grins back. Me? I'm obviously missing something.

"Um, we're not usually here that late," I mention, making sure they remember.

"You go on proper date," Antonio dismisses me and starts picking up the empty plates. Quickly thinking, I grab hold of his wrist to stop him.

"I'll get this; you sit down and eat, talk, or do what you Italians do," I smile and get up to take the washing up over the wash up area. Max joins me a few minutes later, carrying some other bits and bobs.

"Come on. Let's get this done so we can go see how Splinter is doing. You don't want Harlow getting her hands on it; she'll end up keeping it," he chuckles, helping me load the dishwasher.

I gasp, not thinking about Harlow and Thor. As soon as she sees him she's going to fall in love with him. Who wouldn't? Oh yeah, that's right, bloody Max.

"She wouldn't," I affirm, turning to face him and in doing so I bring the jet wash with me, soaking Max to the bone. "Oh my God, I'm so sorry," I choke out, trying hard not to laugh. His t-shirt is clinging to his tight sculptured abs, showcasing every defined ridge on his stomach. His hair is completely drenched; water running down his face, dripping off at his strong, cut jaw. No longer able to hold it in anymore, I crack up right in his face. My laughter loud and shameless and from the look on his face he is not impressed but it just has me bending over, my side hurting from laughing even harder.

"You think that's funny do ya?" he demands, the warning there laced heavily from the tone of his voice. Straightening up ready to give him some sass, I notice his hand moving in my peripheral vision. A startled squeal escapes and my body turns ready for an escape but his hands land around my waist swinging me back towards him.

"Noooo," I laugh when he tries to wet me. I push his hand away with all my strength, my laughter still filling the room when I'm sprayed. My ass slams back into his groin, trying to push him away, but all it does is cause another reaction – a reaction Max likes all too well. The nozzle falls with a thud back into the sink, the loud clang echoing around the kitchen. "Please, I'm sorry, I swear it won't happen again."

"Oh, you'll pay, Lake," he mocks.

When I feel his body heat against mine, I all too soon become aware of how close he's standing behind me, his groin pressed into my ass and his soaked front pressed to my back. Laughter dies in my throat, my body turning so I come face to face with Max. His face has lost its earlier smugness, the teasing expression now wiped away and a hankering of undisguised desire now in its place. We're both silent, both of us lost in our own thoughts. So lost in my own thoughts, my gaze entirely focused on his full lips, I'm surprised when I find them moving towards me as if in slow motion. Then everything falls away and all I can concentrate on is his touch, his lips, and how good it feels kissing him.

I'm so lost in the kiss, in the moment, that I find myself pressing closer to him, wanting to feel his body wrapped around mine and before I can stop myself, I'm throwing my arms around his neck and wrapping my legs around his waist. Also lost in the moment, Max none too gently shoves me into the washer, grinding his pelvis into mine, the contact causing me to moan into his mouth. The hands he has under my ass to support me, tighten to the point his fingers bite into my skin.

Our soaked shirts stick together, my thin top leaving nothing to the imagination as Max glides his now free hand up my ribs to my chest before grabbing more than a handful of my boob. He makes a sound of appreciation at the back of his throat which spurs me on and I find myself rocking my body against him. It feels good. Really good. And with his warm hands touching one of the most intimate places it has me feeling explosive.

I can't get enough.

But it's all too much.

Then a loud girly squeal breaks whatever spell Max has me under. Quickly we break a part, both of us breathing heavily and staring into each other's eyes where again we both begin to feel lost, so lost that when I hear a faint voice, reality comes slamming into me, the force nearly choking me.

"Shit," I hiss, pushing Max away as he slides me to my feet. It doesn't go unnoticed that he keeps me as close to his body as he can and I hate that I liked it. "This can't happen again. We're two different people," I snap, all my anger pushed into those few sentences. It breaks my heart saying them but he needs to know.

I don't let him defend himself; I rush over to where my coat is and grab it before rushing out of the kitchen and into the bar where a waving Antonio is grinning. Too angry and embarrassed I don't stop and give him a snappy comeback, instead, I hightail it out of there.

Back at the house, Joan is in the kitchen finishing off a call. She smiles when she sees me but then her eyes do a double take which has her losing her smile. I'm starting to wish I'd headed upstairs when I first came in but it feels rude not stopping and talking. I should have, though. It's no telling what a mess I look like.

"What's wrong?"

"What?" I ask breathlessly. I hadn't stopped running until I hit the front door, even then I wanted to run through it, up to my room and dive under my cushions.

"You look like you've just run the London Marathon," Joan says, looking at me like I've peed on her floor.

"Oh, spider," I wave her off, still trying to catch my breath. That's when I see

Thor on the kitchen floor coming towards me. I bend down and pick him up, snuggling him in my arms. He immediately falls asleep and my heart soars.

So effin' cute.

"Do you need me to do anything? I was going to go to my room?" I ask, still looking down at the kitten snoring lightly in my arms.

See? Totally cute. He's made me feel better already.

"No, no, dear. Just make sure you're down here for dinner at half five. We're having a family dinner."

The word 'family' hits me in the chest hard, taking my breath away and the need to reach out and rub the ache away is extreme.

"Okay," I whisper, turning and heading back to my room.

In my room I lay down on the bed, bringing Thor with me still cuddled safely on my chest. The minute my eyes close from the emotional exhaustion, the mobile phone Joan had given me the week before beeps from the floor. I know who it is straight away. There has only been one person to even text me since I had it. Since I don't go anywhere no one really has any need to get hold of me.

I did try telling Joan when she gave it to me that it was pointless giving it to me and a total waste of her money but she wouldn't listen to my reasoning. Now I wish I had stuck to my guns and made her take it back.

Getting a text is far worse than receiving a phone call. People tend to write what they really mean on a message, finding it easier to communicate. It can also be interpreted differently and admittedly I'm shit scared of what Max has to say.

MAX: I've never made a girl run from me before.

Breathing in a relaxed breath, feeling that wasn't as bad I originally thought it was going to be, I hesitantly reply.

LAKE: There's a first time for everything.

MAX: Yes, there is. Why did you run?

LAKE: Because I don't want you kissing me.

I type furiously, my temper beginning to rise. Is it so hard to believe not every girl is going to fall for his charms and bow down to him?

MAX: I'd believe you but your moans and groans and the tight grip you had on me tells me something else entirely.

This, unfortunately, is true.

LAKE: You might find this hard to believe but not every girl finds you irresistible.

MAX: Stop lying to yourself, you want me, just admit it.

LAKE: I'm not playing fucking games, Max. Grow up and leave me alone.

I snap and I instantly feel bad about it, but he's becoming more involved in my life and it isn't something I need. I know it's not. I don't deserve anything good and I'm already playing with fire letting Joan take me into her home. Becoming dependent on the emotional and physical support Max brings me won't end well; I can't rely on him for that.

MAX: If that's what you want, fine!!!!!!

My chest aches and my finger inches over the reply button, wanting to take back my words. In just a few weeks that I've known him he's come to mean something to me. Nothing romantic, though, the thought of his body, his cheeky banter and his extremely good looks is making it harder not to think of him that way.

Who am I kidding?

I totally fancy the pants off Max. There's nothing I can do to deny that, yet, anything more is a no go. It just can't go any further.

My eyes close and I return to stroking the little bundle of fur still cuddled up to my chest. The notion relaxes me and it's not long before I fall into a dreamless sleep.

A soft knock on the door wakes me up from another nightmare about my past.

Since moving in with Joan and Mark they've become more and more regular. I know its guilt eating away at me. Why should I live a good life when *he* doesn't have one because of me? That's what it all boils down to. But if I could go back in time and change things, I would. I'd gladly take his place in a heartbeat.

Joan peeks her head in, giving me a small smile when she sees I'm awake. Thor jumps down from the bed and runs out of the room, his little butt wiggling behind him.

So cute!

"Dinner will be ready in five," is all she says before turning and leaving the room. I groan, sitting up, my head is banging.

I remind myself to ask for some paracetamol when I go downstairs. It's not the first time I've woken up from a nightmare and received the mother of all headaches.

Rushing into the bathroom I make quick work of cleaning up before heading back into my room to change.

By the time I make it downstairs everyone is already sitting at the small table in the kitchen. Looking around, my tense body relaxes when I find Max not in attendance. In fact, Maverick isn't here either.

"Hey, Joan, could I have some paracetamol, please?"

"Of course, my dear. You don't have to ask you know, just help yourself. They're in the top cupboard over there," she tells me gently, pointing to the far end of the kitchen. "Is everything okay?"

"Just a headache," I tell her quietly before making my way over to the sink to grab a glass of water.

The water feels cool and soothing against my raw throat, so I take another sip, relishing in the feeling, just as Joan decides to ask me a question.

"Where's Max?"

I choke on my drink, my lungs beginning to burn. I have to calm myself down before looking back at Joan. She's minding her own at the moment but I can tell that secretly all her attention is on me as she dishes out the food.

"I, huh, I don't know."

"He was with you earlier, he texted me," Myles tells me.

"Yeah, he stayed at Antonio's to clean up," I add on quickly, not wanting to be questioned anymore. "So, Harlow, you have your appointment soon, you excited?"

She smiles widely, looking at Malik with adoration. "Yeah. The midwife booked us in for a scan. She said we'll have a proper estimate then for the due date."

"Not so scared then," I state and smile at her. She looks radiant. She's beautiful in every way. The best thing is she doesn't even know it. But don't let her angelic looks deceive you, I've seen her argue with Malik and Denny; the girl has balls.

"No, not now."

"I still can't believe my grandbaby is going to be having a baby. Your mom would be so proud, I just know it," Joan speaks up, her eyes watering.

"Oh, Gram's, don't get upset. And do you really believe that?" Harlow asks, her voice cracking towards the end.

"I know it, baby. She had you so young and I know she never regretted it for one second. She'd support you in the ways I never supported her. I just know it, baby. Call it a mother's intuition," she winks then looks around the table. "I can't believe that boy isn't here. Myles, call him. At least Maverick has a legitimate excuse," she snaps.

"Where is Mav?" Malik asks, taking a mouthful of mashed potato.

"He's clearing out the apartment above the club so he can move a tenant in," Mark answers.

"Why would someone move in there? You'd never get any sleep," Malik grunts.

"It's been soundproofed. With business becoming slow because of Christmas, he needs another income coming in. He's even thought of buying future properties for investment," Mark states proudly.

My ears burn when Myles walks back into the room, his eyes hitting mine briefly before looking over to Joan.

"He's on a date," Myles grunts, frowning.

"That boy," Joan snaps and I feel her eyes on me, but I concentrate hard on my food, trying to look unaffected. Him being on a date shouldn't hurt like this. But it does and I can't deny the sharp pain inside my chest is about anything else.

It was only this morning that he had his tongue down my throat. Now he's on a date. I knew not to trust him. But then, I did tell him to leave me alone. Lads like him can't handle their ego being bruised.

"Denny, how's your brother's girlfriend doing?" Harlow asks Denny quickly and I look over to give her a thankful smile. I know everyone has thought something has been going on between me and Max, although, until today there wasn't anything going on, not really.

God, it's so freaking awkward. I can feel Joan still staring holes in the side of my head.

"She's healed up nicely. She's not his girlfriend anymore, she's his wife. The loons went and got married on their own."

"You've been planning yours now for what? A year?" Harlow laughs. "And your brother gets married within the few weeks of asking her?"

"Don't rub it in," Denny groans. "I'm just happy for them and I said we should do something to celebrate. I know Nan wasn't too pleased about all the rush. But I know she loves Kennedy."

My head feels like it's going to explode listening to them talk back and forth about shit I know nothing about. Obviously I know who they're talking about and what happened and what not, but it's not a conversation I can really be involved in. I'm not family. I'll never be part of a family again and that kills me. More than I care to admit.

Pushing back my chair, all eyes fall on me. "I'm not feeling too good, I think I'm going to get some fresh air," I mumble and before Joan can force me to sit back down or go to bed, I move quickly out of the door, hearing them talk in hushed tones.

Pulling on my sneakers and grabbing my coat I head outside the door. It's times like this, listening to them banter back and forth, that I really miss my family and what we shared. We never sat at a dining room table or a kitchen one but we did sit in front of a television together to eat our dinner every day. We would talk about our days, what we were up to, about a TV show that was on, or just random gossip. It was great.

I took all that away from my family and again today, I took Max away from all of them by arguing with him, otherwise he would be here enjoying his dinner. I ruin everything I come into contact with. It's another reason that is screaming at me, telling me that I don't belong here, that I'm invading everyone's lives.

Hours later the streets are dark, only lit with dim streetlights, as I walk the rest of the way to Joan's house. My feet are killing me and if you ask me where I've been tonight I couldn't tell you. I've been walking around in a daze wondering how my life got so fucked up. But I only have myself to blame. It's the only person I can blame. The only person who *is* to blame.

Opening the front door, I walk in and kick off my sneakers. Joan walks out of the front room with a sad expression on her face but also a look I've come to know all too well. She has something she needs to say. I know she's going to make me cry before she even opens her mouth. I've been on the verge of tears all day.

"Come sit down with me," she orders. I open my mouth to tell her I'm too tired when she raises her hand up, placing it down on my shoulder. "It's not a request."

Sighing, I take off my coat and follow her into the front room. The clock on the wall reads nine o'clock and it shocks the hell out of me. I've been gone for four hours. Four hours of walking around mindlessly not knowing where I was heading or when I'd be back.

"Sit."

Sitting down on the edge of the sofa, I don't relax back into the seat. I need her to know I don't plan on getting comfy, that I want her to get out whatever she has to say. As soon as she does I'll be heading up to my room to wallow in self pity.

"I know you've got secrets, dark ones. I hear you cry in your sleep," she tells me, which really doesn't surprise me that much. I've been waiting for someone to bring up my nightmares since I first moved in, yet, none of them have ever mentioned them once to me. Not that I think Harlow and Malik would hear me, they're too far up to hear anything but Joan and Mark are close by and will have heard me for sure.

"When you feel like you can, I want you to know you're able to come and talk to me. Life is hard but living is harder, and you, my girl, aren't living. You're walking around robotically like anything to do with life or emotion will get you punished."

"Maybe *that's* my punishment," I whisper, wanting to tell her so badly what kind of a girl they've brought into their home.

"I don't believe that for a second. Life is what we make it. But sometimes things are out of our control. We mourn the ones we lose and we greet new life with open arms but when it comes to living, we're walking into it blind."

Her words hit me hard. My nose starts stinging, my throat starts to close up and I know any second I'll be in floods of tears.

"You have a chance at becoming a new person, to change your life, to have something better," she whispers.

I look at her with teary eyes and swallow down the hard lump that's been wedged in my throat since she started talking. "But what if the life I had was the best I was going to get? I did something unforgivable, Joan. I ran from my family instead of staying and facing the consequences of my awful actions. So not only am I a..." I shake my head stopping the next word from forming, the word tasting bitter in my mouth. "I'm a coward. I don't belong here," I tell her, waving my hands around the room.

"Why?"

"Why?" I ask, confused. Out of all that she's only going to ask me *why* I don't belong. She should be more worried about what I did and what brought me to where I am in the first place; not why I don't belong in her world, her home.

"Yes, why?"

"Because I don't," I tell her, struggling to form the words I need to convince her of the fact. "I don't deserve to have warmth, love, or a roof over my head. I don't deserve the kindness you show me, what your family shows me every day," I choke out, feeling my shoulders sag with defeat.

"Oh darling, you belong here more than anyone else. Whatever happened in your past is over with now. You can't go back and change what happened, but you do need to move on, give people a chance. I've seen you with Max, Lake. It's the only time I've ever seen you look alive," she tells me, eyeing me strangely. "Except when you were told you could keep Thor."

My back straightens and I eye the old, sweet lady who is looking at me like she has something up her sleeve. I know when someone is trying to manipulate me.

"What are you getting at?" I ask curiously.

"Just, that maybe Max is your way of moving on; you're light at the end of the tunnel. Your saviour," she answers gently.

"I've got a headache. I'm going to go to bed," I tell her, squeezing her hand before getting up.

"Just remember, I'm here for you, no matter what. You're part of the family now whether you want to be or not," she says and the flood gates open. Tears fall from my eyes in thick streams. I barely make it into my room before the first sob escapes my sore throat. I throw myself down on the bed, smothering the sobs into my pillow.

I think about my family, what I did to them, all the pain I caused them and how much the Carter family have come to mean something to me.

And something inside me feels like loving them is like replacing the family that I lost.

EIGHT

MAX

LAKE: I'm not playing fucking games, Max. Grow up and leave me alone.

F̲UCK HER!
Fuck, fuck, fuck, FUCK, her!

I don't even know why I'm so bothered about the chick. It's not like she's got something other girls haven't. A vagina is a vagina at the end of the day. Every hole is a goal and all that shit. Why she bothers me so much is a fucking mystery not even the Scooby gang will be able to solve.

I text her back furiously then flick through my contacts wondering who I can fuck to get her out of my system. The girl I met the other week springs to mind and I flick through until I come across her name.

MAX: Want to meet up tonight?
GREGGS/TITS: Ye, wanna meet @ Frankies?

Frankie's is one of our local Italian restaurants. If Antonio found out I'd gone to one of his competitors he'd probably slice me up and serve *me* as a pizza. I have no doubt about it. But if I want to get laid and get Lake from off my mind, I'm going to have to suck it up.

And yes, I named her GREGGS/ TITS. It was the only way I knew how to remember her. Names, I don't do. Visuals? Now, that, I can do. It just so happens I met her in Greggs and she had a huge pair of fucking tits. I'm a lad, sue me.

MAX: What time?

GREGGS/TITS: Now?

MAX: I'm on the way.... Shit, I think I've typed your name in wrong, this is the girl from Greggs isn't it?

I'm hoping she doesn't catch on that I'm fishing for her name because I've forgotten, but I can't exactly turn up to a date and not know the girl's name. That would be so awkward. More awkward than walking in on your brother having sex with a girl you've come to love as a sister.

GREGGS/TITS: Ye, it's me, Amy.

Amy... Now I remember.

A FEW HOURS LATER I'M ready to ditch Amy and leave. Not only does the girl have no brain cells, but she hasn't shut up since I arrived.

My phone beeps in my pocket and I know who it is before I even eye the caller ID. Myles is calling. I answer quickly, wanting a reason to get Amy to shut the fuck up for two minutes. That, and I miss the sound of my own voice. Sad I know but I honestly haven't gotten a word in.

"Hello brother of mine," I answer with a grin.

"Cut the shit, dickhead. Joan has prepared a family meal and you don't even turn up. Even Lake showed up and she's not even blood," he hisses down the line.

"She lives there," I deadpan.

"Where are you?" he sighs and my shoulders slump. I hate it when he acts like this. He knows exactly how to act to make me feel guilty and I hate it.

"On a date; I'll be back later," I exclaim and before he can tear me a new asshole, I put the phone down.

My phone beeps as soon as I end the call and I'm about to ignore it when I notice Liam's name come up with a message.

LIAM: Fancy coming to a party over at Hannah's?

MAX: Hell yeah.

Hannah is a girl I fucked back in school. She's a pretty cool chick to be fair and her parties are legendary. Ever since Chris's dad burnt down the Old Gunner's house we've all struggled for somewhere to party. But then Hannah came up with a solution. Her parents are never home, so she throws a party once in a while.

"We're going to a party," I tell my date, Amy.

"Okay. Do I need to get changed? I love parties but I also find I'm always underdressed, so if you want me to..."

I tune her out inwardly cursing myself for inviting her. I should have just told her there was an emergency back at home and left her to it. I throw some cash on the table and grab my hoody.

"Nah, you look fine," I tell her. If she got any more underdressed she'd be dressing for a beach party. How the fuck she's not freezing in her short mini skirt, her high heels and tiny crop top is anyone's guess. I was pretty disappointed when she took off her leather jacket to reveal a short crop top showing her flat stomach instead of her tits. She should show more cleavage. It will get her places in life, I'm sure.

"Oh, goodie. So, as I was saying, my mom wanted me to go to college but I was like, Mom..."

I'VE BEEN WALKING IN silence since we left the restaurant, grunting occasionally so Amy doesn't realise I'm not listening. I tuned her out back at the restaurant but with her voice it's been hard work. Now, standing outside the front of the house where the party is, I grin with relief. People are everywhere. People she can talk to instead of giving me a fucking headache. I hate thinking like a prick, but even a saint would get their hair off with all her talking. She could talk a deaf bloke's ears off.

"I'm going to get a drink, do you want one?"

"Oh, I don't know. What do you think they'll have? I'm not a real beer kind of girl, it gets me too drunk. Anything with vodka makes me frisky and I end up dry humping someone," she giggles.

"How about a fruit cider?" I ask, not really caring; at the rate she's going I'll just hand her a water and be done with it. I honestly couldn't care what she drinks right now as long as I'm not around to listen to it.

"Oh no, I talk too much when I drink cider. My friend, Melissa, told me it puts lads off so I don't drink it. I don't want to come across as a talkative know-it-all."

Seriously? She is really going to say cider makes her talk too much.

"You had one too many today then?" I blurt out, inwardly slapping myself.

"Oh no, I haven't drank anything but water today," she smiles widely.

I groan, raking my hands through my hair. I'm fucked. This chick hasn't even drunk cider and already she hasn't shut up.

Vodka it is. I'd rather a horny bitch on my hands than a chatterbox on speed.

"Let's get you a WKD," I grin, hoping my seductive skills haven't been talked out of me.

She gives me a shy smile, tucking a strand of hair behind her ear, and blinks rapidly like she's got something stuck in her eye.

Lake isn't like this. What you see is what you get. Well, not always. She's hiding some big fucking secret and has demons that haunt her day and night, but apart from that, she's the only girl I know that is real. She's not some girl who has to flash her tits for a lad's attention.

Even with all the baggage that chick has, it would be worth it in the long run. It would also be more interesting listening to her talk about her said baggage than having Amy talk about...anything.

The party isn't even at its fullest and I'm drunk already. Checking my phone I read nine o'clock and groan wanting the party to be over.

Amy is currently grinding down hard on my lap and I can see now why she doesn't drink vodka. I think the girl has gotten off twice just rubbing herself over my dick in the past twenty minutes. When she first started dry humping me I had a boner, sure, but now she's rubbing herself down so hard on my dick that I'm not sure I have any feeling left in my appendage.

Placing my hands at her waist, I try to lift her up to no avail.

"No," she whines, biting down on my ear which causes me to flinch. Fuck, that hurts. "Shall we go somewhere private?" she whispers, trying to sound seductive but her voice is loud and just as annoying as it was when we first met up at Frankie's.

Liam catches my eye from across the room and he shakes his head, grinning like a fucking loon. He's been getting off on watching Amy dry hump me for the past hour. It didn't help I was talking to him the first time she got off. She wasn't even quiet about it. It isn't normal. She's needs help, some serious help with her issues.

"I think you should go home, you're drunk," I tell her, trying to keep the pissed off tone out of my voice. All I want to do is go home and see if Lake is up to playing Grand Theft Auto, or hell, if she wants to watch a lame ass movie. I'd go with just sleeping I'm that desperate to be around her and out of here.

"I've had one drink. I'm just really fucking horny."

"So you don't care you're in a house full of people?" I ask, wondering if I'm hearing this right. How can I be turning down a girl who is ready to fuck in a room full of people? It's like a fantasy come true but for some reason my dick isn't into it.

My hands drunkenly run up her body and she moans, arching into me. Taking that as my cue, I run them under her short top feeling her bare breasts.

When the fuck did she get the time to take her bra off? I look up to her with wide eyes, my hands playing with her nipples as she withers below me. As messed up as this all is, I need to take my mind off Lake and Amy seems willing to help with that.

"Stick your fingers in my ass," she gasps loudly and I notice a few eyes turn our way. Drunk and feeling pretty out of it, I haul her up in my arms and head towards the stairs, Liam on my tail. I knew the dirty fucker would follow. Amy wasn't shy in showing Liam she was interested in him. To be honest, I think she was just interested in getting off, the dirty bitch.

Entering the room I ignore Liam and throw Amy on the bed. She looks up with lust filled eyes before her eyes turn to Liam behind me.

"Oh God, fuck me in the ass," she moans widely and I look to Liam with a grin. He shakes his head but takes his top off grinning as he walks closer to the bed. We've shared before. This isn't anything new to us. The only thing that is different is that Amy is the one to initiate the whole thing, whereas we usually have to sweet talk a girl into a threesome.

"So I can join?" Liam's husky voice asks.

"Yeah, if you let me watch you fuck Max," she moans, touching herself now. "I've always wanted to see two men together."

Liam looks at her horrified before taking a step backwards. I follow his lead wondering what fucking crazy train she stepped off tonight.

"Then I want you to piss all over me," she moans again, her fingers under her skirt playing with herself.

I look at her disgusted and take a leaf out of Liam's book and take another step back, needing to get away. I feel dirty and I don't think a hundred showers a day will make me feel clean after all that shit.

"Fucking gross, man," Liam whispers, now stood next to me, grabbing his t-shirt from off the floor. Amy has her shirt off, her hands playing with her tits. I don't even think she's realised we haven't joined the party. She just keeps touching herself, telling us what she wants us to do, what she wants to see and I swear if I couldn't get a boner before, I wouldn't be able to now she just mentioned fisting.

"I'm just going to get some condoms," I shout over her moaning and back out of the room, slowly, shutting the door behind me.

"Where the fuck did you find her?" Liam laughs once we're outside the shut door.

"Greggs," I shrug, wincing when I hear Amy's moans growing louder.

"No, seriously, where the fuck did you find her? That ain't normal," he laughs, shoving my shoulder.

I sway from the push but catch my balance. "No, seriously, I met her at Greggs. She seemed fucking normal at the time," I frown, wondering if I have something wrong with me.

Lake seems like the type to be into new shit but not the fucking kinky shit Amy considers to be normal. Just picturing being with Lake awakens my boner and I have to fight back a curse.

"What are you going to do?" Liam asks, looking back at the door when another scream wails from the other side.

At least she's enjoying herself. That's what counts, right?

"I think I'm just going to go," I whine, then pause when Liam looks at me like I've grown two heads.

"You can't leave her. At least, not until she's finished herself off. Anyone could just walk in and she'd let them join in," he scolds me.

"If they want to get fisted, each to their own," I shrug.

Just then a scream pierces through the walls, the kinky slut in the other room getting her release. At least one of us is.

"Well, at least she's finished," he laughs and my phone beeps interrupting him. I grab it out of my pocket to find a message from Joan. I'm about to ignore it but Lake's name catches my attention.

JOAN: Lake doesn't seem too good. She's been gone since dinner and she's come back a mess.

The message doesn't elaborate on what kind of mess but it doesn't need to. My feet move, but before I can reach the stairs Liam stops me, motioning to the room Amy is in. The door opens and Amy walks out with a satisfied look upon her face.

"I'll be right back," I tell her before rushing off down the stairs and out of the house. I call a taxi once I'm outside, the night air reaching freezing levels.

The taxi arrives fifteen minutes later, the horn blaring. I quickly get in and fire off my address and sit back in the seat, my drunken state quickly dissipating.

GREGGS/TITS: What's up?

MAX: Lake's upset.

GREGGS/TITS: No, I meant like what are you doing? Where are you?

MAX: On my way home from a party.

I text back, my minds not really registering her texts, it's too occupied on Lake and if she's okay. Maybe I'm still drunk after all because it isn't until I get a text back that I realise who I'm messaging.

GREGGS/TITS: WTF? U left me here on me own?

MAX: No. Of course not. There are loads of people there.

GREGGS/TITS: Fuck you.

MAX: Not into your kind of shit, thanks, and before you ask, no, I'm not into shitting on you either.

I block her number before she has time to text me back. One thing I love about iPhones: I don't need to ring up my network provider to block a number. I can just do it from my phone.

Pulling up outside mine, I pay the taxi driver and walk up to Joan's. The lights are still on and, before I can knock, the door opens with Joan standing there looking pissed as hell.

"I'm sorry about dinner," I start but she stops me by holding her hand up and opening the door a little wider.

Cautiously I take a step inside, looking around the hallway to the living room to see if Lake is there. When she's not, I turn to a pissed off Joan.

"Where's Lake?" I whisper.

"In her room; probably still crying."

I don't wait for her to say anything else or stop when she hisses my name. I rush up the stairs to the first floor, needing to get to Lake. The thought of her crying and alone does something to me. I've only ever had this feeling once before and that was when Myles was in hospital after Kayla's crazy ass mom tried to kill him, or her. Whatever. The point is that it fucking killed me and Lake evokes the same feelings in me.

Slowly, I open the door, hearing sniffling as soon as I enter. "Joan, I just want to be alone," she whispers, not looking up.

I close the door behind me, moving further into the room. I remove my hoody on the way and start undoing my jeans.

"What? Max?" she screeches, jumping up into a sitting position. "What the hell are you doing here?"

"Come to see you," is all I say as I climb into the bed beside her.

"Why are you undressed?" she hisses, her voice croaky.

"Because I'm not leaving you and I'm tired. I don't know why you're upset but I can't stand to see you hurting or knowing you're hurt. Lie down," I order.

"No. You can't just come in here and think you can sleep here. I told you to stay away. It didn't even take you long to get with another girl," she replies bitterly.

"Jealous?"

"Yes! No! Fuck's sake, Max, leave me alone and go home," she huffs out, throwing herself back down and turning to face the wall. I crawl further beside her, spooning her from behind. She tries to fight me by moving away but I pull her body closer.

"Still!" I demand. "I'm not here to piss you off even more. I just want to make sure you're okay. I know I hurt you; you hurt me too," I admit.

"No. You just took a hit to your ego, Max, nothing I've done has hurt *you*," she bites out. A part of me stops to think about it. Am I hurt because she's bruised my ego or because I'm genuinely hurt by her?

"You're right," I start and she humphs in agreement. "But you're also wrong. Yeah, you've hurt my ego but you hurt me too. You're the first girl I don't just want to fuck. I love hanging out with you. I get on with you and don't see you as another fuck. I can get anyone I want, Lake, but it's you I want to be with differently. I don't know what any of it means, I just know I don't want to use you like I use other girls," I admit.

"Max," she whispers, pausing before taking a deep breath. "I like you too, but we can't be anything more than friends. I'm not the person you've all painted me out to be. I've done something terrible. Something I'll never be able to reverse. You don't need that in your lives."

"What are you talking about? Is that why you've been upset?" I ask quietly.

"Yeah and no. I was pissed at you. Pissed that I cared, pissed that you were with another girl, but more pissed at myself for being pissed."

"That's a lot of piss. Should have come to the party tonight, you would have been good to go," I mumble, still confused on what she's trying to say.

"Shut up," she warns before taking another deep breath. "I went out tonight; pissed off about you. But deep down it was more to do with Joan, with Harlow, Malik and everyone else. You all have this tight bond, this deep connection, and it's something I had, yet, will never have again. I'm not after sympathy or a replacement family but I care about you all. I don't even know why."

"It's cause we're a fucking awesome family, that's why," I tell her, chuckling. She playfully smacks my arm that's curled around her stomach and I chuckle into her neck, breathing in her apple shampoo. "So what has you so upset?"

"It wasn't until I got back that Joan made me realise what's really bothering me. It's you. You're making me want to live again and I can't do that, not when I... Not when I..." she stops, her breath catching, and I squeeze her tighter.

"When you did what?" I ask softly.

"Nothing. I can't talk about it. You should go," she whispers: defeated.

"I'm not going anywhere."

"Max, the whore, staying to comfort a girl, whatever will they say?" she teases, still, I can hear the sadness in her voice.

"Oh, I don't know. I met someone tonight much worse than me," I chuckle. "Now go to sleep."

"You're sleeping?"

"Yeah, you've spoilt me too much. I can't sleep without you," I half lie. I haven't had the chance to test that theory but the thought of going home to an empty bed turns my stomach.

"What about your date?" Lake blurts out a few minutes later. My eyes open and I wonder if I should lie but then lying is something I don't condone, not when it's something serious. Something stupid like drawing on your brother's girlfriend's face, however, is another story.

"I was being a dick. Like you said, my ego was blown. Plus, I'm not into pissing on or fisting people," I tell her yawning, the drink catching up with me.

"What?" she laughs, trying to turn around but I stop her, my arms tightening around her. If she faces me and starts talking about all this shit I might get other kind of thoughts.

"True story, one I didn't make up myself."

"Oh my God, she asked you to do...*that?*" Lake laughs, her body shaking beneath me.

"And more," I scoff, thinking back to the remark about watching Liam fuck me.

"Tell me," Lake giggles, relaxing back into my arms.

"No, you're far too young to hear such crude things," I tell her in a posh voice, making her laugh harder.

"Oh, come on, you can't say all that then not tell me."

"Okay, but promise not to get any ideas?" I warn. Half of me is only teasing, though, after tonight with Amy, nothing would surprise me.

"I'm not into fisting and pissing on people, or vice versa," she tells me, grossed out, and it's my turn to laugh.

"She asked Liam, an old friend from school, to fuck me so she could watch."

"Oh my God, she didn't?" she laughs harder but then stops and I brace myself. "Wait. You were going to have a threesome? You must have been in the room alone before she offered up those kind of...*services*," she tells me sadly.

"Liam followed us upstairs after he watched her dry hump me for an hour and get off twice in a room full of people; she wasn't exactly quiet about getting off either."

"I don't even know what to say," she whispers and I feel her body tense up. Shit! I should know by now after listening to Malik, Myles and Mason go on about their relationships that you should never talk about other girls.

"It wasn't like that. At first I met up with her to try to get back at you, or get you out of my head...or something. Then she wouldn't shut up and I kept comparing her to you. She had a bottle of WKD and apparently I should have listened to her when she told me it made her horny. My only other option was to have a more talkative girl on my hand."

"But you went upstairs with her and with a friend to have a threesome," Lake deadpans.

"Yeah, because I had a girl with big tits rubbing herself off on me and I couldn't even get a damn boner. I thought it was because she'd drained the life out of my dick by rubbing herself on me, but it turns out I only get hard for you," I admit, picturing earlier in the day when I kissed Lake. Fuck, I had been so fucking hard just from a kiss. No one has ever made me feel like I could blow my load from just a kiss. I'd been so close. One more thrust into Lake's sex and I would have embarrassed myself in my boxers.

"That does not make sense," she groans.

I push my hips into her, my erection from just lying next her, digging into her ass. "Does that make sense?"

I don't think she realises it but she grinds back into my dick and I bite my lip to stop a moan from slipping out.

"So why didn't you sleep with her?"

"In case you missed it, I'll mention fisting and pissing, that and the fact all I could think of is you."

"I can't be anything more than friends with you," she tells me sadly.

"I'm going to fuck you sooner or later, Lake. I see the way you look at me, act around me, and that you get turned on by me. As for more than being friends, we'll see. You're not the only one with commitment issues. My brothers may have all found the one, or what have you, but for me, relationships, kids, marriage and all that bullshit is what destroys people in the end," I tell her honestly, seeing a case load of blue balls in my future. I hear her intake of breath and realise she's about to ask questions and I'm not ready to indulge more into my fucked up parent's past. Not that she doesn't know almost everything about them anyway. In fact, I'm willing to bet she knows more about my parents than Harlow and Denny put together. "Sleep. We'll talk more tomorrow."

With that, I pull the blanket over us and move further down the bed, snuggling closer to Lake, needing her surrounding me. Any time I think of my parents it's like their ghost is there haunting me, waiting for that one moment to strike and ruin our lives all over again. It's the only thing that can make me angry. They're the only things that can make me lose my temper.

I've gotten into fights, don't get me wrong, but I've never fought angry. It pisses whoever I'm fighting off even more, but that's not my problem. I've never thrown the first punch and I've never caused a fight. Last year, John Gavins got into it with me, trying to rile me up, make me throw the first punch, but I kept joking, dancing around him, making fun of him and having everyone witnessing the whole exchange in fits of laughter. He hated it. He got sent over the edge when

I told him how good his girlfriend was in bed. He couldn't control the anger so I bested him. I won. He still hasn't gotten over it till this day.

My eyes close and I fall asleep listening to the sound of Lake's breathing evening out.

NINE

LAKE

It's been three days since Max confessed all those things to me in my bedroom and also since Joan and I had that heart to heart that honestly seemed to come out of nowhere. It needed to be said, though.

Meanwhile, things have become easier between me and Joan and I find myself becoming closer and closer to not only Joan but everyone around me. I've still not indulged in my past or why I'm here with anyone, but something tells me my secret won't be kept a secret for much longer. With each passing day the urge to tell someone is becoming more and more apparent. It's killing me inside keeping everything I've done bottled up. It's like living with them is a whole lie and once they know the truth it won't mean anything. It's like God is telling me my life isn't punishment enough for the sins I've done.

A knock at the bedroom door has me snapping back to the present. "Come in," I shout, putting down the magazine I was reading.

"Hey, you busy?" Kayla asks, walking in.

"No. You okay?" I wonder out loud, concerned about the colour of her bright red face. She doesn't seem to be short of breath, though, so it calms me down a little. All I need is for her to have a heart attack in my presence. Karma would love that – another way to fuck with my life.

"Yeah, but you remember when I woke up looking like a bloody clown?" she growls and my heart stops for a second. Has Max told her the truth? Or lied and told her it was me? Oh my God, I feel myself becoming hot. I don't want her to hate me. We girls are supposed to stick together and all that crap. You know, sisters over misters. I actually like her and for me to like a girl is actually something new and rare. In the past I never got on with any of the girls at school or gone out of my way and made friends with girls because I found they were all catty. I had my best friend, Emma, and that was it. She was all I needed. Until she moved the year before I ran away.

"Yes," I answer slowly, coughing when my throat feels too tight. Guilt is eating away at me. I should have told Max no, stopped him or, hell, told Kayla the truth, but it was all funny at the time. Now having her standing in front of me questioning me, it's not all that funny. Now I'm sweating like a pig and willing to blurt all my darkest secrets out.

"Well, I'm about to get my revenge, but I need you to make sure Myles is asleep. He text me saying he was watching television downstairs and we all know when he watches evening television after being at college all day he falls asleep."

"So, you want me to go over there and see if he's asleep? Won't I wake him up knocking on the door?" I ask, confused. She could do this on her own. She doesn't really need me. Not for this. Plus, I feel bad playing both sides, but then again, I need to take one for the team. Sisters over misters and all that.

"No, I need you to text Max and ask him what he and Myles are up to, then try and get him out of the house."

"How am I supposed to do that? He'll get suspicious. It's Max. Plus, I never ask about Myles so he'll know straight away I'm up to something."

"Where's your phone?" she asks me quickly and I hand it over to her, not wanting to mess with her. She seems to have a plan and I don't want to get in the way of that. Before I hand it to her the door to my room opens and Harlow barges in.

"God, everyone's boring. Malik's at work, the twins are asleep on the sofa next door, Denny is at her brothers with Mason and Maverick is at work. So it leaves you two. What are we doing and is it going to be fun?"

"Aren't you supposed to be resting?" I ask, at the same time Kayla says, "The twins are asleep?" Kayla grins mischievously and I'll admit it's a scary looking grin.

"Yeah, why? The door's been left open so I just walked in. I didn't bother waking them up because they were watching that cooking programme that they both love. Reading the instructions on a shampoo bottle is more interesting than that show. And no, I'm fed up of resting. I'm pregnant, not disabled," she huffs out.

"I've got a plan. I need to get Myles back for drawing on my face. He's still refusing to admit it was him and blaming Max. But if they're both asleep we might as well get them both," Kayla grins.

"Yes, finally, something fun," Harlow whoops, jumping up and down. I'm too stunned to speak, though; I have to admit the tiny person has me intrigued. "What are we doing?"

"I got these," Kayla laughs, pulling out boxes of wax strips and Harlow and I look to each other and grin.

"This is great," Harlow laughs.

"What were they wearing?" I ask Harlow curiously.

"Myles was wearing shorts, I think, and Max is only in a pair of boxers; the lad is gross. Even in his sleep he can't leave his dick alone," she groans, looking disgusted.

"Eww," I laugh while grabbing the box of wax strips Kayla is handing over to me. "I've got an idea," I tell them and then go into detail about my plan with them both.

"I didn't think of that. I was just going to stick them over his eyebrows," Kayla laughs and we laugh with her. "But this plan is so much better."

I agree. My plan is so much better, plus, I'm still not over Max planning a threesome with another chick. I know I don't have any right to be jealous or have any claim over Max, but deep down I still feel betrayed.

All three of us head over to Max's, taking our shoes off outside so we don't make a noise walking in. Kayla assures us that they're deep sleepers but Harlow and I said we don't want to risk it; not wanting to be caught in the act. It would ruin everything we have planned for them.

Kayla decided she wanted to do Myles and I said I'd happily do Max, so it left Harlow open to share the pile of wax strips she has to do both.

We all bite our lips, fighting not to laugh already. Harlow and I make our way over to Max's sleeping form where he's snoring gently. Harlow stands up at the top end as planned while I get the shitty part.

Harlow's going to do his armpits and his chest hair, while I get the pleasure of getting the crease of the inside of his leg. His legs are already spread wide, one bent leaning against the sofa, the other bent lying flat on the cushion making my job easier. His hand is down his boxers pulling the material away from his man parts. When I see the outline of his dick my breath catches in my throat and I have to shake my head to get rid of all the dirty thoughts running through my mind. As soon as I slowly stick the first wax strip on, I see his bulge clearly stiffen and I gasp. Harlow whispers, 'eww,' when she sees what I'm looking at, but all I can think of is how big it fucking is. Does he take penis enlargement tablets or some shit? No lad his age should be that big. Should they?

Fucking hell, I'm zoning out on Max's dick and not concentrating on the task at hand. Getting with the game I make quick work of sticking on another wax strip, my fingers skimming his ball sack slightly.

My eyes snap to Max to see if he's awake and relax when I find he's still snoring soundly. I kind of feel like I'm violating him, but something tells me if he wakes up he'd see it completely differently and be ecstatic my hands were near his junk.

My eyes slowly rake over his muscled chest. It will never get old looking at his hard, sculptured body; even his wide chest turns me on. It's fucking ridiculous how good looking he is, how well built he is for a lad his age.

Harlow's hand sticking a wax strip on Max's happy trail wakes me up and I move down to his legs, making sure I use all of the six wax strips. When I'm done I admire our masterpiece before moving over to Kayla and Myles.

Like Max, Myles has the crease of the inside of his legs done, his armpits, his happy trail and the hairiest parts of his legs covered in wax strips.

The plan is to wait a few minutes to get the wax strips to work. Kayla can barely hold herself together as she takes pictures of Myles. Harlow already got some of Max as I was finishing up. I'll have to remind myself to ask her to send them to me when we're done. I giggle inside just imagining Max's reaction when he wakes up.

"I've got my video ready to record their reaction," Kayla whispers and Harlow grins, taking her phone out and looking like she wished she thought if it first. I'm wishing I did too. I've left my phone back in my room. It's too late to go grab it now.

"Something tells me this moment is going to be epic," Harlow giggles, setting up the video recorder for when they wake up.

After a few minutes neither Carter brother wakes up. I start to get my hair off.

There's one thing I'm short of and that's patience. Grabbing Harlow and Kayla by the elbows I usher us out the front door.

"What are you doing?" Kayla hisses on a whisper. "It's not payback if I don't get to relish in the after glory of my prank."

"Did it look like they're going to wake up?" I deadpan, making sure the door doesn't slam shut behind us.

"No," Harlow replies slowly looking at me.

"Exactly. Get your cameras ready, ladies," I warn before banging the hell out of the door. Knowing Max as well as one can in the time I've known him, he'll probably be plotting an escape thinking we're the police. "MAX?" I shout, letting myself back in.

"What the fuck?" Booms from the sofa. I stifle a giggle when both brothers are looking down at themselves in confusion. When they see us walk in, Max's eyes reach mine and soften but not before confusion seeps back in and he looks between each of us girls.

It seems Myles is the sharpest as well as the brightest, having already caught on to what's happening, his eyes catching Kayla's and narrowing. But even with his narrowed eyes he still looks like he wants to kiss the hell out of and protect her with his life. It's sickening. Really sickening.

"What. Did. You. Do. Kayla?" Myles bites out and Max, slow as ever snaps his head over to his brother, finally catching on.

"What the fuck did I do?" Max shouts, horrified when he notices the strips between his legs. "Dude, she was near my junk," he shouts just as loud, and an angry noise escapes Myles.

Uh oh!

I didn't see this coming. Myles looks like he's about ready to tackle Max to the floor, even knowing Max is also the injured party. I want to laugh but I'm not ready to draw attention to myself.

Then Kayla steps on my dreams of living in solitude when she turns all her attention to Myles.

"No, I wasn't," Kayla shouts, giving herself away. "Lake was," she adds, dropping me right in it.

Good going, Kayla!

"Thanks," I bite out sarcastically. Harlow chuckles, not caring, and moves farther into the room with her phone still in her hand.

Myles pulls at one of the strips, catching my attention. "MOTHER FUCKER!" he roars and I can't help but laugh and cringe at the same time. It's comical.

"Let me do it," Kayla tells him sweetly but before he has chance to tell her no, she's pulling at the wax strip under his left armpit. He kicks out to thin air, screaming and shouting a bunch of curses through the pain. Laughing, I pull my attention away to see Max's reaction. He's sitting down watching the commotion with an expression full of fear and pain for his brother. It only makes me laugh harder. He's pale, looking completely terrified and frozen in time.

Yep, I still can't feel sorry for him and I can't wait for him to get his taken off either.

"Shut up and let me do it," Kayla snaps, laughing. In my daze watching Max, Kayla has taken off a few more strips. Myles' eyes are watering and I laugh when he grabs at the sofa with so much conviction I'm afraid he's going to rip a hole in it.

"FUCKING HELL," he roars again, making Kayla laugh harder. That's when I notice Max on his phone.

"You're up," I tell him, grinning, but he ignores me, and I bite back a giggle. "Earth to Max."

"I'm on Google," he snaps, typing furiously on his phone.

"Why are you on Google?" I laugh, ignoring Myles' pleas to Kayla for her to leave him alone and that he's sore.

"Trying to find the hospital number."

"Why?" I laugh, holding my side from a sudden stitch.

"Because I'm not going through that," he shouts, standing up and pacing. He lifts the phone to his ear before pulling it away again and pressing some more numbers. After a few minutes someone must answer. "Hello? Hi, I'm calling about myself. Yes. It's not good, no. Sorry, but listen, it's an emergency. My sister-in-law and her psycho friends decided to cover my body in wax strips... How do I safely remove them?" He pauses, listening to the person on the other line before scrunching his face up in horror. "What? They're torture devices. I've just watched my brother, my *twin* brother go through this. I felt everything," he whispers, looking defeated as he plops back down on the sofa. "Whatever. Bye."

"What did they say?" Harlow asks, amused, sitting the farthest away from Max on the sofa.

"To do it quickly," he whispers. "I feel so violated. One is on my ball bag."

I laugh. Hard. I can't help it. It's fucking hilarious. He leans forward, his elbow to his knees and his head in his hands looking like he's thinking it all over.

"Let's get this over with," I smile, enjoying seeing him squirm.

"Please, enjoy yourself; don't worry about me," he waves off, looking at me with disgust.

"Women go through this all the time, Max. I'm sure it's not that bad," Kayla laughs.

"Let's stick one on your most prized possession and see how you react. I can't do it. I can't. Look at him," Max yells, pointing over to Myles curled up on the sofa, his hands cupping between his legs. "He's never going to be the same again."

"Stop bein' a baby," I tell him and quickly grab the one under his armpit while his arm is raised. It pulls the hair with a loud tear and Max screams bloody murder. I have to admit, even I felt that, but it doesn't stop me from laughing hysterically.

"OH MY FUCKING GOD, WHAT DID YOU DO?" he yells and Harlow, Kayla and I both fall to the floor laughing. Oh my God, this is the most I've laughed since... Since forever. I kneel up on the floor and crawl on my knees over to Max who is now lying on the carpet in a ball, his hand cupping his armpit. You'd think I just stabbed him, not pulled some hair out.

My eyes notice a bit of wax strip sticking out of his other armpit and, before Max can dodge my advance, I pull it with full force making him cry out in pain.

"Stop, God, please, just stop," he cries, tears fully running down his face.

"The quicker it's done, the easier it will be," Harlow tells him laughing.

"Quicker? Easier? Are you having a fucking laugh? This shit is serious, Harlow. It's not playing tickle me, Max," he snaps.

"At least let us pull off the ones stuck to your balls before they get permanently stuck," I force out between trying to hold my laugh in.

"WHAT? NO! NO WAY! Stuck? I can't believe this is fucking happening to me. I'd rather have a night with Amy than go through this," he cries, tucking his head back in his hands.

I look to everyone else in the room. Harlow is bending over the arm of the sofa laughing; Kayla is standing by the fire place, close to Myles who is face down on the other sofa. He still hasn't spoken; his whimpers are the only sound to indicate he's even conscious.

"At least let me take the two from off your legs," I plead, trying not to sound like I'm enjoying this too much when I turn back to him.

"Or me," Harlow adds, sitting up straighter. She's looking rather pale and I'm about to ask if she's okay when Max grabs my hand.

"Don't... Don't hurt me," he whispers, his face full of pain and anguish.

I nod my head, keeping my face straight. There's no point in rubbing in the fact that I'm enjoying his pain right now. I'll wait till after.

Men! They proclaim they are the stronger sex but give them wax strips, child birth, and period cramps and they're fucked. Just proves my point that women rule.

"STOP," he shouts, pushing me away. "Do the legs at the same time. Just... Fuck, just do it."

"Okay," I cough out, trying to cover another laugh. He lies back against the sofa, his head resting by the side of Harlow's thighs and his legs sprawled out in front of him.

"On the count of three," I say quietly. "One..." And before he can take a deep breath, I rip them off, falling back on my ass when he flies to the side, screaming in pain.

"YOU MOTHER FUCKING DONKEY," he roars. "My hair, my fucking hair."

"Suck it up," Kayla laughs.

"Suck it up? Suck it up? Kayla, you've damaged me for life. I'll be surprised if my hair grows back," Myles cries, sitting up. "I need some painkillers."

"Just two more, Max," I tell him, ignoring the others bickering.

"No, no more. I can't do it. Not to my balls."

"They've got to come off," Harlow tells him, laughing.

"No, they don't. Can't I soak them in water? Yeah, I'll soak them in water."

"It makes the glue turn harder," I lie quickly and he sighs, leaning back with defeat.

"Just fucking do it," he bites out and sits back down again, this time with his legs spread wide open.

"Bro, just know, I'm here for you," Myles whispers.

"Thanks, Twinny," Max whispers back before closing his eyes. My hand isn't even inches away before he's slapping them away. "Hold on, I'm not ready," he breathes out before giving me a nod to go ahead. I move again, but just like last time he slaps my hands away.

"Stop it," I snap. "The longer you leave it, the more it will hurt."

"I'll do it," he bites out.

"It hurts more when you do it yourself," I tell him. It's like pulling a plaster off. When you do it yourself you tend to do it slowly, making the process more painful. But when someone else does it for you, it's over and done with.

"Just. Let. Me. Do. It," he growls and grabs the wax strip. "FUCK! I can't do this," Max cries, more tears falling from his eyes.

I giggle but it gets caught in my throat when Max snaps his head to mine; his expression stormy and hard.

"For God's sake, just do it already," Harlow says and leans forward, grabbing one of the strips. Max moves as she's doing it so when he slaps her hand away, it's hanging half off. We're all giggling while he screams murder, telling us we're all going to die a slow, painful death and that revenge is a bitch.

While he's still screaming with his eyes closed and his hand waving the stripped hair like a fan, I take the opportunity to grab the other wax strip, pulling sharply so he doesn't have time to smack my hand away. His eyes open wide with horror, his mouth hanging open.

"ARRRGGGHHHHH! WHAT DID YOU FUCKING DO?" he all but roars to the room. "Man down, MAN DOWN!" That's when the front door slams wide open and Maverick, their older brother, comes rushing in.

"What the fuck is going on? Max? Myles? What's wrong?" he asks, concern lacing his voice.

"They've… I can't talk about it," Max whispers, his voice finally calming down, while Myles looks to the floor. Maverick surveys they room, his eyes landing on me and Harlow near Max's legs. Harlow's sitting on the floor now next to me while I'm still sitting between Max's legs.

"Someone tell me what the fuck is going on right now or, so help me God, I will kick every single one of your asses… Not the girls, though," he adds on once he sees the look on our faces.

"We've gone through enough pain, brother," Max snaps, narrowing his eyes on Maverick.

"What the hell is that?" Maverick commands.

"What they took away from me," Max confesses, his head bowed.

"Are you wearing a sanitary towel?" Maverick laughs, pointing between Max's legs and I can't help but giggle. I honestly thought we were in trouble when he walked in. I've not had time to meet with Maverick. He's always busy at work or from what Joan has said, wanting to start another business. He seems pretty cool, though, and hot as hell. His tattoos are freaking hotter than hell.

"No, it's a fucking wax strip," Myles answers for Max, wincing, probably at the reminder of the pain.

"Please, don't tell me this is to make your dick look big? A mate of mine from work does it all the time. It's sick. I don't get why you'd torture yourself just for that."

"What are you talking about?" Max asks, his tone perking up.

"You know Jimmy, the doorman? He removes all his hair down there. Said girls dig that shit and it makes his dick look bigger," Maverick shrugs. He's talking about dicks like it's no big deal. Both Harlow's and Kayla's faces have turned beet red and I'm counting my lucky stars I've never had that problem. Don't get me wrong, I get embarrassed, I just don't turn beet red.

Max's eyes light up, like there's a silver lining now after his temper tantrum. I roll my eyes and to wipe the smile from his face I rip off the last bit of the remaining wax strip Harlow failed to remove.

"Holy mother of God," Maverick mutters, wincing as he stares between Max's legs. "I think I'll get you an ice pack; that doesn't look too good," he adds, looking at where Max has his balls on show, but thankfully, his dick is still covered.

That's when I look, I mean, really look. The left increase of his leg is red and swollen. It's also the side that was mostly stuck onto his ball bag and with it shamelessly hanging out a little you can clearly see it's swollen and red.

"What the fuck have you done to my balls?" he screeches, standing up.

"Go soak it in cold water," Harlow chimes in, looking pale again.

"Are you okay?" I ask her, ignoring Max when he asks me to look up his symptoms.

"Yeah, just tired," Harlow answers, however, from the look on her face I can tell it's more.

"Are you even listening?" Max snaps as Maverick walks out of the room with Myles.

"Your balls aren't going to drop off," I tell him before looking back to Harlow. "Are you sure? You look seriously pale."

"Yeah, you do," Kayla adds, concerned, helping Harlow stand up.

"Do any of you fucking care about my balls?" Max screams.

We all look to him before simultaneously snapping, "No," at him. I turn back to Harlow in time to watch her sway. My arms reach out to steady her but I'm too late and before I know it she's on the floor unconscious.

"Call an ambulance," I scream as Maverick and Myles run back into the front room to see what the commotion is about.

TEN

MAX

I SHIFT IN THE UNCOMFORTABLE seat in the waiting area of the hospital. We've only been here ten minutes or so but already Malik, Joan, Granddad, Mason and Denny are all here. Malik was the only one let in the room with Harlow. The last we heard she was awake still and was waiting for the doctors to see her.

She could be losing her fucking baby and they're making her wait. Shouldn't she be a priority?

"Are you okay? You've not seemed yourself since we arrived," Joan sniffles from beside me. She taps my leg and I wince at the pain it causes between my legs. What a fucking place to put a wax strip. I can feel the rough sting with every fucking movement I make. I'm not even going to go there and describe the pain I'm still in. Getting fisted by Liam and Amy together sounds less painful than what I just went through.

I cough, remembering Joan asked me a question and answer, "Yep."

"You sure? Myles doesn't look right either. You need to know Harlow's going to be fine. You don't need to worry," she tells me but it sounds like she's trying to convince herself more than me.

If only she fucking knew. I was too busy ranting about my balls being sore to notice Harlow was suffering too. I remember hearing Lake ask her if she was okay but I was so self-absorbed in my ball bag that I didn't even stop to register that they were truly concerned.

"I need to just pop to the reception," I wince out, needing an icepack like... now. My balls feel like they're on fire.

"Where are you going?" Lake whispers when I stand up.

"I need something. I can't handle this."

Her eyes soften and she reaches out for my hand. Her touch has me almost forgetting the pain between my legs...Almost. "She'll be okay."

"I hope so; I've got payback to dish out," I tell her, but my voice lacks any conviction. If Harlow is okay, and the baby, there is no way I'll be doing anything to her. Not even putting toothpaste in her hair when she's asleep. After seeing her on the floor unconscious today... It's just knocked me about. I just pray her and the baby are both good and healthy.

Lake rolls her eyes. "So, where are you going? I'll come with you."

"I need to go get something for um... You know..." I cough and look down to my dick.

"Ohhhhh," she giggles quietly and stands up to join me. "This I have to see."

We arrive at the reception desk where an older lady sits typing away at a computer. Her eyes lift up to us when she hears us approaching, her glasses slipping half way down her nose when she does.

"Can I help?" she asks tersely.

"Um, I hope so," I cough, feeling embarrassed and nervous. "My sister-in-law, she was brought in twenty minutes or so ago. Before she had her fall I was in the middle of getting some... um, medical attention." Fuck, this is hard.

"I'm confused," the lady tells me and I sigh, scrubbing my hand down my face.

"What he's trying to say is that he's had a reaction to some wax strips," Lake helpfully butts in. I turn my head to the side and glare down at her. At 6 foot I tower over her 5 foot 5 frame, so I'm hoping my height is enough to intimidate her.

"Let's see," the lady says, moving around the desk. I look wide-eyed at Lake but all I get is her silent laughter. I'm so going to get her back for this if it's the last thing I bloody do.

"It's um... It's," I pause, taking in a deep breath, then lean in and whisper, "It's down there," I point.

"Why on earth are you waxing down… Ohhhh. Well, if you'll follow me I'll get you a bed and you can wait for a doctor to see you."

Not wanting to be away from the others or Harlow, I decline. "I'm sorry, I can't. My sister-in-law was brought it. I was just wondering if you had an ice pack or something until we know everything is okay."

"Very well, but if it gets worse you must see a doctor immediately," she scolds me. I want to reply with something sarcastic but something tells me I'll have my balls handed to me, pun intended. I mean, what does she think I'll do, leave it until my balls drop off? Un-fucking-likely.

"I will, scouts honour," I grin, hoping the dimples get her to hurry up. She just rolls her eyes and tells us to wait where we are while she goes and gets me one. I sigh with relief. I'm not sure how much longer I can handle the fire burning down there.

"That was so fucking funny," Lake giggles and I turn, advancing on her. She loses her smile and steps back. I take one step forward, caging her into the reception desk. I lean down, my mouth hovering over her neck before slowly making my way up to her ear.

"Don't think I've forgotten for one second the pain you inflicted on me. I'm going to make you pay," I whisper huskily, my mind conjuring up all the ways I can make her pay. On her back, legs spread, on all fours, but even better, her pussy waxed and sitting on my face.

Getting a boner right now, in this kind of situation, and not to mention the pain, has me silently cursing, my head moving back to look at her.

"Yeah? How you are you planning on doing that?" she asks with a twinkle in her eye. Little minx.

"Let's just say it will involve a lot less pain, your ass, my hand and you naked on my bed." My voice turns deep, my voice husky as I stare into her deep blue eyes that dilate at my words.

Fuck, she likes the sound of that.

"R-really," she coughs, gaining her voice back.

"Really," I promise, moving closer, my lips hovering over hers. That's when the old nurse decides to interrupt, ruining my fucking moment to get some pleasure after an evening of pain.

"Here, this is all I could do at such short notice," she tells me, handing me a cold press.

"This is great." I thank her.

She gives me a nod and I turn towards the way we came, Lake following beside me as we walk back to the waiting room. I make quick work of placing the cold press inside my boxers, trying my best while moving to put it in the right place. Patients and other people look at me in disgust as we pass them. That's when Lake starts giggling and I turn to see what's so funny.

"What?"

"Well, you are messing with your man parts in the middle of a hospital where sick people are. I'm pretty sure there's a word for it," she giggles and that's when I groan. I've got both hands down my pants and it must look like I'm messing with myself to other people.

"This is great, just fucking great," I hiss and nearly collide with Maverick when he steps out of the waiting room.

"There you are. Where have you been?"

"What's wrong? Are Harlow and the baby okay?" I ask worriedly.

"We haven't heard anything," he sighs sadly. He looks too old for his twenty-four years. He's had to grow up quicker than most people. It's times like this that I notice just how much he has had to grow up. "So, where did you go?"

"To get an ice pack," I admit. Realisation dawns on Maverick and he tries to cover up his deep chuckle by turning his back on us and walking back into the waiting area but I heard it.

Everyone is still sitting in the same position as we left them. The chairs are arranged in a square around the room, then six in the middle, three either side facing away from each other. We're all huddled in the far corner; the only other people in the room are a couple that are sitting nearer the door. The room is cold and not comforting at all which has done nothing to ease the tension in the room.

Joan is still looking out of the window where the rain drips down the window. Another thing that adds to the gloom that surrounds the air in the room. The depressing bloody weather.

I've just taken a seat, adjusting the cold press on my balls when the door opens revealing a pale, dishevelled Malik. Lake gasps from beside me and my fists clench at the sight of him. He doesn't look good which means, whatever he's about to say isn't good.

"Harlow wants everyone in the room. The doctors agreed so she would calm down." Okay, not bad, but then it's not good either. If Harlow wants us all there that means she needs us all there for support.

We all stand up, Mark and Joan asking Malik what's been said. Malik answers but it's short and sweet. They can't find a heartbeat. My body freezes. Doesn't that mean? No! It can't.

I want to punch something. Hit something. My brother, fuck, even Harlow doesn't deserve this shit. After everything he's been through, he doesn't need this. Not now. Not ever.

I thought I had commitment problems caused from daddy and mommy issues, but Malik's issues ran much deeper than mine. Now look at him. He's finally moved forward, found happiness, and now it's going to be ripped away from him, just like that.

"You're hurting me," Lake whispers softly and I shake myself from my thoughts and look to her. It's the first time I notice I'm holding her hand tightly.

"Shit, sorry. Did I hurt you?"

"It's fine," she whispers as we arrive outside Harlow's room. Walking in, Harlow is in a small bed, her back propped up by millions of cushions. Tears are streaming down her face and that's when I notice her attention is on a doctor sitting on a stool by the side of her. My first thought is to punch the fuck out of the doctor for making her cry; the second is to remind myself he's there to help her. It's not easy sitting back and watching the light slowly leaving her eyes.

"I wasn't expecting this many people. Are you sure you want them here?" the doctor asks Harlow quietly. I'd normally take offence to his comment but at the moment the only thing I care about is Harlow and the fact she's in pain. She wasn't in pain before. She clutches her stomach again and I watch, feeling helpless as Malik moves around the other side of the bed, taking her hand in his. He says something to her that we can't hear, but whatever he said seems to have relaxed her somewhat.

Joan moves towards her and from here I can see she's holding it together for Harlow, but even still, you can see the pain clear on her face. She doesn't like seeing her granddaughter suffering and possibly… I choke on my thoughts, a few eyes coming my way, but I don't bother acknowledging them or finishing my trail of thought. My main focus is to stay positive for Harlow and the baby.

"Okay, the gel will be a little cold but you should get used to it after a couple of seconds," the doctor tells Harlow.

The rest of us are standing back against the far wall; not wanting to get in the way.

We all move closer when a thumping drums around the room. We all look to the small screen, all of us preparing ourselves... For what, I don't know. I just know my entire focus is on that screen.

"Oh, look what we have here," the doctor speaks again and everyone's attention focuses on him.

"What, what's wrong?" Harlow demands, her voice filled with emotion. You can see the pain etched on her face, yet, the fear that's filled in her eyes is much clearer and painful to witness.

"This is the baby's heartbeat," he smiles, pointing to the screen. Harlow's moan turns into a sob, her shoulders shaking and her body leaning a little into Malik who is sitting half on the bed comforting her. His eyes haven't left the screen either and from here, I can see he had prepared himself for the worst and not for the positive outcome. The tears in his eyes are a clear indication of relief. Relief Harlow is okay and that his baby is okay.

But then the doctor opens his mouth, moving the device on Harlow's stomach a little. "And here's the second baby's heartbeat," he adds, and everyone gasps, another fast thumping sound echoing around the room.

Malik is frozen in place, however, Harlow's head whips around to the doctor, looking terrified. "How are there two?"

The doctor looks around the room, his eyes staying on me and Myles a second longer and we both grin. Harlow's eyes follow his and when our eyes meet hers she gives us an accusing gaze, her eyes narrowed on us.

"You did this," she snaps, though, her tone has lost conviction.

"Pretty sure I'd remember if I did," I wink, speaking up for the first time. Harlow narrows her eyes then starts smiling.

"Two! Two, Malik," she whispers, looking up at him. Then realising where she is she doesn't wait for an answer before turning back to the doctor. "Are they okay?"

"Yes. Your blood pressure is really low so that could be the reason why you fainted. It's common in pregnancy. The pains in your stomach could be due to your stress levels so I do advise you to relax for a few days. You have no signs of concussion from your fall, so I see no worries," he promises as he passes Harlow a tissue to clean up.

"I need another job," Malik barks out, his face pale. We all laugh but he doesn't join us. "And we need a house, a big one. One with a garden. We'll need a safer car but then, we knew that already. We'll have to get *double* of *everything*. I'll pick up some more work, more shifts and leave college to get a full time job."

My brother's a nut and if he thinks he's going to do this on his own, he's got another thing coming.

"Malik," Harlow whispers, looking up at him with soft eyes. "They're okay, we're okay."

"Yeah, but there's two, babe. Two! I don't think I'll cope if they're boys. Are they boys?" he rants to the doctor.

The doctor smiles before replying. "We won't know the sex until her twenty week scan. Your midwife will already have that booked in. But I would like you to make weekly visits to your midwife in the meantime."

"So, how far gone is she?"

"She's eight and a half weeks. I'll leave you to get cleaned up and a nurse will be with you shortly. You'll be able to go home, but I strongly advise you to have lots of rest, at least until you're feeling one hundred percent better."

"You promise there is nothing wrong?" Harlow whispers, tears in her eyes.

"I can't promise anything. But right now, yes, you and the babies are fine. It's still early on in the pregnancy so anything can happen. Just try to relax."

Harlow nods her head and we're all quiet as we watch the doctor leave the room.

"I cannot believe we're having twins. What are we going to do?" Harlow asks, tears running down her cheeks. "How will we cope? I can't do it. I can't! How am I going to look after two?" Harlow asks, doing a complete three sixty. Not two seconds ago she was on cloud nine knowing that they were safe and everything was fine. Now she looks like she's about to blow.

It's the first time I've seen her lose it like this. No, that's a lie. When some bitch at school took a photo of her in the school showers, that's when I first saw her lose it. She wanted to leave home to move to a new town, pleading for it all to end. It was horrible seeing her crumble like that. We were all worried at first that she would do something stupid. It wasn't just about the photo. She was also having some trouble off another kid at school, she just moved in with her Nan whom she had only just met and was still in the deep grieving stages from losing both her parents tragically.

"Darling, the only other options are abortion or adoption, are you willing to do that?"

I feel everyone's eyes snap to Joan's, furious at her words. How can she even ask that? I'm about to butt in, thankfully, Malik get's there first.

"Joan," he snaps. "That's not even an option."

"I'm asking Harlow," Joan says softly, looking back to her granddaughter.

"Grams, I could never do that. I love them both so much already," Harlow answers confidently, her eyes spilling with tears.

"Then there's your answer. No matter how hard life gets, how hard it will be raising two babies, remember *this* exact moment. Remember the choice you could have made and how that choice made you feel. Always come back to this moment because life, honey, is beautiful. Bringing two children into this world is just magical. It's a precious gift and I have no doubt, no fear, but every bit of faith in you that you will be the best mother you can be," Joan speaks, her voice soft and quiet. It's then the tension in the room eases, my own shoulders sagging with relief. Joan didn't want Harlow to make a choice, she wanted her to realise she was making the right decision.

"Thank you, Grams," Harlow whispers, leaning forward to give her a hug.

"Twins, this shit is awesome," I blurt out. "As long they don't turn out to be girls; then you're fucked, brother."

Everyone laughs, even Harlow who pulls away from Joan to look at me. Malik looks pissed and I can see in his eyes that he's just started praying, no, demanding the twins are boys. Though, they could be like me and Myles.

"Let's just be thankful they're okay and healthy," Granddad speaks up, his voice soft too and looking at Harlow like she's gifting him the world. Sappy fucker.

"Twins! I can't believe we're having twins. It's real, look?" Harlow tells us again, her eyes on the frozen screen of the baby.

"Yeah, Angel, it's real and I promise with all of my heart that I will take care of you. All of you," Malik vows and that's when I decide it's my cue to get out of here.

ELEVEN

LAKE

It's been a few days since Harlow collapsed and everyone found out she and Malik were having twins. She's been in bed for the past few days resting; neither Malik nor Joan letting her lift a finger. She hates every moment and has made sure everyone knows it.

"If one more person asks me if I'm okay, I'm going to snap. I mean really freakin' snap," Harlow growls from her bed.

I laugh. "They're just worried about you," I answer.

We've been watching a TV series called Chicago Fire that we found out about a few days ago. Since then we've done nothing but watch it in Harlow's room on Netflix. It's been addictive.

"There's worried and then there's Nan and Malik. They're in a whole new category of their own. I need to get back to college, work out if I'll be able to take the time off when I have the babies."

"Have you told them you're pregnant?" I ask.

"Not yet. One of the girls in my class mentioned her sister needing loads of time off during her pregnancy and that in the end the college let her go. She wouldn't have passed, but still, I'm scared that will happen to me. I'm only in the early stages and already I've been rushed to hospital."

"You had low blood pressure," I remind her. "And carrying twins."

"True. I'd still rather work with my college teachers so that I don't end up the same as that girl. I need to finish to get my diploma."

"You will," I promise her. "You have a great network of support around you. All of them would help you out any way they could."

"True again. I just don't want to rely on everyone. I guess I want to prove to everyone and all the stuck up people who bitch about young moms not able to bring up their kids properly that I – we – can do it. My mom used to tell me she got a lot of stick from people, even her friends, because they thought she was too young, too immature to bring a child into the world, but she proved them all wrong. She was the best mom I could ever wish for. She'd show me pictures of everything I did from when I was too young to remember doing them. I loved it. I remember always wishing that I would be half the mom she was to me."

"People talk crap. Ignore them. Yeah, some teenagers don't have the maturity to raise a child, yet, most of them raise their kids better than most parents in their forties. A girl, Demy, her mom was like sixty-three. Her mom didn't have her until she had a decent job, money in the bank and in a solid marriage. By the time all that happened she was forty-five. She didn't have the energy to do the things young moms can do. It's not that they neglected her, don't get me wrong, but they weren't as active in her life as other mothers were in their children's lives. She would get picked on a lot too for having older parents. Most people presumed she lived with her grandparents," I tell her. Demy wasn't just left out of sleepovers or having friend's sleepover, she was also left out with up-to-date technology, TV shows and the new fashion.

"You're totally right. I guess it doesn't matter how old you are, to be honest. As long as the child is happy I don't think it matters. And I'm going to love my babies with all of my heart and soul," she smiles.

I smile back. I'm so excited for her. I'm also hoping I'm around to see the twins being born. Sadness creeps in every time I think about leaving.

The door to Harlow's bedroom opens and Malik walks in. He's been at a job all afternoon and is covered in paint.

"Hey," I wave and get up from the bed, knowing he's going to want to shower and want some privacy. "I'm going to head downstairs, I'll catch up with you later," I tell Harlow.

"You don't need to go," she whines, pressing pause on the TV.

My eyes flick to Malik uncomfortably. I don't want to tell her I'm leaving so her boyfriend can have some privacy but I also don't want to get her upset.

"It's fine. I need to check on Thor anyway," I smile.

"I'm still gutted he won't come up here," she pouts, her accusing eyes narrowing on Malik. I hear him chuckle and I grin.

"What can I say? He loves me," I laugh.

"Boo hoo! See you later," she grumbles, making me laugh. I wave bye and head downstairs to my room. Joan should be back soon so I'll have some peace and quiet until then.

When Max walks into my room two hours later he startles me. I look up and my jaw goes slack at the sight of him in my doorway. He's in his dark jeans, a blue hoody, and his Nike trainers and wearing his dark blue Nike cap. He looks more like a boy in this outfit, but if I'm being honest, he looks fitter. I've seen him wearing just his boxers, work clothes, and seen him dressed up, well, for Max anyway, so you'd think I'd get used to the different looks he can pull off by now.

Obviously not.

"What are you doing here?" I ask surprised. He said his granddad was making him go look at a college course that he'd seen in one of the college application course books.

In the end, Max decided to take the sports and leisure course, seeming really interested in it. He hadn't heard of it before, however, if he gets his diploma there's a lot he can do with it. I personally think he'll be good as a football coach. I've seen him with some of the kids in the street playing football. He's pretty good with them.

Thor jumps up on my lap, bringing my attention back to him, and I giggle. He's so freaking cute.

In just the little time I've had him he's already gained a lot of weight. He's also come into himself and has become my cute little terroriser.

"I owe you payback," Max answers after a couple of seconds, walking farther into the room.

My head snaps up at that. I try reading his expression and I can tell he's deadly serious.

Thor runs across the bed before pouncing back in my lap where I'm sitting cross legged. He walks around in a slow circle; all the while I can't keep my eyes off Max who is locking the door behind him.

"W-what do you mean?" I choke out nervously. The tension in the room is thick, not caused by revenge but by lust. I can see it in his eyes, read it on his face and hear it in his breathing as he steps closer towards the bed.

My breathing picks up, the swell of my breasts expanding in my white camisole with each breath I take.

"You see, I've been waiting for the swelling on my left ball bag to go down before I chose the perfect moment to approach you."

That explains why I haven't seen him since the hospital.

"To approach me?" I choke out, leaning back further into the bed.

"Yes, approach you. You owe me," he whispers huskily, his gaze drifting to my lips which has me squirming. My mouth hangs open when he leans into me, his fists to the bed, his gaze searing into mine. Whatever bizarre game he's playing, I don't want to play. Okay, that's a damn straight lie. Whatever game he's playing, at this precise moment in time, I'm in. *All* in.

"Owe you?" I ask, tilting my head a little to the side. A quick grin tugs at his mouth, his dimples showing and melting me right there and then.

"Owe me," he agrees, smirking. Moving in closer, his spicy scent surrounds me. His scent is one of the things that turns me into a blonde bimbo around him. It's so intoxicating, all man, all natural, and all him.

"And what do I owe you?" I ask, showing more confidence than what I actually have right now. I'm really a nervous wreck having him this close, his lips right there in front of me, ready for attack. The urge to grab at him and slam my lips onto his is driving me wild. Ever since we kissed that first time it's consumed my thoughts and my dreams over and over.

"You have to go out with me," he states, moving in closer, his lips hovering over mine.

I take in a deep breath, trying to concentrate but it's hard having him this close. "No."

"No?" he asks amused. "I'm not giving you a choice. You owe me. And I want a chance to prove to you I'm not whatever your mind has twisted me up to be."

"You really thought this through," I snap, my lust and desire evaporating.

"Of course I did. I've been fantasising about you since the moment you gave me attitude at the station," he grins.

I roll my eyes and try to push him away, but his hard body doesn't budge. No, it doesn't budge. Instead he moves closer, closing the little space that is between us, placing his lips on mine. His tongue swipes inside my mouth and I melt into the kiss, kissing him back with such intensity that I moan into his mouth.

When I hear a hissing sound I ignore it, too committed to the kiss, when all of a sudden Max flies backwards screaming. I sit back stunned, wondering what just happened. It doesn't take me that long to guess when Thor cuddles back into my lap, purring himself back to sleep.

I look back up to Max with a shocked face before bursting into laughter when I notice Thor has scratched his throat.

"He tried to slice my throat open," Max hisses, his eyes narrowing on Thor.

I laugh. Hard. And in doing so I disturb Thor and his little cat nap. I laugh at him, stroking his soft fur before looking back up at Max.

"He's a kitten," I scoff. "Stop being so dramatic."

"Are you serious? That thing was a tramp before you took it in. I could have rabies. Fuck! I need to go."

"Max," I laugh, stopping him. "He's had injections."

"Yeah? Well, that makes one of us. Who the fuck knows if my mom or dad fucking bothered to take any of us to get our injections when we were little."

"So, you're saying you're diseased?" I choke out, trying hard to keep my laughter at bay. "That *you* could have given Thor something?"

"No. I'm...What I'm saying is," he pauses looking at Thor warily. "Fuck! I need to go. Look, he's staring at me."

I look down at Thor and notice he is in fact staring at Max; his green eyes focused entirely on him.

"That's because you're being dramatic; isn't it, Thor?" I coo, teasingly. Max grunts and I look up at him from under my lashes and grin.

"Oh, you're enjoying this. I'll be back tomorrow. Be ready for 7."

"What for?" I scoff, still laughing.

"Well, if you're going to go out with me then we need to go on a date," he winks. That cheeky, sly, little sod.

I narrow my eyes. "I'm not going out with you or on a date."

"You will. You won't have a choice."

"We'll see," I sing, still keeping my eyes narrowed on him.

"Stop fighting the inevitable, Lake," he sings back as he walks to the door. He unlocks it, opens it, and steps out before turning back around to face me with an expression I know all too well. "And wear something that will..."

"Stop right there, buddy," I shout, knowing where his dirty mind is taking him. His laugh echoes down the hallway and all the way down the stairs. Once he's out of ear shot, I lie back down on my bed, fuming. I hate that he got to me, that he got me worked up in all the right ways, but mostly because he *left* me worked up in the right ways.

THE FOLLOWING NIGHT I make sure to be gone by five. Knowing Max, he will know I'll be avoiding him and arrive early.

So when five comes along, I grab my coat, say goodbye to Joan and leave in the pouring rain. As soon as I get clear of the street, I begin to relax. Max scares me and not in the way most people get scared but emotionally scared. The scared that has me trying to build my walls back up, yet, every time I'm in his company he manages to knock two-to-three down at a time.

I end up at the cinema, watching some lovesick movie that bores me to tears and has me spending *more* time thinking about Max, my vibrating phone, and what I'm going to do next.

By the time I leave the cinema it's finally late enough for me to go back. I've eaten dinner and watched two movies since I had nothing else to occupy my time.

The lights are on when I arrive back home. No doubt Joan will be waiting up to see where I've been all night. Since arriving I've not been one to disappear or to leave at night. I guess I should have filled her in on the whole Max date thing and me trying to avoid him. But she's done nothing but try and get me and Max together.

When I first found out Max would be doing community service at the church I wanted nothing to do with him. I vowed to stay as far away as possible. But then Joan lumbered him with me at the church and as much as I tried to hate him, I can't. I should but I can't.

Then when we're together, hell, even apart, Joan will find a way for him to do something for me or vice versa. It's obvious where her loyalties lie and I suppose that's why I never really told her what I was planning on doing tonight.

Walking in, I hear someone get up off the sofa and I brace myself. When Joan walks into the hallway I relax slightly until I see the expression on her face. She looks wary, disappointed and, if I'm not mistaken, like she's up to something. She has that look on her face. The one I'm becoming accustomed to. The look that warns me I'm about to get manipulated in some way.

"Hey," I wave lamely.

"Why did you stand up Max?" she asks straight out, no pleasantries.

"It wasn't like that," I tell her quickly. "I never agreed to meet him."

"So, why was he here for three hours waiting for you? He's really upset. Max may come off a charmer, a joker, someone who doesn't take anything seriously, though, deep down that boy has a heart of gold."

"I know and I'm sorry. Look, I'm just not ready to date anyone or see anyone," I begin, feeling uncomfortable.

"I'm not going to be around forever and neither will Mark. Mark was beside himself with glee when Max turned up all dressed up," she smiles sadly.

"He was dressed up?" I ask, feeling shocked he went to any trouble. I presumed he'd take me to McDonalds and watch a film at his place.

"Oh yeah, he looked so handsome. But back to my earlier point, Mark and I won't be around forever. We need to know Max will be happy. He's happy when he's around you," she tells me gently.

See? Manipulation.

"Joan," I start, not wanting to get into this.

"But lucky for you and Max, we've got years left in us so we will put this right. Just cause you missed tonight doesn't mean you'll miss another date. He said he'll be back later or tomorrow."

Later or tomorrow, is the only thing that reaches my ears before a full blown panic attack threatens to surface.

"I'm really tired. I'm just going to go…" I tell her, pointing upstairs towards my room.

"Oh, go on, we'll talk in the morning about what you'll wear," she smiles and I sag with defeat. I'll figure something out later to avoid Max, until then, I just need to get out of Joan's hair.

Nodding my head, I return her smile and make my way up to my room. Opening the door my feet step on something. Flicking the light on an envelope is on the floor beneath my feet.

Opening it up I'm not sure whether to laugh or to be annoyed.

Will you go out with me? Tick one box. Yes or No

I don't want to tick either, but in the end I find my feet moving over towards my bedside table. I grab a pen and tick 'no' before putting the piece of paper back in the envelope and sealing it before I chicken out. I open the door, ready to drop it off to Max when Joan stands there with her hand out ready to take the envelope and scares the bejeezus out of me.

"What on earth, Joan? You scared the crap out of me," I laugh nervously, a hand to my heart.

"Sorry," she laughs. "I knew Max had left something and he did tell me I'd need to return it once you've replied. It's why I'm up so late," she tells me.

I shake my head, handing her the envelope. "He's not going to give up is he?"

"Not likely. When that boy wants something he doesn't give up until he's got it."

"Reassuring," I mutter. "He doesn't even do relationships. The only reason he wants one with me is because I won't give him one. If I was all for being with him he wouldn't be sending little school notes or even trying to get me to go out with him."

"Maybe; maybe not. It's no secret that Max doesn't believe in relationships and sometimes I think he doesn't even believe in the concept of love. He's never really been shown the true meaning. His upbringing wasn't the best. His belief in relationships simmers down from his parents' damaged relationship. Then when he was given a chance to witness a real, loving relationship, his grandmother was taken too soon, bless her soul. I honestly believe when it comes to you he sees past all that because he doesn't just see you as a commitment. He sees you as a friend, a partner, someone he can laugh and joke with.

"I'll let you think it over and I'll get this back to him. Get some sleep," she finishes. She moves forward, grabbing my face in the palms of her hands and pulls my head forward so she can kiss my forehead. My eyes close from the loving touch and when she's gone I still stand there thinking over her words.

I've been too busy thinking about all the reasons why I shouldn't be with Max, what it will do to me that I never really thought about what Max really wanted.

Maybe if we just go out with no labels, no promises, then we will be good. No one will get hurt. Planning on saying yes the next time he asks, I take a step back into my room. I close the door whilst smiling to myself, thinking that my idea could possibly work. But just because I plan on saying yes, it doesn't mean I'm not going to make him work for it. I'm actually a little curious as to what he has planned next.

Waking up the next morning, I listen out for the sound that has woken me up. When scratching at the door begins again, I smile.

Thor!

Jumping up, I rush over to the door and notice another envelope has been shoved under the door either late last night or early this morning.

I quickly snatch it up before opening the door to Thor. He immediately runs through the door, meowing and purring around my feet before ditching me to go and jump onto my bed. There, he moves into the spot I just vacated, getting himself comfortable.

"Morning to you, too," I grumble on a smile. I shut the door behind me before following Thor and jumping into bed with him. He immediately snuggles into my side, not caring I've covered us both with the blankets.

Opening the envelope, I can't keep the giddy smile from off my face. When I open it I burst out laughing.

Will you go out with me? Please tick one of the two boxes ONLY. Yes or Yes.

He's persistent, I'll give him that. Not ticking either box I throw it on my bedside table. For Max to get a date with me he needs to work a little harder than juvenile notes shoved under the door to my bedroom.

Dinner time comes around slowly. The whole day has been spent watching *Sons of Anarchy* in my room; alone. Harlow went off to college around eleven this morning, Malik leaving a few hours earlier than her. With Mark and Joan both out working Thor and I had the house to ourselves and it's been quiet and boring.

I'm so used to having Max's big gob around the house that I've grown accustomed to noise. I've gotten used to talking to someone or another that being alone is actually depressing me. I even fell asleep due to boredom.

Hearing Joan calling my name I get out of bed and grab my hoody off the back of the door. I've not taken one step out of the room before I'm cursing loudly, my toe throbbing from the brick I just kicked.

"What the fuck?" I cry out. Looking down at the floor, there's two weights. One's a small round one and the other is a huge round one, both of them have pieces of paper sellotaped to the top. The biggest and, by the looks of it, heaviest, has a note with the letters, 'NO', written in big red lettering. On the smallest is a similar note, yet, this time the letters read, 'YES'. I grumble under by breath seeing another note in the middle. Picking it up I curse. My foot is killing me. He could have bloody killed me.

The note reads...

Will you go on a date with me? Bring me back the answer, if I don't get one, I'll take that as a yes. Yours awesomely, Max.

I want to kill him.

There is no way I'll be able to lift that fucker with the 'NO' answer on and take it next door. But he's definitely not going to be getting me to take the lightest weight around to him either. The jerk! My foot is still throbbing when I step over both the weights and make my way down the stairs. Malik walks in just in time and an idea pops into my mind.

I must look like a lunatic looking at him then rushing off back upstairs. Joan hears me and shouts my name again.

"In a sec," I shout back down, ripping the notes off both of the weights. I make quick work of carrying the smallest one over to the bottom of Harlow and Malik's stairs.

When I hear Malik telling Joan he'll be back down in a minute I start to panic, wondering how I'll move the other weight before he comes upstairs. When Mark stops him, I sigh with relief and waste no time in trying to move the weight.

Getting on all fours, I slide the weight across the floor, and it works a little, but then I end up falling to the floor in a heap.

Puffing out a breath, and wiping away strands of hair glued to my sweaty forehead, I get down on my ass. With my legs kicked out in front of me, I use the banister for support behind me, and use the strength in my legs to move the weight down the hall. It slides much easier, yet, it's still hard work.

Who the hell could lift this? I know Max is fit and has muscles that will put some boxers to shame, but this shit is enough to snap your arms off. There's no way this weight is legal.

Sliding more towards the weight, I use my legs again, pushing the weight down the hall, and before I know it, I'm out of breath, sweating my tits off, and planning the perfect murder. With the weight in the perfect place I get up and quickly rush back down the hall.

Halfway down the stairs I bump into Malik and I smile. "Hey," I wave lamely. "You okay?"

"Yeah, why wouldn't I be?" I ask enthusiastically. I think I used a bit more enthusiasm than needed because Malik is looking at me like I've lost my marbles. "I best go see Joan."

"Um, yeah, okay," he shrugs, still eyeing me curiously.

Smiling, I move past him and walk down to the kitchen where Joan, Mark and Harlow are sitting around the kitchen table.

"Hey guys," I wave, sitting down in the chair next to Harlow.

"Hey, you have a good day, dear?" Joan asks me and I get a chorus of hellos from everyone else.

"Yeah, I've been up in my room watching TV," I explain lamely. "How was college?" I ask Harlow and for the first time since entering the room, I notice she's looking a little green. "Wow, you okay?"

"Morning sickness! Though, I'm strongly thinking about writing to whoever deals with this shit to change the name. It can't be morning sickness if it lasts all day and night. None of my classes registered today because I was too busy running in and out of them being sick."

"Oh no. Did anyone say anything?" I ask, knowing she's worried.

"Yeah, my main tutor did. She pulled me aside after my last class and asked me if everything was all right. I explained everything, even about having twins, and she was really good about it. Said if I needed an extension on any of the coursework until the sickness subsides then she'll be happy to do that."

"That's good. She seems really nice."

"She is," Harlow smiles but loses it just as quickly. She jumps out of her chair with her hand covering her mouth and takes off for the stairs.

I'm still looking to where she left when Joan interrupts. "I hated morning sickness. Never forget being pregnant with her mom. I was ill with morning sickness up until I was seven months pregnant. With Harlow having twins I won't be surprised if hers lasts that long."

"I thought it was only meant to be for the first trimester?" I ask worriedly. I don't think being sick that long during a pregnancy can be good for the mother or the baby, surely.

Joan must read my thoughts because she pats my hands gently. "It is but in some cases, no. They do say that morning sickness is your body's way of telling you everything is okay, but that's just some mother's myth."

"Hope she feels better soon, though. I know Denny and Kayla have been helping her rearrange some of the hen party plans."

"Oh my, I never even thought about that. I know they're planning on bringing the wedding forward. Denny's worried Harlow won't fit into her dress but, thankfully, we spoke to the designer into making the waist stretchy. It won't be the same as the original but there's no saying how much weight she'll have put on by then."

"I didn't know they were bringing the wedding forward," I tell her surprised. Denny has gone bridezilla on everyone's ass and hates, with a capital H, change. Her Nan, who I met briefly not too long ago, mentioned having a chocolate fountain and Denny went mental. I've never seen anything like it. I bet she's not enjoying this at all. She will have to rearrange everything.

"They agreed last night after much discussion. So the hen party is going ahead as usual but the wedding is being brought forward. I think Denny caved and is finally letting her Nan hire someone to arrange everything."

I giggle. "I bet she's hating that."

"She is," Joan giggles.

Malik walks in with a bright red face, carrying the heavy weight. Holy fucking shit balls. How the fuck has he managed that? His arm muscles are bulging and his neck is straining. He looks hot as fuck. He's even got the smaller weight stacked on top.

Oh my!

"What on earth! You'll break your back," Joan scolds, narrowing her eyes on Malik.

"Fucking Max! I'm going to kill him for leaving this shit outside the door. Anything could have happened. What if Harlow tried to move them?"

Shit. I didn't think about that.

I feel Joan's eyes on mine, but I don't look to make sure. Malik opens his mouth to say something more when Harlow steps around him, still looking green.

"No, I wouldn't have, I'm not stupid so stop overreacting, and go take them back before Max has a heart attack when he finds out his weights have gone. Heaven forbid that boy doesn't get a workout," she scoffs, sitting back down in her seat.

Malik grunts, his face a mixture of anger and sheer determination not to drop the weight on his feet.

I'd laugh if I didn't feel so guilty.

When he turns and leaves through the back door I finally look up. I was right. Joan is standing at the table staring at me with a curious expression.

"I could have sworn I saw them outside your door when I dropped by earlier," she muses.

My body stiffens when all eyes come to me. Mark looks amused, so does Joan, and I don't look to Harlow to read her reaction.

"Nope. Not by my door," I lie, shrugging my shoulders. Joan giggles, Mark chuckles and Harlow keeps quiet. Too quiet. I turn to her to find her staring at me and not with an amused expression. "What?" I snap a little harshly. That gets a reaction. She grins at me, shaking her head.

"Is Max trying to ask you out?" she laughs.

I groan, slamming my head on the table.

"Holy hell, he is. I knew it by the way he's always looking at you. And the weights is something he'd do. Did he give them as a present or something?" she laughs.

I lift my head up and look to her. "No, he used them to ask me out. He wrote a note on them. The heaviest said, 'no' and the lightest said, 'yes' then the note in the middle said to bring one back as an answer. The question being, 'will you go out with me?'"

Her face is blank for a couple of seconds before it softens and she giggles. "That is so freaking cute, I don't even know what to say. What did you reply?"

My eyebrows draw together and I give her a deadpan expression. "Did you not see Malik busting his ass taking them both back over?"

Harlow bursts out laughing, clutching her stomach tightly. "Oh my God, I'm getting baby brain already. As if you moved them. I took one look at them and stepped over them. Even if I wasn't pregnant you wouldn't get me trying to move them."

I can't help it, I laugh. She has the right idea. If it wasn't for wanting them moved I wouldn't have moved them. Hell, the lightest was hard work for me on its own.

"This is going to be so much fun. I can't wait to see what he will do next," she laughs and that's when I lose all laughter. I turn, narrowing my eyes at her and giving her the best glare I can muster.

"How dare you jinx me," I snap seriously, which only causes her, Joan and Mark to laugh harder. I shake my head before slamming it back down on the table. What have I gotten myself into?

TWELVE

LAKE

MONDAY ROLLS AROUND AND we're all summoned to the Carter house on the night to discuss the plans of the hen and stag parties. With Harlow now expecting, Malik wants to make sure he knows her every move and that she won't be in some busy club where she could get knocked around. Sucks for Denny, but no one can argue, what he's doing is for the best and he's making sure Harlow and the babies are safe.

"Does anyone have a problem with that?" Mason asks when he finishes explaining why they need to know what's going on, and to change any plans that involved any clubs.

Harlow sighs next to me. She doesn't look happy at all about anything that Mason just discussed.

"Turn that frown upside down, sister of mine," Max sings, chucking a crisp in Harlow's direction. She looks up, snatching the crisp and crunching it in her mouth. Max laughs but the rest of us look on with concern.

"What?" Malik asks, looking ready for a fight. It's like he knows Harlow's about to blow.

"I just hate that all the hen party plans will have to change while you boys get to do what you want. I don't think it's fair. I'm not disabled. I can take care of myself," she whines crossing her arms over her chest.

"We're not asking you to not go out, just to keep away from any busy clubs. It only takes one person to bang into you," Malik tells her out straight.

"Don't stop you banging into her," Max grins, earning glares from all around the room. Max's eyes reach mine and when he does he winks, sending a flutter to my heart.

Damn him. I've successfully avoided him all weekend. Even Saturday at work we were separated for the first time since he started. Joan had placed me with a new volunteer who wanted some experience on his college applications.

What experience he wanted I will never know. I refused profusely to work with him again to Joan after he spent the whole day making strong advances, crude comments and acted like he was God's gift to women. A bit like how Max acts but sleazy.

Then, Sunday, Max had to help out for the church again. They wanted him to help with the mini football league that they run for kids who are members at the church. By the time he got back I'd already gone to bed not feeling too good.

"What do you think, Lake?" Harlow nudges, bringing me into the conversation. Being so lost in my thoughts over Max I didn't hear what they asked. I look around embarrassed, narrowing my eyes when Max gives me a knowing look.

"Sorry, what did you ask?" I ask, giving her an apologetic smile.

She smiles back softly. "I asked if you were okay with the new plans."

"Yeah, yeah, sure," I agree, not having the giddiest idea what she is on about.

Max laughs loudly while Harlow giggles, looking back down at her lap. Looking around the room everyone's eyes are on me and they're amused; Mason and Maverick both looking like they're ready to burst into laughter and pee their pants.

"What?" I ask slowly, looking to each of them closely.

"We will be meeting the boys at the strip club at the end of the night instead of finishing at Jump, the new nightclub that's opened," Denny answers me, grinning.

"Oh, I really don't mind," I shrug her off.

"I wouldn't mind you giving me a lap dance," Max mentions and I look to him to find him looking at me all lusty, making me want to slap him up the face again.

"Shut up," I bite out, but end up smiling anyway. I'm losing the freaking plot.

"Okay, so now that it's sorted, can we please go out?" Harlow whines.

"Yeah," Malik grins, helping her up.

"See you later," Harlow waves, walking out the door with Malik. We all shout our goodbyes back.

"Who have you invited to the hen party again? I know you didn't want anything big?" Kayla asks. Her voice sounds off like she's been practicing the line all night and has been trying to fit it in the conversation.

"Yeah, it's just going to be me, you, Harlow, Lake, my brother's wife, Kennedy, and Nay and Stace from school."

"Thought you were inviting that chick with the big hair?" Mason asks.

"Mandy? Nah! She's not someone I really speak to anymore. It's usually a text here and there but that's it. I'd rather keep it simple. Nay and Stace have been friends since nursery. I know we don't spend a lot of time together, but they've always been there when I've needed them."

Mason nods and I listen on as everyone else starts to talk about different things. Max jumps up from the floor in front of the fire and flops himself down on the bed next to me. I grunt in annoyance but, in all honesty, it's good to be near him. I've missed him.

"Hey," he smiles coolly.

"Hey back atcha," I grin, nudging his shoulder with mine.

"When these losers go, wanna watch a film?"

"We always watch movies; are there even any movies we've not seen?" I giggle.

"We've never watched 101 Dalmatians," he adds helpfully.

I grin. "True."

"A friend lent me this movie called No Escape; thought we could watch it together."

"What's it about?" I ask, sounding indifferent when really I couldn't care less if it was actually 101 Dalmatians that he wanted to watch. I just want to spend some time with him.

"A family move to China or Hong Kong, I don't know, but basically they move out there and a riot starts or something. I watched the trailer on YouTube and it looks mint to be fair."

"Sounds like a plan," I smile.

"We're going. We need to get Hope to bed. Lake, you want to go shopping for outfits for the hen party tomorrow?"

"NO!" Kayla shouts, shocking everyone. Myles snaps his head to her looking surprised.

"Indoor voice," Max whispers loudly, making me giggle.

"Sorry," she winces, looking red faced. "Leave the outfit. Harlow mentioned getting you this perfect dress, so you can't ruin it."

Straight off I can tell Kayla is lying. Her face gives her away big time and I know Myles has cottoned on because he gives her a questionable look on the sly. When Kayla shakes her head he nods, relaxing, and I know that's a silent communication saying she'll tell him later.

"Really?" Denny asks, looking giddy.

"You don't even need a new dress," Mason moans.

"True dat," Max grunts, making me wonder what that's all about.

Denny narrows her eyes on Max, shutting him up before looking back at Mason and smiling. You know that smile you do when you know you're going to get your own way?

"It's my hen party. I'm only ever going to have one, so I need to have a new outfit. And I don't have loads of dresses," she scoffs.

Max makes this girly screechy noise at the back of his throat before ending up in a coughing fit. I tap his back hard and he waves his hand around, holding his index finger up to give him a minute. Everyone's attention is on Max, waiting to hear what he has to say. Maverick and Myles are the only ones that look amused.

Once he finishes he straightens and looks directly at Denny. She must know what's coming because she juts her hips out and smacks her hand on her hip.

"Let me get this right. Did you, Denny Smith, soon to be Carter, just say you don't have loads of dresses?" he asks, his eyes bugging out of their sockets.

"That's right," Denny replies, giving him a death glare.

Max bursts out laughing, falling to the floor where he continues to roll around looking like a two year old. Not able to hold it in, I laugh with him, even though I find nothing funny other than Max. Maverick and Myles join but Mason, seeming to know something I don't, quietly chuckles instead. He soon shuts up when Denny turns her narrowed eyes on him.

Max gets up off the floor still laughing and holding his stomach. "Denny Smith, soon to be Carter, I do love you but you need to learn the meaning of a little and a lot. You have more dresses in your closet than every girl on this estate has put together."

"I do not," she snaps.

"Babe," Mason grins, looking at her.

"I don't," she argues, looking confronted.

"Babe, you've got more dresses in your wardrobe right now than I've had outfits my whole life."

"No one should have that many clothes. There's only seven days in a week and they weigh a fucking ton, I should know," Max laughs, sitting back down.

"Whatever!" she snaps, making everyone laugh. She stamps her foot before heading towards the back door. Once there Mason rushes over and lifts her over his shoulder before hauling her out of the door, her laughter fading as they move away.

"I need to get to work," Maverick frowns down at his phone, his features tight. He doesn't wait for anyone to answer before he's off, leaving through the front door.

That leaves me, Max, Kayla and Myles sitting in the front room. "Want to go bowling?" Myles asks.

Please say no. Please say no. I hate bowling. I can't bowl worth a shit. I always end up hurting someone. My dad got rushed to hospital the last time we went as a family. The ball flew out of my hand, conking him right in the head. It was bad. Knocked him clean out.

"We've got plans but good luck," Max tells Myles warily, stepping back a little from Kayla. Kayla giggles, noticing, yet, doesn't seem bothered. She must read my confused expression because she turns to me.

"I'm a hazard to anything sporty," she answers my silent question.

"Me too," I laugh. It's a lie, though. It's just bowling that I'm crap at, though, I'm not mentioning that to them; Max would likely have me out the door and to a bowling alley in a second if he knew just so he could take the mick out of me.

"Alright, we'll catch up with you later," Myles tells him, grabbing his coat off the back of the chair. Kayla follows but stops shorts when she gets to me, pulling me into a hug, surprising me.

"See you later," she tells me, pulling away.

That was sweet.

I've felt like an outsider to everyone but Max, but that one simple gesture made me feel like part of the gang. They're all so tight-knit, so loyal to one another. It's hard to be the new girl, the one who has to learn everything new, fit in and be accepted.

"Want a drink?" Max asks once the door shuts behind Myles and Kayla.

"Sure. You got any popcorn?" I ask him, walking into the kitchen.

"Do I have popcorn? I always have popcorn. I need it on tap with all the drama that happens around here," he laughs. "It's in the cupboard up there," he points and I follow his directions and open the cupboard. I laugh loudly when I find several packets of different flavoured popcorn lining the shelves.

"Is toffee okay?"

"Yeah, sure. Um, want a can? We have Fosters, Carling... Oh, we have some WKD left over that Harlow drinks. Want some?"

I consider it for a minute and then think to myself; *why not*. I'm not really a big drinker; I reckon one can of beer will have me feeling merry. Let's just hope I don't get pissed. I remember drinking a glass of wine at some dinner party I went to with my family. I didn't even finish the glass and I was pissed. I'd been so drunk that night it had taken me a week to fully recover.

"Fuck it; why not? I'll have a can of Fosters," I tell him, smiling whilst taking the blue can out of his hand.

"Such a rebel," he teases, grabbing two cans for himself.

We head upstairs to his room and the second I enter, I begin to feel nervous. Not sure where it's coming from I try to ignore it, not wanting to make things awkward.

Max puts the cans down on the side of his bed while I keep mine clutched in my hand along with the popcorn. When he bends his head a little, grabbing the neck of his tee before pulling it over his head, I nearly pass out. His back muscles ripple and flex with each movement and I find it hard to breathe. Only wearing a pair of loose jogging bottoms, he flops himself on his back on the bed, his hands tucked behind his head.

When he notices I haven't moved, he looks at me and grins. It's then I notice my eyes are still riveted to his magnificent body and I swallow hard.

"Like what you see?" he winks.

"You're big," I blurt out, talking about his chest and muscles, but a cocky grin appears on his handsome face making me wish I had kept my mouth shut.

"That's what she said," he laughs before giving me a break. Sort of. "Come on, I don't bite...unless you ask me to," he grins coyly.

I roll my eyes and will my body to move. I place the popcorn and can on the side where Max put his before joining him on the bed.

"Um, where's the DVD?" I ask, noticing for the first time he hasn't moved to put one in.

"It's already set up. I was just waiting for you."

"So, you were planning on asking me?"

"Yeah," he grins proudly. "I figured if you wouldn't go *out* with me then I'd make you stay in with me."

"This isn't a date," I remind him, beginning to feel nervous.

"There's drink, snacks, a movie and if you're lucky I'll let you touch me. I think that is considered a date," he adds smirking.

The little bleeder.

He had this all sussed out from the beginning. He probably stayed away from me all weekend on purpose, knowing I'd miss him.

Crafty sod.

"It's not a date," I tell him firmly, ignoring the butterflies in my stomach.

"We'll see," is all he says before pressing play on the DVD. I take a chance to look at him and wish I hadn't. It takes everything in me not to jump him right now. He looks so hot when he looks relaxed and casual. He must feel my stare before his head turns and he grins. When I quickly avert my eyes, he chuckles but I don't say anything; scared he'll call me out on my ogling.

His arm reaching out startles me but when he manoeuvres me so I'm lying on his chest, his strong arm wrapped around my shoulders, I can't help but relax in the position. I feel so small wrapped up in his arms. He makes me feel loved, protected, and safe and honestly, it feels really fucking good. It's no hidden secret that Max can get any girl he wants, or boy for that matter, but for some reason he wants me. And as much as I try to fight what I'm feeling, he still manages to make me feel like the only girl in the world. He makes me feel special for just being me.

"Stop thinking so hard. It's givin' me a headache," he scolds teasingly.

With that, I look back to the screen; my eyes on the movie that he has made sure will be classed as a date, while wearing a smile upon my face.

I wake up feeling hot and claustrophobic. I kick the blanket off a little but it gets stuck from a large body that is half wrapped around mine.

Max!

His front is to my back, his leg cocked over both of mine and his arm is wrapped around my body, pinning me down. The heat coming off him is suffocating.

I try to move, wiggling away from him, but all I manage to do is rub his groin area with my ass. He doesn't seem to mind, if the tent he's sporting in his boxers has anything to say about it. He groans deep in his throat, the noise sending shivers down my back and all the way to my sex.

My sex starts to ache so I move, trying to ease the pain, but it causes Max to moan out in his sleep.

When his arm tightens around me I know I've woken him up. He presses his groin into my ass and a moan slips free, the sound loud and clear in the quiet empty room. I don't know what possesses me but I press back into him causing him to groan, his hands tightening around me again.

Max moves his hand slowly down my body causing my whole body to burn with heat for an entirely other reason. I'm only wearing his tee, not wanting to go home to change. My jeans had been digging into my stomach and were annoying me half way through the movie. Max noticed and offered for me to put his tee on. It fell to my knees so I agreed.

So when his hand reaches the hem of his shirt that has ridden to my waist, I hold my breath, waiting, anticipating, but also scared about what he's going to do next.

Neither of us speak, like we're too scared it will break whatever the hell this is. When his hands roam under the shirt, his hands pushing my bra down, I moan quietly, pressing my ass into his groin, my head falling back onto his shoulder. He kisses my neck, and the feel of his soft lips at such a sensitive spot is electrifying. I want to touch him, to taste him, but then he tweaks my nipples and I cry out from pleasure. It's been building up for weeks. The sexual tension becoming too much and I know he's going to make me feel things I've never felt before.

His lips carry on their torture along with his hands and I love what he's doing more than anything, but I want to touch him, to make him crazy with need like he's making me feel.

I turn slowly in his arms, my hands slowly reaching for his muscled abs, making sure I touch every part of him.

My lips part when his fingers slide up the inside of my thigh making me delirious. I'm so turned on I could combust and he hasn't even touched me *there* yet. I move forward a fraction, my lips inches from his and he meets me half way and before I know it I'm kissing him with so much passion that I'm about to combust.

His fingers skim my clit over my panties at the same time as I rub him through his boxers and we both moan through our kiss. Neither of us pulling away: not wanting it to end.

It's all becoming too much and when his hand disappears under my knickers I know I'm done for. I rub him a few more times before frantically reaching in and grabbing his large member.

Fucking hell he is huge.

I squeeze him in the palm of my hand and his breathing becomes faster as I begin to pump him. He stops his assault on my sex, his fingers soaked with my wetness as he pants through my touch. When he gains some control back his fingers begin their magic, rubbing in fast circles around my clit before moving down towards my sex where he wastes no time in entering two fingers. I'm shocked at the fullness, my body screaming for release and I cry out with tremendous pleasure.

"Arghhh," I cry out, moving my hips to spur him on.

He groans, obviously liking what I'm doing to him, and I squeeze him harder before moving in for his lips again, feeling close to release. My hand is frantically pumping him up and down, my thumb circling the head of his dick that is covered in pre-cum.

"Fuck," he whispers hoarsely, his voice rough and full of desire. It only turns me on more and I find myself falling closer and closer over the edge. My body is on fire. Tingles after tingles erupt in my lower belly and I can feel it all building and building.

Max stops kissing me, his breathing out of control. He moves his head down and I think he's about to kiss me again, but then his mouth covers my nipple through my T-shirt. The texture of the wet cotton and the heat of his mouth is enough to send me over the edge.

I'm crying out his name, my body jerking with every spasm of my orgasm. Over and over it erupts, the feeling of bliss completely washing over me like nothing else I've ever experienced.

I'm not even down from my high when all of a sudden Max's body stiffens and hot semen shoots out all over my hand, spurt after spurt.

We're both out of breath, breathing frantically as we try to gain our composure. My body is still having little spasms of pleasure and I close my eyes, trying to fight against jumping him and having more of him inside me.

Max is first to move while I'm still trying to comprehend what just happened. One minute I was asleep, the next he was touching me and I wanted it; I was begging for it.

Max turns back towards me and before I can open my mouth he's cleaning his cum from off my hand, throwing whatever he used back onto the floor.

I'm frozen, at a loss of what to say or what to do. My body locks when his arms wrap around me and his hold tightens when he notices.

"Max," I begin hesitantly, but he cuts me off.

"No. Don't. That was the best fucking thing to ever happen to me. Don't ruin it by spouting shit off about you not deserving it. Just go with it. Now go back to sleep. I was in a deep sleep before you jumped me," he teases.

Not fighting it, mainly because I'm still too stunned that I let it happen, I relax into his arms, and before I know it I'm falling asleep cuddled in his arms.

This is not good. Not good at all.

THIRTEEN

LAKE

SATURDAY ROLLS AROUND QUICKER than I expected. The girls and I are all held up at Denny's, waiting for the last of the guests to arrive.

Speaking of... The door knocks and Denny jumps up excitedly to answer it. She's just finished having her hair and nails done. We've just said goodbye to the older woman who came over to do all our hair and pamper Denny: a gift from Mason that none of us knew about until last minute.

"Nay, Stace, you made it," Denny squeals and her excitement makes me smile. They all walk into the front room and I'm surprised when I see them. They're nothing like I presumed they'd be.

"This is Nay," Denny smiles, introducing the tiny girl with raven black hair with the tips died blue. Her blue eyes are heavy in smoky black makeup and her lips are ruby red. She's nothing like how I imagined Denny's friends to look.

"Hey," Kayla, Kennedy and I answer, smiling. Harlow had to run out to grab the outfits for the night: another surprise, but this time one from Harlow. She hasn't showed us yet what we're wearing so I'm dreading it. She said they'd fit but I'm still unsure.

"And this is Stace," Denny finishes and gestures for them to sit down. Stace has bright, short, purple hair and is taller than any of us going out tonight. She's also more girlie than Nay. Her makeup is model worthy and I'm kind of jealous. Denny got the hair and makeup artist to cake the makeup on me when I refused to let anyone touch me. I'm not a makeup wearing kind of girl and as much I was dreading it, it's not as bad as I thought. The only thing that still feels foreign is my eyes. I have thick black eyelashes glued on and heavy, smoky eyes with a lighter shade of red lips.

We all wave, saying hi, when the door knocks again.

"I'll get it," I shout, jumping up to answer the door. I open it to find Harlow standing in front of a million and one bags. "Bloody hell, you buy the whole shopping centre?" I snicker.

"Feels like it. Sorry I took so freaking long. Malik wouldn't let me carry them over here. We argued," she sighs, her cheeks flushed. She looks freaking gorgeous tonight. She's glowing with her hair in thick big curls, her makeup done the same as mine, but her eyes stand out like nothing I've seen. She's beautiful.

"Who won?" I ask, picking up the bags.

"Malik," she sighs again. "He just left with the boys."

I laugh whilst taking the rest and walking back through the door and into the living room. Denny looks to all the bags, her eyes bugging out in surprise and wonder.

"What on earth?" she gasps.

"We couldn't let you have a hen party and not get you dressed up. I remembered when we first became friends and we watched a movie that had something in it that you said you'd love to dress up as. You said you wished you lived in America because they had more fun stuff going on," Harlow smiles and grabs something out of the pink bag and I inwardly groan.

Please, no!

God, no!

"Oh my God," Denny squeals. "We're dressing up as Hooters girls?"

"Yep," Harlow nods, the P popping from her mouth. "This one is yours," she shows her, handing it over to her.

It's then I laugh. Denny holds up the skimpy outfit that is really hot pants and a slim fitting t-shirt. That's not why I'm laughing, though. No, it's because on the front is '#TeamMason' written in bold orange letters. She turns it over and I smile. On the back is written 'Bride to Be,' also in orange lettering.

"These are great," Denny smiles, tears forming in her eyes.

"Don't cry," Harlow scolds. "You'll make me cry."

"And me," Kayla laughs.

"These are awesome," Kennedy smiles.

Harlow hands out a bag for each of us and I silently curse the small woman.

"I need a drink," I groan when she hands me the bag.

"These are the fucking shit," Nay shouts, laughing. That's when I see she's holding the same t-shirt as Denny, but this time it has '#TeamCarter' on the front and 'Bride's bitch' written on the back.

Max is going to get a kick out of that when he sees it. No doubt he'll have something to say.

Speaking of, Max and I have been good. Every time he tries to bring up what happened on Monday I shut him down. It hasn't stopped him from asking me out continuously and making a show of doing so. I just need to know what I want first. I have a lot of baggage and all week I've contemplated whether I should tell him or not. Maybe then I'll be able to rest easy. I don't know. But I know I can't have a relationship when he doesn't know the real me.

"Shots," Denny smiles and grabs some shot glasses.

"Now you're talking," Kennedy laughs and we all move, except Harlow, and take a shot, the liquid burning the back of my throat.

"Right, we don't have much time before we need to leave," Harlow speaks up, her fingers flying across her phone. "Let's get changed. Whoever needs to use the bathroom it's upstairs. There's also Hope's room and Denny's room."

"I'll take Hope's room. I know there's no mirror in there. If I see myself before we go I know I'll get changed," I tell them, making everyone laugh.

"I'll change with you," Kayla tells me and I nod my head smiling. She doesn't seem like the type of girl that wears revealing clothes, so it's nice not being the only one. I've also noticed Kayla doesn't like a lot of attention and when we've been around large groups she tends to stick to Myles or someone she trusts.

We grab our bags and make our way upstairs. When we get into the room, Kayla holds out the tiny hot pants and groans.

"How am I meant to even get these on? They look like they belong to Hope."

"I hear ya," I grumble, holding the tiny pair of shorts.

"Harlow said she got ours bigger than theirs, knowing we wouldn't be comfortable. These don't look bigger," she moans looking horrified.

"Come on, we can do this. If it's bad we'll get Max or Myles to bring us some clothes," I laugh and she laughs with me.

We both turn our backs to each other and start stripping. Pulling the shorts up, there's not as much resistance as I thought there would be and I breathe out a sigh of relief. Twisting my body I look at my backside, thankful the material at least covers most of it. The only thing on show is the globes of my bottom cheeks.

I suppose girls have worn less.

Already wearing the underwear that Harlow instructed we should wear, I pull the top over my head, cringing when my boobs are on full display.

Yep, Max is going to have a field day.

The top has a deep V between my breasts, short sleeves and is cut off at the middle, just above my belly button.

I finish the outfit by putting on the long, knee-high socks. I'm so glad I chose this room now and not one with a mirror. I feel like a drag queen. The clothes are far too small even for my small frame.

"I can't do this," Kayla panics behind me and I worry she'll back out.

"You decent?"

"Yeah."

I turn around to face Kayla and my eyes widen; she looks fucking hot. Her red hair flows in thick loose curls down the middle of her back, her outfit looking good against her nearly pale skin.

"You look hot, girl," I whistle, grinning huge. When she doesn't speak I look at her and find her staring at me with a grin.

"Max is going to have a heart attack when he sees you," she laughs.

"Pft, wait till Myles sees you," I grin back, secretly praying the outfit has an effect on Max.

"Your hair covers more of your ass than your shorts," she giggles and I groan.

"I know. I should get it cut," I frown trying not to mess it up or shove it up in a bobble.

"Don't you dare! I love your hair," she smiles and finishes putting the clothes she had on before into a bag.

"You ready to face everyone?" I ask once we're finished.

"It's now or never," she breathes out looking afraid.

"You look beautiful. Don't worry. Everything will be okay."

"Just not used to the whole going out scene," she confides.

"Me neither. We'll stick together," I promise her.

"Good."

A knock on the door interrupts us and Harlow walks in without waiting for an answer.

"Come on, the limo is here in ten minutes," she hisses on a whisper and my eyes narrow on her.

"Why the hell do you get a full length top?" I growl and Kayla moves beside me, her eyes narrowing on Harlow too.

"Because I'm pregnant and have a bump. I didn't feel right showing it off like that. Now come on, we need to go," she hurries us, making us all rush downstairs.

Everyone is dressed the same when we get down there, making me relax some. They all look good and I'm kind of wishing I looked in a mirror now.

"You two look hot," Denny gushes, handing us another shot. Both Kayla and I look to each other before downing the shot and holding it out for another. Denny laughs, rolls her eyes, yet, still happily pours us another.

My head is already buzzing, but I needed it to relax me tonight. I'd been so on edge about going out, now, adding being dressed up as a… I don't even know what Hooters is, but whatever; it has me feeling more on edge.

"Where did you get your hair extensions from?" Stace asks, walking over to me and Kayla.

"Oh, it's my real hair," I mumble.

"No way! Oh my God; it's so freaking long," she gushes, running her fingers through it. I'm used to this. It's why I normally wear my hair up in a bun. No one can see the length of it then. "Nay, did you know this is real?"

"Really?" Nay asks shocked, smiling. "It's beautiful. My hair doesn't grow past my bra strap."

"Mine neither," Stace adds.

"Everyone, can I have your attention? Denny, your surprise is here," Harlow shouts out smiling.

"What surprise?" Denny asks confused, looking between us all.

"Come and see. We need to go," Harlow says, ignoring her question. We all walk out and lock the door up behind us. I wobble on the high heels bought for me as we walk down the path, everyone laughing when one of us would stumble.

Then we hear Denny. Her screams are so loud I have to cover my ears up to keep from becoming deaf.

"A limo? A freaking limo? This is awesome. Oh my God, I can't believe you did this for me," she tells Harlow excitedly.

"We all chipped in," Harlow smiles and Denny looks around us all and smiles.

"Thank you, guys, and for coming. This is the best hen party anyone could ever have and we've not even got started."

"Let's party," Stace shouts and Denny squeals, rushing into the limo, all of us lining up to follow. Kayla squeezes my hand and I look to her.

"Why do I have the feeling none of us are going to remember tonight tomorrow?" she tells me, but before I can answer, Harlow is dragging us into the limo.

Champagne is waiting for us when we're inside, Kennedy handing out glasses as Nay opens the bottle.

"To the future Mrs Carter," Nay shouts and we all copy, raising our glasses before downing our drinks.

Another glass is poured before I've even put my head straight and I look to find Kayla smirking against her glass. She notices me watching and we both burst out laughing.

Yep, tomorrow none of us will remember any of this.

FOURTEEN

MAX

"WHAT THE FUCK DID YOU DO?" I roar, rushing into the front room. Lee, Mason's mate from school; Adam; Mason's friend from work; Malik; Mason; Maverick; and the fucking culprit, Myles, all laugh when they see me.

I'm literally naked: a white towel around my waist and I'm covered in blue fucking dye from taking a shower. I'm supposed to look slick tonight, not like a blue fucking crayon.

"Payback's a bitch," Myles chuckles. He looks fucking smug sitting there in his chair, all high and mighty.

"Don't look so blue," Mason says sympathetically, causing everyone to crack up.

"Not fucking funny," I growl. "I'm fucking blue. My skin, my eyebrows, my HAIR," I snap at Myles, wondering if I have enough time before the taxi gets here to kick his ass too.

"Even your..." Mav asks, his eyes looking at my dick. I take a step forward, ready to lunge, but Mason slaps his hand down on my shoulder stopping me. I ignore his laughter and turn to my evil twin.

"How the fuck did you do this?" I growl, secretly proud he could come up with something as classic as this.

"I put a blue dye bomb in your shower wash," he states smugly.

No fucking way he came up with that on his own. He had to have had outside help. Kayla... Kayla, the sneaky little bitch. She did this. I'll get her back.

"Why would you do this tonight? I have to go out now looking like Papa fucking Smurf," I bite out. From the look on his face, this was his plan all along. To humiliate me in front of everyone; including Lake. I'll bet any money that he's been sitting on the whole blue dye goldmine for weeks too, waiting for this very moment to use it.

It's Mason's stag party tonight and pranks were meant to be played on him. Not fucking me.

I'd usually laugh this shit off; make a bigger joke out of it, but not tonight. Tonight I wanted to impress Lake, get her to actually agree to go out with me. Now she's never going to take me seriously. Not looking like this. Just thinking about her is enough to drive me crazy and my dick to twitch under my towel. I keep thinking about her smell, the way she felt, and if it wasn't for the fact I needed to be out tonight, I'd be over there and sinking myself deep inside her.

"You need to chill out," Maverick tells me, his lips twitching. I shoot him an angry glare and grab the bags from my earlier shopping encounter. Yeah, this dude went fucking shopping. I grab a fresh pair of boxers, a clean pair of socks and put them on under the towel.

When I grab the new jeans I bought for tonight, another thing to impress Lake with, I pull out the next bag, a big grin on my face.

"Malik, Myles, Mav and I have all got something planned for you tonight. You won't know what until it's time. I'm up first," I grin and if I'm not mistaken, Mason loses some of the colour on his face. If only he knew mine was the easiest out of what everyone has planned.

I grab the first shirt, which is Mason's and laugh when he groans, dropping his head back and looking to the ceiling.

"Please tell me that that's not for tonight," he pleads.

"Oh no, *this* is for tonight, my brother," I grin. "For tonight, you are Clitoris Love-Bandit."

Everyone whoops and cat whistles but Mason just groans, ripping the new shirt he bought for tonight off to put on the black tee I've had done.

"What the fuck?" Mase glares when he sees the picture of a ball and chain on the front. We just laugh, shrugging our shoulders.

"Maverick, you're Judge Lickwood," I tell him, handing him his tee. "Myles, you're Lanky Chaos," I laugh, handing him his. These shirts really are the shit. "Malik, you're Corporal Mangina. What are the chances?" I grin, throwing his over to him. He narrows his eyes on me, but sighs and joins in, putting the tee on. "Lee, you're Comrade Dickless. Adam, you're Durex Manlove and I'm Senator Pantstain," I laugh, not caring how ridiculous we'll all look. I couldn't think of nicknames for everyone; I'm not that bright. Mine kind of sucks, yet, it's actually beginning to grow on me. I would have preferred Fully Loaded, Large Wood, or Well Hung, but hey, can't win them all.

"Where the fuck did you get these?" Mason laughs, looking at everyone's shirts with amusement.

"I found a website that sells them. All I had to do was enter your names and it automatically paired you each with a nickname. It was mint. I had to go collect them this morning; I didn't want to risk them not being delivered on time."

"At least I won't end up in Amsterdam in a hotel, chained to the bed," Mason grins.

"It's WHY I got the t-shirts. Mav knocked down every idea I planned," I huff, still pissed off at my brother.

"They're pretty cool," Adam grins. He would, his name is: Durex Manlove. If his shirt doesn't get the ginger dude laid tonight, nothing will. The poor guy is not a lady's man at all.

"You would say that," Lee laughs, shaking his head at Adam.

"Really, we just wanted you to look like a dick," I add laughing.

"I can't believe you're going to make me wear this," Mason groans and we all laugh at his expense. "If Denny leaves my ass because of this ball and chain, I'm holding you responsible," he warns, pointing his damn finger at me.

I chomp down, growling, pretending to take a bite out of his finger before laughing. I hand out another shot to everyone and finish getting ready. I quickly shove some wax in my hair, groaning when it does nothing different. In the end I leave it looking messy. I don't really give a shit what my hair looks like to be fair.

After spraying on some Hugo Boss, I sit down on the sofa, tying my shoes up.

"Where are we going first? Are the girls leaving soon?" Mason asks and Malik curses at something he sees through the front room window.

"I could fucking kill her," he snaps and moves to the front door like lightning.

Adam and Lee turn to each other, looking confused. "Harlow," we all state at the same time. They laugh, nodding their heads as a horn blares from outside.

"That would be the taxi," Maverick grins and we all grab our wallets and phones before heading outside.

"Did you see the girls?" I ask Malik when he walks down the path. We jump in the back of the cab and he waits until he's in his seat before answering.

"Nah, just Harlow. She was carrying fucking bags full of shit. I didn't even ask what was in there. If it's the outfit that I saw on her computer not long ago, though, I'm going to blow a fuse," he mutters, not looking happy.

"What outfits?" I ask, over-eagerly and he smirks knowingly. "Shut up," I warn him before he can open his mouth.

"You don't want to know," he answers me before resuming conversation with everyone else. I sit back in my seat and hope to Christ Lake isn't wearing anything skimpy, or worse, got her hair down. My body can only hold off for so long when it comes to that girl, but when it comes to her hair... All bets are off. It's my own personal kryptonite. Every time she has it down I imagine wrapping it around my fist and pulling it back while I fuck her from behind. Don't hate on me, I'm just a visual person.

We arrive at Links in no time and all jump out of the taxi. The owner, Tim, is good friends with Maverick and is already expecting us. He is the only one, apart from my brothers, Adam, and Lee, that knows what is happening tonight. We've not even told the girls. We knew if any of them knew they'd intervene or some shit. Plus, we know Harlow hasn't got a simple night out planned for Denny either.

"Look at you," Tim laughs when we enter, his eyes on Mason's shirt. "What will it be, Clitoris Love-Bandit?"

"Fuck you, Tim," Mason laughs. "And a round of shots and Fosters?" Mason asks everyone. We all nod in agreement, not really caring what we drink as long as we end up hammered by the end of the night.

"First round is on the house," Tim grins and smirks our way. He has the first part of tonight's games hidden behind the bar. Don't get too excited, our ideas aren't brilliant, but it's who you play them with that counts. "Why do you look so blue?" Tim asks looking at me and causing everyone to crack up laughing

"Laugh it up, guys. Laugh it up," I groan, keeping the smile on my face.

"You know what I wish I had on CD right now? That blue song. You know:

I'm blue da ba de ba die…" Tim sings, laughing at the end.

Jesus. It's going to be endless blue jokes tonight. I shake my head at them all.

"What do you call a guy with a blue dick?" Adam asks laughing.

Jesus, he's one of those who laugh at their own jokes. To be honest, he probably knows more about having a blue dick more than anyone. Poor bloke. May his balls find peace tonight and his dick find Heaven.

"Tell me, I'm dying to hear it," I tell him dryly.

"A tight fisted wanker," he laughs uncontrollably. Everyone joins him but I think it's more to do with the fact they don't want him looking like a dick laughing at his own joke than actually finding the joke funny.

"Ha, ha, ha," I choke out and Maverick slaps me upside the head, laughing.

"Play nice."

"Okay, I'll be a good boy," I tell him sarcastically, nodding my head. I'm not that bad. I can be nice. In all seriousness, Adam did just call me a tight fisted wanker, I'm pretty sure that earned retaliation, but hey, I'm a nice guy and leaving it alone.

We all take a seat over at a table in the far corner. I slide in before Maverick, knowing his quest for Mason is up next. We all agreed to let him have a drink and shot before we send him off into the dark streets like some hooker begging for her next meal ticket.

"I can't believe I let you four plan my stag party," Mason laughs.

"I can't believe you're *having* a stag party," I tell him.

Mason laughs, shrugging. He doesn't care. Everyone thought he was mad when he told them the news. It was only close family that never questioned it. All of us know what he's been through with Denny and how much they both deserve each other's happiness.

I may not believe in the whole marriage shit, but I believe in my brother. It also doesn't hurt he will have a hot chick in his bed for the rest of his life.

Just saying!

"Wait till you see what's planned next," Malik adds smirking. The fucker wanted to send him out on the river in a little rowing boat to make it look like he was stranded. I voted yes, but Maverick shut us down. Again! Party pooper.

"What do you mean? I thought that we were just having a lads' night out before heading to V.I.P?" Mason says, looking at each of us for answers, none of which he'll be getting until it's time.

"We told you that we all had something planned. We are your best men after all," Myles laughs.

I'd laugh and agree with him, but I'm still upset with my twin right now. I tried for ten minutes to get this dye out before realising the shower gel was making it worse. Then I tried just using shampoo to wash it out, but that didn't work either. When I finally realised I was going to look like a Smurf for the fucking night, one with a skin disorder, because hey, the blue work is patchy, I just gave up and headed downstairs. I knew right away that it was Myles that did it. None of the others would have the balls to go up against me, not when they know I'll retaliate back much harder.

"You goin' to be in a shit mood all night?" Myles asks when he notices I'm not joining in with the laughter.

"Leave him alone," Maverick tells him and I give Myles a smug look. "You can't blame Myles for you having blue balls," he says, looking at me. I groan when everyone roars with laughter.

"I'm sure Lake could help you with that..." Malik ventures off and I shoot him a glare. Hearing him talk about her like that just makes me want to punch his lights out. She's not some slag I want to give a quick fuck then fuck off. She's more. A lot fucking more and I won't have anyone talk less of her, not even a brother.

"Enough with the twin fit and blue balls. What's next?" Mason asks warily. He looks worried about what we have planned for the night, and he has every right to be normally, but in this case we've kept it tame. He's gotten off pretty lucky if you ask me.

Maverick quickly snatches Mason's wallet, his keys and his phone.

"Since it's your last night of freedom, as such, and you can't wait until you've finished your fucking pint to find out, I'll fill you in. As you know I'm next.

"Before you can continue to join the stag party, you have to go out and round up thirty quid. You can nominate Lee or Adam to help, but only one of them, and no, you can't pick a brother. Oh, and if you forfeit you have to down ten shots," Mav grins. Mason looks pale as fuck which has me laughing harder.

This night is going to be fucking epic.

"How am I going to raise thirty fucking quid before the night's completely ended? People are tighter than a virgin around here," he groans.

"Well, we thought we would help you out there. You have to wear this," Lee laughs, walking out from behind the bar where Tim let us store a cardboard notice board that Mason will have to wear over his clothes.

"You have to wear this, and these," Mav grins, handing him the bag of goodies. Inside, Mason pulls out a pink wig, green glasses, red lipstick, and blow up boobs.

"You've got to be fucking with me," Mason groans, laughing. "I can't do this."

"Then ten shots it is, but do you really want to show your wife-to-be you're a quitter?" Mav goads him.

Mason sighs, giving in. He stands up and shoves the sign over his head. On it, it says, 'one pound for a hug, give me some love'.

"Who's going with you?" Myles laughs, taking pictures. Mason has everything on and I can't help but take a picture and send it to Lake.

MAX: He's finding one nyt apart hard nd already looking for some hugging. Howz ur nyt goin?

"Lee, 'cause, he's the fucker that brought this fucking thing over to me," he curses just as an old bloke walks up to him, giving him a quid.

"Fucking brave, my friend," is all he says, giving Mason a big hug and squeezing the breath out of him. I'm laughing that hard I nearly miss my phone beeping from the table.

Clicking the message open, I groan when Lake sends a picture of a limo, but in the picture are her long fucking legs.

Fuck me!

Not wanting to get the shit ripped into me for getting a boner or for texting Lake, I put my phone away, but not before making sure it's on vibrate.

"How long do I have to do this?" Mason groans after the bloke has moved back over to his group of friends, all of them laughing over at Mason.

"Until ten," Maverick grins.

"That's half an hour," Mason tells us, standing up.

When he does, a young woman walks over handing him a tenner. "If a quid will get me a hug, what will a tenner get me?" she flirts and we all laugh at Mason's horrified expression. He just snatches the money and grabs the girl in a tight hug before dropping her to the ground.

"If my fiancé leaves me because of this I am going to kill all of you and it won't be pretty," Mason snaps at Mav, grabbing Mav's pint and downing it.

We all laugh knowing he's going to hate every single hug he has to receive tonight from another woman. He storms out with Lee laughing his ass off behind him.

"How long do you think it will take him?" Myles laughs.

"He'll probably be back in five minutes," Adam grins, still looking at the door where they left. "That guy could pull a gay bird."

"He could definitely have a pull on me," Kevin grins behind Maverick. "What are you fine pieces of ass doing out tonight?"

Kevin's the shit. No joke. He's gay as they come but who gives a fuck. He's funny as shit, can throw a punch, and can drink most lads under the table. He's not bothered about his sexuality either which I admire him for. Not many lads who are gay are like that. Too many dickheads give them shit. To me, you are who you are, same goes for who you love.

Oh, and he's in love with Mason. Well, apart from his boyfriend Mark who has just gone to the loo. Who's also the shit. No one messes with him, though. He's a professional boxer and could probably take on most of the men in this bar at the same time.

"Mason's stag tonight, my friend," I yell out, downing the shot Adam just brought back to the table.

"You break my heart," Kevin feigns hurt and we all laugh.

"Spread the love," I tease, winking.

"Oh, Max, you're too much for me to handle. And high maintenance," he winks back, teasing me.

"You got that right," Maverick laughs.

Kings of Leon's, 'Sex On Fire' starts playing and a big grin breaks out across my face.

I jump up from my chair and belt out, "Youuuuuuuu, your sex is on fire."

Grabbing Kevin, I pull him into a standard dancing position, my hand on his hip, my other hand in his, pointed out. Dragging him around the room I spin him out, my eyes widening when he stumbles into a group of lads walking in from the back room.

"Shit," I grumble, moving quickly when one pushes Kevin off him, sneering at him in disgust.

"Get the fuck off me, fag," a voice I recognise sneers. Taking a closer look around Kevin my eyes widen when I realise it's one of Davis' brother's mates. Most of their crew got sent down, but there were some, like this prick, that got off scot-free.

"Hey, back off," I yell, moving between them.

"Happily. I don't want that Fag anywhere near me."

"I hate that word. It makes me feel like a cancer stick," Kevin mutters, not seeming fazed at the altercation going on at all.

"Shut the fuck up," I snap at the bloke in front of me, choosing not to laugh at Kevin's comment.

"Come on, Tom, let's go," Dan, a kid from the year below me at school, calls from the crowd. I didn't even see him there. It's like he's hiding from us.

The goons have us circled but neither Kevin nor I care. Mav and the rest of them are stood off to the side looking tense. When my eyes find Mav's he shakes his head at me in warning. I smirk, sending him a wink.

"No!" Tom shouts furiously. "Why the fuck should we leave? They can fuck off to a gay bar," he snarls, eyeing Kevin with a disgusted look.

"Are you recommending him one, sugar?" I goad and he turns his disgusted look my way.

"What the fuck you trying to say you little prick?"

"Was I not clear enough?" I ask, tutting at myself. "You obviously know where there's a good gay bar around here. You frequent them often?"

Rage covers his entire expression like nothing I've ever witnessed. I smirk, feeling smug about hitting a sore spot. I just hate judgemental people like him.

Tom's hand twitches and as if sensing the outcome, I duck, just in time to miss his fisting coming towards me. He ends up hitting one of the goons standing behind me. Bursting into laughter, I nearly miss seeing him dive towards me. He must have had a few because at the last second I calmly step out of the way. Tom ends up running into another one of his mates, the one who was distracted by the one who just got punched in the eye, so he doesn't see it coming. They all go down and the bar cheers, hoots filling the air.

"If you wanted them on their knees you should have just asked them more politely," I chuckle.

He stands, his face red with anger, sweat beading his forehead. He tries to make another move for me, his feet unsteady. At this rate he'll take out his entire group of friends. My chuckling just angers him more and he tries to come at me once again and just like before, I jump to the side, laughing my head off at Tom drunkenly try to attack me.

Maverick puts a stop to my entertainment when he holds a hand to my chest and one to Tom's when he tries to come at me again for the millionth time tonight.

"Stop," Maverick demands, his voice controlled, holding authority. "Leave, now."

"They should all be fucking shot," Tom sneers as he turns to narrow his hateful eyes at Kevin.

I laugh when I see Kevin sitting at our table drinking a beer. He doesn't even seem fazed by the chaos going on around him, in fact, he looks like he's watching an MMA match on the tele.

"That's e-fucking-nough, Tom. Get the fuck out before I throw you out. You're barred," Tim shouts, slamming a tray or bottle down on the bar.

"Go on, Peggy Mitchell," I chuckle, earning me a slap around the head from my dearest brother, Maverick.

"Me? You're going to throw *me* out?" Tom shouts, outraged. Everyone in the bar hears him and starts going mad. Most of them cursing him, others chanting for him to get the fuck out. Then all of a sudden the whole bar descends into silence.

Complete and utter silence.

The air in the room changes, the atmosphere turning electric.

"You talk to your sister like that?" A dark, deep, scary voice calmly rumbles from the side of us.

My eyes find Kevin's and his eyes are alight with lust and love as he looks at our new guest. That can only mean one thing.

The new guest is Mark, Kevin's boyfriend.

I catch movement from the corner of my eye and I turn, watching Mark step further into the room, closer towards Tom. His large muscled arms are folded, his stance seeming relaxed but his tense jaw and the dark, cold look in his eyes give away his anger.

"What's my sister got to do with you faggots?" Tom snarls, but his voice shakes as he warily keeps an eye on Mark.

I nearly start clapping with excitement. Mason's stag party is going off with a bang.

Instead of diverting the attention back to me, I take my seat with Mav joining me. I've never had the pleasure of seeing Mark fight before, but I've been told it only takes him one punch to knock his opponent out.

Mark smirks evilly, taking another menacing step forward.

"I wouldn't be surprised if Tom's mom is scrubbing shit stains out of his boxers tomorrow morning," I whisper, making our table chuckle.

"Well, she's gay. She has a girlfriend, one I'm pretty fucking certain she's been with for a long fucking time. What does she think about you spouting that shit out?" Mark asks, a bite to his tone.

"Me sista ain't no leso," Tom barks. He goes to take a step forward, ready to start on Mark, but takes one look at him and takes a few steps back.

"Wanna bet? Want me to ring her girlfriend?"

Thinking about it, what Mark is saying is true. I remember who Tom's sister is now. She's a tiny little thing that got picked on at school like nobody's business. She left in the end when her girlfriend had gotten beaten up pretty badly.

"Yo, trust me, that girl is a lettuce licker. She loves the titties, don't she, Dan?" I laugh, remembering the party he tried it on with her at and she announced to everyone she was into girls. I remember thinking she was the shit coming out in front of everyone like that. I'd say more people should be brave and just come out, but, in my opinion it should be that more people need to accept the same sex couples.

"Fuck off, Carter," Dan shouts. I don't miss the worried look he sends Tom's way.

"Gladly. I was enjoying my night until you two fuckheads started yapping."

"This ain't over," Tom threatens before turning around and leaving. Just as they reach the door I notice him grab the back of Dan's coat and I laugh.

"Fucking dickheads," Mark grumbles before turning to Kevin. "You alright?"

"Yeah. Jesus, you're hot when you get mad. Want to head home for a bit?" Kevin asks and the tone in his voice has me biting back a grin.

"Come on," Mark laughs, looking eager to get his man alone.

"GO ON," I shout, laughing.

"I'll meet up with you later. Where will you be around midnight?" Kevin grins.

"V.I.P."

"See you later, fellas," Kevin grins and Mark shakes his head at his goofy boyfriend, leading him out the back entrance of the pub.

"Well, thank fuck that's over. I was worried about Mason not being here," Maverick mutters.

"Huh? Why?" Malik asks confused.

"Because getting a black eye on his stag night is a rite of passage," Mav laughs.

"The night is still young," Malik agrees and I laugh at their idiocy. Of course there will be more action. We're the Carters.

"Where to next then, boys?" Adam asks, taking a sip of his pint.

"Hold on!" Maverick laughs reading his phone. "That fucker has twenty-seven quid already."

Laughing, we all read the message Maverick shows us and down our pints. "We best get to Bamboos then before he finishes," Myles tells us and we all agree.

It's not even a few hours into the stag party and it's already been an eventful night. There's no telling what the rest of the night will bring or if we'll make it home in one piece.

FIFTEEN

LAKE

My head is already spinning after only drinking two glasses of champagne. The music is booming through the limo, the disco lights adding to the atmosphere. I've never experienced anything like it; I feel like a celebrity. It's exhilarating to say the least.

My phone beeps with an incoming message. Looking at the screen I find it's a picture message from Max. Opening it up, I burst into laughter and lean over the seats to Denny and show her the picture of what Max has sent me.

"What on earth?" she laughs hysterically, then passes my phone around for everyone else to have a look. The picture is of Mason wearing red lip stick, a pink wig and blow up boobs. He's also been covered in a cardboard cut-out.

"I can't believe they've made him do that," Harlow laughs, passing me my phone back.

"As long as no skanks feel him up, I say, let him get tortured," Denny laughs and we all whoop and scream drunkenly. I've never felt so free. Everything feels light, no dark memories weighing me down, and I'm actually glad I accepted the invitation about coming out tonight. For once, I'm acting my age.

"Selfie," Kayla smiles. Holding her camera out in front of us she snaps another picture of us pulling ridiculous faces. I'm used to this now, though. Since we've been in the limo she's taken a million. We've all switched seats at least a dozen times because of this. Thankfully, we're all back in our original seats as we near the club.

"We're here," Harlow squeals and Denny's eyes jump to the window.

"Oh my God, I love this place. It has a jukebox," she squeals. Looking to Harlow, her face relaxes. I could tell she was worried about Denny not enjoying herself earlier on in the day. She's mad for thinking it, though. I reckon we could be sitting at home in front of the TV watching a movie, drinking wine, and Denny would still be just as happy. I know Harlow's just feeling bad because a lot of the stuff we were originally doing has had to be cancelled. But then again, so did the lads' party. We all planned the night accordingly and will end up at V.I.P pretty much at the same time; if everything goes okay and Max doesn't get himself arrested, or anyone else for that matter.

The limo pulls up outside the bar. It's then that I notice Kayla and I are both sitting next to the doors and I glance over at her, feeling panicked.

"I'm not getting out this car first," I shout, just as the music dims. Everyone turns their heads in my direction at my outburst and burst into a fit of giggles. My cheeks heat from embarrassment and I wish I never opened my mouth.

"Me neither," Kayla pipes up loudly, making me relax.

"Well, I didn't put this on to not make an impression," Nay says seductively as she crawls across the limo floor to park her ass nearer the door. We all laugh and I quickly down the rest of my champagne for liquid courage; Kayla does the same thing with her glass.

"Let's do this," Nay shouts and we all scream in excitement, laughter following.

We enter the fairly busy bar and all eyes turn to us. I nervously tug at my shorts, pulling them down. Denny notices and swats my hands away.

"Stop it! You look hot," she whispers in my ear.

"So do you," I smile, grateful that someone as beautiful as her eased my mind.

"Hi, you must be the Carter party," an older lady asks as she walks up to us.

Harlow steps forward to greet her. "Hey, I'm the one that spoke with you on the phone. I'm Harlow."

"Hey, I'm Jackie. Follow me and I'll take you to the V.I.P booth," she tells us, earning grins from all of us. We follow giddily and I can't even hide my excitement.

"This place is awesome," Kayla breathes next to me. Her eyes gaze around the room in awe.

She's right too, it is. The place is huge. And for a Saturday it's looking pretty busy, but not as busy as I expected a bar like this to be. Music is playing quietly in the background but as we venture further into the club bar, and to our round booth, it grows a little louder.

"Vicky will be your bartender for tonight, so if you need anything, please just ask her. The drinks you pre-ordered are ready in the ice buckets on the table, along with some glasses. If there is anything else you need, please, don't hesitate to ask. Enjoy your evening, ladies, and congratulations," she grins at Denny and we all give her our thanks as she leaves.

The bartender, Vicky, asks Harlow again if there's anything she needs and I overhear her ask for a glass of water.

"The karaoke starts in just under an hour. I'll bring the song book and request forms over in just a sec," Vicky announces before leaving us all grinning at each other like Cheshire cats.

"You've so got to sing," I squeal at Denny. I love karaoke. Always have. Any chance I could get when I was younger I'd be on it, hogging the machine and taking all the limelight.

Can I sing? Fuck no! Do I care? Hell to the no. I just love the adrenaline, the high you get, and honestly, I felt like a pop-star holding that damn mic. I laugh inwardly at how idiotic I sound.

"This isn't fair. Kayla can sing like an angel," Denny pouts, amused.

"Want me to sing rock and roll, spice it up?" Kayla laughs, blushing whilst taking a sip of the drink Stace just poured for us all.

"Nope," Harlow butts in. We happily take the folder from Vicky when she arrives back at our table. She gives us all a stern, amused look. "I'm in charge. I'm going to choose the cheesiest love songs known to woman, write them down on a slip of paper, then you'll have to each pick one out of the glass. Whoever fails to sing will have to give the bar a table dance."

"Woman, you are feisty pregnant," Denny laughs, also drinking her drink. I'm pretty sure we're all halfway to being smashed.

"First up, though, is 'the game of truth,'" Harlow grins evilly, pulling out a spinner from her bag.

"You got a kitchen sink in there too?" I laugh, looking over Kayla to see inside Harlow's bag.

Everyone laughs but Harlow just grins back at us while placing a pack of cards on the table. She spins the tiny cardboard spinner and we all suck back a breath. It lands on Stace first who grins excitedly.

"First: rules are you have to tell the truth. If you can't tell the truth then you have to take a shot of this," she says, then holds her hand up, gesturing to Vicky. Vicky smiles as she walks over holding a bottle of Apple Sourz. "Okay, Stace," Harlow begins, picking up a card from the pile. "Have you ever swallowed?" she chokes out laughing.

"Fuck no! If I can help it, I make sure they don't cum in my mouth at all, but if it does get that far, then I spit it out," Stace answers looking disgusted, like she's reliving a bad memory.

"Oh my God! Remember when you gave that doorman a blow-job that once and you only got your mouth around his dick when he shot his load?" Nay laughs.

"I spat it all over his trousers. He took me off guard," Stace laughs remembering. We all laugh and I find myself enjoying the fun and games, enjoying life. A part of me feels guilty but their happiness is contagious.

"Okay, next," Harlow announces, still laughing. "Ahhh, Denny. Have you ever done it in a car?"

Denny laughs, her cheeks flushing and everyone starts giggling at her reaction. "We tried. It didn't go so well. I ended up with bruised knees. People on the tele make that shit look easy," she giggles.

"I've done it in a car with Evan," Kennedy pipes up, laughing. "It was one of the best moments of my life," she grins.

"Eww, that's my brother," Denny laughs, smacking Kennedy lightly on the shoulder.

"Stace, it's you again. Have you had sex with more than one person at a time?"

We all lean forward, obviously all wanting to know what her answer is going to be. She looks at all of us before finally leaning forward like she's about to reveal the dirtiest secret ever told.

"Nope. I wouldn't have a clue what to do." She laughs when she sees all the disappointed looks on our faces. It's like she's just announced that Santa Clause isn't real.

"Lake, have you ever fancied your best friend's boyfriend?"

I think about it for a moment and realise, no, I haven't. There's no one I can think back to and say, hand on heart, that I fancied their boyfriends.

"Nope," I grin, taking a sip of my drink.

"Damn, next is…" Harlow starts but is interrupted by Nay.

"Hold on, what about you, Kayla? You're dating Myles, right?"

"Yeah," Kayla smiles widely.

"Do you fancy Max, too?"

My head snaps to Kayla, my interest piqued. Does she? But then I think about Myles and as good looking as he is, he's not Max. I honestly think it's the personality that makes a person who they are. After all, most incredibly good looking guys can be assholes.

"God no! No offence, Lake," she adds quickly.

"Wait, you're with Max?" Stace asks open mouthed.

"Evan didn't tell me that," Kennedy adds looking surprised.

"No, we're just… Just friends, I guess," I shrug, wanting the conversation to be over. When it comes to me and Max, it's private. I know he hasn't let anyone see the real him, the person I see, so revealing that would feel like I was betraying him.

"I don't get it. How can you not like Max when he looks exactly like Myles? They're twins."

"Easy. They're two completely different people. I don't just like Myles for what he looks like but for who he is. He's nothing like Max. Yeah, they have some similar qualities, but that's as far as it goes for me," Kayla answers perfectly. It's how I would describe them too.

"Who's next?" I ask, wanting to move on.

"Kennedy, where is the weirdest place you've had sex?"

Kennedy blushes looking around the table. "I don't think we have had a weird place. I guess if I had to say which was the scariest, because I thought we would get caught, is at the hotel we stayed at after we got married. We were in the pool late at night and things got heated," she starts, her face heating. You can see it even with the dim lights.

"My ears are bleeding," Denny howls horrified and we all laugh.

"Helloooooo, welcome to The Fire Inn. We have a special crowd with us tonight," the DJ shouts, earning hoots and hollers from around the pub. "A hen night if I'm not mistaken," he calls again and the lads in the pub start whistling. "I'm also told the first six songs will be sung by them, so give it up, guys, for Team Carter," he shouts in the mic. We all cheer at the table, all of us banging our glasses on the table and stomping our feet on the floor.

Harlow quickly scribbles the rest of the songs down on the slips before scrunching them up and throwing them in a pint glass. She gives them a quick shake, looking to Denny.

"You're first, bride-to-be," she winks at Denny. "Pick a song."

"Oh my God. I've got *Celine Dion, Because You Love Me*," she giggles, standing up. We all cheer her onto the stage, all of us stomping our legs and whistling. Harlow grabs her phone and when she catches me looking she grins evilly.

"Got to get the proof," she winks and turns back to the stage.

Denny hands the slip over to the DJ and he smiles, nodding his head. She then continues to walk over to the centre of the stage, where the mic is grinning ear to ear. Looking up at the huge TV screen up on the wall, she bites her lip before taking in a deep breath. She looks petrified but excited at the same time.

"Come on, Denny," Stace shouts, her hands cupping her mouth just as the music starts playing. We're all smiling and laughing, shouting encouragement as she sings through the first verse.

Some lads sitting at the far back start hollering, "Get ya tits out, get ya tits out, get ya tits out for the lads."

Denny stops for a second, looking completely shocked, but then grins and shouts back and all of us join in with her.

"Get ya peckers out, get ya peckers out, get ya peckers out for us gals."

The DJ, grinning his head off, shakes his head but leans over to the mic as the song finishes. "Please don't. I don't need to see that shit."

We all laugh like drunken idiots, hooting and hollering.

"Your turn," Nay shouts and Harlow grins, grabbing a folded piece of paper from the pint glass.

"Oh shitting hell, I got *Aerosmith, I Don't Want To Miss A Thing*," she pouts. "Don't blame me when the cats start lining up outside to get in." With that she steps up onto the stage, smacking Denny's arse on the way. Denny comes and sits down, gulping down her drink at the same time as the song begins.

Just like we did with Denny, we all cheer her on, ignoring the cat calls and whistles from the lads sitting at the back. I don't know about the others but I don't want to give them the ammunition to come over.

We're all laughing throughout the song. Harlow wasn't kidding about the cat comment. If cats aren't swarming the area outside wondering where their mother is, I'd be shocked as fuck. She's basically screaming down the mic towards the end but it doesn't stop us all from singing along right with her, all of us so out of tune and sounding worse than nails scraping down a chalkboard.

"Thank you, and goodnight," Harlow shouts, laughing and sounding so out of breath I begin to worry she's going to pass out.

"Who's next?" Kennedy asks, grinning and shaking the pint glass. She's gone from merry to being pissed in the space of two songs and I can't actually blame her. We've been drinking shot after shot and that's not including the drinks we've been sipping on.

"Kayla, you're up, babe," Nay grins at her.

"It's so unfair that we'll all most likely sound like strangled, tortured animals and you'll sound like an angel," Denny pouts, her words beginning to slur.

"I've got *Christina Perry's, Thousand Years,*" she grins looking pleased.

And I find out why when she gets up on the stage and begins to sing, making the song her own. Her voice is husky, soft. It's spectacular.

"Fucking hell! She sounds freaking amazing," I blurt out, making everyone laugh. I don't care; it's the first time I've heard her sing and it's the most beautiful sound ever.

"She's really good," Kennedy whispers in awe. "I'm actually pretty scared about going up next."

"She is awesome. Look at her blushing. I don't get why, she owns it. She's got such a fantastic voice," Harlow mentions and I agree, looking back to the stage to where Kayla is slowly finishing the song.

A round of applause erupts from around the bar when she finishes and we all stand up hollering and shouting. She laughs, throwing her head back on the stage, before stepping forward and taking a dramatic bow.

"Quick, Kennedy, you're up next."

Kennedy reluctantly shakes the glass before taking one of the slips out. "You were amazing, Kayla. I don't think I'm gonna top that. No one could top that performance. You should have gone last."

"Knock um dead," Kayla laughs shaking off the compliment, and I move out the booth to let her sit back down.

"I got *Bruno Mars', Marry you,*" Kennedy giggles. "I freaking love this song." We all laugh and cheer her on as she jumps out from the booth and up onto the stage: her earlier reluctance gone.

We're all clapping when she starts singing. Then Denny has a bright idea as the song really gets going, Kennedy enjoying herself up on the stage.

"Let's dance," Denny grins and we all smile in agreement.

We all jump down to the little area that has been cleared and start to dance, singing along with Kennedy who seems more relaxed and is working the stage, making us giggle.

'I think I wanna marry you,' is sung and we all point to Denny, singing the words to her and she throws her head back laughing.

I grab Kayla's hands and start swinging her around, jiggling my hips and body to the music. It's the most fun I've ever had and I feel so free, so alive, and I'm having the best time of my life, finally feeling like I belong.

The song finishes and we all take our seats, laughing. I soon lose mine when I find out it's my turn next.

"Damn it," I mutter, then grab a slip and groan loudly throwing my head back. "You've got to be kidding me."

"What did you get?" Denny laughs.

"*Whitney Houston's, I Will Always Love You,*" I groan but move out of the booth and take the slip to the DJ. "Don't suppose the mic broke before I got up here?"

He laughs, shaking his head. I flop my head back groaning and take the stage. I send Harlow a glare but she just laughs along with the rest of the girls. I feel like I'm in the spotlight, which I guess I am, but more so wearing a hooker outfit that shows more skin than a bikini.

"Come on, Lake, work it, baby," Nay shouts, making me laugh. Then I begin to sing. The song isn't that bad at first and I don't feel like I sound like a drowning cat. But then the song continues and the notes get higher and my voice begins to crack and get out of tune.

Just when the highest note of the song begins, I burst out laughing. Denny, Harlow, Kennedy, Kayla, Nay and Stace are all standing up, swinging their arms from side to side and screaming out the song for me.

I end up finishing the song in a fit of laughter but no one seems to care; they all seem to be having as much fun as the rest of us.

When I jump down from the stage, Nay is already making her way up, her hips jiggling from side to side as she walks.

I grin when she gives me a high five and a hip bump. "Knock um dead," I laugh, carrying on to my seat.

I flop down on the seat, feeling myself becoming hotter: sweat starting to bead my forehead and the back of my neck.

"You were brilliant," they all cheer when I finish downing my drink and wishing I didn't when a sudden dizziness hits me.

I wave them off with a grin. When I realise the song Nay has picked out, I sigh. Lucky cow!

"Let's dance," Denny shouts again and we all hit the make shift dance floor and wiggle our hips to the music.

Crazy in Love by Beyonce begins to play and we're all shaking our hips to the beat. Nay, on stage, starts singing and she actually sounds okay. She works the stage walking back and forth like a real pop star, making us all giggle and sing along with her.

She starts full on dancing at the chorus, copying the moves that *Beyonce* does in the video. When she starts twerking, her hips twisting all the way to the floor then snapping back up with her ass in the air, we all scream. Lads start hollering and I'm pretty sure they're having the night of their lives. They're basically getting a free show with the way Nay is working the stage in that outfit. She looks pretty fucking awesome up there.

"Whooohoooo," I shout, cheering her on, but the girl doesn't need it. She's got it going on.

"This night is so awesome," Kayla slurs in my ear and I giggle, swinging my hips up against hers in a sexy way. Both obviously not used to the nightlife, we end up giggling, tripping over our own shadows and falling to the floor.

We both land with a loud umph but end up in a fit of laughter. It's then I realise Nay isn't singing anymore, the song now finished. She's joined the other girls and is laughing down at me and Kayla.

"You said knock um dead, not over," Nay laughs which makes us laugh harder. It takes them a few attempts to help us up. Finally back in our seats we all look to Stace.

"You're next," Kayla shouts, pointing a finger right in Stace's face.

Stace laughs, knocking her hand away before picking the last slip out of the pint glass.

"Oh my God, I love this song," Stace shouts squealing. She doesn't give us chance to ask what it is, she's out of the booth and running up on the stage, handing the DJ the slip.

When the song begins we all look at each other and grin. Jumping out of the booth, we all head back to the dance floor.

We listen, sing and dance as Stace sings *Dirty Dancing's, Time Of My Life*. Just like Nay, she works the stage. We all laugh at her facial expressions. She's proper getting into the song.

"I wonder what the boys are up to?" Kayla shouts and I smile.

"Let's see," I answer with mischief in my voice. I grab my phone and hold it up, trying to get a selfie to send to Max, but it doesn't work. Every time I think I've got the picture I take a look and find the picture a complete disaster. On one, half of our faces are missing and on the other, neither of us end up in the shot at all. We both laugh at my failed attempts at photography.

"Here, I'll take it," Nay laughs, grabbing my phone. Kayla and I wrap our arms around each other, posing for the picture. Nay snaps the picture, winking when she hands me my phone back.

"We're heading to the next club," Harlow shouts, warning us to finish our drinks.

I make quick work of uploading the photo. Writing a message out, though, turns out to be a little more difficult whilst intoxicated.

Me: Having thee timeee of myyy wife. Wifi. Duck sake. Wife. No. I'm having the dime of my lifeeeeeeee.

Laughing, I send the message. "Ha, I rocked that message,' I tell Kayla, but when I turn to face her, she's gone.

SIXTEEN

MAX

I'D BE A MILLIONAIRE BY NOW if I had a pound for every time someone has mentioned how blue I'm looking. I've been able to forget about my skin deficiency, but then some little fucker would bring it up making me feel small. Like a gnome.

Like now.

"Aww, you look like Papa Smurf," a drunk, giggling girl snickers with her mates.

"Aww, you look like Joker from Batman," I tell her dryly. Her friends all curse and call me names but I carry on walking, ignoring them. Okay, staggering, towards Bamboos.

"I think we should have skipped that last bar," Myles laughs as he steadies Adam who is two sheets to the wind.

"It was Malik's idea. Blame him," I chuckle.

Malik had suggested heading into another bar while we waited for Lee's message to say that they've finished. That other bar ended up being another three. Poor Mason and Lee will have to catch the fuck up when we reach them.

Rounding the corner, I see Bamboos up ahead of us. A large queue is lining up outside and I inwardly groan. Hopefully someone we know is working the door tonight because you can forget about me waiting in that line.

"There's Mason," Maverick laughs and we all look up and follow his line of direction. And there he is. Mason. His body rigid, stiff as a board. He's giving some stocky built girl a hug. His face is scrunched up in distaste, while Lee is laughing his ass off beside him, taking a picture for evidence.

"How much are you charging tonight, bro?" I shout, laughing when his head snaps up and he glares over at us.

When we're closer we all notice his cardboard cut-out is looking a little bent out of shape. His wig has disappeared, along with his fake boobs. And if I'm not mistaken, his lipstick is looking a little smudged.

"What the fuck happened to you?" Malik laughs, stepping closer for a better inspection.

"I'm never, and I mean, never, going to forgive you for this. I feel violated. That last girl stunk like a sewer. I'm not even going to get into how many times I've been groped and touched in places I didn't give them permission to touch," he whines. Taking off his cardboard cut-out he shoves it at me.

Laughing my head off, I grab the cardboard cut out and hand it over to the girl that he just accused of stinking like a sewer.

"You look like you could use a hug," I wink. I wince when she smiles, her teeth looking like they've been brushed with a mouldy banana.

I dry heave and Mason gives me a sympathetic look like he knows what I just witnessed and how I'm feeling. Which I suppose he does. He did just get up close and personal with her.

"What's next? Please say it involves a lot of alcohol," he pleads, turning his back on banana teeth girl.

"It does," Maverick laughs. "You've got a lot of catching up to do." He gestures to Adam who looks like he's about to pass out and we all laugh.

"But first, the next part of tonight," Myles chuckles.

Mason groans, throwing his head back. "Please don't make me wear any more stupid shit."

"You won't be," Myles laughs. "When I shout 'ants' you guys have to hit the deck, waving your arms and legs around in the air. Failure to follow through will earn you a punishment."

"But I can drink?" Mason asks, double-checking.

"You got a drinking problem, bro?" I ask chuckling.

"Fuck off."

"Elliot is on the door tonight. He's got a new doorman working for him but he said we can go right on through," Maverick adds as he holds a drunk Adam up. I follow behind for backup. There's no guessing when Adam will lose his footing. I want to be ready with my phone to capture the epic moment.

"What the fuck? Why you lookin' so blue? Are you tryin' to be an Avatar?" Elliot, the big, burly doorman, booms. His deep laughter rumbles through the air and I tip my head back to the tall fucker and smirk.

"What the fuck? Why you looking so big? Are you trying to be The Rock?" I reply sarcastically. Taking my teasing in goodwill he just laughs me off, slapping me on the back.

"Easy there, tiger. *Some* might call that assault," I groan, twisting my shoulders. Shit that hurt.

'Ants,' is shouted and I groan. I'm standing in front of two massive doormen and have a queue of people behind me and he decides to shout 'ants' now.

Yep. It's official. This game sucks for me.

Making quick work of dropping to the floor, I begin waving my legs and arms around. Myles didn't mention for us to do anything else, or for how long. So once I've made a show of myself, I get up acting like nothing happened.

Elliot is staring at me like I've lost the plot. People from the queue behind me are shouting and laughing. And when I look around Elliot I notice my brothers, Adam and Lee all laughing their heads off with their phones aimed in my direction.

"You fuckers," I rumble.

"I'm the only one who can shout it," Myles laughs.

"Sorry," Mason grins, looking smug, and I know then it was that fucker that shouted ants.

"Payback's a bitch," I remind him; pointing my finger warningly towards him. Turning around I face the queue and give them a bow. "Thank you, Coldenshire, and goodnight," I boom, earning a few more giggles and laughter.

Walking past Elliot towards the rest of the group I swear I hear him mumble about mental institutions, but I can't be sure. Maybe he has a relative in one.

"That was fucking classic," Mason roars over the loud music. He's still laughing at my expense. Fucker.

I jump on his back, causing him to stumble. "Giddy up. It's party time."

"I'll get the drinks. You fuckers go grab that table bar over by the dance floor," I shout.

The place is packed. People are huddled at the bar waiting to be served but I push my way through until I'm happily at the front. The girl next to me sends me a glare but I just wink, blowing her a kiss.

When I see one of the girls I've fucked before I shout her over. I can't really remember her name. I'm pretty sure it begins with a D but it could be anything. I just don't want to risk calling her the wrong name and not being served.

One thing I'm short of and that's patience. I can't stand waiting in line for anything. Even at a bank when there are more than two people in front of me, I'll leave.

"Hey, gorgeous," she purrs, leaning over the bar. Her heavy breasts squeezing together and with the small tank top she's wearing, I get more than a good eyeful.

"Hey, Da- darling," I greet smiling. I try to recall her name again, but I'm getting nothing. I just hope the whole darling thing worked. When she smiles I take that as a good sign and that she hasn't caught on that I have no idea what her name is.

"What can I get ya, Senator?"

I grin. "Can I get seven vodka Red Bulls, fourteen shots of whatever you have and four shots of the strongest liquor you have," I wink. Mason needs to catch up but he also needs to learn the concept of revenge.

"Walk to the end of the bar," she shouts over the music. Handing me my change, she picks up the tray of drinks. I nod my head, knowing the drill. Whenever they have a big order they always ask the customer to head to the end of the bar. That way the drinks won't get spilt trying to get out of the crowd of people waiting to be served.

"Call me. I finish at three," she winks, leaning in to kiss my cheek. My mouth, for once, stays shut. I'll probably end up wearing the tray of drinks with the comebacks flying through my mind right now. Instead, I give her a tight smile and walk off. I don't even know what I'll be doing at three, but one thing is for certain, I know who I'd love to be doing at three and it's most certainly not her.

"That was quick," Mason comments as I place the tray down.

"That's what Denny said about you," I smart off. Clearly not amused, I carry on. "Joking. People just separated to let me through. They were lining up to serve *me*," I tell him.

"Dickhead," he mutters.

"Did you buy the bar?" Maverick shouts over the music.

"These are Mason's," I shout. Picking up the four shots the D chick poured. I hand them over to Mason with a grin on my face. "You need to catch up."

He nods grinning. Poor sod really does look like he needs a drink. He takes the first shot and ends up bent over coughing his lungs up.

"What the fuck is that?" he wheezes. I slap his back hard while trying to control my laughter.

"That, my friend, is payback. Here, take this. It will ease the burn," I lie.

Not reading into my lie, Mason happily takes the shot glass from me, downing the drink quickly. His eyes shoot wide open, a look of horror crossing his face. I burst out laughing, no longer able to control it. His cheeks are puffed out like a hamster and I'm pretty sure I'll be seeing steam shooting from his ears soon.

"Two more," I shout, grinning.

"You're an ass," he growls but takes the two shots anyway. I laugh when he starts coughing again. He grabs for the glass of vodka Red Bull, downing most of it in one go.

"Bottoms up," Maverick shouts, holding one of the shots up. We all follow, grabbing our own and shooting it back.

"Ants," Myles laughs.

I groan, but then the seven of us are on the floor with our legs and arms flapping around. I'm pretty sure Adam was already playing Ants before we even dropped the deck, but it all happened so fast I can't be sure.

Getting back up I begin to feel a little wheezy. It's then I realise the gist of the game. The quick movements are guaranteed to get us pissed quicker.

"You sly dog," I laugh at Myles who just salutes me with his drink, pocketing his phone. Mason and Maverick are helping Adam up, leaning him up against the post next to the dance floor.

"He's not going to last the night," I point out to anyone who is listening.

"We'll drag him with us anyway. He can be like our mascot or something," Lee grins, grabbing a pen out of his pocket.

"You carry a colouring book in there too?" I ask, leaning back to see.

"No," he laughs. Walking over to a swaying Adam; Lee begins to draw on his face. I laugh. So cliché.

Dick move. But still funny as fuck.

Walking over to Lee, I snatch the pen from his hand, ignoring his protests. He was in the middle of drawing a moustache. It looks more like a two year old has been scribbling on his face, though, I don't tell Lee that in fear of hurting his feelings. "What's his number?" I ask Lee. He rattles it off while I copy it down on Adam's head. 'Call me in the morning' is written above the number and I step back, admiring my handi work.

"He's going to kill you," Mason chuckles as I pocket the pen, hoping it will come in handy later on.

Maybe that's why Lee had it, I think to myself.

I shrug. Then I hear it. I jump in the air, twisting around mid jump to face the others and start going crazy.

My fucking song!

I love this tune.

"Ooooh watch me, watch me," I sing and start throwing down some moves. Everyone moves out of my way as I jump up the two steps leading to the dance floor.

Everyone cheers me on and I grin, busting another move as the song continues.

Myles and Lee join me, showing off their own skills, but Mason and Maverick watch on laughing. They move their bodies every so often but, apart from that, the two look like two stiff robots.

Dorks.

Adam. Poor Adam. He's standing against the pole, nodding his head with heavy, jerky movements. Every so often I'll see him try to move his arms in the air, but it doesn't happen for the poor lad.

Bless him, he does soldier on.

The song finishes and a girly song comes on but it doesn't stop me. Helping me, Lee and Myles grab Mason onto the dance floor. I try to grab Maverick but the 'fuck off' look he gives me has me dancing backwards, hands in the air, back to the others.

Back in the group huddle, I start jumping around Mason shaking my chest as Jessie J and Ariana start talking about banging some chick. Drunk, and feeling stupid, I keep pretending to shake my tits at him. He shakes his head amused. But then hands Maverick his drink to hold and starts shaking his ass.

"Whooo, Clitoris Love-Bandit is getting married next month," I shout over the crowd.

"Two months," Mason laughs, correcting me.

"And you're having your stag now?" Lee asks laughing.

"We didn't want hangovers on our wedding day," Mason shouts back, then starts twerking like a fool.

Laughing hard, I copy, bouncing my way around our small group. A few girls try to join in by acting like retards. It's like they're thinking if they can dance like us they'll be accepted, but it doesn't work like that. You have to be a special kind of retard to join our huddle, they just look like crazy clowns on drugs.

Listening to hollers around us, I look up and notice we've formed a nice crowd. None of us seem to care. Even Maverick has joined us. He's not exactly busting any moves but at least he's not robotically moving his shoulders from side to side anymore.

"Ants," Myles shouts, roaring with laughter.

"Fucker," Maverick growls as we all throw ourselves down on the floor.

"I'm going to need some back physio after tonight," I groan, waving my legs and arms around.

"You should be used to being on your back," Lee comments snidely.

"Nah, your mom likes me on top," I shoot back.

"Wanker."

People are careful not to step on us. A few of them even stop to stare down at us as if we're fascinating creatures on display.

"What? You never seen an epileptic ant before?" I shout.

Getting up off the floor I wipe off the back of my jeans, groaning when I feel the back of my jeans are wet.

"Great," I moan and Mason and Maverick turn in my direction.

"What?" they ask simultaneously.

"I'm soaked. I landed in a drink," I tell them, turning around for them to see.

When they begin laughing I turn back around to face them. "What? Please tell me it's beer and not some other bodily fluid."

"At least you've lived up to your name, Senator Pantstain," Maverick laughs. I groan, not finding the fucker funny.

"Where do you think the girls are now? Harlow hasn't texted me back," Malik shouts, ignoring Maverick and Mason laughing at my suspense.

"You going to be pussy whipped all night?" Lee asks.

Shit.

He didn't just say that.

"Shut the fuck up," Malik growls. One thing you should never do and that's make snide comments about his relationship with Harlow. Yeah, he's pussy whipped to fuck, but for Malik, it's love and he's proved over and over that it is. He'd do anything for her. Has been like that since the day he met her.

"Hey, just asking," Lee laughs, holding his hands up, not realising how close to death he just got. "Hey, a shot, girl. Let's grab a few shots and head to the next bar."

"Yeah, it's getting on. Didn't realise how long Mason took to raise some money," Maverick laughs.

Now Malik has mentioned the girls, my mind turns to Lake. Grabbing my phone from my back pocket I unlock the screen. One message pops up and I grin when I see it's from Lake.

A picture downloads of Lake and Kayla and my eyes pop out of my head.

What the fucking hell!

Why are we here and not with the girls?

Do the lads know what the hell they're wearing? Or not wearing shall I say.

Holy fuck, her tits. Her legs. Fuck me, her hair. It's wild and down, falling to her luscious ass. Not that I can see her tight ass in the picture, but the picture is grabbing at my imagination. The shorts look like they're painted on her, they cling that tight to her body.

"What has you looking like you're about to blow your load?" Myles grins, staggering up to me. He looks quickly down at my phone but then from the corner of my eye I see his head snap back down. His hand shoots out snatching the phone from my hand as he inspects the picture at a closer range.

"Holy fucking Christ," he shouts, his eyes bugging out. "Did you know what they were wearing tonight?" he asks Malik.

"What?" Malik asks panicked and grabs the phone from him. He looks at the screen and turns awfully pale. For a second I think he's going to pass out like good ole Adam. But instead, he hands Mason the phone and gets his own out. He pulls the phone to his ear and curses when he doesn't get an answer.

"He really wants to fuck her right now doesn't he?" I muse loudly, earning a growl from Malik. "What? I'm hard from just a picture," I laugh.

Myles slaps me. "That's my fucking girlfriend."

"Huh?" I wince, rubbing my sore head.

"Kayla," he deadpans. "In the picture."

"Like I give a fuck. My eyes were on the prize, bro," I wink and he just shakes his head.

"Come on. We need to move on before the bouncers come and kick sleeping beauty out," Maverick laughs. He's bent over helping up a sleeping Adam.

"I'm up, mom," Adam slurs and we all look at him laughing.

The atmosphere in the club turns light again and we all laugh trying to help Adam up.

"Shouldn't this be me you guys are carrying?" Mason wheezes, tucking his shoulder under Adam's.

"Oh, give it time. Give it time. The night is still young," I warn and follow them out.

SEVENTEEN

LAKE

"Hey, isn't this Maverick's club?" I ask the girls when we pull up outside MC5. Max had mentioned the clubs his brothers own a few times during conversations.

"Yeah. It's above VIP, the strip club," Kayla giggles. Bless her. Her face is all red and everything and she only said, 'strip club'.

"I thought they were two different clubs," I think aloud. It's pretty impressive. Getting out of the limo I take in the scenery. Queues of people line the street, waiting to be let in. Lights stream through the windows of the club and the music blares from the inside.

"This is amazing," Nay squeals, stepping towards the club. Seems Nay is a squealer and a happy drunk. She's been hilarious since we drunk our last drinks at 'The Fire Inn'.

"It's impressive," I agree, grinning. Grabbing my arm, Kayla pulls me towards the front of the queue. Denny and Harlow are already stood at the front doors, laughing and joking with one of the doormen. I hear him congratulate Harlow on the pregnancy just as we arrive, so they must be familiar with him.

"You ladies stay out of trouble tonight," the doorman winks.

"Oh, you can restrain me if I get into trouble," Stace flirts, winking back at him.

Turning towards her, I burst out laughing. She's eyeing him up like he's something to be devoured.

"He's not a pizza," I whisper yell in her ear. Everyone laughs. The doorman just smirks, eyeing the tall, model beauty.

"Ohhh, but how I'd love to have a piece of him," she breathes. My eyes fall on the tall, burly doorman again and I can see her appeal. He's a good looking man if you're into the whole scary looking, muscled man. And from the way he and Stace are eyeing one another, I'll take a huge guess and say they're both into each other.

"Have a good night," he chuckles. He removes the red rope letting us step past. A few people in the queue protest but a deep growl from the doorman shuts them up right away.

Kayla and I giggle. We follow the girls into the club, both of us in awe as we take in the atmosphere and our surroundings. Everyone in the club is dancing, having fun and drinking. Just walking in I can feel the buzz coming from everyone else, the feeling contagious.

"Oh my gawd, this is amazing," I giggle excitedly, my hips moving to the music as we follow Harlow. "Where are we going?" I shout.

"We've got a private area blocked off for us tonight. Mason handled it all," Kayla answers, her head nodding to the beat of the music.

Holy cow!

Mason is the shit and has just become my favourite Carter brother. He's cornered off the far end of the club for us. It's roped off, a doorman standing near the makeshift entrance.

"Hey, Mason has had Tony prepare you some drinks. They're on the table. He'll be over soon, he just got called away," the doorman rumbles to Denny.

"It's fine," she waves him off and we head into what is now our space. I feel special, like a celebrity, as we enter the roped up area. Nearby people begin to stare, most likely wondering the same thing, I'm sure.

As soon as we're seated, Nay is pouring us drinks and handing us some shots. Tony even prepared Harlow some cool refreshments. A coke, water and an orange juice are all in a bucket of ice. Mason really thought of everything for his girl and her friends. He went all out.

Kennedy hands me another shot, I take it, knocking it back. Surprisingly

I don't cough, which is a first for the night, even the taste doesn't bother me anymore: I've drank that many I'm immune to the strength of them.

"This is the best freaking night ever," Denny screams over the music. "Thank you so much. I love you guys so much." Her eyes begin to water and my own eyes start to soften.

"Aww, we love you too, babe. And we're having a blast too," Nay replies.

"And coming out isn't exactly a hardship," Harlow laughs.

"Nope, I'm having the time of my life," I salute, holding my glass up. Don't ask me what we're drinking. I have no clue. All I can tell you is that it's fruity and yummy as hell.

"You guys are going to make cry," Denny pouts. We all laugh at the sulky expression she's trying to pull off.

"Stop with all the emotional stuff. We're here to have fun," Harlow shouts over the loud booming music. "But just so you know, I love you too, bitch."

"Hell yeah," Nay shouts, shaking her raven black hair.

"We've played the truth game but what comes with playing truth?" Harlow asks with a cheeky grin as she eyes us.

"Dares," Stace answers, grinning like a fool. She looks excited at the possibility of getting down and dirty.

"I'm lost," I declare loudly, my drink sloshing a little over the side of the glass. "Whoops."

"I'm with Lake," Kayla laughs. "Literally."

I laugh at her goofiness. She's so darn cute. "Thanks," I grin.

"Truth and dare. We've played truth, now it's time to get down and naughty and play dare," Harlow giggles, her cheeks blushing.

"Did you practice that speech?" Denny teases.

"Every day in the mirror," Harlow answers seriously. Giggling, I take another sip of my drink, readying myself for what Harlow has up her sleeve for dares. Because there's no doubt that she has been planning the best dares her masterful mind could conjure up.

"Who's up first?" Nay asks. Her ass is literally hanging off the edge of the seat and her hands are rubbing together excitedly.

"I'm out with this one. The place is too packed for me to join. Not only would Malik get pissed but I'm not willing to risk my babies."

"That's okay. You'll have fun watching us make fools of ourselves," Kennedy giggles.

"True," Harlow winks. "First up is the bride-to-be. And your dare is…" Harlow pauses. She grabs something out of her bag which looks like a box of nail filers.

"I don't think now is the right time to do your nails," Denny laughs.

"Oh, these aren't nail filers. These are your dares," she winks. "And yours, my friend, is to: photo bomb at least three photos, pulling some sort of face, or joining in."

The table erupts with laughter and Denny giggles, downing the rest of her drink. I'd die if that was my dare. Not only do I hate having my photo taken but I hate making nice with strangers. I just don't have it in me. Then again, tonight, I am feeling overly friendly.

Standing up, Denny walks off with a swing in her hips.

"She's going to do it," Kennedy hoots.

"This one was one of the easiest. Wait till you see the rest," Harlow laughs. Slowly, we all turn our heads in her direction, a worried look upon our faces.

"Please tell me no one has to get naked?" I plead. Not that us stripping would make much difference when we're barely wearing anything anyway.

"No. Oh my God! What is she doing?" Harlow laughs, her hand covering her mouth. We all turn to look in the direction she's looking and all crack up. Denny is standing at a pose, her hands on her hips and has accomplished the 'duck face' like she was born to do it. But what has us laughing is the fact she's doing it behind some chick who is trying to pull off the same pose but failing miserably.

When she's done she wanders off, her hips moving to the beat of the music as her eyes scan the rest of the dancers. When she catches someone, she moves quickly across the dance floor.

"She wouldn't?" I laugh when she saddles up next to a couple taking a selfie of themselves kissing. She's literally shoved her head in the picture next to them, like they're not sucking face and smiling. The couple haven't even noticed, or they've chosen to ignore her, because she's gone before they have chance to separate.

"That is so fucking funny. I wonder when they'll notice," Stace laughs.

"I cannot believe she just did that. She went right up close to them," Kennedy adds laughing.

"I thought she was going to join in," Nay pipes in next, chuckling.

"Me too," Kayla giggles drunkenly.

"Me three," I say, waving my hand in the air. I soon stop when I nearly take out Kayla's eye with my finger. "Sorry."

"It's okay," she giggles again, turning back around to watch Denny. She's moved further into the club, so we've lost sight of her. We all stand up searching through the sea of people to find her.

When I see the orange writing on her top glowing in the dark, I laugh. "There she is," I point.

"What on earth?" Kennedy squeaks. Even my eyes widen in shock. She's managed to get a lad to lift her up onto the bar. I notice the bartender shouting something at her but Denny ignores her and leans to the side with one hand thrown in the air like she's trying to pose like a starfish.

"She did it," Harlow laughs.

"Uh-oh. The doorman is getting her down," Kayla smirks, biting her lip.

"So jealous," Stace sighs beside me. That's when I realise it's the doorman that we met outside.

"When Denny gets back it's your turn, Kayla. Remember you don't have to do any of them. Some of these can be a bit... I dunno. A bit much. Don't feel bad if you don't want to do one of the dares."

Kayla nods at Harlow looking kinda pale. "You okay?" I shout.

"Yeah," she nods. "As long as it doesn't involve a male I'll be fine."

"It will be okay," I assure her, praying like hell I don't get a male dare now that she's mentioned it. Now I'm thinking about it, the more nervous I become.

Denny finds her way back to the table, laughing. "I did it," she sings happily. "I swear that couple were doing more than kissing," she shudders, making us all laugh.

"Eww, that's gross," Kennedy chuckles.

"Who's up next? This is so much fun." Denny bounces up and down excitedly before moving around the table, taking her seat.

"Kayla. And she has to: pinch a guy's ass and walk away. What will it be, Kayla, dare or shots?"

Kayla stands up surprising me. I have to suppress a grin when I see the determined look on her face. She looks so freaking cute; her button nose all scrunched up and her fists clenched with a fierce look upon her face.

"Why not? I'm going to do this. Damn it, yes, I'm going to pinch some guy's bum and love it," she declares.

"Maybe not too much. Myles might get jealous."

"Oh," she says, her facial expression falling. "Do you think he'll be mad?"

"It's for my party. Of course not," Denny answers shocked, but fighting a smile. When I'm around Kayla, I feel more worldly.

"Then I'm going to do it," she says firmly and nearly trips over one of the chair legs when she starts to walk away. It doesn't deter her from her mission, though. She marches right out into the sea of people with a look of determination, making sure to stay in the line of our sight.

She must have her eye on the target already because the next thing I see is her running back towards us laughing her head off. A bloke standing where she once was is looking around curiously but the only people that are behind him are a group of lads. When he walks off in a hurry it makes me laugh harder.

"Did you see? Did you see?" Kayla laughs bubbly. She looks so freaking pleased with herself like she just accomplished a life goal. Then again, from what I've learnt about Kayla over the months I've known her, I can see why this is such a big deal for her. She's always so quiet. She keeps to herself and I know from what I've heard the others mention that she's been through a lot.

"Well done. Did you see his face?" I ask, grinning from ear to ear. I'm so happy for her. She's deliberately moved out of her comfort zone by doing this dare. Maybe that's what I need to do for once. Just let loose.

"Of course I didn't. I ran like a vampire was chasing me," she replies.

"Have you seen the vampires now on TV? Why the fuck would you run? Damon Salvatore could bite me any day of the week," Nay grins.

"Oh, I'm team Stephan," Stace laughs.

"He's a boring old fart," Nay protests.

"I'm more of an Edward Cullen fan," Kayla adds, earning nods from Denny and Harlow.

"Well, fuck you guys, I'm a werewolf fan. Jacob Black all the way," I grin. God, he's so gorgeous it hurts to look at him. All that golden brown skin, tight muscles and that smile is enough to make any girl melt.

"I'm more of a superhero fan," Kennedy pipes in. "I love Thor."

We all laugh and agree. *Chris Hemsworth* is to die for.

"Okay. Settle down. Settle down. Nay, you're up next," Harlow grins. She's already holding up one of the nail filer sticks so I reckon her grin has to do with what is written on it.

"From the look on your face I can tell mine isn't going to be easy," Nay whines but is smirking at Harlow.

"Damn right. Your dare is to: find a condom."

"Please tell me it doesn't have to be used?" Nay pleads, looking as grossed out as the rest of us.

"Eww," I add, hoping she doesn't need to find a used one.

"No. The rules are, unused, and it says you're not allowed to purchase one."

"I can do this," Nay tells us. She pours herself another shot, knocking it back in one.

"Oh and you have ten minutes," Harlow shouts after her.

We lose Nay in the crowd, but less than ten minutes later she returns from the club waving a foiled wrapper around.

"How did you get it?" Denny laughs. Her eyes are wide with surprise. We're all surprised. We were talking about it while we were waiting and decided it couldn't be done. Harlow told us there were harder ones, but still fun to try.

"It took me a while to pick out the players. When I did I looked for the easiest one. I walked up to him, flirted, then said, 'Did you know you can guess the size of a lad's dick by what condom he uses?' He couldn't wait to flop that bad boy out," she giggles, throwing the foiled wrapper onto the table.

"How did he measure up?" Stace laughs.

"Thinks he's big but it's all talk."

Joining in the laughter, I feel a stitch begin to ache in my side from all the laughing we've done tonight.

"I'm going to do Kennedy and Stace together. Stace, you have ten minutes to collect a man's pair of boxers. Kennedy, you have to collect a girl's bra."

"No way. How am I supposed to do that?" Kennedy screeches, throwing her head back.

"Flirt?" Nay answers grinning.

"I can do this, easy." Stace's voice is firm and challenging when she looks at Kennedy. Kennedy, rising to the bait, stands up with a determined look on her face.

"So can I."

"First one back wins?" Stace grins.

"Deal," Kennedy agrees.

In a flash both girls have rushed from the roped up area and disappeared into the roaring crowd that are partying hard.

"Hey, Harlow, the boss man wanted you downstairs in the next ten minutes. Is that okay still?" the doorman standing near the tables asks, pressing an ear piece closer to his ear.

"Yeah. We'll wait until the other two girls we're with come back and then we'll head down."

"You'll have to take the back stairs," he tells her, nodding to the exit.

Harlow nods her head, okay with the plan. I sigh with relief when I realise I've gotten out of doing a dare. I don't think I'd have the courage or the attitude to get someone to give me their boxers or bra.

"Don't look relieved. You're next, Lake. I'll read the dare before we head down. Yours will be harder cause there's less people in V.I.P."

"Fantastic," I answer dryly.

"This night is so freaking awesome," Kayla sings, throwing her hands up to the music. I nod, agreeing and begin wiggling my hips in my seat, loving the music they're playing.

Kennedy jumps out of nowhere, swinging a bra around her head. "Whoohooo. I won! I fudging won. Whooohooo," she cries laughing.

"How did you manage that?" we all ask shocked.

"You didn't give us rules. I found someone I knew and told her what was going on. Her mate, Emily, happily gave me her bra. Said it was doing her head in anyway," she cheers laughing.

"There were no rules," Harlow laughs, throwing the bra on the table after Kennedy throws it at her.

Next thing I know, Stace jumps up behind Kennedy. "Noooo! I lost! How long have you been here?" she whines, grinning.

"About a minute or two," Kennedy laughs, fist pumping the air.

"You're joking?" Stace giggles. "I promised the doorman a blowjob later if he lent me his boxers. Remind me to give them him back later," she winks.

"You didn't?" Denny gasps.

"Of course I fucking did. Did you see him? I'm still dreaming of my mouth around his..."

"That's enough visual right there," Harlow interrupts laughing. "We've got to head downstairs. It's getting busier up here. Lake, your dare is to give the bride-to-be a lap dance."

"How fitting," Kennedy laughs.

"This is awesome," Kayla giggles, slapping my arm playfully.

"Bring it on," is what comes out of my mouth and I'm shocked. I've never been so bold before.

"Hit me with your best moves, baby," Denny hollers and I start to giggle.

"Come on, let's go."

We all follow Harlow and Denny down some darkened stairs. She said this was to prevent us having to walk back through the crowd to reach the front entrance. These stairs are for the staff to use or something. It also has another corridor for when a fire occurs.

We walk into V.I.P and it's nothing like anything I had pictured a strip club to be like. There aren't any seedy men drooling all over plastic enhanced women, and there isn't smoke choking the air in the room.

I guess it's true what they say. Never believe everything you see on the television. The place is a pretty classy establishment, especially since it's run by two young males.

The room is painted a dark red with black woodwork. The bar itself is also black with what looks to be twinkle lights built inside it. Behind the bar it's lit up enough for the bartenders to see but still enough to keep the sexy, raw, romantic atmosphere to the room.

The stage is red, and again, the outer wooden edge is painted black. A pole sits at the end of the rectangular stage that leads off from a half-moon shaped stage. There's two smaller half moon shaped stages positioned on either side of the main stage, both also with a light up pole fixed to it.

Tables and booths scatter the floor in no particular setting and as we're lead to what will be our seats for the night, I notice only a few patrons sitting around.

"It's quiet," I whisper yell as we take our seats. The girls all giggle but take notice of everything around us, just like I am.

"The next show is at one. I heard Maverick mention having the performances on late tonight because of us coming. He wasn't sure if we would end up here before now so he made sure to only let the regulars in," Harlow tells us.

"This place is the shit. Do you think they'll mind if we test out the, uh, the equipment?" Stace grins, winking at Harlow.

"Yeah," Harlow laughs in return. "I told Maverick he was being stupid warning me to keep everyone off the stage. Now I can see why he did."

"Party pooper," Stace pouts playfully.

"I'm pretty sure you owe someone a dance," Harlow grins, tapping her chin with her index finger.

"I need a drink first," I laugh, looking around for the bar. I move to stand up but Harlow stops me. She waves her hand to someone standing near the bar. A woman clad in a short, revealing top, similar to ours, prowls over. Her mini skirt just covers her womanly parts and I have to give it to the woman, she's rocking her outfit. She doesn't look slutty but she doesn't look classy either.

"Hey ladies, what can I get ya?" she asks smiling. Well, if she's shocked a group of women are here in a strip club to party, she doesn't show it. In fact, she doesn't even blink.

Harlow orders another round of drinks, making sure to order herself a pop. The music turns up a little louder and we have to shout to be heard.

Just as the drinks arrive a song comes on that everyone loves and we all get up and start dancing. None of us care that there isn't a dance floor and that the men in the room could be watching us. We just shake our hips, our drinks in hand, and dance to the beat.

I'm so lost with dancing I don't notice the song has changed or that Harlow has dragged a chair to where we've all formed our little circle. Nay, Stace and Harlow all throw their shoes in the middle.

The girls begin to clap when Denny sits down, laughing her head off in the chair, her hair flying forward when she tries to cover her face in embarrassment.

"I'm the one giving you the lap dance," I laugh. "Why are you embarrassed?"

With the alcohol in my system it gives me a confidence boost. I don't even care if I look like a fool, or that there are professional dancers just behind the black and red curtain.

Seductively, I move forward, swinging my hips from side to side as I make my way towards Denny in the chair. The girls are all laughing and I fight hard to try and keep my expression neutral. But it's hard to when you're giving one of your friends that you've not known long enough a lap dance. Even so, I can't deny I'm having fun and the look on Denny's face is priceless.

Laughing, I put my hands on the back of Denny's chair and grind my hips into her. We're both laughing hysterically. My nerves are shot by the alcohol so I boldly wiggle my hips down in front of Denny. Both my hands reach out to her bare thighs and with only a few stumbles I wiggle my hips back up, flicking my hair in her face as I do.

The song changes to Christina Aguilera's, Dirty, the beat faster than the song before and it spurs me on. Turning so my back is to Denny, I bend over so my ass is in her face, wiggling from side to side as seductively as I can in my state. Running my hands up my body, I close my eyes, letting the music seep into my bones. My hands move into my hair as my ass wiggles down into Denny's lap.

The hairs on the back of my neck rise and a tingle shoots up my spine, suddenly aware someone is watching me.

And not just anybody. My body only ever reacts like this for one person.

When my eyes open, they reach *his* straight away and my body tightens. I've never seen a look so raw, so primal before. He almost looks like he's turning blue from holding his breath but it could just be the lighting in the club.

Max's eyes look almost black, dilated to the point of no return. My body lights up like it's aware of Max and is beckoning for him to come to me.

My body seductively moves back up, my fingers running through my hair, but my eyes stay fixed on Max's, feeling like I'm only dancing for him now. It's like I'm in a complete trance. Even my heart is pounding harder than it was before.

I watch, transfixed on Max, as something snaps behind his eyes. A shiver runs up my spine, heating my whole body.

My head is screaming at me to step back, to stop goading him, but instead of listening to my inner warning I stand frozen, waiting for him to make his move.

Then suddenly he does and all bets are off.

Something tells me I won't be able to handle the Max I'm finally about to meet.

EIGHTEEN

MAX

THE WALK TO SNOOPS IS TAKING us forever. Thankfully, the walk has sobered Adam up a bit. The rest of us, however, are pissed as fuck, staggering along the pavement.

"I'm surprised Max hasn't brought his own music along with him," Mason grunts, smirking.

"Fuck off, dickhead."

"Why would he bring his own music?" Lee asks amused.

"No reason," I snap, not wanting to get into this. The way they've picked on me tonight you'd think it was my fucking stag do.

"He's not into the whole RnB shit. He's more into Disney, Taylor Swift and all that bollox," Mason laughs, punching my arm playfully.

"Seriously? Assault," I warn, my eyes snapping to my arm. He just chuckles, ignoring my pain.

"No way?" Lee and Adam laugh.

"Hysterical," I snap dryly. "Oh, look, Snoops."

"Sing the way for us," Lee adds.

"Nope."

"Come on," Maverick urges, grinning at me like a drunken fool.

"Can we go drink like men, please," I tell them. "I'm beginning to wonder why we're even out. If you all wanted a pamper party I'm sure the girls would have loved to have organised you one."

"Aww, come on, bro, show us what you're made of," Myles teases.

"Sugar and spice and all things nice," I wink.

"Spoil sport," Mason laughs.

"Don't forget you've still got one task to complete before we can meet up with the girls," I add, making Mason lose the grin.

"Fuck!"

I laugh, giving him a punch in the same place he gave me mine. It's Malik's task next. This fucker had help from Harlow, though. She let it slip one night when she told us she already knew what Malik had planned 'cause she helped plan it. We all let him have it, though, all of us ripping him a new asshole. None of us consulted with outsiders or the hen party so it felt like he let the team down when he went running to his girlfriend.

"Hit me," Mason says, motioning his hands towards himself.

Punching him in the arm again, I get a grunt of pain from him. I grin; pleased with myself.

"What the fuck was that for?" he shouts as we stand outside Snoops.

"You told me to hit you," I tell him slowly, wondering if I hit him too hard the first time. I roll my eyes at him and move away slowly.

"I meant hit me with the next task, asshole," he growls, raising his fist.

"I've got ChildLine's number on speed dial," I shout, moving away quickly. The guys laugh, shaking their heads, but Mason just rolls his eyes before turning to Malik.

"Come on then. What bright idea did you come up with?"

"Now, don't go giving him the credit," I start, but a slap around the head from Maverick shuts me up. "Shit. I'm seriously hoping ChildLine is twenty-four hour," I groan, rubbing my sore head.

"Basically, when I shout 'selfie' you have to take a selfie with the person to your right. Doesn't matter who is there. You have to do it," Malik grunts, smirking.

"Seriously?" Mason laughs. "That's not as bad as the 'ant' game."

We all look away, not bothering to tell him Malik plans to shout 'selfie' at the worst possible time. There isn't a queue outside Snoops. There rarely ever is, but with the limited clubs in town, we had no choice.

Walking up to the doors, a large doorman stands with his arms crossed across his chest, looking intimidating while talking to some bloke in a suit. He's around six foot five, has muscles that out rank any wrestler I've ever known about, and has hands the size of my head.

I take a deep swallow before making sure I'm the furthest away from the beast. The rest don't seem to be fazed, but then I notice everyone is hanging back a little. I know why when I hear Malik shout, "Selfie," at the top of his voice.

"Fuck no," I hear Mason groan and I laugh. He pulls his phone out of his pocket and, unbeknown to the doorman, Mason walks right up to him and stands up on his tip toes before snapping a picture. The doorman notices the flash and looks to Mason with an angry glare.

"What the fuck?" The doorman grumbles looking pissed.

"Mason, it's good to see you," the bloke wearing a suit greets, laughing. "Oh, it's the stag party tonight. Tim did warn me."

"Yeah," Mason laughs. "Sorry, mate. These fuckheads have me doing shit," Mason explains and the doorman nods his head in understanding but still doesn't look too happy about having a selfie taken with Mason.

A laugh rumbles up from inside me and everyone's attention turns to me. "Don't mind me. Just remembering this movie I watched last night," I lie.

"What? Tinkerbell?" Mason laughs.

"Fuck off."

"So, what have you troublesome lot been up to?" the suit guy asks.

"Well, first I looked like a homeless prostitute looking for some cheap lovin'. Then we played 'ants' which is the cause of the dirt on the back of my tee and trousers," Mason laughs.

"Sounds fun," suit guy laughs. "I'll let you guys get back to it. Have fun. Oh, and here, first round is on me," the suit says, handing some cards to Mason.

"Cheers, Chris." Mason pockets them and shakes Chris' hand.

The club is actually pretty busy for Snoops. One of the reasons we put Snoops down was because it rarely got busy and we knew Malik wouldn't last long until he wanted to be with his baby momma. They must have some promotion on tonight to have brought in this many people. Looking around the club I notice a bunch of hot girls dancing on the stage to my right. My eyes only linger long enough to see that they're hot. They're just not hotter than Lake. Especially since I've got the image of her wearing that barely there outfit.

I don't think I'll ever manage to erase that image from my mind, but just in case, I'm glad I have it saved to my phone. May as well save it under spank bank.

Grabbing another round of drinks we stand around near the bar talking shit and having a laugh.

More drinks are poured and more shots are taken. Girls have tried to come up and chat with us but, apart from Lee, no one has engaged in any of their conversations. Adam, the poor lad, tried a time or two but ended up with a drink in his face. It was probably the closest to a reaction he's got from a girl.

Maverick, who I thought would jump at the chance to get laid, has even sent girls away. He looked at them with boredom and disinterest. It makes me wonder if my eldest brother is gay. It would explain why he's always single, that's for sure.

"What you staring at?" Maverick asks, looking at me strangely.

"Sorry, just thinking about boys," I tell him happily.

"What?" he asks, his drink spraying from his mouth.

I roll my narrowed eyes, wiping the drink from my face.

"Thanks," I say dryly.

"Sorry," he shrugs, not looking remorseful.

"Anyway, as I was saying. I just think it's a good thing when lads can reveal their true feelings to one another."

"I think you've had one too many," Maverick responds, looking at me like I've grown two heads.

"Nah, bro. I just want you to know that I understand. I don't mind. Women can be a huge hassle. You get in there, bro. I know a few lads that might be interested. Ash tried setting me up with a few."

"Max?"

"Yeah?"

"Lay off the fucking drink. You're talking shit," is all Maverick says before turning back to the group. I grin thinking I've helped. I should become a councillor like Kayla. I'd be good at getting people to open up about their true feelings, guessing what they really want for life.

When 'selfie' is shouted, I react out of instinct. My phone is already in my hand and I end up grinning, open-mouthed, holding my thumb up and snapping a picture.

When I'm done I look back to the group and notice them all staring at me with amused expressions.

"What?" I ask, holding my hands up.

"You do know Mason is the one to do the selfie?" Malik asks, laughing.

"Yeah," I lie. "I just wanted to post a picture on Facebook," I shrug.

"Okayyy," Malik says slowly.

I shrug then turn to Mason. "You do your selfie?"

"Yeah," he grins.

"Then we're good," I grin back and bob my head to the music.

"This is meant to be a lads night out and you guys are moping around thinking about your girls," Lee comments.

"Or men," I add for Maverick's benefit. All eyes land on me but I shrug. I'm a loyal brother. When Maverick's ready, he'll let us know he's into dick.

"I'm starting to worry about you," Maverick shouts and everyone nods in agreement.

"I'm just saying. It's okay to like boys, ya know?"

"Yeah, but I thought you were straight as a ruler?" Maverick asks, mimicking the very thing I said to them when Ash tried to set me up.

"I am. But maybe some people aren't," I answer, widening my eyes a little so he knows I'm talking about him.

"What?" Maverick shouts, holding his hands up. The others are talking amongst themselves about the girls and what they're up to. Don't blame them. I can't wait to meet up with them either. Okay, I can't wait to meet up with Lake and see her outfit with hands-on experience.

"They'll understand," I whisper yell, leaning in closer.

"Understand what?" he yells back. His pissed off face fills with anger and frustration. There are two ways I could go about this. Argue it out until he owns up, or, I could call him right out on it and ask him.

"I know," I tell him, wiggling my eyebrows.

"Give me strength, Max. What the fuck do you know?"

"Seriously, calm down. I'm just saying I know why you don't date girls," I shrug, opening the conversation up for him.

"And why is that, Max?" he bites out. Jesus, he seems to be getting more pissed by the second. He really is that deep in the closet; he's forgotten why he's in there.

If I just give him a little push...

"Because you're into men," I smile, making sure he knows I'm okay with it. I don't understand the pleasure in it. Not that I've tried it. But a girl only tried to put her finger there once and I nearly cried like a baby.

"Max. Get the fuck out of my face," he bites out, moving away.

"What's up?" Mason asks, noticing the tension coming from Maverick.

"Nothing," Maverick sighs. Looking back at me he shakes his head, exasperated, like he doesn't know what to do with me. He looks at me like this a lot.

"It's not nothing," I trail off smugly. It feels great finally knowing something before the others. I'm usually the last one to find out.

"What the fuck are you talking about now?" Myles grins.

"He thinks I'm gay because I don't date," Maverick laughs. His eyes are still hard but clearly he's playing it off amused.

"You think he's gay... because he doesn't date?" Mason laughs. "He doesn't date because..."

"Because I have to look after your dumb ass," Maverick butts in.

"I'm confused. Are you telling the truth or are you still hiding in the closet? You should know that none of us would care."

"I'm not fucking gay," Maverick sighs and then punches me in the arm. "Now come on, this place is shit. And you've ruined the fucking mood."

"Sorry, I just thought..."

"You thought with that brain of yours. I know. But I'm not fucking gay, okay?" he says sternly, his eyes narrowing on mine. Looking, I can see he's telling me the truth.

Well, shit!

That's awkward.

"Okay. Well, let's get these pussies to their girls," I say, rolling my eyes.

"Like you're not excited to see Lake," he laughs, pushing me forward.

I manage to finish my drink before we reach the entrance. Mason, however, is stopped short when Malik shouts, 'Selfie,' laughing his head off.

Turning on the stairs at the entrance, I look over to Mason's right and burst out laughing. I'm literally doubled over on the stairs. The people that are walking past me look at me curiously and I wave them off; clutching my stomach.

On Mason's right is a sweaty, older and larger woman, dancing. Usually, I'm all for a bit of weight on a girl. It doesn't bother me. But this woman has taken her weight to a new extreme. She's obviously not looking after herself and the full pint of beer in her hand is just another indication that she doesn't. She could probably out-drink most men.

She's wearing a black tank top, her humongous breasts spilling over the top. Paired with that she's wearing what I think are leggings, but I'm not sure, she could have just painted her legs black. You can see everything, and I mean *everything*.

You know the saying, 'I look like a beached whale? I'm pretty sure if you Google imaged that, her face would be plastered all over the screen.

Don't get me wrong, I know I sound like a complete wanker, but I call 'um as I see 'um.

Mason hesitantly walks over with his phone clutched tightly in his hand. His face is one of horror and I can't help but laugh harder. He looks scared as fuck.

He steps beside the woman who's dancing and gets knocked out of the way from her jiggling her hips. He flies across the room, stumbling into a few people before looking to us for some sort of help.

Malik shakes his head 'no,' pointing his finger back over to the woman. I can only laugh harder. I'm pretty close to pissing myself. Malik isn't going to let him sit this one out. He proves that when he gives Mason a gentle nudge.

"First... Let me take a selfie," I shout, using a girlie voice and swinging my head to the side whilst pouting. A group of girls walking out of the club, giggle, eyeing me up and down with appreciation. "Sorry, ladies, I'm spoken for," I half lie. I am spoken for. It's just Lake who doesn't know it's because of her. This relationship bullshit is a new thing for me. But with Lake I'll try. Frankly, if I can get her to agree to go out with me then it will be a damn fucking miracle.

My eyes flicker to Mason again to check his progress and they go wide when I see the woman has him in some sort of headlock.

"Man down, man down," I shout at the top of my voice. Jumping down the last few steps I land next to Maverick and Myles.

"No, no, leave him," Myles wheezes, holding his phone up: recording.

"I don't think he can breathe," I tell them, kind of worried about my big brother. Okay, I'm not worried. This is funny as fuck and I end up taking out my own phone to record the disaster happening before my very eyes.

The woman has her hand around Mason's neck, his face swallowed up in her ample cleavage. His arms are flapping around everywhere, gaining attention from other dancers. The woman keeps him in line, though, dragging him with her as she dances.

"One of us should save him," Lee flinches. When the woman's hold on

Mason tightens, even I have to admit I'm feeling kinda sorry for him. The woman looks sweaty. Her wet hair is stuck to her head and her body is glistening under the club lights.

Classy!

All of a sudden, Mason escapes unscathed, but from the look on his face, a lot of therapy is going to be needed. He looks like he's just survived *The Hunger Games* but is still reeling from the after effects.

"You doing okay there, bro?" I ask.

"Get me out of here before she comes back with drinks," he whisper yells, his voice hoarse. He hasn't blinked or looked at any of us and I'm beginning to wonder if more happened to him than what we witnessed. I look behind him into the crowd and laugh when I see her holding two beers in her hand. She's dancing towards us with a huge grin on her face.

"Love-Bandit, come to mama," I hear shouted and Mason looks at us with wide, horrified eyes.

"Go! Go! Run! Evacuate the building," Mason shouts. He's running up the stairs before any of us manage to take a breath. When he's gone from sight we all look back to the woman. She's still heading our way with a determined look in her eyes. I think quickly, not wanting her to swallow all this hunky goodness up in one gulp. I push Myles in front of me in the line of fire before turning and following Mason as fast as my legs will take me. I'm out the door before the others have time to catch on, but it's only seconds before I hear their footfalls behind me.

I'm not sure how long we run for but by the time we stop we're in the town centre, not far from MC5.

"I cannot believe you would deliberately push me in front of her line of sight," Myles growls.

"Payback's a bitch," I wink.

He growls. "She would have eaten me for dinner, or worse, made me her bitch."

I laugh as I picture Myles becoming her bitch, my chest hurting with exertion. Everyone's silent for a few seconds, trying to catch their breaths when Mason interrupts.

"I'm never going to forgive you," Mason growls. He's bent over, his hands on his knees trying to catch his breath. It's pretty hilarious to be honest.

"She seemed…nice," Malik chuckles, his dimples on full display.

"Nice?" Mason shouts. "I can still taste her fucking skin in my mouth."

"Um. Why were you eating her?" I ask hesitantly.

Mason's head snaps to mine, a growl rumbling from his chest. "I was in the middle of asking her for a photo when she grabbed my head. I was swallowed up, open mouthed and she was *sweating*. At first I thought it was spilt beer but then I managed to get my mouth closed," he tells us, and closes his eyes like he's trying to block out the horror he just suffered. "I don't want to talk about this, ever again."

"Let's go see if the girls are having a better time than us," Myles laughs. We all agree and follow his lead, crossing the road and heading towards the club.

"How you doing, Adam? You feeling queasy still?" I ask, a smirk on my face. He's not as drunk as he was before but he's also not sober. He still has no idea he has permanent marker scrawled across his forehead and a bad drawing of a moustache.

We'll wait for him to find it himself before giving him shit about it.

"Yeah, I'm good. Happy. I can drink all you fuckers under the table," he slurs, holding his hands up in triumph.

"That's where you've been most the night," I snigger teasingly.

He looks confused at what I said, which just makes me laugh at him.

"Hey, Josh. The girls downstairs?" Mason asks the doorman when we walk up to the main entrance of V.I.P.

"Yeah, I think Todd is taking them down now," Josh tells us. He speaks into his mic before listening to what someone is saying on the other side. "He's just left them down there. There are four doorman on downstairs until one but then me, Todd and Jerry will be down at around two."

"Good, good."

"You look a little pale, boss. Are you okay?" Josh asks Mason and we all snicker in response.

"Don't ask. I'm hoping I wake up and not remember this night. At all."

"That bad?" Josh laughs. "Well, enjoy it, boss. It seems your girl and her friends have been having fun themselves. I'm still waiting for my boxers back."

"Boxers?" I ask wide-eyed.

I notice Myles, Malik and Mason all clench their fists, and decide it's something I should be doing too. I mirror their stances, wondering why they're all on high alert, but then Josh's next words clue me in.

"Don't worry. It's a tall beauty with purple hair that has 'um. Think they called her, Stace. Not sure," Josh nods and my brothers instantly relax, so I do the same.

See. I can do this boyfriend shit.

Now I just need to prove to Lake that I can. If I can get her to see I'm taking this seriously then maybe she'll finally go out with me.

Fuck! I sound like a fifteen year old boy.

"I don't even want to know," Mason laughs. "I'm gonna go sneak up on them. See what they're up to."

Passing Josh, he gives all my brothers a fist pump but when he gets to me I quickly duck down, making him punch Adam, who's currently wobbling behind me, in the face. I turn whilst laughing my head off.

Adam looks confused for a second before realising what just happened. "What the fuck, Josh?"

"Sorry, Adam," Josh winces, sending me an angry glare.

"Fuck! That hurt," Adam curses, rubbing his jaw.

"Thought you were tough?" I tease, feeling Josh's pissed off gaze on my back.

"He's got huge fucking knuckles, did you see?" Adam mumbles.

"I didn't. You seemed to have gotten a closer look, though," I laugh.

When we arrive at the main entrance, Maverick is standing to the side talking to another doorman so I use the chance to sneak up to the front. When I walk into the room I'm caught off guard at what I see.

When I was told we'd end up in a strip club my first thought had been tits. Then I found out the girls would be here and then I just thought how awkward tonight would be. But then this...

I blink making sure my eyes aren't deceiving me. When nothing changes, I scrub at them hard, wondering if I'm hallucinating.

Nope. Definitely not hallucinating. Denny is sitting down in a red chair and is currently getting worked over by Lake.

If that wasn't bad enough, Lake's long assed legs in those tiny shorts killed it.

Fuck! Her body is a work of art. Beautifully sculpted to perfection. Her wild hair flies back, showcasing the curve of her neck to the V line of her cleavage perfectly.

I gulp, picturing her in that same position but with me in Denny's place. Oh, and both of us naked.

I'm completely frozen to the spot. I can't move my eyes away from the way her body sensually moves to the music. How seductive she looks running her hands up her body, tangling her fingers into her wild mess of hair.

I take a deep swallow.

My jeans feel tight against my groin, the pain welcome as I try to think of what to do. But then her eyes reach mine and all thoughts, but her, are gone.

My feet move. One after the other and before I know it I'm standing in front of her. Not wasting any time I grab her thighs; her legs automatically wrap around my waist and I move, heading towards the hallway in the direction of Maverick's office.

Neither of us speak; me because I'm too lost in the feel of her tight body wrapped around mine to even conjure up a single word.

But as soon as I kick the door to Maverick's thankfully empty office, I'm on her, not holding back.

It's time for Lake to see the real Max Carter. I'm not holding back any more. This girl is mine and I'm about to show her exactly what being mine really means.

NINETEEN

LAKE

Holy smokes!

I've never seen this primal look in Max's eyes before. He looks like he's about to tear into me. Rip me apart and put me back together again. The sight is so erotic I can barely breathe.

The feel of his large calloused hands on the bare skin of my ass sends a new kind of shiver through my body. My nipples are hard; aching so badly like they're pleading to be touched. The wetness between my legs is unmistakeable. I'll be surprised if I don't already have a wet patch showing on my skimpy shorts.

The door to the room Max has carried me into slams shut. The sound causes a jolt of desire to run through my body. Then he turns and before I know it my back is slammed against the door and his lips are on mine. They're hard and aggressive and I find myself fighting against him for more.

I've never been like this with anyone. Never felt this need; this raw, passionate need. It feels like I can't get him close enough; that my body can't get him close enough. Everything inside me is screaming at him to touch me. To touch me and make me feel things no other has ever made me feel. I want to scream at the top of my lungs that it feels so good and beg him to never stop. The tingles in my lower stomach magnify.

The kiss turns aggressive. My hips rock involuntarily, my sex aching at the emptiness. He feels so good and boy can he kiss. Fuck, can he kiss.

Everything after that becomes a blur. Our hands and mouths are a tangled mess as we ravage each other's bodies. A wave of pleasure sweeps me away, freeing my head of all darkness and taking me to a place where only Max exists.

Before I can open my mouth to beg him for more, we're on the move again. He sweeps my body up like I weigh nothing at all and carries me over to the desk where a single dull lamp is shining. I don't get to see much of anything else because my ass is being planted on the desk and Max's lips are back on mine. He rubs his hardness against my sex causing me to cry out. I feel like I'm going to combust. My sex is clenching so badly it hurts.

"Fuck, you feel so fucking good," he rasps against my mouth. His breath is a mixture of mint and Red Bull, but mostly Max, and I moan into his mouth.

In hurried, jerky movements he has my skimpy shirt up over my head so I'm left wearing my lacy bra that leaves nothing to the imagination. You can literally see my nipples through the thin fabric and I know the moment Max notices. His eyes turn molten and a groan erupts from his mouth. I move back on my elbows on the table, my behaviour bold and nothing like me at all.

His eyes narrow, looking pained. He rips his shirt off like the Incredible Hulk, throwing it behind him aggressively.

"I need you," is all I hear him say before his mouth is slamming against mine. I'm not sure how to respond next. I need *him* to make the next move. I'd beg him but I'm so lost in him that he's left me completely speechless.

I bite his lip, teasing him. I'm enjoying the fact that it's me bringing this reaction out of him, that he's feeling everything that I am.

My hands grab onto the back of his head, pulling him down to kiss me again. When he moves suddenly, I grab onto his flexed biceps.

My pulse races when one of his hands snake up my body. His rough fingertips skim across the swells of my breasts. Then I lose his mouth at my neck when he moves down, kissing between my breasts before lightly moving his hands around my back, unclasping my bra.

A moan escapes and I'm desperate for him. Just like he's desperate for me. I can feel just how much against my leg.

Everything seems to be moving quickly. The second the cool air hits my hot nipples, Max moves down my body trailing wet, open kisses until he reaches the top of my shorts. Then they're being ripped down my legs with urgency and it has me catching a breath.

"Oh, God," I moan when I feel cool air hit my heated sex, my core tightening.

Max rises up; a cheeky grin plastered on his face. "Now's not the time to be calling me some other fucker's name."

A laugh slips out but soon turns into a moan when I feel his fingers running through my wet slit.

"I want to savour this moment but I need you. I can't wait any fuckin' longer."

My eyes close and my pulse races when I hear the belt to his jeans unclasp and then his jeans fall to the floor in a heap. I'm lying bare, vulnerable and naked on the table. Anyone could walk in at any second but I don't care. The thrill of being caught just heightens my need for him.

The distinct sound of foil crinkling has my eyes opening. It's going to happen. Right here, right now. The first wave of nervousness seeps through but when I look down, getting a glimpse of him rolling the condom along his long, thick shaft, it all disappears.

My mind has no time to think. As soon as he has the condom rolled on, he's inside me; in one long, hard stroke, he's inside me and I'm suddenly full. The feel of him stretching me has my inner walls clamping tightly down on his erection.

We both release a desperate sound, both of us overwhelmed by the sensations coursing through our bodies.

His breath is heavy against mine and I'm afraid I've done something wrong when he doesn't move, but then his eyes flicker up to mine.

"I'm going to fuck you so hard. You're never going to want anyone else but me," he rasps out, his voice trembling with certainty and need.

"Please," I shamelessly beg him.

The words barely leave my mouth when he pulls out; slamming back in, his head flying back and releasing a loud growl. My body arches off the table and I find my fingers gripping onto the back of his head, just as his mouth reaches down to take one of my hard, ready nipples into his mouth.

The pressure between my legs is building with each hard thrust and it's becoming unbearable. I can't take it. My hands fly out, trying to grip the edge of the table, but my hand hits something else. The small lamp falls from the table, along with some other things. The room dims a little and a raspy chuckle escapes

Max, but it doesn't stop him.

He lifts himself up, his movements quickening as he looks down at me. I feel like I'm on display and I have a fleeting moment where I feel self-conscious. But then his expression changes to pure desire. His hands slide up my body, covering my large breasts. His thumbs sweep over my nipples and my core tightens further. I'm close. So fucking close. This has never happened before.

"Yes," I moan, the sound echoing around the room.

"Fuck, yes," Max grunts and then a sharp pinch to my nipples is what sends me over the edge. I'm screaming my release; my body reacting like it's got a mind of its own. My back bows off the desk, my toes curl together tightly and I swear to all that is holy that I see stars.

"Max."

"I'm coming," Max roars. His thrusts become jagged and with one last deep, hard thrust, he's coming. And God, it's a sight to see. His beautiful, hard chiselled face locks up, his eyes closing from the pleasure overwhelming his body.

His abs tighten, each muscle flexing and I can't help the sudden rush of desire already heating my body back up.

Max drops his head to my chest, both our breathing laboured as we try to come down from our high.

Everywhere is still tingling, my sex still sensitive and I cry out when he shifts, the aftershocks too delicious to ignore.

"I'm never letting you go," Max whispers. Then his eyes harden when a banging causes the room to rattle.

"Bro, come on. Gavin made his specialty," Maverick shouts through the door and a hot flush of embarrassment hits me.

"Oh my God," I cry out, pushing Max away. I moan when his large dick slips free from my sex.

"Wanker," Max calls back, and is left with a deep chuckle echoing down the hall as Maverick leaves.

"Do you think he heard?" I ask, embarrassed.

"I'm pretty sure the entire club upstairs heard us," he winks and I punch his arm as I grab my bra from the desk.

"I can't believe we did that," I tell him, finally feeling shocked at our actions.

"What? Don't tell me you regret it," he says, sounding clearly upset.

"What? Of course not. I'm just... I'm embarrassed. Now, where did you throw my knickers?"

"They're still in your shorts. Which brings me to this; how have none of you been arrested for indecent exposure?"

I laugh, I already expected him to ask something like that. I'd mentioned it at the beginning of the night to the girls.

"No," I tease, then pause, looking at him. "Why the hell are you blue?" My God. I thought it was the lighting in the club, but no, Max is definitely changing colour. Either that or my eyesight is playing tricks on me.

"Oh... Yeah... Nothing contagious," he grins.

Fully dressed, I run my fingers through my hair with my back turned to Max. I hear his raspy chuckle and the hair on the back on my neck stands on edge.

"Bride's bitch, huh?"

"Yep," I laugh, looking at him over my shoulder.

"Hmmm," he murmurs after a beat. Then I feel him step forward, his front a breath away from my back. His fingers reach up, sweeping my thick, wavy hair to the side, sending a wave of shivers down my spine.

He steps back and I miss his body heat. When he begins to mysteriously run something across my back, I frown.

"What are you doing?" I ask, trying to turn around. His hand on my hip stops me from turning around.

"Stay still," he rasps. Then moves his other hand to finish what he was doing. "All done."

Turning, he's wearing an amused smirk which has me worried. In fact, I'm always on high alert when it comes to Max.

"What did you do?" I ask him, looking around the room for a mirror.

When I don't find one, I look for anything that will get a reflection but see nothing. I sigh, and give him a pointed look to tell me. Grinning, he shrugs and holds his hand out for me to take.

Forgetting all about the t-shirt, I grab his hand grinning, nearly tripping over my own feet in the process. I giggle catching my balance. We walk to the door but instead of opening it like I thought he would, Max turns to me, pulling me into his arms.

"I meant what I said. I'm never letting you go. So you're going to have to go out with me," he smirks, leaning down to kiss the tip of my nose. The gesture is both sweet and cute.

"We'll see," I tease, rolling my eyes. Shaking his head at me he gives me his trademark smirk, his dimples causing me to release a dreamy sigh.

When we reach the others, everyone's eyes are on me and Max. My face must redden because Stace and Nay start giggling.

"I'll take that twenty now," Maverick smirks at Lee.

The Lee guy, who I've not met, glowers at Maverick. "You cheated. You banged on the fucking door."

"They were already finished. Right, Max?"

That's when my brain catches up with me and I realise they're talking about me and Max doing it. Knowing Max wouldn't reveal such personal information, I relax.

"We finished a second before," Max offers, sitting down.

My head snaps to him and I give him a glare. "Max!" I yell, not believing he just said that.

"What?" he asks astonished. "Honesty is the best policy."

"Yeah, if you've cheated, lied or stolen. Not about this," I screech. The girls begin to laugh while I slowly sink myself into the chair next to Max.

A drink is handed to me by Stace. "You look like you need a refreshment," she chuckles.

I narrow my eyes but there's no denying the fact that I'm parched. I gulp the fruity drink down in one go, choking when I pull away.

"What on earth is that?" I wheeze out. Everyone laughs. If I wasn't buzzed before, I sure am now. The alcohol warms my throat all the way down to my stomach and the buzz I already had going begins to intensify.

"Gavin's speciality," Myles chuckles.

Looking around the table I notice Malik and Harlow have disappeared, along with the bride and groom.

"Where are the others?" I ask, my voice sounding a little slurred.

Maybe I shouldn't have drunk that last drink. My head is spinning. Needing my bag, for no reason, I get up, sweeping my hair to the side as I move over to where I was sitting before.

When a round of laughter erupts from behind me, I wonder if I've dressed properly or if I stumbled.

"What?" I ask, feeling wobbly on my feet as I turn back around, giggling when I find my bag. I pick it up and make my way back to the table.

"Max's bitch, huh?" Lee chuckles.

"What? No? Is that what he's telling you?" I shriek. Turning to Max I narrow my eyes and lean in close to him. "What are you telling them? I'm no one's bitch. If anything you're my bitch. Yes. You're my bitch," I state proudly.

"I'm not the one wearing the t-shirt," he grins, leaning in. His lips are a breath away and I groan.

"Get those lips away from me," I grumble, making him chuckle. "And what t-shirt? I don't have a t-shirt."

"The one you're wearing," Kayla giggles.

"Huh?" I ask, looking at her confused.

"It says Max's bitch at the back instead of Bride's bitch," she giggles and I snap my head to Max in fury.

"I cannot believe you," I growl.

"Baby, I call 'um as I see 'um," he winks.

"Fuck, yes! Another twenty quid please, lads," Maverick chuckles proudly, taking another twenty quid from Lee and the other bloke sitting next to him.

Wondering who else ducked out for a quickie, I turn in my seat. That's when I see a blushing Denny and a grinning Mason, who is currently adjusting his junk, walking towards us.

"Bro, something you want to tell us?" Max calls out grinning.

"What?" Mason asks, not bothering to look offended. He sits down next to Kayla, pulling Denny into his lap.

"You're walking funny," Max snickers.

"Well, yeah, some fucker took the office," Mason growls, looking at Max with a pissed off expression.

I giggle, not able to hold it in. I don't even know *why* I'm giggling. The look Mason throws Max's and my way should embarrass me, knowing they all know what we got up to in the office, but it doesn't.

"That still doesn't explain the walking," Max laughs, taking a sip of his drink, looking relaxed.

"That would be because I had to…"

"Don't even finish that sentence," Denny giggles, smacking Mason on the arm.

"Let's just say, outside wasn't as fun as I thought it would be," Mason grunts.

"Why didn't you use the toilets?" Max asks.

"'Cause Adam *was* throwing up in the bloke's and Malik beat me to the girl's toilets," Mason groans.

Everyone laughs and a moment later Malik and Harlow walk around the corner laughing. I've never seen Malik laugh. It's a sight to see that's for sure. He acts so broody all of the time; it's nice to see him look carefree for a change.

"Took you long enough," Max grunts, looking put out by their lack of presence.

"Says the person who couldn't get his girl out of here quick enough," Malik grunts, sitting down. When Malik tries to pull Harlow down on his lap she slaps his hand away, dragging an empty chair closer to him before taking a seat.

"So, what did you boys get up to? Myles won't tell me," Kayla asks, her words slurring slightly, wobbling to her seat.

The boys laugh. "Not a lot."

The comment has me more interested. I can tell by the looks they give each other that *something* happened.

"Come on…" I start, but then a male voice has me pausing.

"Ohhhh, we caught up to you hunk bunches."

I twist around in my chair, smiling when I see a good looking bloke basically skipping towards us. Already I can tell he's gay and the fact he's mentioned catching up to these 'hunk bunches' has me grinning. Did they pick him up or do they know him? That's the million dollar question.

"Kevin," Max shouts, bursting my ear drum. "I knew you missed me," Max grins.

"Oh, you wish," Kevin flirts, his eyes raking over the rest of the group before landing on Mason. He lets out a dramatic sigh. "You break my heart, sugar bunch."

"Sugar bunch?" I whisper to Max, who chuckles.

"He's got a thing for Mason," he answers, not caring who hears.

"Kevin," Mason greets, smiling. "Where's Mark?"

"Left him in bed exhausted," he winks. "Jealous?"

"He should be. He left me still walking," Denny laughs. Mason turns, scowling at her, but I can see amusement lighting up in his eyes.

"Oh, I like her. She's feisty," Kevin tells Mason before approaching Denny. "If I wasn't gay I'd be totally all over you."

"And if you wasn't gay and I wasn't in love, I'd be all over you," Denny winks.

"That's my future wife you're talking to," Mason growls at Kevin, then narrows his eyes at Denny.

"Ohhh, it makes me hard when you talk to me in that rough tone," Kevin flirts and the group laughs.

His attention zones in on the rest of the group. His eyes land on Kayla and he grins. "My, don't you look like a fairy princess?" he gushes.

"Thanks?" she replies, blushing which makes me giggle. My giggle causes his attention to snap to me and my giggle stops short causing me to choke.

"And hair on a stick. My lord, you are beautiful, girl."

"Thanks," I giggle.

"Watch it, I'll start getting jealous," Max teases.

"Why, she your girl?" Kevin asks. He actually looks shocked. Not that I can blame the guy. What stops me is the 'your girl' comment. I'm not sure what I am to Max, I wouldn't put a label on it.

"Yes, but I love the attention you give me," Max winks at Kevin, making the burly man blush.

"And you. My, you are tiny. Malik, stay calm, boy, I mean no offence," Kevin warns Malik when he walks over to Harlow; reaching down to touch her stomach. I notice Malik's body tighten when he does and it's sweet. It's blatantly obvious these guys know Kevin and know he's gay, yet, Malik is still defensive when it comes to Harlow. It's goddamn adorable. "You *are* pregnant. Congratulations, I love babies," he gushes, causing Harlow's face to light up.

"Do you plan to have your own someday?" she asks sweetly.

"I'd be up the duff already if I had the right equipment, sweet cheeks," he smiles, though, it looks sad.

"Want some of Gavin's speciality?" Maverick asks, his words also a slur. It could just be my hearing because a constant buzzing keeps ringing in my ears. Especially now they've turned the music up a notch.

I look around the darkly lit room and gasp when I see a half dressed woman on the stage, dancing.

"Holy crap." I'm amazed that's the only thing that has come out of my mouth. The woman dancing on stage is barely dressed. She's got on some corset, laced knickers and to complete the hooker outfit, she's paired it with thigh-high, leather boots.

"Oh my God, I want to have a go," Denny laughs.

Everyone's attention turns to the stage. We talk, laugh and listen to Kevin as he argues with Maverick about getting some male strippers in. Us girls all agree with him wholeheartedly.

It's not until Myles drunkenly pulls out a slip of paper that everyone stops talking to hear him more clearly. It must be important because Kayla's eyes soften, her eyes watering when she sees what he's holding.

"Is that a copy of *the* list?" Kayla asks Myles.

"Yeah, babe. We can tick some of these bad boys off," he chuckles.

"What list?" Denny asks, leaning over from Mason's lap. She nearly topples over but Mason's grip on her thighs stop her.

I'm pretty sure we're all pretty much as wasted as each other at this point. The only two that seem to be sober is Harlow and Malik. But then, I've seen Malik consume the same amount of alcohol as us.

"Charlie wrote me a bucket list in her letter to me. Things she wanted me to do. Getting drunk was one of them."

"Name one you haven't done?" Harlow asks, smiling softly.

"Tattoo," Kayla grins.

"I want a tattoo. I've always wanted one," Denny gushes.

Drunkenly, Maverick sits up grinning from ear to ear. "Want me to call my mate? He does mine."

"What now?" Denny grins mischievously, looking to Mason for his input.

"Yeah. When do you think I get the chance to have mine done when I'm busy running this place and looking after Max?"

"Myles is sitting right there," Max growls, pouting.

"Yeah, but he doesn't need babysitting."

"Neither do I," Max replies, outraged.

"Max, shut up. Maverick, call him. I want a tattoo," Denny shrieks giddily.

"Babe, I don't think you should get one whilst you're drunk," Mason comments, but he doesn't seem too worried. He's grinning like a mad fool watching Denny's face light up.

"No…" she whines. "It's a great idea. I'm so excited."

Maverick grabs his phone out, pulling it to his ear. After a few minutes of talking to someone he turns back to us and smiles.

"He's coming with a mate of his. He needs the extra cash."

"Oh my God. Whoohooo. Best hen party ever," Nay hoots.

Kennedy and Stace are over near the stage dancing in front of the stripper without a care in the world. Giggling, I get up and rush over to join them. Nay and Kayla are hot on my heels and we start dancing to the music blaring through the speakers.

Sweat is rolling down my body and I'm dying of thirst, but I'm too drunk to care. My head is spinning, or the room is, but it's nothing to how freeing I feel. Nothing seems real. Everything feels and looks light, like it's floating in the air. And when two hands slide around my waist, I know it's Max straight away. I decide to tease him by grinding my ass into his groin and a deep growl vibrates from my neck down my back.

Wrapping my hands around his neck I dance as seductively as I can. We've been trying to get the dancers to teach us some moves but the grumpy doorman kept moving us back. Even when Denny joined us they kept telling us to keep back. You'd think with her connections they'd let us dance on the stage. But noooo...

The hands on my hips push me a way a little before turning me around. Coming face to face with Max I'm hit with the beauty before me. He's so fucking gorgeous it's a crime.

"You having a good time?" he grins, moving his body closer to mine.

"Yes. You?" I ask, my eyes fluttered closed.

"Better now," he rasps, close to my ear. "So, when are we going out on a date?"

I pull away frowning, my body stumbling a little. "You don't want to go out with me," I tell him seriously.

"Why not?" he asks in a teasing tone.

"Because."

"Give me one good reason why we shouldn't," he demands, moving closer so that his mouth is hovering over mine.

For a second I forget what he asked me from having his lips so close, yet, somehow I manage to answer.

"Because I'm a murderer. I murdered my brother," I tell him truthfully. The words are a huge slur and I'm not sure if he made out what I said. I don't get chance to look at his reaction because I'm being pulled away.

"Look at my badass tattoo," Denny gushes and lifts her shirt a little. Underneath her right boob is a heart lock on a chain with the words, *'one love,'* scrolled next to the chain. It's beautiful.

"That's gorgeous," I gush, bubbly. I've never had a tattoo and I honestly believe I'd pass out before the needle even pierced the skin.

"Mason has got one on his ribs too. His is a key on a chain with the word, '*heart,*' written next to it."

"Getting matching tattoos," I tease, rolling my eyes. "Whatever next... Marriage?"

She giggles just as Kayla comes dancing over to us. I haven't seen her in a while since I've been lost in my own mind and dancing.

"Hey," I slur happily, rushing over to her and hugging her. "I love you. You're a good friend."

"I love you too but you're hurting my tattoo," she giggles, swaying slightly.

"You got a tattoo, too?" I sing.

"Yeah," she grins and pulls her top down revealing her collarbone. On it is, '*never a victim, forever a fighter,*' scrolled in beautiful italic writing and birds flying up onto her shoulder. It's truly beautiful and it brings tears to my eyes.

"It's beautiful," I tell her, wishing I had half of her strength.

"Guys, I have the best plan. I just spoke to Jill and..."

"Hold up," I laugh, holding my hand up to stop Denny. "Who's Jill?"

"The dancer," she waves me off. "Anyway, she said if we go around to the side of the curtain over there, that she'll unlock the door for us."

"And why would she do that?" Kayla laughs.

"So we can go on stage," Denny says, giving Kayla a duh look.

"I'm not stripping," Kayla shrieks, but then quietens her voice when she notices people are listening. "I cannot take my clothes off."

I can't believe we're actually talking about this. I just listen. I'm not stripping but I'm up for riding along with them.

"I'm not stripping either," Denny says looking offended. "I'm just going to try on the outfit and walk onto the stage. By then I'm hoping Mason will carry me off the stage and take me home," she giggles.

"What if he doesn't?" I laugh.

"Then he's getting one hell of a show," she giggles then runs off leaving me and Kayla with our mouths hanging open.

Warm hands circle my waist again and I grin. "Miss me?"

"Fuck yeah," he slurs, a slight edge to his voice. "What will it take for you to open up to me?"

"Why?" I flirt, turning around.

"Because I want you. I want you to agree to go on a date with me. What will it take?" Max grins. "I'm even willing to dry hump Mason's leg."

I scrunch my nose up, earning a chuckle from Max, but then an idea forms in my mind.

"I don't think you have the balls to do what I want, though," I play innocently.

"What? I have big balls. Huge balls in fact," he shouts, outraged, and a few customers turn our way smirking. "I do," he tells them offended.

"If you say so," I mutter, looking away, biting my lip to cover the smirk.

"Tell me. What do I need to do?"

He's so eager to please me I feel bad for a second for even thinking of doing what I'm about to do. But knowing Max loves a good prank, I lean up on my tip toes and whisper in his ear.

After that he nods his head, looking far too pleased and eager. He's out of the building before I even have chance to tell him I've changed my mind, but then the spotlights on the stage stop me from going after him.

Kayla comes rushing over to me, nearly making us go ass over tit doing it. "Oh my Lord, she's doing it."

"What is she doing?" Kennedy slurs, her whole body swaying from side to side. She's completely wasted.

"Come on, sexy," I cheer, cupping my hands over my mouth.

Decked out in a small leather crop top, that should really be classed as a bra, and a pair of leather pants and the same hooker boots the stripper had on earlier, Denny starts swinging her hips, walking down the stage to the pole.

I turn in time to see Mason's reaction. He's standing near the bar where the rest of the group are now located. Maverick slaps him on the back looking alarmed. Maverick's lips don't move but when he points over towards Denny, Mason's eyes follow. As soon as he sees Denny who is now swinging her hips down the pole, his jaw goes slack. Before we know it, his feet are moving and he's sweeping Denny off the stage in a fireman's hold.

We're all laughing and cheering them on as he carries her out of the bar.

Maverick walks over with Lee who is sucking face with Nay. "Where's Stace?" I ask in a cheerful voice.

"She left about ten minutes ago with the doorman," Nay winks and I burst out laughing.

"Where's Max?" Maverick asks looking around.

I think for a second. I know I spoke to him not long ago but can't figure out what we talked about. "I don't know," I shrug, frowning.

"He left. I saw him run out of here like they were about to perform Hocus Pocus on the stage," Myles laughs, pulling Kayla to his chest.

Maverick laughs. "Come on. We're all heading back. Harlow's tired. And the bride and groom have left."

"I'm sleepy," I yawn, wobbling on my feet. I knock into some table and chairs on the way out. Maverick sweeps in, chuckling. He picks me up, cradling me in his arms and I yawn, cuddling up to his chest. He doesn't smell like his brother. And I don't feel right in his arms like I do Max's. But I'm too tired and too exhausted to even whine about it. I mumble something but it's lost to my own ears.

I end up falling asleep listening to laughing and talking from those around me.

TWENTY

LAKE

U GH.
What on earth is that noise?
Make it stop. *Please! Just make it stop*, my head screams. The room spins when I blink open one eye, the movement causing a wave of sickness to hit me. Groaning, I close my eyes, willing the room to stop spinning.

The last thing I remember from last night is the dares. I remember dares, lots and lots of dares. After that everything is a huge blur. My brain hurts trying to conjure up a memory. Any memory would do, but the only thing that comes to mind is a dream I must have had last night about Max filling me, his body thrusting inside me with so much force it drove me wild. I've had dreams like this before but none have felt as real as this one.

The noise level downstairs continues to rise, but instead of going down to see what all the drama is about, I throw the pillow over my head to try and block out the noise.

I feel like I'm going to throw up.

That's when I hear angry footsteps marching up the stairs. My ears perk up and when the sound gets closer to my room, I begin to panic. What did I do? Is someone hurt? Did I open my mouth last night? I try everything in my power to remember something I said that would cause someone to stomp up the stairs after having a blow out with someone, but nothing comes to mind.

The room to my door bursts open and I throw the pillow from my head, wincing at the sunlight streaming through the curtains, momentary blinding me.

Max stands in the doorway wearing the tightest pair of trousers I've ever seen on him and an even tighter top that reads, 'Girls gone wild'.

"What the fuck, Max?" I grumble, feeling queasy again. "What the hell are you wearing and why are you so blue?" I gasp. I'd laugh if I didn't feel so sick and pissed he interrupted my pity party. But know, I am laughing deeply on the inside.

"*Live out my wildest fantasy*, she said. *It will be fun*, she said. *I'll make it worth your while*, she said. What she didn't fucking say was that she'd leave me butt naked, freezing my balls off at Hawthorn Farm while she slept snuggled up warm in her bed," he grits out, looking kind of pissed.

"I love Hawthorn Farm," I smile, cheering up. I remember staying there when I first arrived in Coldenshire. The place had so many barns full of animals and hay, that it kept me there out of sheer fascination. The animals had been so friendly. I really loved it there, but it was short lived when the owner found me sleeping in the barn. He didn't get mad like I thought he would, but he did tell me I couldn't sleep there anymore; that I needed to find somewhere else to squat. That's when Antonio found me hunting for food and directed me to Joan and the church.

"I know," he bites out. He opens his mouth but Joan walks in with flushed cheeks and stops him. He turns around, sees her and groans. "Not now, Joan."

"Get out of Lake's room, right now," Joan hisses but her eyes flick to me before narrowing back on Max. "Now look what you've gone and done. You've woken her up."

"If I'm going to get my ass reamed then so is she. This is all her fault," Max cries, aghast.

Me? What did I do? My head ping-pongs to and from the other as they argue, wondering what alternate universe I've woken up in. Have they lost their complete minds? And why am I even involved.

My head is spinning trying to work out what is being said and what my involvement is. But if I'm honest, I'm more curious as to why Max is dressed between looking like a really bad drag queen and a Smurf.

"Because you got arrested. Again!" Joan shouts, throwing her hands up in the air. My ears perk up at that. I didn't catch the first part of the conversation, but at this point, I don't think it matters.

"He was arrested?" I ask shocked. Why, when the first time I met him he was being arrested, I don't know. I guess I thought he had learnt his lesson. I sit up, the dizziness hitting me with force once again.

"What did you think would happen?" he shouts in my direction and I blanch. There he goes again, blaming me. What the hell did I do last night?

"Don't shout at her," Joan yells at him, shutting him up. "You've got no one else to blame but yourself, young man."

"It's her fault," he whines, pointing at me.

"Me?" I yell, wincing at the noise.

"Yeah. You! You told me to go there..." he stops, looking at Joan before groaning. "Can I please have some other clothes? My dick can't take anymore."

"Here," Joan snaps. Clucking her tongue she hands him a pile of clothes and scissors.

What on earth is he going to do with scissors? I grab my wild, tangled hair and scrape it to the side, hoping he doesn't have any ideas.

When he starts cutting the tight top off himself, I giggle. Oh my Lord. Only one snip and the poor, strained material bursts right open. He really is confined and restricted in those clothes.

"Don't," he warns, narrowing his eyes on me.

"Ignore him," Joan says. She clearly dismisses Max when she turns her back to him and it makes me want to giggle again. For such a tiny person she's so full of energy and sass.

"Why was he arrested?" I ask her, hoping I'm not to blame like Max is accusing. That would really suck.

"He was caught jaywalking drunken and disorderly down the Galsby Road from Hawthorn Farm," she tells me, looking back at Max in disappointment. "Now he's trying to blame you for it."

"It was her fault," Max grunts, his voice sounding out of breath.

"He's blamed me?" I ask Joan, ignoring Max completely. "Why would Max jaywalking have anything to do with me? I've been here all night. I *have* been here all night, right? *How* did I get here last night?"

My mind begins to panic at all the various possibilities. Was I with Max? Is that why he's saying this is my fault? I start to feel sick but it's not from all the drink from last night. It's from the fact I don't remember anything about how I got home.

"Maverick, ever the gentlemen, carried you home from the club. Apparently you passed out asleep in his arms." Joan's words soothe me instantly and I feel my shoulders sag with relief. Maverick is one person I'd trust with my life. Something about him draws you to him. Don't get me wrong, he's scary as hell because he's so secretive and broody. But when you look in his eyes you can see the fierce love, and loyalty he has for his brothers and those closest to him.

"What were you doing in his arms?" Max shouts outraged.

"Bless him. Hope I wasn't too much trouble for him," I smile at Joan, hoping I remember to thank him when I next see him.

"Not at all. I've also popped a few painkillers and a glass of water on the side," she says. Her eyes flicker to the bedside table before coming back to me. "I see you haven't taken them."

"I didn't see them," I tell her, looking to the side to see them. I don't waste time grabbing the two pills and downing them. The water feels cool and soothing down my dry throat. I feel like I've got a fur ball of Thor's stuck down there it's that dry and scratchy. "Thank you so much, Joan." My throat clogs up at her thoughtfulness. She's taken care of me so much already and now this.

"Oh, yes. Nearly there," Max grunts, the sound off-putting. My eyes flicker over to him to see him struggling on the floor trying to do something with the jeans he's got on.

"Why are you wearing those clothes?" I ask again.

He grunts. Narrowing his eyes on me he answers. "Because, it's all they had at the police station. Whatever. The fucker was probably still pissed at me for throwing up on his shoes."

"I'm not surprised. You were rude, Max. You... I don't even know what to say to you."

"How about; are you okay? Would you like me to get you some painkillers, my lovely, dearest, Max?"

Joan just stares at him before turning back to me. Instantly her expression softens. "It seems you're not the only one with a hangover."

"No shit. I am here," Max grunts, still trying to pull the jeans off while trying to use the scissors at the same time. It's an accident waiting to happen. I want to warn him to be careful but the way his eyes are narrowed on the jeans, and how much he's pissed at me right now, I don't think anything I say will be helpful.

I'm just grateful Joan brought up a spare set of clothes for him. And for the fact he's used his brain and used a towel to cover himself up for when his trousers do come off.

"Why? Who else isn't feeling good?" I ask her. As soon as it escapes my lips I regret asking. It's pretty obvious we were all hammered last night except Harlow. Only due to the fact she didn't drink. So unless someone is immune to alcohol, we should all be dying this morning, bar Harlow.

"Denny's the worst I've seen this morning. She came rushing over at a God awful hour, crying and screaming."

"Really?" I ask. My eyes wide. The only thing stopping me from worrying is the fact Joan looks amused and not concerned. "What happened?"

"Could someone help? How the fuck do girls wear these things?" he mutters, sounding out of breath. "Is there a fucking technique I don't know about?"

"She thought she cheated on Mason last night," Joan answers, rolling her eyes. Why on earth would she get that crazy idea in her head?

"What? Why?" I shriek, immediately covering my head in agony.

"Keep it down. I'm suffering enough over here," Max snaps, cursing.

"She didn't. She woke up wearing half of a hooker outfit. Her words, not mine," Joan grins. "But she couldn't remember what happened last night and Mason wasn't there when she woke up. There were also other things that made her think it but none of what she said sounded logical. It didn't even make sense," Joan cackles. "It all got sorted out, thank heavens, when Mason came back with coffee and a McDonalds breakfast," she waves off. Looking to Max when he makes a strangled noise in the back of his throat, she shakes her head in disappointment before turning her eyes to me.

"So what happened?" I ask, dying to know. I'd rather be in bed asleep so I can sleep the whole hangover away, but this seems too good of a story to miss. I'm afraid if I don't get the deets now I'll forget all about it when I wake up.

"I thought getting them over my ass was the hard part. It's like they're glued to my fucking legs," Max growls frustrated. He's been twisting and turning and making a racket on the floor trying to yank those trousers down for a while. When I look he's only managed to get the jeans over his ass. You can see the slashes in the denim where he's tried hacking away at it to no avail.

Joan laughs and at first I think it's because of Max. "Turned out Mason was the bloke she hooked up with. Neither can remember where she got the outfit from, though. Shame, I was going to see if they had it in my size."

I giggle. I'm used to this side of Joan now and none of it surprises me anymore. I lift the blanket up to reveal my outfit and wonder if she's talking about this exact outfit.

"Was it white and orange?" I ask her.

"No, black leather. She had the whole thing back on, covering it with a dressing gown, before running over here," Joan cackles, the noise making my head spin.

"Seriously, could you please help me?" Max groans from the floor.

"So glad they sorted it. I honestly don't remember much myself. When my friends used to tell me they never remembered the night before I always thought they were liars. But after last night, I'm proved wrong." I shake my head, wishing I could recall some more of it. "Most of the night is pretty much a blur."

"I'm glad you had fun, sweetie. I've been scrolling through Harlow's videos and photos," she giggles.

"I don't want to see them," I groan, falling back onto the bed with a loud yawn.

"I'll leave you to it. Take some more of those pills in a few hours and get some rest. Do you want some breakfast before you sleep?"

"I could eat a full English," Max answers, pausing at what he's doing.

"I'm fine," I groan. "I can't even think about food right now. It's making me feel worse."

"Okay. Get some rest," she smiles and turns to leave but Max calls out her name, stopping her. "What?" she huffs.

"Are you making me breakfast?" he asks, his eyes drooping half closed and giving her a Carter grin, full dimples and all.

"No. I'm not happy with you right now and neither is your grandfather. You're lucky I'm allowing you to be in this room. You've disturbed everyone's morning enough already, you don't need to disturb Lake's too."

"But it was Lake's..."

"I don't want to hear it," she snaps but there's no aggression behind it.

I grin when she shuts the door behind her before turning to look at a stunned Max.

"What?"

"How the hell do you do it?" he growls.

"Huh?" I ask, looking at him confused.

"You're the reason I got arrested, yet you're shitting golden eggs."

"I am not. I don't even know what happened last night," I groan.

Max stands up in a huff. "These are a fucking nightmare. I can't even cut through them." I watch him stand trying to yank them down but it doesn't work. When he falls over to the floor, I begin to laugh.

Feeling sorry for him I swing my legs off the edge of the bed and grab the ends of the jeans. Pulling with what little strength I have left, I get them loose enough for Max to get them off. He stands up with the towel still wrapped around his waist but as soon as he tries to pull his boxers up, it falls loose. I get a glimpse of his impressive dick before he covers it with his boxers. He pulls on a t-shirt covering his rock hard body and I feel slightly disappointed. The naughty dream I had about him last time floods through my mind and I remember the feel of his muscles beneath my finger-tips. I also remember how good it felt when he was inside me. Not that I'd admit that to him.

I must have been staring for a while because all of a sudden Max lets out a deep chuckle.

"If I wasn't so hungover and so pissed off with you right now, I'd be getting you on your knees with my dick deep in your throat. Or maybe I'll fuck you on the dresser. You seem to have a thing for desks," he rasps huskily.

My eyes widen in shock. He couldn't possibly know about my dream or where I fantasised having sex with him. In the dream we had sex in Maverick's office. It was rough, it was fast, but mostly it was so fucking good.

"Don't look so innocent, you begged for it," he winks and climbs over me to slide into bed.

"What? We had sex? It was real?" I choke out.

"My ego can't take the hit right now. I already got arrested having the worst case of a shrivelled up dick because of spending the night in the freezing cold."

"About that," I begin, going back to him being naked. "Why were you there? And why is it my fault?"

"You really don't remember?" he asks, looking into my eyes carefully. Most likely for any signs that I'm lying to him.

"No, and how are you not so hungover? And how do you remember everything when I don't?"

"Well, shit. Now I'm going to see if we can use Maverick's office for twenty minutes to re-enact the best sex of my life," he grins.

I roll my eyes. "Only twenty minutes?" I tease.

"Babe, I just said my ego was bruised. Now it's fucking crushed." He fakes hurt and I smile. We both turn to our sides so we're facing each other.

"So? How do you remember everything? And explain about the whole naked thing and why you weren't near your clothes."

"Because I only had one of Gavin's fucking *specialities*. That stuff is fucking lethal. It seemed you girls were drinking it before we arrived."

I remember the fruity drink I had last night. It was yummy and didn't taste of alcohol so I drunk more than I normally would.

"Okayyyy," I nod, wanting him to continue.

"Anyway, all this happened after we had the best sex ever and you told me some nonsense, but I'll go into that when I'm not sporting the worst headache ever. We were dancing and I asked you out. You told me if I made your fantasy come true you would. So I did."

"What was my fantasy?" I ask, unsure if he's pulling my leg. I yawn, feeling really tired all of a sudden.

"To fuck under the stars against a tree. I found the tree but you never arrived. You told me where to go, what to do, the lot. I could have woken up to being raped by an animal."

I choke out a laugh. "You did not just say that."

"I fucking did," he growls. "I woke up to a fucking dog licking my face. It could have been my dick."

"Oh my God, stop," I laugh, holding my sides. The room still feels like it's spinning and laughing isn't helping the nauseous feeling in my stomach.

"I must have thought I had gotten the wrong tree and moved on, leaving my clothes behind. I don't remember. I was too cold and fucking tired by that time. I won't be surprised to find my junk on Facebook or Twitter. I had to walk down the main road," he growls.

I'm still laughing. I can't help it. It's fucking hysterical. If what he's saying is true, and I did indeed say it, I can't believe he followed through just to go out with me.

"I can't believe you did that," I laugh.

"Told you last night and I'll tell you again since you're having a case of amnesia; I'm not letting you go now. You're mine."

"Max," I say softly but stop. It's not that I don't like him, I do. We've grown closer than I've ever been to anyone but he doesn't know the real me. He doesn't know what I did.

"Nope. Not listening to your bullshit. You got me arrested. I had to face my granddad and tell him what happened and *why* I was buck naked. To make it worse, Malik and Mason went along for the ride and took loads of pictures of me."

I laugh, putting away that timid bit of information so I can remember to get copies from Malik.

"Now sleep. I woke up with bark and leaves in places they shouldn't be and pains in places I never knew existed," he growls.

"Okay," I giggle, rolling over so my back is to him. Not seconds after his arms wrap around me, pulling me snug against his chest.

WAKING UP, MY BLADDER screams in pain, needing to be relieved. It doesn't help that I have a huge, muscled arm wrapped around my waist, pressing heavily down on my bladder.

Not wanting to wake him I silently slide out from under him. He grunts when I'm free and rolls forward so he's lying on his stomach, his arms curled around the pillow I'd be using.

He looks different sleeping. I've thought this before. His lashes are ones girls would cry for: long, dark and brushing across his cheeks. His full lips make even myself envious. They're full, plump and have a natural redness that beckons even the strongest of women to want to kiss them.

He really is beautiful. Not that I'd ever tell him that. I'd never live it down. He'd never see it as a compliment either, just another hit to his massive ego.

Stumbling out into the hall, I make my way over to the toilet, bumping into a hard body on my way.

"Fuck. Sorry," I croak out hoarsely, looking up to find an amused Malik in front of me.

"You look worse than Denny," he chuckles.

"Thanks," I mutter dryly, causing him to chuckle more.

"Is Max still passed out? I'll go give him a Carter wake up call," he says, grinning evilly.

Before I can stop myself I reach out and grab his arm. "Please don't. I can't deal with him just yet. Please let the beast sleep," I plead.

Malik laughs, throwing his head back. "Just this once, Lake. And only because I know how hyper the little fucker can be, even with a hangover."

"Tell me about it," I groan. "I think my headache is more from him blabbering on this morning."

"The arrest?" he asks.

"Yeah. Can you believe he blamed me?" I ask shocked. I'm bouncing from one foot to the other now, desperate to empty my bladder. Malik looks at me with amusement and steps to the side.

"I'll see you later. Let me know when he's up, I want some payback," he winks before moving off to his and Harlow's room. I don't even wait around to question him about the payback. It could be over anything with these brothers. They fight and prank each other on a daily basis just for funsies.

I moan as I empty my bladder. Once I'm done I wash up, cleaning my hands, face, neck and other parts of my body before brushing the God awful taste out of my mouth. My morning breath is deadly on a normal basis, but having hungover morning breath? It's enough to wipe out the entire population of Coldenshire.

The worst is my hair and makeup, though. My mascara and eyeliner are smudged down my face in an unattractive way and my hair looks like it's been in a tornado and dragged through a bush backwards. It's horrendous.

Walking back to my room I begin to shiver. The door below slams shut and everything in the house turns silent. I rush into my room, jumping in my bed, forgetting about Max for that split second.

"I'm up; I'm up," he grumbles sitting up in the bed. The blanket falls from his chest and I enjoy staring at his ripped muscles. It's another thing women would kill Max for. He has a tendency to eat twice his body weight but still doesn't put on an ounce of fat.

I'm glad I'm not one of *those girls*. If I get big, I get big. We only live our lives once so we shouldn't waste it by suffering through diets. Be who you want to be is what I say.

"Jesus, what time is it?" Max rasps, looking at my outfit. I look down and blush. I didn't realise I was still wearing the skimpy outfit from last night.

I groan, realising Max had seen me dressed like this, my hair wild and my makeup a complete disaster.

I look over on the nightstand as I snuggle into the blanket. "It's after one."

"I feel like I've had no sleep," he groans, scrubbing his hands down his face. "Be back. I need to piss."

"Classy," I grunt, watching his fine ass jump out of my bed, loving how his ass looks in those boxers. I can't help myself. I bite my lip and gasp when he turns around, showing me his impressive package tenting in his boxers.

Coughing, I look up to find his amused eyes concentrating on me. Blushing, I narrow my eyes but he just chuckles.

"What?" I snap, picking at the blanket.

"Nothing, Babe. Nothing at all," he chuckles, amusement laced in his tone. "Be back in a few. Need to wet the whistle while I'm up."

I fall back on the bed with a sigh when he finally leaves, shutting the door behind him. I should probably get up and get changed but my body feels too weak to move.

I'm thinking about what superpowers I'd pick if I had a choice when Max walks back into the room holding two glasses of fresh orange juice.

"Please tell me one of them is for me," I moan, feeling parched.

"Sure is, Babe."

"Thank you," I grin, grabbing the juice from him. It's gone within a second of the glass reaching my lips. It feels like heaven having the cold liquid pour down my sore, dry throat.

"Thirsty?" he rasps out and my eyes shoot to his. They're dilated and his eyes are transfixed on my throat. My throat bobs, swallowing the last gulp of orange juice. Neither of us looks away, not until Max takes my glass from my shaking hands, putting it on the bedside table.

"W-what?" I stutter, pausing when he reaches for me. He places a hand on either side of me on the bed, his eyes molten as he appraises every inch of my body. Well, of what he can see anyway. The blanket is covering my bottom half but it doesn't make a difference. I can feel everywhere his eyes are looking as if he were touching me instead. Wetness pours between my legs and I have to clench my thighs together. He notices. I can tell. His grin turns into a mischievous smirk, his eyes darkening, the colour almost black.

"I think it's time I show you exactly what we did last night, play by play. Show you how hot you were for me and how hard I was for you. I'm going to have you screaming my name and trembling with pleasure beneath me. I'm not going to let you come up for air until you beg me and only then, I may let you," he rasps out, his voice hoarse. Tingles shoot between my legs, pooling in my belly like a thousand butterflies fluttering inside me.

I may have had a mini orgasm from just his words.

"I... I," I start, shaking my head when nothing comes out. I feel like a teenager having sex for the first time. But this isn't my first time and the promise in Max's eyes tells me this won't be my last either.

"Oh, babe," he whispers huskily before capturing my mouth in a heated kiss. I moan into his mouth, my arms reaching up and grabbing onto his large shoulders.

Lord, he can kiss. Fuck, just his kiss is driving me wild. I'm scared at what the rest of him will do to me.

His knees hit the bed, his body looming over me. When he pulls my wrists a whimper leaves my mouth leaving me breathless.

I can't seem to control my body. My eyes stay glued to his and another whimper escapes me when he presses my wrists to the mattress above my head.

There's a gleam in his eyes when he takes in my new position, his eyes lingering a little longer on my chest.

"Fuck! You're so fucking beautiful."

"Did you say this last night?" I ask breathless.

"If I didn't then I'm a fucking wanker."

"That you are," I grin. But lose it as soon as his lips tenderly pepper kisses across my neck. The feel of his full lips against my skin snaps the last bit of control I had.

My hands fight loose from his hold and I run my fingers through his hair, pulling at the strands, bringing his mouth to mine.

He kneels between my spread thighs, his body moving over the top of me. When he pulls at my top I lift my arms in the air, shivering at the cold air hitting my chest. My bra is next and I hear Max suck in a sharp breath.

I'm surprised when he doesn't immediately touch me. He just stares down at my chest with a pained expression. If it wasn't for the tent in his boxers I'd think he was repulsed.

Then he surprises me, he kisses me again with more force. He tastes like mint and Max, the taste powerful and addictive. I feel like I'm high right now, I'm so drunk on him. His bare chest presses against mine causing my nipples to throb almost painfully. Letting out a curse, I rake my nails down his back, loving the groan he makes when I do.

Naked from the waist up, I should feel exposed but I don't. If anything, it makes me feel sexy and bold. Bold enough to grab the waistband of Max's boxers and begin to pull them down.

His lifts up a little, helping me remove them from his luscious body. My eyes widen when his dick springs free, thick, long and slapping against his abdomen.

He grins. "Like what you see?" he asks, grabbing a hold of his large cock, giving it a few strokes before a groan slips out.

His fingers slip into the tiny shorts, slipping them down my legs along with my knickers. The cool air hits my heated sex and I have to bite my lip to stop the loud moan from escaping.

"Touch me," I blurt out, the desire ruling all my senses.

"Fuck! I wanted this to last, but if you keep talking to me like that I'll blow my load before I've even got my dick in your tight pussy."

"Max," I moan.

He reaches between us, his fingers slipping through my wet sex. He leans down capturing my lips in a kiss while he continues to tease me between my legs.

"God, you feel so fucking good. So fucking wet."

"Please," I beg, my hips arching to meet his. His dick brushes against my clit and I let out a whimper, the sensation overwhelming. My eyes meet his and my breath hitches. His eyes are darker now, the colour black, and I feel powerful that it's me doing this to him.

I reach down, needing him to stop teasing me, grabbing his dick in the palm of my hands causing him to hiss in a breath.

"That feels so fucking good," he grunts, his hips moving back and forth. "I've got to have you."

Finally!

My mind is screaming at him to hurry up and when he bends over the bed I'm confused for a moment, but then he produces a foiled wrapper and I smile.

"Where did you get that from?" I tease, wondering where the hell he could have gotten that. He has obviously lost his wallet and his other belongings, yet he's managed to get a condom.

"You don't want to know," he grunts, rolling the condom down his engorged length.

"I do," I grin, his fingers continuing to torture me.

"Let's just say my granddad is a dirty old man. I didn't even know they used condoms at their age," he grunts before shaking his head. "Stop making me think about it."

"Okay," I giggle, before reaching for him, needing to have his lips on mine. He gives me what I want, his lips pressing hard against mine, before he sucks my tongue into his mouth. I moan, grabbing onto him with such strength I'm worried for a second that I hurt him. Thankfully, the noises coming from him are only those caused from pleasure.

The tip of his dick presses against my opening causing my body to shiver as he slams into me with one hard thrust. My eyes roll to the back of my head and a silent scream leaves my mouth. I feel full, my sex stretched causing a slight burn. It's a good kind of burn, though.

He stills, sweat beading across his forehead, his jaw tight as he concentrates on not blowing his load.

"Fucking hell, you're as tight as I remembered."

Not knowing how to answer that, and not really wanting to talk right now, I move my hips. His hands at my waist tighten but it doesn't stop me. The ache between my legs is building and I make a frustrated sound in the back of my throat.

"I'm hanging on by a thread, babe. I don't want to hurt you."

"Fuck me," I curse at him.

His eyes watch me for a few more seconds before he gets up on his knees, lifting my legs with him, pressing them against my chest. The new position causes him to go deeper and I have to bite my lip to stop myself from screaming. I'm so lost, so lost in him that I should be bothered I'm having sex in someone else's home.

His hands hold my legs in position, his eyes dilated as he stares down at me. I wiggle my hips, needing him to move. It must snap something inside him because the next thing I know he's pulling out and then slamming himself back inside me, causing a tight tingle to start in my lower stomach.

"Oh my God," I scream out.

"What is it with you and that guy?" he curses, slamming himself back inside like he's trying to punish me. God, with each thrust he's lighting something up inside, something I've never felt before. It's building and building; I don't know how long I'll have until it explodes. He feels so good.

I ignore his words and just admire his beautiful body. Sweat is glistening on his tight chest and his muscles flex with each thrust. He's so sinfully sexy, it's unfair.

I match his movements, meeting him thrust to thrust, both of us breathing heavily. One of his hands reaches between us, moving up my taut stomach before reaching my breasts. With one pinch of my erect nipple, I'm seeing stars. I scream out, my eyes rolling to the back of my head and my whole body tightening as my body arches off the bed almost painfully.

"Fuck! Fuck!" Max roars above me, slamming his hips one more time before his cock pulses inside me. I'm still sensitive, my body still pulsing with pleasure and feeling him come inside me has my core convulsing again.

"That was…" I start but don't finish. I'm out of breath and feeling exhausted. I don't even complain when Max drops his body weight on top of me with him still semi-hard inside me.

"Mind-blowing?" he finishes but I don't answer. I'm not sure there's a word in the dictionary that could describe how that felt.

His body weight begins to feel too much, the pressure weighing on me. Before I have a chance to ask him to let up, he's screeching in pain.

"Stupid fucking rat. He's attacked my balls," he yells, rolling off me. I wince from the loss, but more because of the sudden movements.

"What are you talking about?" I ask, holding back laughter when I see the pain in his face.

I look down in time to see Thor jump across the bed onto Max's foot. He squeals in pain falling from the bed. I roll over and watch in horror as he bangs his head on the bedside table before falling into a naked lump on the floor.

Thor walks to the edge of the bed looking down at Max. "Meow"

"Fucking rat," Max hisses getting up. He grabs his boxers still keeping an eye on Thor.

"Come 'ere, Thor," I coo, picking the ball of fluff into my arms. He begins to purr, rubbing his cute little face against my chest.

"We got problems," Max starts, still eyeing Thor warily.

"Max. You're exaggerating. He's just playing," I tell him.

"Splinter has it out for me. Did you see what he did to me the other day at dinner? He nearly pissed on my leg," he hisses.

"No, he didn't," I chuckle. "He was just rubbing himself against you."

"No, Lake, he wasn't. He has it out for me. I swear he's the reason my trainers were wet inside too."

"It was wet outside."

"Stop sticking up for Splinter. Just admit he has it out for me. He doesn't attack anyone else or stare at them until they look away in fear," he shudders and I giggle.

The other week Max had stayed to watch a movie with me, Harlow and Joan. Thor had been on the floor but once Max came and sat down next to me he jumped up onto the arm of the sofa and stared Max down. In the end Max had walked out, muttering about having to do something. Thor had instantly jumped in his place, curling into a ball and falling straight to sleep.

"Stop being so stupid."

Thor jumps down from the bed and Max screams jumping backwards. Thor only stops for a second, looking at Max in annoyance before heading for the door.

"Can you let him out?"

"I'm not going anywhere near Splinter," he shudders, moving slowly back to the bed. I shake my head and grab my pyjama top that I keep under my pillow. When I'm dressed I jump out of bed, nearly tripping over when Max pushes past me to get to the safety of the bed.

"God, you are such a baby," I grumble, opening the door to Thor who rushes out as soon as it's open.

"Thank fuck he's gone."

"Seriously, Max, lay off my cat or we're going to have serious problems."

"Yeah, we are," he grunts, moving the blankets.

"Shit, Lake. Were you a virgin?" he asks and my face flushes beet red. I walk over to the bed to see what he's looking down at and find spots of blood on the sheets. "Why the fuck wouldn't you tell me? I was rough with you. Shit," he hisses, pushing his fingers through his hair. "I'm not cut out for this shit. It was my first time. I've never taken someone's virginity before. How could you not tell me?"

I stare at him for a few seconds before snorting. I've most likely bled because he's bigger than my ex-boyfriend. Someone I don't even want to think about let alone talk about. It's not because I had a bad experience, I didn't. The sex hadn't been pleasurable but he never took advantage of me. He'd been my life for so long, but it was all a lie. He wasn't who I thought he was. No one knew the real him. Not until it was too late. He's the bane of my existence. Just thinking about him is bringing back too many bad memories.

"Say something," Max groans, looking red. "Were you a virgin?" he asks again, pointing down to the little red stain. It's no bigger than a dot, but I could use it to my advantage. He should have asked me this last night. He should have respected me to at least ask me first. Last night still feels like a dream to me.

"I was, but you changed that last night," I grin, lying through my teeth. Jumping over him, I move the pillows against the headboard and lean back on them, getting comfy. When Max doesn't speak I turn to face him, wondering what's going through his mind.

His face is a picture. He's staring down, looking into space, a million emotions running across his face. It makes me want to giggle.

"I can't believe I was drunk for my first time," he whispers, sounding genuinely upset.

"Your first time?" I ask, trying to cover up my amusement.

"Yes. I've never taken a virgin before. I should have took my time, sweeten the moment, it should have been romantic and not in some bloody office. I can't believe you'd do this to me."

"Um. It was my virginity, Max," I tell him, smothering a giggle.

"Not everything is about you," he snaps and I burst out laughing. He looks at me like I've grown two heads which only causes me to laugh harder. This is so fucking funny. He's actually more upset that I didn't make my first time special *for him*.

"Why are you laughing?" he growls, looking annoyed with me.

"I'm lying," I wheeze through laughter. "I lost my virginity with my ex boyfriend."

Still laughing, I don't notice the sudden change in Max until I feel him move to face me. His body tenses and when I look over at him his face is like stone.

"You weren't a virgin?" he grits out, causing me to laugh more. He needs to make up his mind which he's more pissed about. The fact we're even having this conversation right now is just ridiculous.

"No, Max, I wasn't. Were you a virgin?" I ask teasingly.

"Fuck, no. I lost mine..." he loses his grin before his eyes turn sharply at me. "This isn't about me. If you hadn't just fucked me senseless I'd spank your ass."

I just roll my eyes punching his shoulder lightly.

"I'm fucking serious. If you and I are going to work out we need to be able to communicate. Joan talked to me about the importance of a relationship the other day and communication was on that list. If we can't communicate we aren't going to work out," he mutters, shaking his head like he's disappointed in me.

"You're acting like we're boyfriend and girlfriend," I tease, shoving his shoulder a little.

"Um, that's because we fucking are," he grunts and my heart stops. My hands are frozen in my lap and I can't look at him in fear of what he'll see. I can't be with him like that. I can't get attached to him, but even thinking the words I know it's already too late. If he knew the real me, the person I've hidden, the person who I will always be, he wouldn't be with me. He wouldn't want to sit in the same room as me. I've seen the way he is with his brothers and how loyal he is with them. There is no way he'd understand that I didn't mean to do what I did. If I could go back and change that night I would. I would do everything, from the second I read that text, differently.

Max still talking snaps me out of my own thoughts. "You need to be a good girlfriend, though. You have to have sex with me whenever I please or when you're in the mood. If you want to wake me up by wrapping your mouth around my cock, I'm game. Just saying. Or if you want to sit on my face and shake me awake some time, I'm good with that too. Okay, I'm game with anything that ends with me deep inside you. I reckon we should have rules..." he stops when he realises I haven't spoken, giving me a look that breaks my heart.

He looks so happy. I know being in a relationship is the last thing he ever wanted and what he's giving me is something I should be treasuring. Instead, I'm about to throw it all in his face, something I'm sure he's been scared of.

But we can't be together. It's better to end this now before we get too invested. I can't hurt him like that.

My heart feels heavy and I swear it's breaking in two from just watching him trying to figure out what's going on inside my head.

"Why aren't you saying anything? You can't agree to all the terms, you're a woman. You argue over everything," he mutters, looking at me closely.

"I..." I begin, but my throat is clogged up with emotion and I have to clear my throat. "We... I... I can't be in a relationship with you, Max. I can't be your girlfriend. This," I gesture between us. "Can't happen again. I'm so sorry."

"Why?" he asks quietly and it breaks my heart even more. I can feel my eyes flood with tears as he stands up, grabbing the t-shirt from off the floor. "WHY?" he roars, looking upset.

"Because it won't work. You don't know me, Max, and if you did you wouldn't want to be with me."

"So, tell me. Tell me whatever this fucking big secret is that you keep bottled up inside you. I know it haunts you. Maybe getting it out in the open and talking about it will help."

"What? You mean like you talk about your problems?" I snap. I shake my head not wanting to hurt him further, but I couldn't help the question coming from out my mouth. Ever since I first met Max I knew he had dark secrets behind those brown, soulful eyes. I knew he kept things hidden and disguised his true feelings by acting like the charming, fun loving Max everyone knows and loves. But I see beyond all that. I see the scared little boy who just wants to be loved. He wants what everyone else around him has but for some reason he's scared of having it, or wanting it.

"This isn't about me, Lake. This is about you pushing me away."

"I'm not pushing you away, Max. I'm telling you we can't be in a relationship. I don't want to be in one," I lie, feeling the first tear fall from my eyes. "You'll never understand."

"No. You're right. I don't fucking understand. You let me believe you wanted me, that you felt for me the same as I felt for you. Was it all a lie?" he asks, his voice rising with each breath he takes.

"No. No," I shake my head, tears falling freely. I stand up trying to calm him down. It's killing me see him breaking inside. I didn't want this. I didn't want to hurt him. But it will hurt him more knowing he's been sleeping with a murderer.

"You're full of shit. You're so fucking scared of telling the truth you're willing to lose me. You're willing to throw what we have away all over something you won't talk about. You don't even know what I'll think. You can't decide that for me," he shouts.

"Yes. Yes, I can. You don't know anything," I sneer, feeling anger rising.

"Because you won't talk to me," he roars, throwing his hands up in the air.

The door bursts open. Malik stands there looking between me and his brother with concern and curiosity.

"Come to see how the mighty have fallen?" Max sneers at him and I flinch at the same time Malik does.

"Bro, what are you talking about?" Malik asks gently and I notice Harlow behind, tears filling her eyes as she watches Max heave with anger.

"Take a picture. Or get a good fucking look. I guess mom and dad were right,

I'm not worthy of love," he laughs bitterly and my heart completely stops and a sob breaks free.

"Come on. We can go downstairs and get a drink," Malik offers, but Max snorts in return.

"Fuck you. Don't baby me. You all knew this would happen. You all warned me that my whoring around would come back to bite me in the ass. Guess what? You were right. First girl I've ever pictured a future with and I pick a scared coward who doesn't want a relationship," he bites out.

My breath hitches again listening to him. I want to reach out to him, to tell him I take it back and that I'm sorry, but I'm completely frozen. I never realised how deeply he felt up until this moment and now I've ruined it. I've ruined my life for the second time in my life.

"I'm not, bro. But you need to calm down," Malik warns him, his tone still gentle.

Max looks behind Malik to Harlow, a pained noise rising in his throat when he takes in the pregnant girl crying, her hand covering her mouth. His pained eyes reach mine again and I break down sobbing. He looks so hurt, so betrayed that I don't think I'll ever be able to make this right. I hear him push past Malik before storming down the stairs. Next I hear Harlow whisper something quickly before the door to my room shuts.

A strangled sob tears through my throat as I collapse to the floor, burying my face into my blanket. The smell of Max still lingers and it kills me more. The pain is too much. It's unbearable. My chest feels tight like I can't breathe. I try to catch my breath but another sob catches in my throat taking my breath away. My vision starts to become blurry through my tears and my whole body heats alarmingly.

"Hey, calm down," Harlow whispers soothingly. Her voice makes me jump. I had thought she had left when Malik and Max did. I didn't think she'd stay, not when I broke her brother-in-law's heart.

"I... I..." I start but I can't breathe. It all feels too much. I rub at my chest trying to catch my breath but it doesn't help. A surge of overwhelming panic takes over and I try to suck in a deep breath and fail.

"Lean forward and put your head between your legs. You're having a panic attack," Harlow tells me gently, moving me so that my head is placed between my legs. She keeps a soothing hand on my back, rubbing up and down with little pressure. "Now count with me. Even if it's in your head," she tells me. "One. Two.

Three. Four. Five," she counts.

I listen to the sound of the voice counting with her in my head while I try to calm down my breathing. We get to twenty before I'm able to sit back up, my body shaking.

"What have I done?" I ask her, holding a hand to my chest. It still feels tight but not in a suffocating way like it was before.

"Lay down for a minute," she whispers, pulling the blanket back. On wobbly legs I do as I'm told, lying down facing Harlow. Her eyes are still tearstained and her expression is full of concern and sorrow.

"How am I going to make this right? I broke him," I sob, clutching the pillow that smells of Max.

"Do you love him?" she asks quietly, running her fingers through my knotted hair.

I nod shakily. "Yes, I think I do. So much."

"So what happened?" she asks looking confused.

"Me. I happened. I do nothing but cause destruction. If Joan wants me to go can you come and let me know? I don't think I can handle it if she asked me herself to leave," I sob, crying harder.

"She wouldn't want you to go. Please, don't think that. We will sort this out," she promises. I ignore her, closing my eyes, letting grief consume me.

As soon as I close my eyes all I can see is his stricken face, the heartache so clearly written in his expression and how angry he was. His words about being unloveable cause the ache inside my chest to tighten. If only he knew just how loveable he truly is. Anyone who comes into contact with him falls easily into his charm and easy-going attitude. There isn't anyone I know immune to it. Not even me who promised to never get close to anyone ever again.

What have I done?

TWENTY-ONE

MAX

"Are you sure about this?" Liam asks from his desk.

"Yeah, man. I need answers," I grumble, feeling exhausted as I settle back on his bed waiting for him to find out what I need.

Walking out of Lake's room last week had been one of the hardest things I've ever had to do. She broke me in ways I never thought possible. I'd gone straight to my room where Malik followed, Maverick shortly after when he heard me begin to smash my room to shreds.

Maverick had pulled me away from punching a hole in my wall, pinning me to my bed before growling some shit in my face. It wasn't until I calmed down that I realised why I was reacting the way I was.

I loved her.

I fucking loved the crazy bitch that has more secrets hidden behind those big round eyes than an entire class at Grayson High. She's so fucking stubborn, hard headed and so sure of herself that she acts like she doesn't need anyone. I see behind all that crap. I know she craves family. I see the way she looks at Hope, at Joan and at me and my brothers. She couldn't hide her longing any more than I could hide my boner for her.

Once things had settled down and my brothers had left me to deal with my self-pity party, I remembered everything from the night before. I don't just mean how fucking great she felt when I was balls deep inside her. Just from that alone, though, should have proven she was just pushing me away. But then I remembered the dribble babble she spouted off when we were dancing. She said she killed her brother.

At first I wasn't sure if she was having me on. I mean, it wouldn't be the first time that girl has pulled some crap to play me up. It's like foreplay for me. I guess being hammered made me brush it under the rug. I even made myself think she said, 'I could kill your brother'. I mean, the music was loud and I was drunk as fuck. But as soon as I began to think about it, the more I was sure she said she killed her brother.

So that was how my week started. I avoided her at all costs, even forgoing family dinners and opting to eat out.

On Wednesday I went to Hope's birthday party and was surprised to find Lake wasn't there. When Harlow mentioned to Denny that they hadn't seen much of her my gut twisted, thinking the worst. Was she running? Was she seeing someone else? What the fuck was she up to? It was then I knew who I needed to go to get some answers.

It was Friday and we'd been working non-stop for two days trying to figure out what happened.

"Here's another newspaper article," Liam calls, grabbing my attention.

I jump off the bed and walk over to his desk. Looking over his shoulder at the computer screen, I grimace. On the screen is a picture of a wrecked car being pulled out of a flooded stream.

"Zoom in," I ask Liam, looking closer to the screen. Reading through the article, my gut twists. This has to be it. A link attached to the bottom of the article confirms that. "Click on that link," I tell Liam, pointing to the highlighted link.

"Jesus!" he hisses, his eyes meeting mine. "Is this her, the girl you've got a boner for?"

"Yeah," I whisper, my gut clenching.

The more I read the sicker I feel. I'm willing to put my life on the fact she doesn't know any of this. She couldn't. There's no way she'd be here if she did.

"Find me everything you can on the family. I mean everything."

"It could be a while. Do you want to stay or do you want to go do something?"

he asks, his fingers clicking a mile a minute on the keyboard.

"Can I hang out? I'll be going out of my mind if I go home and probably call you every five minutes to find out what you found."

"What exactly am I looking for? I can pull up their information easily but I'm guessing you need more?"

"Yeah, mate. I need to know that there isn't another reason she's running. Her family could be abusive, we don't know. If you can find anything out about the brother, his background and shit, let me know."

"Like I said it might take some digging and a few phone calls to his old school. I can only do so much from here, though."

"You should get a job with Denny's brother. He's a PI or some shit. You'd be good. Want me to hook you up?"

"They couldn't afford me," Liam laughs. "But I guess working for someone will help keep me out of jail. Some of what I do is illegal."

"You wouldn't make it in prison. You've got a Beyonce ass," I chuckle.

"Why the fuck you staring at my ass, mate?" Liam asks disgusted.

"Can't help myself. I'm an ass man."

"Are you sure you're not gay? Ash's cousin is an alright guy," Liam tells me like it's something I need to know.

"He doesn't have the right equipment," I growl. Liam chuckles, holding his hands up in surrender before he carries on typing.

"Fuck off then. Go play Call Of Duty or something. I can't work with you breathing down my neck," he growls.

"No need to get snippy," I mutter, moving over to the bed and grabbing the controller.

Five hours later I'm sitting in front of my own desk typing out an email. I just hope none of this backfires on me. She already hates me enough right now.

My first thought after finding out everything I needed to know was to go find her and tell her. But from what I've learnt over the past few months of knowing Lake, she won't believe hearsay. She will want proof. So I'm doing what I can to give her that.

I'm just finishing off the email when my phone starts ringing. Groaning, I pick it up and see Joan's number flashing.

"Hey, beautiful, you miss me?" I tease.

"Now, now, Max. You know I miss my troublemaker. You keep me on my toes."

"I'm pretty sure my Granddad does that," I chuckle.

"Oh, he does more than that," she laughs.

"TMI, Joan. We've talked about boundaries. You and Granddad are a huge boundary for me. Now what can I do for you? And if you want to talk dirty to me, I've told you, my ears can't take it."

"What will I do with you?" Joan giggles.

"I'd rather you didn't tell me," I reply quickly, my lips pulling up in a smirk.

The phone cuts out and I smile down at my phone shaking my head. Grabbing a fresh t-shirt, I pull it on over my head before grabbing my trainers.

The house is quiet when I walk through it which is unusual. Maverick and Myles both said they'd be home tonight. Personally, I think they've just wanted to keep an eye on me. Well, balls to that. I can look after my own goddamn self.

Tripping over the threshold I grab a hold of the door to steady myself as I leave the house.

Goddamn it. That's the second time in three days that I've done that. Maverick really should get that looked at.

"Well, if it isn't one of them," Miss Davis from next door snarls.

"There's only one of me," I shout back smirking. "Trollop," I whisper under my breath.

"All you Carters think you can take what you want when you want. I'm telling you, you'll regret the day you ever met me," she hisses.

Shaking my head, confused, I wave my hand to her, giving her an attentive smile. "We already do," I reply back before letting myself into Joan's. "Joan," I shout, walking down the hall. "You need to tell Granddad about your obsession with me. I keep telling you, we can't have an affair. It will break the ol' man's heart and we both know he's getting on a bit. The ticker might stop ticking."

Reaching the kitchen I open the door to be greeted with four unamused gazes.

"Well, shit. Guess I let the cat out of the bag," I smirk, looking apologetic.

"Sit down dic-" Maverick starts. "Ouch!"

"Maverick," Joan warns, looking at him sternly. Jesus, she's scary when she looks pissed.

"Sorry," Mav mumbles, putting his head down like the naughty boy he is.

"What did I do now?" I ask, looking around at their faces. When Granddad, Maverick and Joan are together you know I've done something. Although, I can't think of a reason why they'd willingly invite Myles when they know we do nothing but argue when I've been in trouble. The only thing is, I can't think of what I've done. "If this is about the hole in the wall, I told you, I'll fix it."

"Just sit down, son. We need to talk to you about something really important and we need you to hear us out," Granddad says softly like he's talking a Rottweiler down from biting a chunk out his ass.

Shit, he looks really serious. What the fuck could they possibly need to talk... Oh shit!

"Oh my God! You're knocked up?" I gasp in horror, staring at Joan before turning my accusing eyes to Granddad. "How many times? If you're not going to sack it, go home and whack it? And how many times have you told me no balloon, no party? Fuck! I can't have an uncle or auntie younger than me," I ramble, thinking about what people would say when they found out.

"Shut up and sit down," Joan snaps, rolling her eyes at me.

She seems to be taking the news better than most women her age would.

"Love it when you talk dirty," I wink, taking a seat. "But seriously, when are you due?"

"Max!" Myles shouts, shutting me up. "She's not fucking pregnant."

"Touché," I sing, holding my hands up in surrender.

"Just listen to your grandfather," Joan says, gesturing to my granddad who now has his head in his hands.

"Alright. Alright," I tell her, officially all ears.

"With the twins arriving in no time, Joan and I were thinking about space. The house next door has-"

"Holy crap! You're kicking us out? Is it because of the hole in the wall? I told you I was going to fix it. And plus, how much room can two mini Malik's take up?" I argue, outraged.

"Now, now, dear. Firstly, watch your language. Secondly, we're not kicking you out," she begins and my body relaxes back down in my chair. "We've bought the Davis' old house."

My mind immediately goes back to the comments she made when I left the house. It all starts to make sense.

"Well, that explains the cranky bitch's comment when I walked out the house before."

"They're not *exactly* happy we've bought the property," Granddad explains with a grimace.

"Mark, darling, it's not our fault their landlord is selling the property or that they couldn't keep up with the rent. They've given him grief for years," Joan says, her hand rubbing soothingly over Granddad's hand.

"Bollox. If they give you any shit, let me know. I can take the bitch down," I say before pausing. "Okay, I'll get someone else to take the bitch down."

"Max, heaven, language," she warns.

"Max is right. Not about taking her out, but if there is any trouble you need to let us handle it," Maverick adds. As soon as the words leave his mouth it gives me a sense of pride. I sit up straighter in my chair, a smirk playing on my lips. It's good to be right. But it's fucking amazing when your brother announces it.

Yeah, take that.

"Okay," Granddad agrees, nodding his head.

"Not to put a damper on the issue but the Davis' place is a shithole. Not really a place to bring up two babies. It's a health hazard," Myles tells us.

"Look at you getting all social worker on us," I grin, getting a glare from Myles.

"Oh, that's why we wanted to meet with you boys. It will be you three moving into the Davis' place," Joan smiles.

"What? You said you weren't kicking us out. You can't make me move. I'm not good with change," I cry out.

"You have a new girl in your bed most nights," Myles mutters, looking displeased.

"Not lately," Joan mentions, sounding smug above her cup of tea.

"What can I say? I like variety but that doesn't mean I can move. I just can't," I explain.

"You moved into Malik's old room the minute he started packing," Maverick adds, putting his pennyworth in.

"That's not the same," I snap, sending him a glare.

"The sale is still going through," Granddad explains, trying to ease the tension.

"So there's still a chance we can stay?" I grin, feeling better.

"No, son. We've got the house. The Davis' have just over a month left to move out. When they're gone you boys can start the renovations."

"So why can't Malik and Harlow move in?" I ask.

"Because they'll want everything ready for before the babies come. We can't risk the house not being ready in time. You can live there if necessary, if the work isn't done. Plus, Joan and I think it will better for them to be close by. They'll need help with the babies."

"Whatever. We just built a freaking house," I grumble, feeling grumpy.

"Mason and I built a house," Maverick amends.

"Whatever," I yell. "I watched you build it. I don't want to have to do that again."

"So you'll move in here then. You can take Harlow's room," Joan tells me.

"You'd do anything just to spend time with me wouldn't you, Joan?" I tease.

"It's you that doesn't want to move. This is the only other option you have. There will be rules. No staying out late. No loud music. And you'll have restrictions on your computer games. I know how much they cost to run."

"Fixing a house up actually seems like a fun idea," I add quickly, smiling.

"So it's settled," Joan claps excitedly. "We haven't told Malik and Harlow the good news yet. We're meeting with them later. We wanted to run it by you three first."

"We won't say anything. I know Malik will be thrilled having not to worry about where to live. He's been bending over backwards to raise money. His talk of dropping out of college is really pissing me off," Maverick tells us as my phone starts ringing.

Seeing Lake's number flashing on the screen has my heart skipping a beat. I haven't spoken to her since Sunday morning after our argument. Should I answer it? What would I say?

"Are you going to answer that?" Myles snaps groaning. Poor lad. He hasn't gotten over his hangover from last week.

"Um, yeah," I stutter, getting up from the chair. I move out of the room, leaving the four of them to talk about arrangements. "Hello?"

"Max?"

"Antonio?" I answer surprised. What the fuck is he doing with Lake's phone?

"Yeah. Lake is..."

"Is she hurt?"

"What? No!"

"Oh my God, has some lad tried it on with her. I'm telling you now, if he so much as lays a finger on my girl, I'll knock his teeth down his throat."

"No, Max," he says sounding frustrated.

"What then? You're killing me," I growl.

"Well, she's um, she's drunk. I think you'd better come and get her. She won't leave," he says, sounding sad. I know he cares deeply for Lake. They've built a relationship over the time they've known each other. Can't say I blame him. Everyone has mentioned more than once that she's been acting differently.

"I'll be there in fifteen," I tell him before ending the call. "Fuck," I hiss, wondering what the fuck I'm going to tell her. She needs to know what I found out. There's no way I can't tell her. She'll hate me forever if I don't and for some reason my chest hurts just imagining her hating me.

TWENTY-TWO

MAX

WALKING INTO THE BAR I SPOT Lake immediately. She's hunched over the bar with her hand waving an empty glass in the air.

Shaking my head I make my way over. Antonio walks out of the kitchen just as I'm coming up behind Lake.

"Max, what a surprise," he smiles but it doesn't reach his eyes as his gaze reaches Lake.

She spins around on her stool with a wide smile on her face. But it doesn't match the sadness swimming in her eyes.

"Max," she shouts, causing a few people sitting at nearby tables to turn and look. "Heard you're like a stallion in bed," she giggles, confusing me.

"That I am," I chuckle dryly.

"I know!" she huffs loudly. "Christie told me all about it. How you were with her on Tuesday night. How magical it was for you and how much you were meant to be together," she sings like she's reciting poetry.

"Who the fuck is Christie?" I ask confused. I went with Liam to a party on Tuesday but left after a few minutes of arriving. The place just wasn't my scene anymore. I wanted to be at home with Lake, curled up in bed watching some lame ass movie.

"Don't worry. She still wants you, she's over there," she giggles looking at something behind me.

I turn around looking in the direction she's pointing in and find Christie Harold sitting with a few of her mates. Her brother is the biggest dickhead I know. We went to school together and never got on. I had won captain on the football team at school and found out that Brad was taking drugs. The P.E teacher found out before I could tell him and all hell broke loose. He blamed me ever since. Like I give a fuck. I never even corrected him when he thought it was me who grassed him up.

As for Brad's sister, I've never even talked to the bitch. She's a year younger than me, that's all I know.

"Wait here," I growl and prowl over to their table. Christie's head pops up and her eyes widen when she sees me. I'm pretty sure the angry pissed off look I've got going on is telling her the reason I'm here.

"Why the fuck are you telling people we slept together?" I growl, my voice raised.

"Because we did," she smiles sweetly, her cheeks turning pink.

"No, we didn't," I growl, sounding pissed.

"Max, you don't need to lie anymore. It happened," she tells me and I can't believe the little cow is lying right to my face.

Her friends all giggle, whispering to each other as they look on curiously. An idea forms and I smile sweetly at Christie. Her expression immediately becomes wary and I smirk.

"You're right," I smile, gaining the full attention of her friends. Now that they're all ears I smirk evilly, watching Christie take a huge gulp. "I just didn't think you'd want everyone to know that you screamed your brother's name when I made you come. You said you felt ashamed and didn't want people to know about your incest activities."

Her friends gasp in shock; their eyes locking on their friend. Christie stands up, her face scrunching up in anger.

"What? No. He's lying," she tells her friends quickly before turning her glare towards me.

"Now, now, Christie. You don't need to be ashamed. It was an okay night," I shrug.

"We didn't even sleep together," she shouts, throwing her hands up in the air. Her friends gasp again. Christie looks down at the table looking ashamed.

"My work here is done," I smirk. "Ladies," I nod to her friends before walking off.

"You're a prick. Who would want to sleep with you anyway?" she shouts at my retreating back.

I ignore her bitchiness and carry on walking towards the bar where Lake is sitting open mouthed.

"Now that that's settled, how about you tell me why you're here getting drunk out of your mind?"

"I wanted to have some fun," she tells me defensively.

"Liar," I whisper, leaning in close. The smell of her strawberry shampoo has me wanting to pull her closer. I love her scent. She always smells good.

"Taxi is outside," Antonio tells us, interrupting mine and Lake's stare off.

"Thanks, man. Come on piss head. Let's get you home."

"I don't have a home," she moans. I pull her into my arms and her arms wrap around my neck with no hesitation before shoving her face into my neck. "I want another drink. I love Malibu. It's yummy," she giggles.

"We'll see in the morning if it's still 'yummy,'" I chuckle.

"I will. I really, really will," she tells me. The feel of her lips against my neck and the feel of her breath whispering across my skin is sending chills down my spine. I have to bite back a groan when my dick twitches.

Not now, Big Max. Not now.

"In you get," I tell her as I set her in the taxi. I walked here but didn't want to risk an accident on the way back if I let her walk in the state she's in. It would probably be better if I let her walk the alcohol off but I just want to get her back home.

"No, you get in," she pouts, looking cute when I put her back down on her feet.

"Well, I will when you get in. Ladies first," I smirk.

"Then by all means, I'll get in," she huffs, her back straightening. She doesn't even make it a step inside the taxi before she's tripping over her own shadow.

"Easy there," I chuckle, grabbing her hips. Her body melts against me causing me to tighten my hold against her. Once she's steady I lift her by her hips and help her into the waiting taxi.

"Not easy," she mumbles, then looks to the taxi driver with a stern expression. "I'm not. I'm definitely not easy. He's easy. A girl only has to say you, me, and he's on it like a car bonnet."

I laugh when I notice the old man driving blush, not answering the drunken fool. I ignore her, giving the poor bloke my address.

"Easy there, tiger. We're not in Gone In 60 Seconds," Lake giggles. "SIXTY SECONDS," she bursts out. "That's how long you last, isn't it, Max?"

My head whips around to her, my amusement washed away by her words. "No, I fucking do not. I'll have you know I can last a long time," I defend myself.

"What? It's like *4,3,2,1* in bed with you," she giggles, using another movie quote.

"Hardy hah," I mutter, then notice the taxi driver grinning in the rearview mirror. "I last longer, I swear. I can call around and prove it."

"He could. He's been around the block," Lake snorts.

"No, I haven't. I've just had a few… more than a few relations."

"Relations?" she snorts again, a hiccup escaping her, making her sound cute.

"Well, I can't say fucked. My Granddad and Joan would have my balls if they knew I had spoken like that to someone their own age."

"You do have 'Monster Balls'," she giggles, throwing her head back like she's been told the funniest joke.

"What is with the movie quotes?" I grumble, hating that the taxi driver is laughing quietly. Probably at my *monster* balls. And the fact he thinks I only last sixty seconds.

"Why do we do anything? Why tomorrow? Why today? Why yesterday?"

"Now what are you talking about?" I ask, feeling as lost as ever. The sad look on her face as she eyes me causes my chest to ache. She looks so fucking lost and it's not even me talking crap. I want to reach out and hold her but I have a feeling she'll either pull away and it will kill me or she'll pounce on me and we'll fuck, for longer than sixty seconds, and she'll end up regretting it in the morning. Either way I don't fucking win.

"Life sucks. It really sucks. Me and Malibu came to the conclusion that life isn't for me. I should have ended everything when my life turned to shit."

"Don't say that," I snap, feeling angry towards the long haired beauty for the first time. "Never fucking say that."

"Why? Because it's wrong? Because there are people out there who would love a chance for another day with loved ones? Why? Because right now I'd happily take one of their places, give them the life I lost."

"SHUT UP!" I roar, gaining her attention. Her back straightens and a sobering look crosses her face.

"I'm sorry. I didn't mean that. I'm being selfish and ungrateful. I just... What am I going to do?" she asks, her eyes watering.

"First, you're going to talk to me," I tell her softly, taking her hand in mine. She doesn't pull away and I relax, letting out of the breath I didn't realise I had been holding in. "We're here."

She doesn't say anything as she waits for me to pay for the taxi. Thankfully Maverick left his wallet out for me this morning in the kitchen: unattended. It was begging to be taken. I wanted to go get a new computer game but ended up at Liam's instead.

Helping her out of the taxi, I'm glad she lets me guide her to mine instead of back to Joan's. I need her to talk to me. Something has being haunting her from the very moment I met her but I knew deep down she didn't need saving, she just needed someone, *anyone* to make her feel less lonely.

"Do you want a glass of water?"

"Do you have anything stronger?" she sighs, still wearing that lost look in her eyes.

"Water it is, you rebel," I smirk.

Once I have her drink poured, we head upstairs to my room for some privacy. I'm not expecting Maverick back until morning and Myles said he was sleeping at Kayla's.

"Do you want a t-shirt?" I ask her, knowing she hates sleeping in her clothes.

"Please," she tells me softly.

I hand her the first t-shirt my hands touch in my drawer and watch her leave to get changed. I make quick work of stripping my clothes off and grabbing a pair of shorts. I turn the television on, leaving the volume low.

When Lake walks back in wearing my t-shirt my mouth falls open. I'll never get tired of seeing her in my clothes. It falls loosely to her thighs. She looks like she's being swallowed. I give her a small smile hoping to ease some of her nerves. Her hands are visibly shaking and her face has turned a shade paler.

"Are you okay?" I ask gently.

"No, I'm really not okay. I've lived for so long believing that a miserable life is what I'm worth but I can't live like this anymore. I need to pay for what I did," she sighs, looking down at her feet. She still hasn't moved away from the door and I badly want to get up and take her in my arms. The vibe she's giving off, though, has me staying sitting on the bed.

Then her words replay in my head. *I need to pay for what I did.* This is about her brother. I need to tell her. Maybe then she can finally move forward.

I stand up ready to take a step towards her but a choking sound leaves her throat and she looks up at me, her eyes pleading and her hand held out in front of her for me to stay where I am.

I do what she wants, although every instinct in my body is screaming at me to move, to open my mouth, to tell her.

"Lake, I have so-"

"NO! No, I need to say this, I need to get it out before I finally lose my mind. You've drove me insane from the minute I saw you. You've gotten under my skin. You're like a rash I can't get rid of."

"Thanks?"

"What I'm trying to say is; before you I didn't let anyone in," she breathes.

"You let Kayla and Joan in," I remind her, not wanting to be put this high on a pedestal. I hate heights.

"Not like I let you in. I've told you more than I've told anyone I know. But there's something you need to know," she tells me taking large gulp.

I take another step forward, my gut not able to handle seeing her struggle this much. It's killing her and she hasn't even told me anything.

"I know everything," I tell her, wanting, no, needing her to know.

"No, you don't know anything. I killed my brother," she blurts out, tears falling from her cheeks. "I killed my brother," she sobs and falls to the floor. My legs move before my brain even registers and I have her in my arms and across the room back to my bed. I tuck her against me, her head in my shoulder. Hearing her sobs rake through my body are like torture. I can't take much more.

"Baby," I whisper soothingly.

With each sharp intake of breath and each sob escaping her body, the more I realise just how much she needed to get this out. Whatever I have to tell her can wait until after. It's clear whatever I tell her now she isn't going to believe anyway. Not when she really believes she killed her brother.

"I had been so wrapped up in my new boyfriend that I didn't realise until it was too late. I had been one of the popular kids at school but even that status could never get the attention of Darren Young. He never dated anyone from school. If it wasn't for the fact he was seen dating college chicks we would have thought he was gay," she starts.

Hearing her mention another man in her life has my fists clenching at my sides. I'm so caught off guard that I miss what she says.

"What?" I ask. "Sorry, I'm still processing you having a boyfriend," I tell her honestly.

She chuckles dryly. "Do you want to hear it? It's not pretty?" she whispers.

"Yeah, baby. But first you need to realise life isn't pretty. Life is the hardest thing anyone will have to do. We make mistakes, we learn from them, but we can also misjudge situations. Like my Granddad believed he was the reason for my mom's behaviour, that it was his fault, but it wasn't. It had nothing to do with him or the way he raised her. It was what it was," I tell her. Hoping she understands. "Okay, that wasn't really a good way of explaining what I'm trying to explain. But yeah, I'm going to shut up," I grumble, feeling like a twat. Jesus! I can talk the fucking ear off a McDonald's worker, but when it comes to some serious shit I come up with that.

"Are you ready?" she whispers, snuggling closer to me. My arms around her tighten and I kiss the top of her head, inhaling her strawberry scent that I love so much. It helps calm down my raging heart. I'm sure she can feel how fast it's strumming with her head against my chest.

"Yeah, babe. Tell me everything from the beginning," I tell her, knowing what I read today isn't half of what happened.

TWENTY-THREE

LAKE
One Year Earlier

*T*HE PICTURE SENT TO MY PHONE IS ALL the proof I needed. My boyfriend, soon to be ex boyfriend, is a drug dealer, maybe murderer, and is currently the reason for my brother's behaviour.

I'm already pissed. Darren, my so called boyfriend, and I got in to a fight tonight at prom. It was meant to be the one night he didn't ditch me to do whatever it was he did when he disappeared. But no! All night the jerk has disappeared, leaving me sitting at the table all alone while everyone around me were having the time of their lives.

Now I know the answer to all my questions, I'm triple fuming.

My Mum is already suspecting something is going on with me and Darren, especially when I came home early throwing a tantrum. I literally ran right up to my room, undressed and brushed my stupid hair-do out. I know as soon as she finds out I'm going to get a big fat, 'I told you so,' from her.

Most of all she is going to lose her shit when she finds out about Cowen, my brother. My infuriating twin brother, who has been moody, bad tempered and acting like a complete wanker for the past few months which is so unlike him.

We used to be so close. We would tell each other everything and we hung out with the same crowd at school and out of school. But for the past few months he's been secretive, avoiding me, and no longer hanging with any of our friends at school. When he does show his face he does nothing but throw insults and start fights.

It all started when his ex-girlfriend broke up with him. He just changed. He wouldn't even talk to me about why they broke up. He just shouted at me to mind my own business.

I kept blaming his moods because of the breakup still being so fresh but over the course of a month his behaviour changed drastically. So drastically I began to worry myself sick.

That's when I started watching him more closely and found drugs in his room. He denied it at first, telling me they were his mates. He forgot that I knew all his mates; they were my mates too. It's the first time he ever lied to my face and I won't lie and say it didn't hurt because it did. It hurt me deeply. After that I watched for other signs and they were there. The dilated pupils, the nose bleeds, his mood changes, it was right there. He may as well have carried a neon sign around saying, 'I do drugs'.

Looking back down at the picture of him buying drugs from my now ex-boyfriend brings tears to my eyes. I guess I didn't want to believe it even though deep down I knew I was right.

Emma, my best friend in the whole world, lost her sister eight weeks ago. She was sold drugs that ended up killing her.

It's how the picture came to be on the screen of my phone. Emma and I have been doing our own investigating. She couldn't get over her sister's death and wanted answers. Drugs weren't her sister's thing. All we knew was that the night she died, she was out to meet her secret boyfriend.

Rumours were flying around the school about who sold Maisie the drugs and when Emma heard a few she came up with this master plan.

My phone rings, snapping me back to the present. Emma's name flashes on my phone and I rush to answer it.

"Are you okay?" I ask frantically, knowing she went to the after-party tonight with her date. I ended up staying home, not wanting to be the third wheel.

"Yeah," she sighs, tears in her voice. "I just don't know what to do, Lake. Can they even arrest him for selling her drugs? It's not like we have proof he was the one who sold them to her. He killed my sister," she whispers, a sob escaping.

I sigh, feeling angry on her behalf and hurting for her. She's my best friend. When she hurts, I hurt.

How could Darren do this? Yeah, he's always been a bit of a bad boy but he's also one of the most popular boys at school. All my friends are jealous. He's never dated anyone from school before. He always dated girls from college. There were even rumours he dated someone's mum from school. He never confirmed or denied. But even with all the stuff I know about, I never thought he'd willingly sell drugs to someone. He's been known to take something on weekends but I've only ever seen him smoke weed.

A sniffle down the phone wipes any thoughts of past Darren away.

"Of course they will, Emma. He's committing a serious crime. We need to go to the police right away."

"But what about your brother?" she sniffles.

"He made his bed, he can lie in it."

"Oh Lord!" she whispers. The fear in her voice has my back straightening.

"What? Are you okay? Did Darren hear you?" I rush out in a panic.

"Um, Lake, I think you need to come and get your brother. Like, now."

"Oh no! Why? What's happening?" I cry, a sick feeling hitting the pit of my stomach.

"He's climbing on the roof," she tells me quickly. "Someone stop him!" I hear her shout before she talks back into the phone. "He's completely off his trolley, Lake. I think he's on something."

"No. Please, no," I cry. "I'll be there soon." I end the call before she has chance to answer me.

I grab my brown leather boots and pull my feet into them, zipping them up before I stand.

My mum is so going to freak out when I tell her.

"Mum," I shout at the top of my lungs as I run for the stairs.

"What on earth?" she asks, rushing out of the living room with her hand on her heart. "What is all this yelling, young lady?"

"It's um," I stop, pausing to think about what to say. "Cowen. Yes, Cowen. He called me and said he needs us to pick him up from Banner's party," I lie, hating every second of it. It's one thing we don't do with our parents. Lie. We've always been brought up feeling safe enough to talk about anything. We know no matter what we'll never lose the respect or love from our parents but I'm scared if I open my mouth and tell mum what Cowen has been up to she'll look at him differently.

Maybe when I've talked to Cowen, found out how bad it is and what else has been going on, we can sit down with mum and dad together.

"The weather is pretty bad. Linda mentioned she hired a gazebo. Hope their night isn't ruined," she mumbles, her voice full of worry.

"Yeah," I agree, remembering the storm I felt brewing yesterday. It hit yesterday and hasn't eased up. It's another reason I didn't want to go to the after party. My hair can't take it. The length is a few inches above my waist and when it's wet the knots are a killer to brush out.

"Well, come on then, Lake," Mum chuckles, snapping me out of my daydream. Looking over I find she's already got her shoes on and is currently pulling her coat on.

The drive over is silent on my part. Mum must sense something is going on and bothering me because she lets out the 'mum sigh'. The one that warns me I'm about to get a lecture any second.

"I can't take it. What is going on, Lake River Miller?" she sighs, using my full name. God, I hate when she pulls out the full name card. Not only because it's a ridiculous name but because I know she means business.

When I don't answer right away, I feel her glance my way, scrutinising my expression before she shifts in her seat a little.

"Does it have anything to do with your brother's weird behaviour lately?"

Lately? Where has she been? I know she's noticed. Her and Dad have both tried talking to him but it's just caused fights. Another thing that is unusual in our house.

"Yeah," I whisper. I know I need to tell her the truth and I will, eventually, but my twin bond is what is stopping me. You can't understand until you have that strong bond, that tight connection.

In the end I tell her what I can that's as close to the truth as I can get without losing my brother for good. "He's been drinking a lot," I tell her, which is the truth. He has never been a big drinker. He's just changed so much. I miss my brother.

Tears have filled my eyes and I turn my head towards the window so my mum can't see how much he's hurting me.

"That boy! Since he broke up with May he has been acting out of sorts. Your father and I were talking about confronting the issue again. Last time didn't exactly go very well, but I just presumed it was because of the breakup still being so fresh. It's been months. I didn't even think they were that serious. I just don't understand what is going on with him," she sighs.

Drugs!

That's what is going on with him, but I don't say that out loud.

We turn onto Banner's road and as soon as the house comes into view, both mum and I gasp, horrified. Cowen is standing on the garage roof, swaying.

"Oh my Lord," Mum gasps, her one hand not on the wheel reaching for her chest.

As soon as she pulls up to a stop we rush out of the car. The wind and rain whips my hair around my face, loose strands covering my eyes.

"Cowen Daniel Miller, get your ass down here, right now," Mum shouts over the rain, a thunderous expression on her face.

"Burn," someone shouts. "She used the full name." Drunken laughter erupts from the growing crowd and I look around wondering why no one stopped him before he made it up. It's not like there aren't enough people here.

"MUM! Come up here and join me," he grins, holding his hands out, palms up, and lifting his face to soak in the pouring rain.

"Hi, Miss Miller, we're just getting the ladder out of the shed to get him down," George Banner tells Mum, handing her his umbrella with a sheepish smile.

"Thank you, George," she smiles sadly, gratefully taking the umbrella from him.

Normally I'd snicker at hearing Mum calling him George. I think, apart from his parents, Mum is the only other parent to call him by his given name. Everyone else calls him Banner.

Mum and I watch in silence as Banner rushes off to his mates who are already getting the ladder ready. The rain is pouring heavy and my heart stops in my chest hoping nothing happens. It isn't until he's on the ground that I begin to relax.

When he staggers closer he notices me standing slightly behind mum and a furious expression grows on his face.

"Should have fucking known you were involved," Cowen snarls, running his fingers angrily through his soaking wet hair.

"Do not talk to your sister like that," Mum snaps, handing Banner his umbrella back before grabbing Cowen's arm and dragging him towards the car.

'Sorry,' I mouth to Banner, knowing he and his parents spent a fortune on this party only to have Cowen ruin it for everyone. He gives me a chin lift before heading back towards his group of friends.

Following Mum and Cowen, I catch up pretty quickly. Just as I reach the car a hand grabs my elbow, startling me. When I turn around I expect to see Emma but instead Darren stands there dripping wet, his slick black hair looking wild, giving him a darker edge to his already bad boy image. He's wearing his signature leather jacket and his black boots, not what he was wearing a few hours ago when we went to prom.

"What?" I snap, my lip curling in disgust at seeing him. Just looking at him and being near him has my skin crawling. Whatever did I see in him? He gives me a confused look, like he doesn't understand the reason for my hostility. If I didn't have the picture proof and people's word that he sold drugs to them, I would believe he was innocent.

"Hey, what's wrong, baby?" he asks sweetly, his voice carrying a rough tone to it. He steps forward trying to take my hands in his, but I step back moving my hands away.

"Don't touch me," I hiss, ignoring the sounds of my mum and Cowen arguing in the car, their voices rising.

"What's going on?" he sighs, the sweet facade disappearing and a bored expression now taking its place.

"I know," I tell him firmly, not breaking eye contact.

"Know what?" he cries, throwing his hands up in the air.

"That you're the one selling drugs to people at school and whoever else. You're the one who got Maisie killed," I snarl, leaning in closer so my mum doesn't happen to overhear. That's all I need.

He steps closer and a chill runs down my spine. "Watch your fucking mouth, Lake. You have no idea what you're talking about," he barks, his voice above a whisper. I take a step back out of fear. I've never heard him talk like that to anyone before. Also, the thunderous expression he's currently supporting is kind of scaring the crap out of me. He looks like an entirely different person. Not like the Darren I had a crush on all throughout year nine.

"Tell that to the police," I hiss, finding the courage to stand up to him before turning to storm off. The minute my body turns, I'm swung back around sharply, my shoulder screaming in pain from the force.

"Let go of my daughter, Darren," my Mum shouts, stepping out of the car.

Seeing my mum for the first time he lets go of my arm quickly, but not before giving me one last painful squeeze. Taking the opportunity and needing the space put between us, I rush around the car, jumping in the passenger seat.

As soon as the driver's side door slams shut and mum has her seatbelt on she's pulling away from the curb, nearly hitting a parked car in front of us.

"What was that about?" Mum asks softly, her eyes flickering to me briefly before turning her eyes back to the car.

I look away, my gaze staring out the window, watching the streets pass us by. My brother snorts from the backseat which has my back straightening. I turn around giving him a glare, still pissed off at him. Not just for the drugs but for putting himself in danger. He's my other half. Without him I'm just a shell of a person. As much as I hate who he's become, I love my brother with everything inside me.

"Grow up, Cowen," I snap.

"Fuck off, Lake," he laughs dryly. "We can't all be a goody fucking two shoes like you," he replies sarcastically.

"Watch your mouth, Cowen. You're not too old to put over my knee," Mum warns him, her eyes looking at him through the rear-view mirror.

"Goody two shoes? Are you high right now?" I ask him, my eyes widening in horror when I realise what just slipped out of my mouth.

"You're such a fucking bitch," he shouts, leaning forward to get in my face.

"Will you two shut up, right now," Mum shouts but both of us ignore her.

"I'd rather be a bitch than a loser like you," I growl, my eyes watering. We've never fought before and I never thought we would. Truth be told, though, I don't think he's a loser. Yeah I think he's heading down a darkened path but I know this is just a bump in a road, that there's more to him than this. I just want to hurt him the way he's been hurting me. Selfish and childish, I know.

He laughs bitterly. "Wonder if Mum and Dad would still kiss your ass if they found out you've been fucking a drug dealer?"

"Cowen," Mum cries mortified. But then I see her face register what he just said and she looks over to me briefly, disappointment and concern shining in her eyes. "Lake?"

I turn further in my seat, pulling the seatbelt as far as it will go and turn to my brother with eyes rimmed with tears. "I hate you," I cry, angry. "I didn't know until today. And you should know all about him being a drug dealer since you've been buying drugs off him," I shout, leaning over and smacking him in the arm.

"Is that true, Cowen?" Mum gasps. "Lake, sit back down." I turn in my seat, a few tears leaking down my face.

"You just had to open your big trap, didn't you?" Cowen yells. A punch to my shoulder has me cursing, pain radiating down my arm and up my neck.

"I hate you," I scream, turning back around I hit him over and over with my free hand.

"You two stop it, now!" Mum screams, the car swerving a little before she straightens it back up.

Cowen and I both ignore her, the two of us pushing and shoving each other across the seats.

Mum keeps screaming at us to stop, to sit back down in our seats, when the car swerves sharply knocking me a little into Mum. When her scream turns fearful I move quickly sitting back down in my seat in time to see the car swerve again in the rain. I also notice we're going a lot faster than we were when we started out.

The street lights are limited on the road we're on so the darkness and rain makes it harder to see, but when I notice a flicker of light coming towards us I scream out. "Mum, look out," I tell her, gripping my seat. The car in front tries to swerve to miss hitting us but with the rain and slippery roads the car hits the back end of the car causing us to tailspin.

I hear Cowen grunt in pain from the backseat and I turn to find him passed out, his head dangling lifelessly to the side as blood oozes from his head.

Just when I feel like the car is coming to a stop, another car hits us from behind. My body shoots forward, the seatbelt locking and knocking the wind out of me. From the side I notice Mum shoot forward, a scream escaping her throat as the car lurches forward. My head turns and my whole body freezes when I find we're heading for the edge of the old wooden bridge.

A scream is lodged in my throat and I close my eyes as tightly as I can, hoping to make it all disappear and pray we all come out of this unharmed.

Everything seems to happen in slow motion, nothing registering until it's too late. The wood splitting reaches my ears, causing a cold chill to run through my body.

"Mum," I scream, fear seeping through my bones. I've never been so scared in my life. I hold my breath as I feel the car hit air and I know we're going over. There's nothing to prevent what is going to happen.

It's my last thought before I hear the loud splash, the force of the car hitting the surface of the flooded stream knocking me out, darkness filling everything around me.

Groggily, I wake up wondering what the hell Emma and I drank last night. I'm pretty sure we didn't even plan to drink.

Confused, I open my eyes, but then panic, a hoarse scream leaving my throat. Water has filled the car, reaching my waist. It only causes me to panic more and I rip the belt from my body. I look over at Mum first, my eye sight blurred from the tears.

"Mum! Mum!" I sob, shaking her still body that is hunched over the steering wheel. The side of her face is smothered in blood and her wrist doesn't look normal.

Nausea rolls through my stomach and I'm about to check on Cowen when a cough escapes Mum's mouth. I know the minute she gains consciousness. Her whole body locks up, before she must realise where she is, and what happened. Her head snaps to me, her eyes filled with fear. As soon as she see's I'm okay her body relaxes but only by a little. She tries to turn to check on Cowen, but she winces, the seatbelt keeping her body in place.

"Lake? Are you okay? Is Cowen okay, baby? Please tell me you're both okay," she cries and a lump forms in my throat.

"I'm here mum. We need to get out, though. It's not safe," I tell her, probably something she already knows. The water is rising, if only by a little but it's enough to bring on another panic attack.

"Cowen?" Mum calls.

With everything still in a blur, I forgot to check on my brother. Painfully, I turn my body to the side, checking on my brother. I gasp when I see him slumped to the side, the water slapping up his body against his face. I begin to struggle, moving my legs so I'm kneeling on the seat.

"Mum, can you move? Do you think you could climb out your window?" I rush out, noticing her window has broken from the fall.

"I think I broke my arm," she whispers; now holding it limply against her chest.

"Mum, I need to get to Cowen, but we need to get out first," I tell her, my voice choked up. I feel under the water, ignoring her cries for Cowen until I find the plug to her seatbelt. It comes undone easily enough and I free her from it.

"I need you to climb through the window," I tell her, hoping my voice doesn't sound as scared as I feel. "Come on, Mum." I help guide her through the window, my eyes flickering to Cowen every few seconds. I feel torn on what to do, but I know I need Mum to go get help.

The wind grows stronger as Mum falls with a splash outside the window, a cry of pain leaving her mouth.

"Are you okay, Miss?" I hear asked, but I don't wait around as I climb over the seats to get to my brother. The water is rising quickly and when I see Cowen is now under the water I scream.

"Miss, do you need help?" another voice asks and I breathe a sigh of relief.

I struggle to hold Cowen's head up above water, and I cry out with fear. "Cowen! Wake up. So help me, God, if you don't wake up I will kill you myself," I shout.

"Help! Help!" I shout when no one comes to the car for us. The water around us moves in angry waves and a dark figure sticks his head into the car window. When he spots us in the back seat, he curses.

"My brother, he's stuck. Please help," I cry out.

"Hold on," he shouts through the window and moves to the back of the car. He's by the window and I notice he's trying to open the door. I want to scream at him. He must know he's never going to get that open with how powerful the water is flowing. When it doesn't budge, he curses before moving back to the front of the car, sticking his head in the window.

"I'll be back. I'm going to get something," he shouts. I cry out to stop him, begging him not to leave us, but he doesn't listen.

I move so Cowen's head is leant against me, but his seatbelt is restricting his movements. Manoeuvring us so his head is leant against my neck, I find his seatbelt plug and undo it. When it doesn't come unloose the first time, I try again, fear seeping through my bones. My heart is aching, but I don't feel it. I'm too scared. I could lose my other half. I won't be able to live without him. There's no me without him. There's a reason people tell you twins have a special bond. This is one of them.

I pull on the belt strap as my other hand presses down on the plug. After a few presses the belt comes free and Cowen's body slumps forward into the water.

I reach out to catch him but his body is too heavy. I lift with everything I have, my whole body fighting to keep him above water.

"Please! Somebody help me!" I scream, tears rushing down my face. "Please, Cowen. You need to wake up. Don't do this. I need you. We need you. You can't leave us," I scream.

"Cover your faces," is shouted through the window. Before I have chance to realise what is happening the back window is smashed. I watch with relief as he removes as much of the glass as he can before leaning through the window.

"Can you move him towards me a little more?" the man wheezes out, just as a younger man arrives behind him.

"Yes," I shiver, my teeth chattering together. "Help him," I beg them and with the help from the two men I get Cowen out of the window. The two men hold Cowen: one is carrying his feet while the other holds him by the shoulders. I stumble out of the car window, cutting my knee on some broken glass still lodged into the door. No one pays attention to me as we make our way to the bank.

My mum is on Cowen the minute the men gently drop him on the grass. Paramedics run out of nowhere causing me to jump.

"He's not breathing!" My mum suddenly screams, tears falling from her face.

"No!" I whisper, stepping backwards. He can't be dead. He can't. Oh my God! This is all my fault. If I didn't drag my mum out in this we wouldn't be in a crash and Cowen would most likely be sleeping off his drunken behaviour at Banner's.

"What did you do? What did you do?" my mum chants over and over, her head turning towards me before she falls onto my brother's chest.

"Miss, we need you to step back," a paramedic shouts as he starts compressions on Cowen's chest.

A sudden pain in my chest causes me to silently cry out, my eyes never leaving my brother. With each deep press on his chest another agonising pain hits my chest knocking the wind out of me.

"Still nothing," the other paramedic calls, checking for a pulse.

My mum is still chanting, 'What did you do?' and it all becomes too much. I find myself taking another step back and then another: before I know it I'm running, leaving the sounds of my mother's gut-wrenching screams begging Cowen to come back to her.

TWENTY-FOUR

MAX

"SO THERE YOU HAVE IT," she whispers. "I killed my brother."

I reach out, laying her on top of me to hold her closer. She needs to know. "No, you didn't," I begin.

"Yes, I did. You weren't there, Max. Had it not been for me he would have been okay. I caused the crash by leaning over the seats and fighting with Cowen. I shouldn't have told my mum about what was going on," she tells me, her heavy sobs breaking me.

"You're wrong, baby. Did you stick around after the paramedics got there? Did you go home?" I ask her, needing her to think clearly.

"No, I went straight home, packed a bag and left. Hearing my mum, seeing that broken look on her face and knowing I did that to her... I couldn't stick around. Without Cowen I wasn't me. I felt him die inside my chest. The pain had me falling to my knees on the side of the road gasping for breath. I knew then in my heart, that I had lost him forever."

Hearing her telling me this has me imagining losing Myles. As much as the fucker can be a pain in my ass, the thought of living in this world without him is enough to kill me.

When Myles got run over and I didn't know if he was okay or not, I felt the very pain Lake is describing. I can relate to the pain she felt but she needs to know she didn't kill her brother.

"Lake," I whisper.

"Make it go away," she begs, looking at me with pleading eyes.

"I don't know how," I tell her honestly, forgetting everything I was going to say to her.

"Kiss me," she whispers, her eyes darkening a touch.

She moves up my body a little, her luscious curves causing a growl to rumble through my chest. My hands move to her hips, gripping her tightly.

"I don't know if that's a good idea," I tell her, knowing she's been drinking and has just emotionally exhausted herself. She's not in the right frame of mind.

"It's the best idea," she whispers, her lips hovering over mine. The second her soft lips touch mine I'm lost in her. My hands move up her body, one diving into her hair and the other holding her neck, tilting her head to the side so I can deepen the kiss. I lose my breath with each stroke of her tongue massaging against mine.

When her body begins to thrust and rub against mine my hard on turns painful.

"Lake," I whisper, breaking our kiss. When I see how turned on she is, I roughly turn us so I'm the one on top, so that I'm the one in charge.

My lips hover over hers before I nibble her bottom lip into my mouth. She moans, her body trying to seek out what she needs as she thrusts her hips up against me, growling in frustration when I move my hips away. If I didn't I'd most likely blow my load.

"Are you sure?" I ask her, needing her to be one hundred percent.

"Never been so sure about anything in my whole life," she mutters, grabbing me at the back of my neck and pulling me down on her. Not wanting to be a jerk, I comply, my lips slamming hard down on hers as I slide my hands down her body, my fingers gripping the thin tank top before lifting it up over her head. As soon as she's free her lips are back on mine, her hands touching every inch of my body causing me to lose my ever-loving mind.

Trailing my lips down her neck, her body arches at my touch. Chuckling, I nip at the skin before soothing the sting with my tongue.

"Max," she moans, her hands gripping my hair.

"Babe, I'm not into being bald," I chuckle, looking up at her through my lashes. She's so fucking beautiful. Her eyes are half open, her skin flushed, her cheeks pink and the swell of her breasts are falling and rising with each breath.

"Sorry," she whispers, letting go of the hold on my hair.

"How about you tug on something else," I smirk, my lips hovering over the swell of her breasts.

She shakes her head whilst rolling her eyes and I chuckle.

"How about you hurry up and get inside me already," she tells me, being her usual bossy self.

"I feel like I'm being taken advantage of," I mutter, teasing her.

She playfully slaps my arm but I move back up her body, my lips taking hers in a hot, searing kiss.

Before I know it we're both naked, our bodies slick with sweat. Rolling a condom on, I position myself at her entrance, my eyes locking with hers. Her eyes look up at me full of trust and desire and it takes my breath away, twisting my stomach up in knots.

Moving, I plant myself inside her, both of us hissing at the pleasure. My eyes close tightly, trying to gain control of my body that is throbbing with need.

Lake digs her nails into my ass, moving her hips at the same time and my eyes roll to the back of my head. Moving in and out I hit the right spot, watching smugly as Lake starts to lose control. Her breathing picks up and with each thrust a strangled moan leaves her mouth.

Picking up my speed, my thrusts become harder. Lake cups her sex, her finger swirling around her clit. My body instantly jolts with jealousy and I'm pretty sure my eyes darken as I watch her touch herself intimately.

"Stop," I rasp out when her sex tightens once more around my cock. "Touch your tits," I plead, taking one in my mouth before she can move. I feel her body obeying my command and I grin around her nipple, nipping lightly before pulling away.

My eyes stare down at her, her body stretched in front of me, writhing with pleasure and a surge of warmth spreads through me, along with a feeling I'm not accustomed to, scaring the shit out of me.

Not knowing what else to do or how to explain the feeling surging through me, I lean forward, capturing her lips with mine. My body feels like an inferno and with each thrust inside her and with each meet of our tongues, sparks shoot through my body and I growl out with pleasure.

I'm surprised Lake can keep up, her hips rocking against mine, doing everything she can to match me with each thrust.

My vision begins to blur and I know I'm close and if Lake's breathing and moans are anything to go by, then so is she.

My heart feels like it's going to explode in my chest when I look down at her. Desire flares in her eyes and a look I've seen on Denny's and Harlow's faces when they look at my brothers crosses her features causing a wild fire to burn through my body.

My hips pumped inside her harder, harder than I've ever taken her before and my eyes never once leave hers. She must feel what I'm feeling because she looks just as lost in me as I am with her. Heated tingles erupt suddenly; the same time Lake tightens her legs around me, her sex clutching me so tight in her grip, that my release causes me to see fireworks. My body stiffens from my release, an animalistic growl erupting from my chest at the same time Lake screams through her release, her back arching off the bed.

Both of us are shaking from our release. Adrenaline pounds in my ears as I try to catch my breath. When the tingles in my lower stomach begin to ease off I lower myself on Lake, our sweat-slicked bodies coming together. I breathe in her scent, my head shoved into her neck.

"I think I love you," I blurt out, panicking when her body freezes against mine. "Best sex I've ever had," I add on quickly, causing her body to relax.

A yawn escapes her mouth, her breath blowing on my shoulder causing shivers to run up my back.

Rolling onto my side, I pull the condom off, tying it off before throwing it into the bin next to my desk. Pulling the blanket up I cover me and Lake before turning and pulling her against my chest. She willingly obeys, wiggling her ass against my groin, causing my semi-hard dick to become fully erect.

"Again?" she whispers amused, her voice tired.

"I'm always hard when it comes to you. But sleep. You've worn me out," I tease.

"No stamina," she mutters, already half asleep.

"We'll see," I chuckle, pulling her tighter against me. I'll wake her up once I've rested my eyes for a little bit and show her just how much stamina I've got.

I wake up in the middle of the night needing a piss. Once I relieve myself I make my way back to my room. When I pass my desk I notice my laptop is still on and when I wake the screen up it's still on my emails and a reply message is in my inbox waiting for me.

My eyes widen as I read the message, my hands scrubbing my unshaven jaw. Fuck!

I didn't want to believe Lake but I also didn't want this to be true either. I feel like I'm being torn in two. Either way I'll lose Lake.

If someone told me a few months ago I'd be going crazy over a girl I'd tell them to get clean off the drugs making them high, but then I met Lake and everything changed.

Yeah, I've always wanted to fuck her but she's more than that. I love hanging out with her. Even if it's just watching stupid ass movies or that TV series she's got into. I don't even mind when we play Grand Theft Auto and she stops at every red light. I just make her believe it annoys me when really I think it's fucking cute as hell.

She makes me laugh, she doesn't expect anything from me or anyone around me, and she doesn't have fantasies about 'happily ever afters'. But for once I'm cursing myself and her for not believing in it because at this precise moment in time I want her to want a happily ever after.

Maybe it's me. Maybe I'm not supposed to have love in my life in any other form than brotherly love.

Rereading the message again, my heart begins to ache and I shove away from the chair needing a stronger drink.

Once I'm downstairs I walk into the kitchen, jumping when I find Maverick sitting on the barstool at the breakfast bar looking at his laptop.

"What are you doing here?"

"What are you doing up?" he asks, eyeing me funnily.

"I was coming to get a drink. What about you? I didn't think you were here tonight."

"Got some shit going on at the club," he sighs, running a hand over his tired face.

"Everything okay?" I ask worriedly, noticing how tired he really looks. He's been working more than normal lately, but I don't think that's it. I know he's been getting called into work a lot lately over certain things happening. I just hope it's nothing serious, not that he'd tell me anyway.

"Yeah, it's just been a long fucking week," he grunts. "What's up with you? You look really pale."

"I've been meaning to complain about the weather," I mutter.

Rolling his eyes he gives me a pointed look and I sit down across from him and sigh. "I found something out and now I don't know what to do with the information I got."

"Does this have anything to do with Lake and why Liam accidentally text me saying he sent the information to my email address?"

"Fucking prick," I mutter, cursing Liam. "Yeah."

"So? Are you going to tell me?"

"She told me she killed her brother," I blurt out, keeping my voice down.

My brother's eyes widen, his mouth open in shock. "What?"

"Yeah, but there's more," I tell him, feeling my palms begin to sweat.

"Don't tell me she killed all her family. She doesn't seem like the kind of girl," he chokes out, looking behind him like Lake will be standing there with a butcher's knife.

I snort. "No, jackass, she didn't kill her brother either but she thinks she did."

"Now I'm fucking confused."

"Welcome to my world," I mutter.

"You were born confused," he tells me and I grin.

"You got jokes."

"Learning," he winks. "But seriously, what's going on?"

"Long story short, she thinks she caused a crash that caused her brother's death. Not just a brother but her twin brother," I tell him, watching his eyes go as wide as saucers.

"Holy shit," he whispers.

"I know, right? That's her side of the story anyway. She ran away when the paramedics were there and couldn't revive him," I tell him, pausing. As soon as I've said the next part it's all going to be true and that I'll have to do the right thing. No more pretending I don't know what I know.

"And? I'm guessing there is more," Maverick says, pouring us both a glass of Jack Daniels.

I grunt, nodding my head. "Yeah, I got Liam to look into her. When we had that fight last Sunday I remembered something she said to me on the Saturday.

He finally found some newspaper articles. Her brother didn't die and Lake is a missing person. They are still searching for her. They've even got a ten thousand pound reward for anyone who can tell them her whereabouts."

"Shit!" Maverick mutters. "What happened with her brother?"

"I'm not sure. She's pretty sure he died. But in the article it says they brought him back but he sustained long term illness," I shrug.

"Why do I have the feeling you're still keeping something from me?" he asks.

"Because I am. I emailed her parents. They confirmed everything. Lake is their daughter and they want to come meet her. But I tried telling Lake earlier and she didn't listen," I mumble, knowing I didn't try hard enough.

"I'm pretty sure fucking her brains out isn't trying to tell her anything," Maverick says, rolling his eyes.

"I did fuck her brains out," I grin proudly and Maverick leans over and punches my shoulder. "Ouch. Jackass."

"So, what are you going to do?"

"I dunno," I shrug, downing my drink and pouring another.

"You're worried about losing her, aren't you?"

"Well, aren't you the mind reader tonight," I mutter sarcastically.

"She deserves to know," he tells me, his voice softer.

"Yeah, but something tells me she won't believe a word I have to say. She's had to live with this, thinking she killed her twin brother."

"So invite them down here, make her see."

"Then she leaves with them," I grumble but I already know I need to do the right thing. I meant what I said earlier, I love her. "Suppose it's true what they say: If you love someone they will go."

"I'm pretty sure it's, if you love someone, let them go," Maverick tells me.

"Same thing," I wave at him, pouring another drink. Maverick slides the bottle away from me, out of reach, and I roll my eyes at him.

"No, it's not. Things might not change, Max, but you need to do the right thing."

"I know," I tell him, downing my drink before slamming the glass on the side. "I'll see you in the morning. Well, in a few hours."

"Night," I hear him say before I'm walking up the stairs, the alcohol spreading a warmth through my body.

Making my way upstairs, I press reply to the message I was sent by either Lake's mom or dad and send them a reply.

Once I'm done, I check out my Facebook, not having been on there for a while, when my laptop message alerts dings. I wasn't expecting a response from them until tomorrow so when I see it's them, I'm shocked.

Now all I have to do is pray Lake doesn't hate me when this is all over. Come Sunday she'll be reunited with her parents. Let's just hope I'm doing the right thing.

TWENTY-FIVE

LAKE

STRETCHING MY SORE LIMBS, a groan erupts loudly from my mouth from all the aches and pains throughout my body. Max kept me up until the early hours of this morning making love to me. Okay, not making love, but I couldn't call it fucking either. It was somewhere in between and it was freaking epic. He knows how to light my body up and make it explode into a thousand pieces. He had me seeing stars every single time.

Last night we couldn't get enough of each other. It was all hands, all mouths, neither of us getting our fill until we completely exhausted ourselves, and even then, temptation was too hard to resist.

Ever since I spilled my guts out to Max on Friday my mind and body has felt so much lighter. I've felt it with every step I've taken and I'm positive that everyone has noticed the change too.

This morning, though, I've woken up with a queasy feeling in my stomach and not the butterflies I woke up with yesterday when I woke up in Max's arms, feeling accepted and wanted, even after telling him my darkest secrets.

What has me on edge is in the change of attitude in Max. He's been acting stranger than usual and not at all like himself. I've worried myself sick that he hasn't accepted me the way he made me believe, but then I remember his touch, his whispered words and how gentle he was with me.

Every time I questioned him about his behaviour he'd distract me with kisses, amongst other things. Not that I'm complaining. I feel like a totally new person. Like my life is finally on track and I'm where I'm meant to be, even if it means I have to live the rest of my life without my parents.

Opening my eyes I have to squint at the alarm clock to see the numbers and groan. It's half eleven. I've slept in once again. I promised Joan I'd help her this morning with an extra delivery arriving at the food bank. It's too late for me to do anything about it. She's most likely already back and downstairs making tea.

I didn't even hear Max leave the bed this morning but what surprises me the most is the fact Max even got out of bed. He wore me out last night, just as much as I wore him out, so how he's found the energy to even move is shocking. That boy loves his sleep.

Sliding my legs out of bed I get up, grabbing some fresh clothes before heading into the bathroom down the hallway.

Whispers are coming from downstairs when I walk across the landing and I hope it's not Max getting told off by Joan about sleeping over. Not that she's minded before. She seems pretty lenient for a parent and is trusting when it comes to letting boys stay. When Max told me Malik slept over all the time when he first met Harlow I was surprised. My parents would go ape shit if I brought a boy into my room, let alone sleep over. Then Joan filled me in on why and told me if she thought Harlow had betrayed her trust in any way or if she thought Harlow wasn't mature enough to have a boy over, she wouldn't allow it. But there's a time in a parent's life where they have to let their child grow up into an adult and start making choices. She also said she'd rather Harlow was safe than running around behind her back, doing God knows what.

I make quick work of showering, making sure to not get my hair wet before getting out, drying myself off and getting dressed. Once I've brushed my teeth I head back to my room to grab a pair of socks and to run a brush through my hair, not bothering with makeup like always. Thanks to Joan taking me to a hairdressers I managed to get a few inches off my hair without having to worry about someone chopping it all off. Don't judge, it happens. One time I went I asked for a trim, the woman ended up taking off six inches. It broke my heart. Thankfully, the hairdresser Joan took me to know the meaning of a trim and did a fantastic job.

She even gave my long, straight locks some shape and put in some layers and feathered it around my face. It looks amazing.

Walking down the stairs, the whispered voices coming from the living room stop me from taking another step down. My stomach coils and I wrap my arms around myself feeling queasy and suddenly cold.

Max chooses that moment to walk out of the front room. When he sees me he stops, coming to a sudden halt, his face paling as his eyes move from the front room before coming back to me.

"Is everything okay?" I ask, curious to his weird reaction. Not that he's normal by any means.

"Yeah, um, can we talk in the kitchen?" he asks, avoiding my eyes.

A cold shudder runs up my spine and I have a sinking feeling that whatever he's about to tell me is going to tear my world apart... Once again.

Following Max into the kitchen I wipe my sweaty palms down my jeans, ignoring the way my legs are shaking and the way I start to become lightheaded. My racing heart does nothing to calm my nerves down and when Max keeps quiet as we enter it only makes it that much worse.

"What's going on, Max? You're scaring me. Is this about what I told you Friday?"

"Yes," he whispers looking pained and if I've read his expression correctly, a little guilty. "But..."

"What did you do?" I ask. My eyes harden a touch, knowing I'm not ready for what he's about to say. If he's told someone after I specifically asked him not to I'll wring his fucking neck and let Thor have his way with him.

"Just hear me out before you start thinking of doing something drastic to my manhood," he says looking frantic, holding his hands up like he's warning me off.

My eyes don't leave him as I stand there waiting for him to say something. When he still doesn't explain himself I step forward threateningly. "Talk."

"Okay, okay. Stop pushing me. You're making me feel under pressure. I can't take it. I'm surprised I'm not breaking out in acne. I can't take it. I just need you to listen," he whisper yells, his gaze flicking behind me towards the kitchen door.

"If you haven't noticed I've been listening the whole time," I snap.

"Jesus, is it wrong you look hot right now?" he smirks and my temper begins to rise. Why can't he ever do anything simple? He has the attention span of a two year old kid.

"Fucking talk, Max, before I hurt your manhood."

"That's playing dirty and you know it," he blinks, turning his junk away from me.

"Max," I growl, my foot tapping restlessly onto the kitchen floor.

"THEY'RE HERE!" he blurts out, turning around so his broad back is facing me while running his fingers through his hair. When he faces me again, he looks apologetic, guilty, and I know straight away he's talking about my parents. I know he is. A sickening feeling in my stomach tells me I'm right.

"How could you?" I whisper, feeling hurt. I try to process everything, to truly understand what he means, but I can't get past him going behind my back, sticking his nose in.

"Please don't hurt my dick," he pleads. "Or balls. You told me about your brother the night of the hen party. When you broke up with me my ego got hurt. But then I remembered everything you said at the hen party and what you said the morning after and it all began to make sense, so I got Liam to do some digging. Babe…"

"Don't you dare 'babe' me," I snap, pointing at him. "How dare you?" I ask again, tears filling my eyes. My heart hurts from his betrayal. I thought he cared about me. He must have known doing this would kill me inside. He knew I'd been struggling to come to terms with losing them all and now he goes and does all this. "I told you all that because I trusted you. Not so you could bring my parents here. Do you think I want to see the shame, the disappointment and blame in their eyes? How could you, Max? Honest to God, I trusted you and I've not trusted anyone in so long. So fucking long."

"You didn't kill your brother," he snaps. His eyes are heated, the colour darkening as he steps towards me. It doesn't matter. I can still see the hurt and a tiny bit of regret flash in his eyes before he manages to hide it. "If you would just stop for one fucking second," he begs. "Listen to me. Just listen. You didn't kill him…"

"Don't you dare tell me what I did or didn't do. You weren't there. You didn't see my brother's lifeless body lying there covered in mud, soaked with rain and turning blue. You didn't have to hold his dead weight to keep him from choking on more water. You weren't there when my mum turned around, asking me over and over again what I did… Put your hand down, Max, I'm not finished. How the hell could you do this? Do you have any idea how much this is killing me? Where are they? Do I at least have time to escape?"

"They're in the front room," he whispers. His eyes look unsure as he scans my face before flickering back to the floor.

Thor, rubbing himself up my feet, shakes me from the storm brewing through my body. But not even Thor can keep me from moving. My body is heading towards the backdoor before I can even think about the consequences. I don't even reach the back door before Max is grabbing me around the waist, swinging me around.

"Let me go," I cry, my voice rising.

"No, you can't keep running."

"Says you? You've ran from relationships every single day of your life. You make a joke out of every situation just so you don't have to deal with the emotion. Don't talk to me about running," I snap, wiping furiously at my eyes.

"Stop deflecting," he snaps, his hold on me tightening. My body struggles to get out of his grasp but he's much stronger than I am, so fighting him is useless.

"What on earth is going on?" Joan hisses as she storms into the kitchen. My head bows in defeat, falling limply to my chest. I never wanted Joan to find out about my past and see me differently. I feel like a bigger fraud of a person now she's seen the real me.

"I'm sorry," I whisper. "I'll be going as soon as Max lets me go," I tell her, elbowing Max in the stomach. He grunts but doesn't let me go, frustrating the hell out of me.

"At least it wasn't the balls," he groans, more to himself than to me.

"Let her go. Lake, your parents really want to see you, sweet girl. Your brother should be here any minute," Joan tells me and my head snaps up to her. Did she just say? No, she couldn't. I heard her wrong, I must have. I saw him die. I was there. I lived it.

"What?" I whisper hoarsely, trying to shake the fog from my brain.

"They're in the front room. I had to talk them down from coming in here when we heard you pair start arguing. I did explain arguing is like foreplay to you both but it would be better if I checked out what was happening first," she says to me like she didn't just dump a huge bombshell on me or tell my parents arguing is like foreplay to me.

I shake my head. No. None of this is real. It's not. I'm oversexed, exhausted and tired. Closing my arms I pinch myself, praying I wake up in my bed, Max curled up next to me.

"We did go for hours," Max agrees and I realise I just said that out loud. My cheeks flame, the heat causing me to feel a little dizzy.

"It's real. Now come on. You need to talk to them, sweetie. They have been going out of their minds for a year now, wondering if you were alright. Sweetie, they love you and miss you," Joan says stepping forward, her finger running down my cheek, her thumb wiping under my wet eyes. But it's no use. The tears keep falling faster down my face. My breathing escalates and I feel like I'm on the urge of a massive panic attack. My palms are sweating, my body shaking and before I do something stupid like pass out, my whole body sags back against Max's hard chest. He supports my weight immediately like I weigh nothing at all. And for a second I feel safe, forgetting that he betrayed me.

"My brother? He's alive?" I whisper, all the blood draining from my face.

Thor begins hissing at Max's feet, clawing at his jeans like a mad cat and Max curses.

"Splinter, fuck off," he hisses but I don't miss the quiver of fear in his voice. In the end Max picks me up, taking me over to the table where he sits down on a chair, pulling me into his lap. I don't bother fighting it and instead follow, feeling numb. My mind is still trying to process what all this means. It's not every day, after living a year thinking your brother's dead, that you're told he's really alive. Shit like this doesn't happen in real life.

My heart and head still doesn't believe it, not being able to wrap my head around it all. My mind is still picturing his lifeless body, my heart feeling the crippling pain from when the paramedics tried to resuscitate him but failed. It all becomes too much. Nothing makes sense anymore. None of it. How can he be alive and I not know? How did I not feel it?

"Yes, didn't Max tell you?" Joan asks softly, but I hear the glare in her voice as she addresses Max.

"I did. I told her more than once so don't blame me for this one. She doesn't listen... at all," Max defends himself.

"No, you didn't," I snap, turning to face him, accusing him with my eyes.

"Don't look at me with that tone," he begs. "I did. I said, 'You didn't kill your brother.'"

"Yeah, and I thought you meant, 'you didn't kill your brother, it was an accident," I hiss. "I didn't think.... Oh my God, he's alive. He's really alive?" I ask again, looking deeply into Max's eyes. They soften and he nods his head.

Mark walks into the kitchen, his eyes softening when he takes me in, unfortunately still sitting in Max's lap. He looks to Joan briefly before walking further into the room and coming to stand in front of me.

"Lake, girl, your parents really want to see you," Mark tells me gently. "Come on in to the front room so that they can explain everything."

I nod my head numbly, standing up. Max grabs a hold of my hand and I cringe when I feel how sweaty they've really become. I'm pretty sure if you looked my underarms would just be as bad. He doesn't seem to mind, though. Not that I care if he does either way. I'm just undecided if I'm angry at him still or if I'm happy. My mind isn't made up.

My shaking legs carry me down the narrow hallway towards the living room. The minute I enter the living area my eyes immediately seek out my Mum and Dad. My Dad has his arms pinned around her: stopping her from escaping? Or running? Whether that's away from me or to me, I don't know. But I guess I'm about to find out.

A sharp intake of breath has me stepping back, my back hitting Max's hard chest once again. His hands grip a hold of my waist, sending shivers down my spine. It also gives me the little bit of strength I need to face my mum and dad. The two people I love most in the world and who I let down greatly.

"Lake," Mum gasps, her voice filled with pain. Her expression is stricken with pain, relief and love. The second my dad lets her go, seeming frozen as he stares at me, I'm grabbed by my mum, her arms embracing me in a warm, tight hug. It feels surreal. Every day for a year I believed I'd never feel this again, the love, the warmth and the safeness that my parents provoke when they're near me. They've only ever shown me and my brother love and when I left it was one thing I missed the most. Having my parents love me.

A pained sob leaves my mouth, a pain in my chest that I've never felt before as I grip my arms tightly around my mother. It's like a year of excruciating pain has built up only to explode in this moment. I feel everything and from the pained sobs coming from my mum, she must be feeling the same way.

Another set of arms wrap around me and I instantly smell my dad's signature cologne, his natural scent comforting me instantly.

Safe. That is what I feel having my parents here, their arms wrapped tightly around me, protecting me from everything outside.

"It's really you," Mum cries, gripping me tighter like she's scared I'll disappear.

"LeLe, we've missed you so much," my Dad tells me hoarsely, tears in his voice. My breath catches hearing him use my nickname and I find it hard to breathe for a split second. Then a smile touches my lips briefly before I'm grabbing both of them tightly, never wanting to let either of them go.

"I've you missed you so much too. I'm so sorry," I tell them, needing them to know I never wanted to leave or to cause them pain but it was the only way they would've moved on.

"Oh, honey," Mum whispers, moving back a step and taking my head in her hands. "We've missed you. Why did you ever think I'd blame you?" she asks me, sadness in her tone.

"You kept saying, 'what did you do? What did you do?' over and over again. The look in your eyes," I shudder, remembering the way she looked at me like I ended her world brings all that pain and heartache back.

She tries to cover her sob with her hand, tears rushing down her cheeks. "No, darlin', I was saying it to myself. I was the one driving, the one responsible for you. Not just as a driver but as a mother. I should have pulled over until you two had stopped arguing. The only time I remember looking over at you was to make sure you got out of the water safely. Please believe me when I tell you I never, not once, blamed you or Cowen," she pleads, her hands now holding mine.

"You didn't?" I whisper, my whole world falling apart once again. How did I mix everything that happened up? "You really don't blame me?"

"No, we've been searching every day for you," Dad chokes out, taking one of my hands out of Mum's grip. "We needed you to know that you weren't to blame. We did everything from newspaper articles to online support pages just so you would come home, but everything lead to dead ends. Well, not until this young man emailed us asking if we were child abusers," Dad smiles, his eyes shining with amusement when he looks at Max behind me.

I turn my head around to Max, glaring at him. "Child abusers? Really?" I snap, pissed he'd think my parents were capable of such a thing. The only thing my dad has ever hurt, and that's only because my mum has a phobia, is when there's a spider in the house and he has to kill it for her.

"How else was I to know you weren't going back to get whipped and chained in the basement?" he tells me, holding his hands up. He looks like he believes he was doing the right thing, but Jesus, a child abuser? Did I look like an abused child? He can be so dramatic sometimes.

"A basement, really? What childhood did you have?" I ask but then regret the words immediately. "Sorry."

"No. No." He waves me off, not caring that I just mentioned his childhood. I know he hasn't had the best time and understand now why he asked my parents. He was just being...Max. "The tales of Max Carter can wait, the door's about to knock," he winks.

"W-what?"

The door knocks before he can answer and my heart literally stops. Not because Max predicted the door was about to be knocked but because I know who it is. For some reason I can feel him, I know he's there. My heart is beating ten to the dozen and I don't know if I can do this without passing out.

"That will be Cowen," my dad announces and I become dizzy, my body swaying slightly. Max notices and supports my weight, keeping me upright.

"Cowen," I whisper under my breath, unmoving. Everyone shifts around me, yet, I'm too scared to move. Voices start up near the front door, but it all sounds fuzzy due to the buzzing ringing in my ears.

With shaky hands I tuck a loose strand of hair behind my ear; a nervous habit that I picked up in middle school.

"Lake," a deep rumble is said from behind me. My body is completely frozen. I'm too scared to turn around to see that it's really him, though, deep down I know it's him. The feeling of familiarity is stronger than earlier. My eyes are cast down to the floor, my hands shaking so badly I'm worried I'm still going to pass out.

A large shadow looms above me, two large feet stepping into my line of vision and I visibly tense. I can't do this. I can't. What if this is just a dream and I wake up any second? It will be like losing my brother and family all over again. I can't do that.

"Lake, look... Look," he clears his throat, his body shifting, a nervous energy coming from him, but I still don't look up. "Up. Look Lake up," he tells me and the stutter in his voice confuses me enough to look up.

My breath hitches on a sob as I take in my twin brother. His features seem younger but aged at the same time. He's bigger than he once was if that's possible. His muscles are more defined than what they were last year, but something about him, something I can't put my finger on is different.

"Cowen," I whisper, reaching up with my fingers to touch his cheek, needing to feel that he's real, that this isn't some fucked up dream to punish me further.

He doesn't flinch or move away and I take it as a good sign. When he covers my hand with his and gives me a toothy grin more tears fall from my eyes.

"Mum. Lake. It's Lake," he smiles and my eyes pull together in a frown. I look to Mum for answers to see her hand covering her mouth, tears still pouring down her cheeks.

"Mum? Dad?"

"Cowen has aphasia. It's a brain injury caused from the crash. He took most of the impact when the car hit the back end the first time. Lack of oxygen to the brain didn't help his recovery," my dad answers sadly.

"What does that mean?" I ask, looking back at my twin brother who doesn't seem bothered we're talking about him like he's not here.

"It means you're awesome and I'm not," he laughs, making me chuckle, but then frowns, shaking his head. "No, I'm awesome, you're not," he nods, looking proud for saying it right.

"I like him," Max chuckles behind me sounding genuine. I don't turn around to see his reaction, the sincerity in his voice is enough for me, but more than that, I can't keep my eyes from my brother.

"You are awesome," I smile, leaning in and giving him a hug.

"Ugh," he complains. "Mum. No hugging brothers," he moans and I burst out laughing.

"Will he be okay?" I ask, looking back at my parents.

"He's fine. He has episodes where it gets bad. Mostly when he's nervous," Mum giggles, looking adoringly at Cowen.

"Like when I asked my girlfriend not to marry me," Cowen says proudly and my mouth gapes open.

"What? Did he... Did he just say what I think he said?"

"Hi," a voice squeaks from behind me and I jump, making Cowen laugh.

"Fu...," he clears his throat, looking uncomfortable for a moment like he's thinking too hard. "Funny. I missed you," he whispers, tears forming in his eyes.

"I've missed you too," I tell him before turning back to the girl who said hi. "I'm Lake."

"I'm Marybeth," she smiles holding her hand out for me to shake and I smile. I like her immediately. She's a tiny little thing with short brown hair and a round, hour glass figure. But that's not what grabs my attention or the reason why I like her, it's because of the kindness and gentleness shining in her eyes that has me warming instantly to her.

"I'm Max," Max boasts, holding his hand out to Cowen.

"I'm Cowen. I'm a twin," Cowen answers and Max grins.

"No shit? Me too," Max grins, high fiving my brother. My brother looks at Max like he's just told him he's Batman and my heart warms.

"Not really? A girl one?" Cowen asks. It's weird that no one has asked him to repeat what he's said. Everyone can still understand him. Even though he's mixing his words up I can still understand what he's trying to say.

My heart is hammering in my chest having him standing in front of me when I never, ever, imagined this would happen again, not even in my dreams. The only dreams I ever had of Cowen were nightmares and were of him dying in front of my eyes all over again. And just like the first time, it killed me reliving it.

"Nah, he's a boy, but he does act like a girl sometimes," Max grins, winking at Cowen.

"Your eye moved," Cowen blurts out whilst laughing, causing me and everyone to giggle.

"Hey, Joan, do you have any milk? Oh, sorry, I didn't know you had company," Myles says, stopping short when he sees the living area filled with strangers.

"Mum. Dad. Look. Two. Look," Cowen shouts excitedly and Marybeth moves forward towards my brother, smiling.

"How cool?" she asks him, looking as pleased as he does but I can also see she moved to calm him. It makes me jealous for a second, but then I remember she's been there for him when I haven't. She knows Cowen better than me at this moment in his life.

"Two," he nods. "You look the same."

My eyes fill with tears. He's not the brother I left two years ago, but he's still there inside. He has the same sense of humour, similar facial features, but it's like he's a whole new person. I hate that I wasn't there for him. I hate that he needed me and I ran away. Even though I left believing he was dead, I feel even more guilty for not being there for him or sticking around. I just presumed the worst and left. I ran the first chance I got. Some more tears spill down my face and no matter how quickly I try to wipe them away, they are still seen.

"No! No! She's crying. Stop it," Cowen shouts at me and Max laughs.

"She leaks a lot, mate. Don't sweat it."

"I'm no sweating no more," he tells Max before looking to me seriously. "Stop leaking."

"You tell her. This is my twin brother, Myles. Myles, this is Cowen, Lake's twin brother. Those two lovely looking people standing over there are her parents... and they're not child abusers," Max adds quickly like he's reassuring him for his own safety. I have to roll my eyes at his antics.

"Hi," my parents wave at Myles whilst still grinning at Max and Cowen.

"Brother? Twin? Why didn't we know?" Myles asks looking hurt, which puts more guilt on my shoulders. They deserved to know about my life, after all, they've shared theirs with me for months and months.

"I knew," Cowen tells him, putting his hand in the air.

"Shall I come back?" Myles asks, looking at my red rimmed eyes.

"You can stay if you'd like?" I whisper, looking away.

"I better get back to Kayla before she kicks my balls."

"I love playing with balls," Cowen tells Myles, walking up to him. "Can I play?"

Myles chokes on his laughter while Max grins evilly before turning his smothering eyes to me. "I love him," he mouths and I shake my head amused.

"Maybe another time?" Myles says, still looking confused. He walks over to me and kisses my cheek before moving to whisper in my ear. "You have a lot to tell us. The girls won't be happy."

I nod my head feeling ashamed. I should have told them all by now about my family, about the accident, about everything.

The fact Joan has been okay with everything just shows how truly kind she really is. I shouldn't have judged her, thinking she'd turn her back on me. I should have known she would stand by me and help me.

"Mark and I are going to make some pancakes and tea. Why don't you catch up and we'll be back in a minute with food," Joan smiles and I relax, loving how welcome she's being to my family. "Max?" she calls when he doesn't move. Mark and Myles have left but Max doesn't even blink. In fact, he doesn't look like he's about to move at all.

"No, I need to catch up with my twin from another mister," Max grins, taking my brother over to the sofa. "Cowen, do you want to tell me all the embarrassing things about your sister?"

"NO!" I shout, startling everyone.

"She wet the bed. She said to tell people because she hated being embarrassed,"

Cowen tells him smiling.

"You wet the bed too," I defend myself, pouting, hoping my face isn't as red as it feels.

"No, Marybeth, I don't do I?" he asks, seeming unsure.

"No, baby."

"See," he grins and my breath catches at seeing some of the old Cowen. His grin. It was always boyish with his dimples and cheeky charm; it made all the girls at school swoon when he would grin their way. And from the looks of it, it works on Marybeth too. She's gazing lovingly up at him, adoration shining in her eyes. I'm glad my brother has that, especially after everything he's been through.

I take a seat on the sofa opposite Max, Marybeth and Cowen, my parents taking a seat on either side of me, both taking a hand in their own.

"What about the time you fell out the tree and lost your jogging bottoms and boxers, showing everyone your junk?" I laugh, remembering the time one of the girls from school sent him to get a cat down from the tree. He only agreed because he wanted to get in the girls pants so badly and said it would give him some major man points with all the other girls. Only, we ended up having to call the fire department to get *him* down, it was the talk of the school for months.

"It was freeing," he grins, a tinge of pink showing on his cheeks.

"I've done that a time or two," Max nods, agreeing with Cowen's comment. "Nice to get a little air down there."

"You need to be my…" Cowen clears his throat, looking to Marybeth for help but she just smiles and nods encouragingly.

"I reckon me and you should be best friends," Max grins and my heart warms at seeing how gentle he's being with my brother. It's like he knew what my brother was trying to say and instead of helping him out and embarrassing him, he turned it around so it was him asking. Pretty fucking sweet if you ask me. "What do you think?"

"I think… I think it's… It's great."

"Goody," I clap, rolling my eyes at Max. "He needs more friends," I tell Cowen.

Max and Cowen begin chatting about other friends; Marybeth joining in every so often but seeming nervous around Max. I don't blame her, Max can be too much for anyone at times.

My dad squeezes my hand, grabbing my attention. Turning towards him I find he's still got tears shining in his eyes, causing mine to start up again. I think I'm still in shock that they're here, safe, alive, and just... Fuck... Just here.

"Never leave us again. We've missed you, missed you so much. Please tell us you've been safe, that nothing bad has happened to you?" he chokes out, his face paling like he's waiting for me to tell him bad news.

"I've been fine, Dad," I half lie. I want him to rest easy, not feel bad over everything that went wrong in my life. I've had some ups and downs, but what teenager living on the streets wouldn't? He can sleep easy now knowing nothing terrible actually happened to me. What matters is that I was taken in by one of the most caring, most generous families I've ever known. I'll never get over everything Joan and the Carters have done for me.

"You look so different, so grown up. Your hair is much longer, your body fuller and I swear you've grown ten inches," Mum says, her words laced with sadness and she looks me over once more, her eyes glistening with more tears. After today I think I'll have cried myself dry.

"I'm sorry I ran away," I tell them, feeling ashamed now that I know the true story, wishing I had just stuck around a moment longer.

"Baby, we found you, that is all that matters."

"What about Cowen? Is he really okay?" I ask, turning my watery eyes to my mum.

"Yes, sweetie. He wasn't at first but he's improved so much over the year. He suffered with some dark depression at the beginning, but once he started going to speech therapy he began to recover."

"I think meeting Marybeth at the centre helped him. It showed him life didn't need to change just because of his injury," my dad adds.

"Marybeth?" I question, wondering why she needed speech therapy. Granted, I've not heard her speak more than a few words but she doesn't seem like someone to need it.

"She would take her little brother while her mother worked," Mum answers smiling.

"She seems really nice," I admit, smiling over at my brother, Max and Marybeth.

"She is. She's so good for him."

We sit in silence, all three of us just processing everything when my mum's hand reaches out of nowhere, touching my cheek.

"I just need to touch you," she breathes out.

The evening wears on and my stomach rumbles ready for dinner. I'm too scared to say anything about it just in case Mum and Dad decide to leave. It's who they are. They've never been ones to overstay their welcome and I know if they think we're not eating because they're here then they will leave. It's short-lived, though, when my dad clears his throat, sitting forward in his seat, looking reluctant to say what he needs to.

"We should be going. We need to find a bed and breakfast or a Travelodge to stay in," he says, looking like he'd rather do anything else. I don't blame him. I don't want them to leave either. They just got here. I'm also glad they're not heading back home right away and that they planned to stay.

"Nonsense. You can stay next door at Mark's old place. The boys still live there but there is still plenty of room for you all to sleep."

"We couldn't," Mum says, waving Joan's invitation away.

"But you can," Joan winks. "Believe me, it's fine. You should all be together as a family. Now, I'm going to order in some dinner as I don't have anything prepped. Is there anything you guys would like or something you don't want?"

"No veg," my brother grunts, then blushes when everyone turns his way.

"We're like twins," Max says in awe.

"We are twins," Cowen tells him smiling.

"Veggies are good for you," Joan reprimands, giving Max the eye like he shouldn't be encouraging Cowen.

Both boys groan, shaking their heads, and I laugh. My brother turns in my direction and his face falls a little. He's been doing it a lot since they arrived. I've also noticed Marybeth whisper to him, seeming to be encouraging him do something. Just when I think he will say or do what he needs to, he sighs in defeat and looks away from me sadly.

"Can Lake and me talk outside?" he asks, and although it sounds like he's asking for permission, he's actually addressing me when he asks.

"We can. Do you have a coat? It's pretty cold out this evening," I tell him.

He nods his head and gets up. He grabs his coat that's hanging on the door and steps towards me. I move out of the living room, grabbing my coat from the hook in the hallway by the front door.

Outside, I gesture for Cowen to sit on the wall, knowing there's nowhere else we can go and have privacy since Denny is at home and so is Myles with Kayla. We sit in awkward silence for a while until I hear Cowen clear his throat, shifting his ass on the wall.

"I'm sorry for what happened to you," I start, my throat clogging. "If I had gotten to you sooner..."

"Don't blame you. W-we don't blame you. I was a wanker all the time."

Opening my mouth to interrupt him, not wanting to listen to him beat himself up over something that doesn't matter anymore, he surprises me by placing his hand over my mouth, shutting me up. Just like when we were younger I stick my tongue out, licking his hand.

"Eww," he laughs and before I can pull away in time he's wiping salvia down my face with the hand I just licked.

Laughing, I shove him away playfully. "Don't," I squeal causing him to laugh harder.

"Can you shut up so I can talk," he says softly, but his words rushed, coming out slightly harsh. "Nicely," he smiles, but it's sad. "I want to get you on your own. The reason I behaved like a wanker was because May... May... She." He stops, taking in a deep breath, looking frustrated with himself. Placing my hand on his knee I smile softly at him. His hands clench into fists as his mind ticks over. I can see it in his eyes that he's struggling.

"Take your time. There's no rush."

"No rush," he agrees. "May killed my baby," he blurts out, his face flushed red. His eyes glisten like saying it out loud has taken him back to that time.

"What?" I gasp, tears filling my eyes. How did I not know this? Why didn't he ever talk to me? No wonder he was acting like he was. Everything begins to make sense. Why she broke up with him out of the blue and why he seemed so cut up over it when he had never been one to wallow over anything. It also explains why May left school and wouldn't return my calls.

"I'm sorry for all of it. S-she told me, Cowen, that she would let me keep baby, that I could be the dad. That I'm the dad. I was excited and scared, so scared, but I wanted a baby," he sighs, looking down at his hands that are folded up in his lap now. I take one in mine, squeezing it reassuringly.

"You will be a good dad, Cowen. The best. Why didn't you tell me?" I ask, the hurt evident in my voice.

"Because she killed it. She had... She had a," he grunts, scrubbing his face as he tries to get his words out. Even only being in his life again for a short amount of time, I know he wouldn't want me to help him, to speak for him. We're alike in a lot of ways.

"I know," I tell him, knowing what he's trying to tell me. She had an abortion. "Do Mum and Dad know?"

"Yes. Now. They cried. A lot. Do you like Marybeth?" he blurts out, looking deeply at my expression for an answer.

"Yes," I smile widely. "She's amazing. Do you like Marybeth?" I tease.

"I loveeee Marybeth," he grins. "She loves me. She doesn't think I'm a... a... a spaz."

"You're not a spaz, Cowen. You might have trouble remembering words or getting them out, but that means nothing. Even normal people can get stuck sometimes. In fact, I prefer this new you. You seem more relaxed, happier, and you don't act too cocky," I grin.

"I'm cocky to Marybeth. She thought I played."

"Played?"

"No. Player. She thought I'm a player."

"Ha. She's right. You were. But now you're not. I can't believe you're getting married."

"I want babies with her."

I laugh, loving this new side to my brother. It's like he doesn't have a filter. It's also a sad reminder of everything that happened and everything I caused.

"I'm so glad you're happy."

"I want to talk to you," he tells me again and I wonder if he's forgotten about our talk already. "Talk more," he adds breathlessly.

"Okay," I nod.

"No one is to blame for the crash. If there was then it would be. But it was an accident. I'm sorry if you left because of me," he tells me sadly.

"I left because I thought I lost you. Without you there is no me. And the look on Mum's face when the paramedics couldn't revive you will stay with me forever."

"I'm sad," he tells me and I give him a sad smile, resting my head lightly on his shoulder.

"Hey," a chirpy Harlow greets, walking down the street towards us wrapped up in hat, scarf, gloves and a woolly coat.

"Hey," I smile and frown when I notice her eyes narrowed on Cowen. It's then I realise she doesn't know who he is or that I've even *got* a brother. "This is my brother, Cowen. Cowen, this is Harlow. She's Joan's granddaughter and Malik,

Max's other brother's, girlfriend."

"Hey," she smiles but she can't hide the shock on her face. I shake my head subtly hoping she understands that I'll explain everything later.

"I'm a twin," he greets holding his hand out.

I giggle at her expression. "We're twins," I add, easing her confusion.

"Max is my friend and he's a twin too," Cowen adds, looking flushed. "Nice big baby."

Harlow laughs. "Yeah, two very big babies. I'm having twins too," she smiles, proud of her unborn babies.

"No!" Cowen shouts, jumping off the wall. "Two? Twins? Max, Lake and me are twins. We're all twins," he smiles, genuinely happy about the fact.

"Max got this excited too," Harlow tells him.

"Can we see Max now?" Cowen asks, now looking at me. "We can tell him she's having twins."

"Come on then before Marybeth comes and kicks my ass for taking you away for so long."

"Marybeth won't hurt no one," he tells me sternly, looking unpleased at the suggestion.

"I'm joking," I tease, nudging him with my shoulder.

He laughs. "I can joke good," he tells Harlow and helps her up the walkway to the door. I follow with a Cheshire grin upon my face.

I thought I felt free on Friday, but having my brother and parents here, nothing could beat that. All that pain, all that sorrow from believing my brother was dead and I was the cause finally leaves my body. And I know the second I walk over the threshold my life will begin again. I just hope I don't lose anyone else in the meantime.

TWENTY-SIX

LAKE

Having my family back in my life has been a whirlwind since the second they arrived. I haven't had time to really process anything or what it means, them being here for me. It all feels like a foggy dream and I keep expecting to wake up any second.

At times it feels like old times, falling into old habits, laughing and joking. It's hard to believe it's been a year since I last saw them. It's like we've never been apart. But then there are times when everything stops and I look at how much has changed, how much they've changed, and it all floods back, feeling like it's been far longer than a year.

Max has been great. He's supported me since their arrival and has made sure I'm okay with everything and him after he went behind my back and called them. At first I was angry but now I know that he did it with good intentions. It also helps knowing everything that really happened and that I didn't lose my brother. I kind of owe him my life. I'll be forever thankful for what he did for me, for my family.

He's also been great with Cowen. They've hung out like they're old friends, played football, played the Xbox and even gone out together to do *boy stuff*. Even

Mum and Dad have both commented on how happy they are at seeing Cowen so happy, glad that he's finally interacting with someone other than them and Marybeth.

It worried me that he had no one other than those three during such a hard time in his life and even asked my parents why none of his friends were there for him. She explained how he pushed everyone away after the accident due to the deep depression he was suffering with. Even after he got better he refused to make new friends, scared of what they'd think of him or that they'd think he was an invalid. It kills me knowing I could have been there for him, helped him through it all.

I'm just glad he met Marybeth. She is genuinely the kindest person you could ever meet. All the girls have welcomed her into their fold and have kept her company while Max has been out with Cowen and I've spent alone time with my parents.

I've also gotten to know Marybeth, not as well as I would have liked, though. But even if I didn't, just listening to her talk about my brother or the way she looks adoringly up at him any time he is near would tell me everything I need to know about her. She truly does love my brother and he loves her and she doesn't seem bothered by his illness. She's also given me another perspective on my brother, filling in things Cowen couldn't talk to my parents about during the time his illness was at its worst.

And although the past few days have been a blast, a sickening feeling that it's all about to come to an end is churning in the pit my stomach. I don't want my parents to leave and I don't want to leave Joan and everyone else. It's tearing me up inside.

It's the fourth day of having my family here and Joan has arranged a meal for everyone over at her house. We've all stayed at Mark's the past four days, even me, only going back to my room for a change of clothes. My parents didn't even blink when they found out I was sleeping in Max's room which surprised me.

With there being such a large number of us, Mark has had to pull out the large table, my dad helping him set it up with the extended middle to make it bigger. It barely fits in Joan's large kitchen.

My heart warms watching and listening to my two families laugh and get along together. It's true what they say, not all family is through blood. Sometimes a family is those closest to you. Joan and the Carters have been a family to me since I was found in the shed at the church. They've done nothing but show me kindness and love and I don't know if I'll ever be able to thank them enough.

"You look so different with your guard down," Kayla tells me, walking up to my side. Turning my head to the side, I look at her, my eyes pulling together in confusion. Out of all the girls Kayla is the one I'm closest to, second to her is Harlow but that's only because we live together. Everyone else is busy with their lives, work and college.

"What do you mean?"

"Before your family arrived you were so secretive, always on guard. It was like you had the whole world on your shoulders, always checking over your shoulder, worried about what was following you. The guilt you carried in your eyes, the pain and sorrow would make me catch my breath every time I saw you. Now you're relaxed, light, free, your eyes softer and that strain you carried in your expression has now gone."

"WOW! You make it sound like she looked constantly constipated," Max tells Kayla, jumping behind us.

"Shut up," I laugh, turning to slap him on the chest. For some reason he doesn't get on my nerves as much as he used to. I've also found myself acting like a thirteen year old teenager with a huge crush when I'm around him. It's sickening really.

"God, no!" he says looking horrified. "Imagine the constant awkward silence," he tells us, exaggerating.

"Yeah, but think of the silence," Kayla giggles, moving over to the table and taking her seat.

"Where's Denny?" Joan asks Mason as he walks through the back door, catching mine and Max's attention.

"She's about a minute behind me. Evan and Kennedy just picked Hope up for the night," he answers, giving everyone a chin lift.

"I got friends," Cowen tells Marybeth as they walk into the kitchen, sitting down at the table.

"Yeah, you do," she smiles, leaning up to kiss his cheek.

"Your brother fucking loves me," Max whispers in my ear, causing me to shiver. With my parents under the same roof, I've not been able to explore Max the way I would have liked. We've touched each other but it's never gone too far. So after four days of constant foreplay between the two of us, I'm craving him like a pregnant woman does her food. My body is always hyper aware when he's around and I've found myself damp just looking at him.

A joke about my brother's head injury is on the tip of my tongue, using that as an excuse as to why my brother likes him so much. Feeling ashamed of myself I shake my head, turning to Max with a smirk gracing my lips.

"Someone needs to," I tease.

"You love me more," he jokes, moving and taking a seat next to Cowen, high fiving him which has become their normal greeting for each other.

"Twin, five, high," Cowen laughs, his eyes shining brightly when he sees Max. My eyes water watching them playfully high five each other, Marybeth shaking her head at their childish antics.

Pulling a chair out, I sit opposite Max, my dad to my right at the head of the table and my mum to my left.

"I love my daughter," Denny shouts as she walks through the back door with an evil grin upon her face.

"What did my girl do?" Max chuckles. He really does love his niece. It still surprises me about the way he is around that little girl. It just adds to his hotness in my book. I'm still gutted I missed her birthday party. I was too wrapped up in my own shit, but it's still no excuse. I felt so ashamed the next day when Joan asked me where I was. I ended up going over to Denny's to apologise. Even though she waved it away in understanding, guilt still gnaws at me.

"I think...thought Lake w-was your... Um... Your.... Um.... Love?" Cowen says, looking frustrated. He gets frustrated a lot but the only time he's flipped over it is when he wanted ketchup the other night at dinner but couldn't say that he wanted it. In the end Mum had answered him and just like I predicted he flipped a lid, saying he wasn't a baby.

"Oh, she is," Denny winks at Cowen, causing him to blush. "We're talking about my daughter, Hope. She just did a nice big poop for her uncle Evan, my brother."

Cowen laughs then falls easily into conversation with Marybeth and Kayla, telling them all about the football game he and Max played the other day.

"Won't Kennedy just change her?" Mason asks, biting his bottom lip. "What if he doesn't clean her properly and she comes back with a rash!"

"He has a daughter that he changes daily. I'm pretty sure he knows how to change a nappy, Mason," Denny replies, rolling her eyes. "He lost a bet and has to change nappies for the day as punishment," she grins.

"Unluckyyyyyy," Max hoots, laughing.

"Dinner's done," Joan announces, moving towards the table with serving dishes full of delicious smelling food. The roast she's spent the day cooking smells divine and I can't wait to dig in, my grumbling stomach agrees. How she managed to cook enough to feed fifteen of us is anyone's guess. Her appliances are only small, yet, somehow she still managed to cook more than enough.

"Do you want any help?" I ask, feeling bad that I've not offered to help until now.

"Ass licker," Max mutters under his breath, but loud enough for everyone to hear. Joan hears him and smacks him lightly across the head. "Harder," he smirks at her, giving her a wink. She just shakes her head and grabs some more dishes.

"No thank you, sweetheart," Joan smiles.

"Lick ass," Cowen chuckles, grinning at me, a look I know all too well crossing his features. I know exactly what he's thinking about. Call it twin intuition if you like. I glare at him, warning him to keep it shut, but he just chuckles, shaking his head. Thankfully, Marybeth distracts him from saying anything more.

When I was in year nine I basically did everything in my power to get our drama teacher to like me. She'd always get me to do the shitty jobs, ones involving painting, making props or helping backstage. It was so boring. I had to watch paint dry for hours.

It didn't matter how nice I was to her, how helpful I became, or that I'd bring her treats every drama lesson, she'd still never give me the leading role as Juliet. My frenemy, Alishia Cole, got the leading part all the time, even though she did a terrible job.

With the table buzzing with a million and one conversations, I'm worried no one heard that dinner was ready. It's only when Joan finally sits down that everyone turns quiet and begins to help themselves to food.

Looking around the table I bite my bottom lip, worried. For some reason the tension in my shoulders has not left me today and I'm beginning to feel uptight about it. It doesn't help everyone is here, together, for the first time since my family arrived. I'm worried they're not going to like each other. I don't think I'd cope if they never got on.

"Please don't make me say a prayer," Max whines when everyone has their plates nearly piled with food. Confused, I look up, wondering what on earth he's going on about. Joan has never made anyone say a prayer at dinner before. I should know, I've lived here for months and months.

"It would be good for your soul," Joan teases, rolling her eyes at him.

"Are you going to whip me again as punishment if I don't?" he asks, his bottom lip quivering. He asks the question with such sincerity that *I* almost believe him.

Cowen's eyes are wide with fear and Marybeth, bless her heart, looks confused as her eyes bounce back and forth between Max and Joan's conversation. My parents, however, are shifting uneasily in their seats, looking like they're ready to run for the hills, grabbing me and Cowen with them.

"He's joking," I assure them quickly, glaring over at Max, warning him to shut the fuck up.

Max gasps at my spoken words, a fearful expression still on his face as he keeps one eye on Joan. "I do not joke about the whiplashing. I can still hear the sound of the leather whistling through the air, the sound of it hitting my skin. The pain, Jesus, the pain," he shudders, his eyes looking lost for a minute or two like he's actually reliving the traumatic event. "It's okay, though. It's still not as bad as when she made me be a naked slave for the day, all her friends trying to take a turn."

"He really is joking," I tell my parents, but don't focus long enough on them to gauge their reaction. My eyes are completely focused on one subject, Max, wishing I could sew his fucking mouth shut. Why is he doing this right now? He's behaved as much as Max can all week and I've been thankful for it. I don't want my parents thinking I've been living with a crazy person.

"You wound me," he says, sounding genuinely hurt.

"I'll wound you in a minute if you don't shut up," I bite out. Images of jumping over the table and wrapping my hands around his throat are running through my mind. And as if reading my thoughts, an amused smirk tugs at his lips, making me growl under my breath.

The table has gone noticeably quiet, however, I'm too pissed to be embarrassed right now. My parents are going to freak out any second. I can see it now. They may be easy going parents but even this is something they wouldn't expect someone to joke about. They don't even know Max well enough to know he has an abnormal sense of humour, or that he tends to be over dramatic.

"She got to you didn't she?" he asks me, his voice above a whisper. He looks sad as he moves his food slowly around his plate with his fork, his hands shaking now and again.

"Dick-"

"Language," Mum warns, and I bow my head embarrassed. Max chuckling breaks into the silence. He slowly begins to laugh which causes me to snap my head up. As soon as I do everyone else is joining in with him, laughing their heads off at my reaction.

"You could have kept going for a while longer. She looked ready to smash her plate around your head."

My glare turns to Mason, not caring that he's right and that I was ready to smash a plate around Max's head. That's when I realise everyone knew what he was doing, even my parents. I wondered why no one had stepped in to shut him up. Growling under my breath, I narrow my eyes at everyone.

"Not funny," I grumble, my lips twitching.

"We had to do something. You look like you've got a stick up your ass," Max says ever-so politely.

"She whips you?" Cowen whispers, moving his chair away from Joan's general direction.

We all laugh then, the mood light and carefree. Marybeth explains the joke to Cowen but he still keeps one eye trained on Joan, watching for any sudden movements. I swear, every now and then he'll jump when he see's Joan move, looking afraid that Joan will grab a whip out of her back pocket and whip his ass. It's hysterical.

The rest of the dinner is pretty much everyone stuffing their faces and chatting mindlessly about anything and everything. It's one of the best days of my life.

Everyone is finished when my dad clears his throat. Turning my head I notice he's shifting uncomfortably in his chair, looking like he'd rather be somewhere else.

"Dad?" I call nervously, wondering what's on his mind.

"We need to talk to you about a few things. We just need you to know it wasn't our intention to keep anything from you," Dad chokes out, looking to my mum for help.

"Mum?" I ask her, my voice pleading. My body heats, trembles raking through my body as I anxiously wait for her to answer. She looks to my dad before looking my way again, her eyes softening when she sees my panic stricken expression.

"What your dad is trying to say is that we were going to tell you. It's just, we've only just got you back. We didn't want to be a bearer of bad news."

"Emma," Cowen blurts out, then looks down at the table shamefully. Marybeth rubs his back affectionately and I sit up straighter in my seat, my eyes watering.

"What about Emma?" I choke out and I hear Kayla gasp from the other side of my mother. I know she's thinking the worst, the same as me, after all, she knows what it's like to lose her best friend. Max filled me in on some of what happened but Kayla filled me in the most about Charlie, Kayla's best friend, and the heart condition that she suffered with before she passed away from complications.

"After the accident, Darren, he um, he kind of lost it. It was the same night everything happened. It was Banner that found her before it got too far," she tells me.

"What do you mean? What did he do?" I plead. My fingers bruise from digging my nails into the wooden chair but it's the only thing keeping me grounded.

"He attacked her," Cowen says, looking at me with sad eyes.

"But she's okay?" I ask, not believing something has happened. Not to Emma. Not when she lost her sister not long before.

"Yes, she's okay now… kind of. Darren attacked her, he tried to…" my dad starts to explain.

"I get it," I tell him quickly, not wanting to hear the word 'rape'. All I want to do is get in a shower I feel that dirty. I loved him or I thought I did. I gave myself to him and never realised just how sick he was. The drug dealing thing I could move on from, but this… This is something that I blame myself for. I taunted Darren the night of the accident, I told him we knew and that Emma was going to the police. How many lives have I destroyed? I shake my head, a few tears falling free.

"She's okay, but she wasn't for a while. She wouldn't leave the house or let anyone in to see her. She's attending a community college near home for now but she still needs a lot of support."

"Why didn't you tell me sooner?" I whisper. I feel bad that the past few days I've enjoyed being around my family, happy to know I didn't tear us apart or lose my brother. When all along I did ruin someone's life, it just wasn't who I thought it was.

"We wanted to tell you at the right time. We wanted you to be surrounded by the people you love," Mum tells me softly.

It's then the silence in the room becomes too much and I look around the table giving everyone a small smile.

"I can talk to her soon," I nod, needing to make all this right, and honestly, not wanting to talk about it in front of everyone. I don't need them to know how much of a failure I really am.

Not only had my brother needed me by his side, but my best friend had also. God, she must have suffered. Then something occurs to me. "What happened to Darren?"

"He was arrested, put on trial and got found guilty. He got five years," Dad fills in.

"For good behaviour he gets two," Cowen snorts, his jaw clenched. I know his pain. Even though Emma was my best friend, she was also close with Cowen and even admitted to having a crush on him a time or two. Nothing she'd ever play on. She valued our friendship and knew being with my brother would ruin that. Back then he never stayed with a girl long. He usually got what he wanted and moved on. If he did that to Emma it would have caused tension at home and I'd most likely lose my friend because of it.

"I hope he stays there," I bite out.

"Hopefully his parents can only afford soap," Max adds, lightening the mood. We all laugh, Cowen chuckling louder than the rest of us.

"You said a few things?" I tell Dad while everyone begins conversations: filling the silence.

"Yeah. We've got to go back tomorrow. We want you to come with us," he tells me and my heart stops. I knew there would be a time they'd have to leave but I didn't want to process it. How could I? I have a life here, a new family, but I also don't want to lose my real family now that I have them back.

"I don't..." I shake my head, looking to Max for answers. His eyes are on me and I know from the sadness flashing in his eyes that he heard everything my dad just said.

I have to admit, a huge part of me wants to stay because of him. He believed in me when I didn't believe in myself and he's also been through a lot, he doesn't need another woman in his life leaving. But not only that, I can't picture my life without him in it. We've spent nearly every moment together since I moved in. Losing him would be like losing Cowen at this point. That's how close we've become.

My dad's expression falls when I stay silent and my mum's hand grips my leg under the table. I know they'll let me stay if I asked, but I also know it would kill them. I've missed out on so much already. But they don't know how much Joan and her family have done for me. Everything here feels right. But if they leave, it won't. Either way I don't win. I'll be losing someone who means the world to me.

"What time do you have to leave?" Max asks my dad, his expression changing. It's not his normal light, carefree face. His face has hardened a touch and his eyes have turned cold.

"We need to leave before midday," Dad answers.

"You should go," Max tells me, nodding his head. "You've finally got your family back. You should stay with them."

"But..." I start, but his expression has me shutting my mouth, my eyes watering.

"But what? When I called them I knew you'd leave with them. Have you not thought of that before now? I've got to meet Lindsey tomorrow around half eleven, so it works out perfectly. I won't get accused of anything."

"Jackie?" I ask, my voice laced with hurt. Why is he doing this to me? I don't understand.

"Yeah," he smirks, leaning forward on his elbows. "She's a chick I met at Antonio's. Hot piece. Big jugs," he tells me, his eyes cold and distant. This isn't the Max I know.

"Max," Maverick warns, moving back in his chair.

"What?" Max asks, looking offended, a huge smile on his face, although it doesn't reach his eyes.

"You know what," Maverick snaps back; his voice louder.

"Why are you doing this?" I ask him, moving my chair back ready to escape. I look around and although everyone avoids my eyes the humiliation of what Max is doing still hits me, my cheeks heating in embarrassment.

"How else am I going to get rid of you? I've lost my player status since you arrived," he snarls yet a flash of hurt and regret flickers in his eyes.

"That's enough," Dad snaps, beginning to look red. His hands are clenched into fists on the table but my mother's soothing voice calling his name relaxes him.

"Sorry, sir, but she needs to know she has to go. I can see love hearts in her eyes like a poxy emoji and I'd hate for her to lose you again because I'm awesome," he snickers.

"Max. Don't do this, please," I beg, not understanding why he's pushing me away.

"Do what? Tell you the truth," he laughs, his head thrown back.

"Max, get the fuck out now!" Maverick roars, slamming his cup down on the table. I'm surprised it didn't smash.

"Why?" Max asks cockily. My brother next to him is fuming, his eyes narrowed angrily up at Max. Marybeth is trying to calm him down. Seeing everyone like this is making everything that is already happening worse. Devastation and betrayal hit me in full force and I have to take in a deep breath to try and calm down.

"You're going to regret ever saying any of this in the morning. You don't mean it. Stop being a jerk and let Lake make up her own mind."

"For fuck's sake, she already made up her mind. Everyone leaves, brother, you should know. You were good at it," Max snarls and Maverick looks like he's been hit with a sledge hammer and the hurt that washes across his face has me wondering what Max meant. "I'm doing her a favour. I'm not the bad fucking guy here. Fuck it. I'm going to meet Lindsey. I'll see you assholes in the morning," Max snaps before rushing out the room.

The room goes completely silent as I sit at the table with tears running down my face, my heart hurting painfully at Max's departing words twist the knife he already stabbed in my heart.

"Lake," Mum whispers, her hand on my thigh rubbing gently.

Snapping out of it, I jump up from my seat. "I best go pack then," I mutter before rushing out of the room.

In my room I head straight for my phone, praying Max has sent me a text message saying it was all a lie and that he was joking or he didn't mean any of it. When there's nothing I sink down on my bed and burst into tears. I grip my chest letting the pain consume me as a strangled sob breaks free from my throat. For the first time in a while I let the pain consume me, feeling everything enough for it to break me, my body falling limply onto the bed from exhaustion.

Not much time passes, maybe twenty minutes at the most, before someone comes knocking on my door. I half expected someone to come up and check on me but I guessed they'd have come sooner.

"Go away," I sniffle, not wanting anyone to see how humiliated I'm feeling right now. It would just be another knife to the chest.

Max deliberately caused that scene downstairs, knowing what it would do to me and how I would feel. He didn't care either way. It has me wondering, though, if he had planned to do what he did all along. He didn't seem to hesitate or mull over what he was going to say next, it all came out naturally like a rehearsed speech.

The door opens even after I protested, telling them to go away. I'm about to ream out whoever's brave enough to go against my wishes but when I'm met with Maverick's dark, nearly black, eyes staring back at me, I'm startled into silence.

Out of everyone Maverick is the last person I would have guessed to be the one coming to check up on me. We've never really spoken. He's given me more dirty looks than the girls at the church food bank.

I've not really seen him since Denny's hen party. From what I overheard Mark telling Joan last week, Maverick has something going down at V.I.P and it's causing him stress.

"Hi," I whisper, wiping tears from my eyes and my runny nose along the sleeve of my t-shirt.

"How are ya feelin'?" he asks me gently, stepping further into the room and taking a seat on the end of my bed.

"Oh, I'm fine. Not like Max didn't just rip my heart out in front of everyone I care about," I bite out sarcastically. My body sags immediately for talking so rudely to him when he's just checking up on me. "I'm sorry."

"It's fine," he tells me gently, his eyes staring at me intently, searching for what, I don't know. Shifting on my bed, I avoid his intense stare. I've always been intimidated by Maverick. Out of all the brothers he seems to have a dark edge to him, something cold and dark lurking behind those dark brown eyes of his. It actually reminds me of when I first met him and I thought his eyes were black. God, how long ago that was now?

"It's not," I whisper after a few awkward moments of silence.

"You do know he didn't mean any of what he said down there, don't you? He's just scared, as much as it would pain him to admit," he tells me and my eyes reach his. Looking at him closely I can tell he genuinely believes what he said. It doesn't matter, though. Max can't take back what he did or said to me. It's engraved in my mind, playing over and over like a broken fucking record.

"Didn't he? Want to bet he's already with *Lindsey* right now?" I bite out, my face scrunched up in pain. "I thought I meant something to him," I tell Maverick without meaning to. It just slipped out. But I meant every word. I did believe I meant something to him. I thought we shared something special.

"Deep down I think you know how much you really mean to him. You're just angry and upset right now. He knew you'd be leaving."

"How? I didn't even know until he made the choice for me. And why do you care? You've always seemed wary of me."

"I guess I predicted this would happen. I know my brothers. They're good men and I knew the first time I met you that you were running from your family. Whether it was from a broken home or something else, I didn't know. The minute one or more of my brothers found out they'd want to fix it. Max fixed it," he shrugs. "He didn't grow up with a family like you did. All he's ever had is us and Granddad. Everyone else left. He doesn't realise how fortunate we are our mum left, but that loss hits him whether he admits it or not. Our dad was killed, leaving us. Even if he was an evil prick we were together. Then we moved in with Granddad and our Nan. Then she died, leaving us again. We've watched people leave us our whole life. It's why he never lets anyone in. He never even got close to anyone to push them away before until he met you."

"What about Harlow, Denny and Kayla?" I whisper. His words roll around in my head and I never really thought of it that way. He never seemed to care that he lost his parents. In fact, he always made me believe it was a blessing and from what he told me about them, it was a blessing.

"He knew they weren't going anywhere. Have you seen the way my brothers are with those girls? They'd die before they'd let them leave. Denny left once, when Mason fucked up, and although she was with Mason, it killed Max. They were close and he felt that loss when she left."

"Why are you telling me all of this," I whisper, conflicted about what to do.

"Because I need you to know my brother loves you, even if he hasn't said those words out loud. I'm hoping this isn't the end of us seeing you and that you'll come back."

"Wouldn't that be harder?" I ask him, searching his expression.

"Maybe," he shrugs. "But what's the alternative? If you stay then you'll miss more time with your family. Max out of all people should know what it's like to be apart from your twin. Or you could go, keep in touch and try to balance it all out."

When I don't say anything he reaches into his coat jacket, pulling out a card with the club logo on. When he hands it to me I look at him confused.

"Call me. If you ever need anything, no matter what, call me."

I nod my head, tears filling my eyes once again. "What am I going to do about Max?"

"Forgive the prick. He's probably at some bar drinking his sorrows, regretting what he did."

When he leaves I stay sitting on my bed thinking about everything he just said to me. Either way I'm going to be destroyed, but at least if I leave with my parents I'll feel wanted. Grabbing my phone from the side I pull up Max's number, sending him a message.

LAKE: I'm sorry

I fall asleep holding my phone to my chest, waiting for Max to reply. But when I wake up the next morning, there are no missed calls or messages, sealing my fate.

TWENTY-SEVEN

LAKE

Bags packed and loaded up in the car, I sit in my bedroom, taking in my room once more before I leave.

My parents waited as long as they could for Max to return home, but it's midday and still no word from him. Everyone has tried to get in touch with him with no luck. They've tried to play it off but I'm worried. We're leaving in fifteen and I've still not said goodbye.

My door opens and I wipe my tears frantically, stunned when Joan walks in with some tissues.

"Thank you," I smile.

"You're not leaving us for good, sweetheart. This isn't goodbye, it's I'll see you later," she tells me, causing me to burst into tears. I wrap my arms around her neck, holding her tightly. I'm going to miss her so much.

"Thank you. Thank you so much for everything you've done for me. You're the Grandma I never had. I love you," I choke out between sobs, hating that I'm leaving.

"Sweetheart," she sighs, rubbing her cold hands down my back. "I love you too, but thank you. Thank you for coming into our lives. We've loved having you and you'll always, *always*, have a home here. This room will always be yours. So you can come and stay whenever you want. You'll always be welcome."

"Why isn't he here?" I ask after a few minutes of just holding each other. I pull back looking at her sad expression.

"I don't know, sweetheart, but I will tell you he's got me to answer to when he finally resurfaces."

I give her a weak smile. "I'm really going to miss you guys."

"We're going to miss you too. I've packed you some chocolate mousse cake for the drive home, it's in the kitchen."

I begin to cry again and Joan pulls my head on her shoulder. I knew today would be hard but not this hard. I can literally feel my heart cracking in two, being pulled in two different directions.

The door knocks again, opening to show Denny, Harlow and Kayla. Denny and Kayla have both got tears in their eyes but Harlow is full on crying.

"Damn hormones," she sobs, walking into the room. Joan stands, pulling me to my feet.

"I'm going to make sure your mother doesn't need anything before she leaves," she smiles, then pulls me in for another hug. "See you soon."

"My hormones can't take this," Harlow sobs close by and I pull back, laughing through my tears.

"Com' 'ere," she sobs, pulling me into a hug, her bump pressed against my stomach.

"I'm going to miss you," I whisper, holding her tighter. She's been like a sister to me, one I always wished for growing up with a brother.

"I'm going to miss you too. It's not going to be the same around here without you," she tells me sadly. "But I know if I had a chance to go back to my parents, I would. I miss them every day," she vows to me. "Max will get over it soon," she promises.

"My turn, bitch," Denny tells Harlow, bumping her lightly with her hip. "Don't be a stranger, girl. We'll hunt your ass down otherwise," she tells me, her voice choked up with emotion.

"I won't, I promise," I giggle, wiping my eyes once more. God, I didn't think I had any tears left after I cried myself to sleep last night. Obviously I was wrong.

"What she said," Kayla smiles sadly. "I don't want you to go, but if I had parents like yours, I'd want to spend every waking moment with them."

"This is so hard," I cry, sitting down on the edge of the bed. Kayla moves behind me on the bed, Denny sits to my right and Harlow to my left, and they all envelop me into a tight hug.

"We love you," Harlow whispers as the door to my room opens once more. I don't have time to turn my head before large bodies are squashing us to the bed. Harlow moves out of the way quickly.

"Arghhh, you fat bastards," Denny cries, half lying on me still.

"Group hug," Mason chuckles, smacking a kiss on Denny before lifting up along with Myles, Malik and Maverick. Jesus, how did they not suffocate us?

Seeing Myles has a pang hitting my chest. I keep expecting Max to turn up and seeing his face is just another reminder that he's not coming.

Kayla barely makes it off the bed before Mason and Myles are jumping on me again, squashing me into the mattress. The girls begin to giggle while I try to puff out a breath.

"Seriously, you guys weigh a ton," I wheeze out.

"We're going to miss you," Myles tells me, leaning in to kiss my forehead. My eyes water again and I roll my eyes.

"Don't leak on me," Mason tells me seriously, making me giggle.

"Sorry. I'm just going to miss you guys," I babble, balling my eyes out once again.

"Now look what you've done," I hear Maverick mutter. Strong arms lift me up from the bed and fold me into a hug. "It's going to be okay. Do you still have my card?" he asks, his voice below a whisper so the others don't hear. I nod my head and hold him tighter for a second before pulling away.

"I best go then," I tell them and all of them rush towards me, engulfing me into a tight huddle.

When they pull away, Malik clears his throat seeming uncomfortable with all the emotion going on in the room. It makes me smile.

"I'm going to go... Go do some shit," he says, causing Harlow to giggle.

"Let's go see if they need any help," Harlow tells him.

Everyone starts filing out of my room and I'm the last to follow, my eyes taking in the room once more before I shut the door, emotion clogging my throat.

We're all outside saying our goodbyes once more. Denny has Hope wrapped up in her winter coat, standing next to Mason. Myles has Kayla wrapped up in his arms, her head on his shoulder and Malik has his arms wrapped around Harlow from behind, his large hands rubbing her pregnant stomach. Maverick is standing next to Mark who has a weeping Joan in his arms.

My hands are full, holding two containers of my favourite chocolate mousse, when an idea occurs to me.

"Wait, I need to do something," I tell Mum and Dad. Everyone stares as I step away from the car, a smile tugging at my lips.

"Where are you going?" Mum calls.

"Just need to leave something for Max," I call back, hoping he'll understand.

When I'm done I can't help but cry. I'm about to leave Max's bedroom when one of his t-shirts catch my eye. Checking the hall to make sure no one is there, I grab it, folding it up and hiding it underneath my coat.

It might be creepy stealing his clothes, but I need something to remind me of him. The thought of never smelling his scent again causes an ache to form in my chest. Just like the thought of never being able to see him again.

Walking out, Mum and Dad are in the car; Marybeth's already gone.

"Where's Cowen and Marybeth?" I ask as I walk up to the car. Joan moves away, coming to hug me one more time.

"They've gone ahead, sweetheart," Mum tells me.

I nod, getting into the back of the car, strapping the belt around me. Everyone is standing outside the window and I wave, smiling sadly.

"You ready?" Mum asks.

No. No, I'm not. Instead, I whisper, "Yes."

She starts the car and tears begin to fall faster. I wave at everyone standing there and watch the girls and Joan break down in their men's arms. A painful sob tears from my throat and I can't hold back any longer.

"Oh, honey," Mum whispers, looking at me through the rear-view mirror.

"It will get easier," Dad says from the passenger seat, looking over at me sadly. I give him a weak smile as I rest my head against the window, watching the rain begin to pour.

It feels like I've just left my other half all over again, splitting me in two. When my phone dings I grab it out of my coat pocket, thankful that Joan let me keep it.

My breath hitches when I see Max's name and I find it hard to breathe as I open the message.

Max: I'm sorry.

I don't text back, my heart hurting too much. I should be over the moon that he's sorry but it just makes leaving that much harder.

All I can do now is pray my heart recovers, but deep down, without Max, my heart will always be torn in two.

TWENTY-EIGHT

MAX

It's been a week since Lake left and nothing seems to be getting easier. Joan has tried to keep me busy, or punish me, but it doesn't matter, she's always on my mind. No matter how much I drink at night I'll still fall asleep thinking of her, dreaming of her and wishing I didn't fuck up as bad as I did. But if I didn't I know she would have torn herself apart making a decision. We hadn't talked about it, but I knew it was there in the back of her mind. Pushing her away was the only way and I regret how I did it, but not doing it... I couldn't be the reason she stayed apart from her family, not when I know how I would feel if someone ever tried to take my family away from me.

I had planned to say goodbye, to tell her I'm sorry, but I passed out at Antonio's place and never woke up until late midday. I woke up to a bunch of missed calls and messages off everyone, telling me what a prick I am and that she left. I immediately texted her, telling her I was sorry. But it was too late, even I knew that. But saying it, even if it was through text, was something I needed to do.

Finishing up the last of the washing up, I dry my hands on the tea towel. Joan takes that moment to walk in and I groan. I had hoped to sneak out and head over to the pub. I'm not in the mood to do shit today other than drink.

"I'm off to the pub," I tell Joan before she can rope me into anything else.

"Nope, you're folding these clothes and putting them away," she tells me, throwing a sock at me, the offending item smacking me in the face before I grab hold of it.

"Master has presented Dobby with clothes. Dobby is free!" I shout and grab my coat from the back of the kitchen chair and run out the backdoor, ignoring Joan's furious calls for me to go back.

I take the shortcut to MC5 and get there in record time. Luckily Mason isn't working today and Maverick will be downstairs sorting whatever shit is going on with V.I.P. I'll have time to wallow in my own self pity without having them all watching me like a hawk.

"Double JD and coke and a straight double of JD," I tell Jax, one of the new bartenders Mason hired.

"Sure," he nods and makes quick work of making my drinks. I don't bother moving away from the bar. After downing the first double shot of JD I order another and another. Soon I'm swaying myself over to an empty high table, struggling to sit straight on the stall.

"Shit, this fucker's high," I mutter, chuckling to myself and feeling drunker by the second.

"Hey, handsome," a young girl with a friend flirts as she walks up to my table. "You want some company?"

"I need something," I mutter to myself and wave my arm at the two empty chairs. They both share a grin before taking a seat. "Well, hello beautiful ladies," I grin, faking my charm.

"So what has you drinking all alone this evening?" the other girl says. She's a curvy girl, works it well. Freckles cover her nose and cheeks and she has her hair up in a messy ponytail, the blonde box job she's got needs some serious work. I think she's got more roots than blonde.

"Do I look lonely to you?" I smirk. "You know, Lake would never come get drunk with me," I tell them heatedly. "NO! She'd make me watch lame ass movies, which I'd enjoy but didn't want to."

"Huh? Who's Lake," the girl who first approached me asks. She's slimmer than the bad-blonde girl, has sharp blue eyes. She tries to give me a seductive smile but all I can do is hold back a cringe. She's got a gap between the top two front teeth, making me feel sorry for the next fucker she gives a blowjob to.

"The girl who left me. Would you leave me? I bet you wouldn't leave me. SHOTS!" I shout across the bar and Jax, the bartender, rolls his eyes looking like he wants to refuse. Still, it doesn't stop that fucker from making me my drinks. "Don't forget one for these young ladies."

The girls giggle and I give them a drunken grin. I can do this. I've got the charm. I've got the love. I can rock their world.

"I'm Em and this is Kim," Blondie tells me.

"Max," I grin but a frown soon replaces it.

"So who put a frown on your face?" Kim asks, still trying to be seductive, bless her heart.

"Lake. Can you believe she put shit in my boxers?" I tell them, both girls looking thoroughly disgusted.

"Not real shit," I slur, rolling my eyes. "She left mousse in my boxers. Not just one pair but every fucking pair. Everyone thought I had the runs. Couldn't even get the stains out," I chuckle, remembering when I got home the day Lake left.

I'd gone straight to my room after getting my ass handed to me from everyone. Literally. They all took turns getting their anger and frustration out on me. Harlow even got physical before she suddenly burst into tears. Don't even get me started on Maverick. He's been giving me the eye all week and I know he's itching to kick my ass. Not that I blame him.

Anyway, I'd gone to my room, showered and headed back to my room. When I went to grab a fresh pair of boxers, I found out the hard way just how much I hurt Lake.

After taking a second shower, rinsing chocolate mousse from my ass crack and balls, I headed back into my room for another pair. Only, the sneaky bitch ruined every single pair in my drawers.

Everyone had thought I'd shit myself. It took me shoving a pair in my brother's face to prove I wasn't having bowel problems. Of course, I'd already tasted the offending mess; it's how I found out it was Joan's famous mousse recipe.

Crazy bitch.

"You know how to get over someone?" gap girl flirts, her finger running up and down my arm.

"Fuck two girls senseless at the same time?" I ask, but there's no heat in my words. I probably wouldn't be able to get it up for them and not just because I'm two sheets to the wind. Doesn't mean I won't make a fool of myself trying.

The girls giggle and I fight hard not to roll my eyes at them. Movement on the DJ stage catches my eye and I notice some blokes setting something up.

"What's going on?" I shout over to Jax who's walking over with our drinks.

"It's karaoke," he rumbles, not seeming impressed with me.

Neyo's, So Sick starts playing over the speakers, grabbing my attention. Jax huffs seeming pissed at my sudden dismissal. Fuck, if only he knew how heartbroken I am.

Neyo starts babbling over the speakers about not being able to move on, feeling ridiculous about not getting over her even though it's been months. Then he mentions being stronger, not wanting to walk around being blue and it hits me. I have to sing a hate song or something powering to help me move on. The more the idea swirls in my head the more sure I am it will work.

"I need to sing a hate song. It will help me move on from her," I tell the girls, but they're too busy chatting to each other. I fall in a heap on the floor, bruising my ass, and the girls look over the table at me seeming amused.

"I need to sing. I'm good. I'm good," I slur, getting up and moving over towards the stage. I nearly knock over a few chairs on my way but luckily people were sitting in them, stopping them from going down.

"Mate, I think you need to go home and sleep it off," Jax tells me and I look at him like he's got two heads.

"Why don't *you* sleep it off," I snap, pointing my finger at his chest.

"Because I'm not drunk or falling over customers. You just groped a lady's chest," he tells me, rolling his eyes.

"Pft, please," I roll my eyes. "I landed on them, not like I did it on purpose."

"You gave them a squeeze."

"They felt soft," I defend.

"She's in her sixties," Jax tells me dryly.

"Then she just got the thrill of her life."

"What are you doing?" he asks, sighing.

"Singing. I need to sing Lake a hate song so I can get over her for leaving. She left. Just left. Everyone leaves. Did you know…"

"Mate, just sing your song," he tells me, moving out of my way. Well, isn't he a chatty chappy.

Grinning in triumph I make my way up the stage and flick through the song book until I come across the perfect one. I take the book over to the DJ and he looks at me like I've lost it. Maybe I have.

"This one?" he double checks, looking uncertain with my awesome song choice.

"Yeppers," I grin, feeling happy about my decision. I needed this. To get her out of my mind once and for all. Shit, maybe I can sing *Kylie Minogue's, I Can't Get You Out Of My Head*.

"Alrighty then," he chuckles, before handing me a mic.

Gloria Gaynor's I Will Survive starts blasting from the speakers and everyone in the bar turns to me.

Some laugh when I start singing but I don't give a shit. I need to feel empowered, strong and what better way than *Gloria Gaynor's I Will Survive*? I just hope I don't fuck up when I get to the chorus and sing 'I will survive, as long as I've had Weetabix, I know I'll stay alive' from the Weetabix advert years ago.

My voice is high as I sing the lyrics, demanding someone to walk out the door, to not turn around, that I don't need them anymore.

It feels good, refreshing, and I start to get carried away, pointing to people in the bar, singing louder as I stare at them. My hips start jiggling and I find myself moving across the stage, nearly flying backwards when the wire of the mic stops me short.

The song comes to an end and everyone cheers. I take a dramatic bow, nearly falling face first off the stage. Luckily, I manage to catch my footing.

Jumping down from the stage, I grin big as I make my way back to the table, to the two girls sitting with a fresh round of drinks. I smirk as I arrive, downing the drink in one go.

"What shall we sing next? I reckon we should sing some Taylor, or hell, maybe some Bruno Mars and Celine Dion. Come on, I'm feeling energetic," I rant, feeling excitement bubble inside me for the first time since Lake left.

"Maybe we could go do something else?" she suggests, waggling her eyebrows at me. I laugh at the two caterpillars before leaning over the table like I'm going to tell them a big secret.

"What you thinking? *My Heart Will Go On*? *We're Never Getting Back Together*?"

"I was thinking more along the lines of being naked," Kim flirts, giggling.

I look between the two, weighing my options. I've been in this situation before and it didn't end well for me.

"Few questions first," I tell them, watching their eyes light up. "You into threesomes? Spanking?"

The girls nod, looking at each with a scrunched up face. I ignore it, carrying on. After all, we're talking about my safety here.

"What about fisting, soiling on each other? Anal?" I ramble, taking another gulp of my drink. When I open my eyes the girls are rushing away.

"Well, shit," I chuckle and then look around the room, looking for someone to help sing my problems away with. When I see another group of girls, I smack my glass down on the table.

Sha-tttting!

Staggering over to the group of four girls I put a wide grin on my face. They see me approach and a few run an appreciative eye over me.

Well, look at that, I'm in, I grin, tripping over my own feet and bumping into two of the four girls.

"Shit, ladies, I'm sorry. Bartender spiked my drink," I joke. The two I bumped into don't look too pleased and start to move away from me. The other two are giggling, looking amused. At least someone appreciates my moves.

"Hey, I'm Amber," the chick with brown hair, blue eyes and a rack to drool over greets.

"Well, hellooooo, Amber," I smirk, my eyes zeroing on her two beauties. "Want to go and sing with me? We could rock this place."

"What were you thinking?" Amber asks seeming into the idea.

"Maybe *Taylor Swift*, *One Direction*, or maybe some *Celine Dion*, 'My Heart Will Go On', what do you think?"

"Who's *Celine Dion*?" she asks and I look at her appalled.

"Are you fucking with me? I'm only eighteen and even I know who *Celine Dion* is," I tell her, eyes wide. I don't bother to mention my nan listened to her constantly and that the chick kind of grew on me. I could sing a bit of Celine better than most people.

But seriously, has this chick been living under a rock?

"You been living under a rock?"

"No," she snaps dryly, the seductive look she was giving me now wiped from her face. Well, shit. Maybe the other chick will be game. When my eyes turn to the side my body sways and I think I've drunk more than I realised because all three of the other girls have disappeared.

"Magic," I whisper, rubbing furiously at my eyes. Nope, still gone.

"What?"

"Nothing, so... Taylor? One D?"

"Um..." she starts, but something behind me catches her eye and I watch them widen before dilating into lust.

What crab ass is trying to steal my singing partner? Turning, I watch as Maverick struts over, an angry glare in his eyes.

Jesus, he's acting like he owns the place. *That's because he does, fuckhead.*

I chuckle before turning to greet my brother full on, my arms open wide for a hug. He doesn't even blink at my hug offer. He just nods to the girl behind me with disinterest, making my earlier gay comment fitting.

"Max," he snaps. "What are you doing here? Shouldn't you be at home doing chores for Joan?"

"Bro," I call excitedly, throwing my hands around the girl beside me. "Didn't you hear? I'm a free elf. Master presented Dobby with a sock, Dobby free," I laugh, the girl laughing beside me.

"Can you give us a minute?" Maverick asks the girl, and the look he gives her doesn't leave any room for an argument. She disappears and I watch her walk away pouting. That is until she sits at a table with a bunch of other girls, one looking familiar.

"Hey, doesn't she look like a rougher version of Kayla?" I whisper like it's a conspiracy, whilst looking over at Kayla's rougher looking doppelgänger. I even point in her direction in case Maverick missed her while he was doing a cat walk over here, but he slaps my hand down looking embarrassed.

"Pack it in," he hisses, looking unamused. Leaning forward he grabs my arm, pulling me through the bar towards the back.

"Hey, I was trying to find my score for the night," I snap, my words slurred and honestly? Uncaring. "Hey, are you drunk?" I ask, wondering why he's zigzagging me through the bar.

Maverick whirls on me, his face thunderous. "Shut the fuck up. We need to talk," he booms, shoving me into the unoccupied booths.

"I'm not a fucking rag doll," I snap, rolling my eyes dramatically. "If you're here to give me the lecture on the usage of protection, I got it covered. If you want to give me some sexual pointers, one ewwww, and two, I don't need any. This bad boy can go all night," I grin, thrusting my hips, managing to catch my groin on the table. "Fuck."

"What the fuck is going on with you? First you're a jerk to Lake, embarrassing her in front of everyone and her family..." he starts, making my hands fist together under the table.

"*WE* were her family too," I shout, my blood raging. How dare he bring her up, how fucking dare he? He doesn't know fucking shit. He doesn't know that I acted like a dick to protect her, to give her what she wanted, what she needed.

My brother sighs, his eyes softening for a moment before looking at me with a pitiful look.

"Don't do that," I warn him, not needing him to take pity on me. After a second I plaster on a fake smile, looking at him like nothing ever happened. "Want to sing a song? We could duet you know. Maybe some breakaway pop hit," I tell him seriously, wondering if it will be okay for men to sing together.

He ignores me, a sad sigh escaping. "If you didn't want her to leave why did you push her away?"

"As riveting as this conversation is, I'd rather be getting another drink and getting into that one's pants," I tell him, pointing to the hot blonde that has been eye fucking me from across the room. She winks when she sees me pointing, so I return it with a wink of my own.

Maverick turns to look: hey, he's male, don't judge him. His eyes widen before snapping back to me with an expression I can't decipher.

"That sixty year old woman?" he asks, with a slight squeak to his voice.

"What?" I ask confused, shaking my alcohol induced head. That's when I see her, the old lady whose chest kept me standing earlier on my way to the stage. "Nah, not her," I chuckle, amused. "Already felt that up."

Maverick doesn't seem too impressed, in fact, he looks down right horrified and if I'm right, a little pissed.

"Why are you doing this?" he asks, looking defeated and older than his twenty-six years.

"'Cause I need to get laid? 'Cause I need someone to fuck Lake out of my fucking mind?"

"For fuck's sake, Max," he roars, slamming his fist on the table. "For once in your fucking life be honest. Tell me what's going on in that warped ass, crazy mind of yours. One thing I never pictured you as and that's a coward."

Anger fills my veins, fuelling my temper which I don't lose often. It takes a lot for me to get angry, but he's going too far. I'm no fucking coward. I stand up suddenly, leaning menacingly over the table, getting in his face.

"Don't you fucking dare, Mav. If anyone's a coward it's you," I snarl, bringing up the time he left when we were younger.

His short fuse blows and he pushes me back down, taking his turn to get in my face before sitting back down. "That's unfair and you fucking know it," he snarls and the dark look that crosses his face has me sobering, sitting back in the leather booth. I've seen him angry but I've never seen him like this. His eyes are completely void of any emotion, a dark, cold look smothering his features. His eyes have turned completely black, scaring the shit out of me. "You have no idea, no fucking idea what I went through living in that house. You think you guys had it bad? I had it ten times worse, Max. But that's not why you're pissed is it? No, it's about Lake leaving, not me. Now fucking admit why you're so worked up over her leaving."

"Because I fucking love her," I roar, and everyone's eyes fall on me. Ducking my head, I lower my tone to just above a whisper. "I love her," I finally admit, feeling deflated. I've never loved anyone as much as I've loved her. I might have pushed her away for her own good but in the end she would have made the same choice, leaving me anyway. I just made it easier for her, even if it killed me inside.

I've come to blows with Mav before, but nothing compared to this. Ever. He's also never talked about his childhood before either which is shocking. He might not have revealed much to some people, but to me, it's more than he's ever shared before. He, Mason and Malik stay closed off when it comes to growing up, but Maverick, he shuts down anything to do with him and his upbringing. So knowing I've caused him to blow up like this, to talk about his past, makes me realise how much I've really fucked up this past week.

"So go get her back," he tells me after a few minutes, only our heavy breathing filling the silence.

His complete one-eighty personality change causes a wave of dizziness to hit me. He's acting like we didn't just hit each other with emotional abuse. My eyes warily watch him, trying to see if he's going to jump me the minute I step out of the booth, but all I see is concern and worry, looking at me like I'm going to break at any second.

"How?" I ask, my voice weak. I don't have the energy to fight with him anymore; it's exhausting. That and all the alcohol consumption hasn't helped my energy levels.

"It's not going to be easy. First you need to sober up."

I was afraid he was going to say that.

"Okay, but first, stop spinning the room, it's making me feel sick."

TWENTY-NINE

LAKE

I WAKE UP WITH RED PUFFY EYES from crying all night. I'd literally fallen asleep sobbing my eyes out.

When we arrived home yesterday my stomach was still tied up in knots. I felt so sick and it wasn't from the car ride. It only got worse the second we pulled up to my childhood home.

My mum and dad neglected to tell me they had organised a surprise 'welcome home' party. I knew they planned it out of love and wanted me to feel welcome but it just felt like an ambush, one that suffocated me from the second I walked through the door.

Family and friends passed me around like some rare antique. They asked me question after question, some even going as far as to send me disapproving looks. After listening to my uncle Ian give me what for, reminding me how much I put my family through running away, I kindly excused myself and rushed up to my old bedroom.

I fell apart as soon as I opened the door. It's like everything hits me at once seeing my old room. Mum and Dad hadn't moved or changed a thing. Not one thing. Everything is how I remembered it to be from the night we left to pick

Cowen up from that dreadful party.

My prom dress was still hanging up on the wardrobe door, my school uniform folded on my chair and even my mobile phone, nail polish and magazine was still lying on my bed like I had only been gone away a day and not a year.

All that ran through my head was, 'They never gave up on me'. Not once. It broke my heart knowing they lived life expecting me to return at any second but each day passed with no word from me. It was just another hard reminder of how badly I've messed up.

This past year I've spent every day wishing I could change that tragic night. I prayed that I could save Cowen, bring him back to life and that life would go back to how it was supposed to be. The guilt over that night ate away at me until there was nothing left of me.

Then I met Joan. She was so kind, so gentle, and never pushed me. She breathed a little light into my life, showed me a world where people were worse off than me. It gave me a reason to live again. If I couldn't make my own life better then the least I could do was try to help other people make their lives better.

But then Max happened and I wasn't prepared for him. I never expected he would be the one to breathe the life back into me. He brought me to want to live again, to love again, and by God, I love him. I love him so much that the pain from him not being in my life has left a hole in my heart and it's slowly killing me inside and out.

A knock on my bedroom door shakes me out of my thoughts. Quickly, I sit up, leaning back against my cushions before wiping at my tears furiously. I don't want my mum or dad to walk in and see the mess I'm in and think I don't want to be here. I'm trying so hard to not show how badly I'm missing Max, missing Joan and the rest of them, but it's so hard when it's breaking my heart. They all became such a huge part in my life that not having them around anymore is making me feel lost. It's tearing me apart inside because it's the same feeling I had when I ran away.

It's like I'm being pulled in two different directions. One part of me wants to be back home with Max, with Joan, but the other is hanging on tight to stay with her parents, with her brother.

"Come in," I call out, my voice hoarse.

My door opens revealing an apprehensive looking Marybeth. I'm actually surprised it's her and not my mum or Cowen. They've done nothing but smother me, asking if I'm okay every five minutes. I'm glad my dad gives me a wide berth but I think he's only doing that because he knows I need some space.

"Hey, can I come in for a little bit?" she asks quietly, looking unsure.

"Sure! Sure!" I tell her, gesturing to the end of the bed for her to take a seat.

"Are you doing okay? I heard you crying when I went to bed last night," she admits, watching me with a deep expression.

"Yeah," I nod, not meeting her eyes. When she doesn't say anything I look up. She's looking at me with a soft expression, one that says she doesn't believe me. "I miss them," I blurt out, feeling guiltier now I've said it out loud. My parents are going to think I don't love them.

"You're bound to. I don't know much about them or how you all met, but from what I saw and heard from my time there I could tell how much you meant to them and how much they meant to you. They were your family so of course you'll miss them."

My eyes water despite my protests. "It's not just that they were family. We were all so close. But it was more. I miss them all so much already and I've been gone a day. It feels like I'm losing my family all over again," I sob, clutching my chest. "I feel like I'm betraying my own family somehow. It hurts. It hurts so much."

Marybeth rushes to sit down next to me, rubbing my shoulder soothingly.

"It's all going to be fine, Lake. You'll be able to see them soon," she assures me.

"It won't be the same, though. I'll be visiting my cat that's not really my cat anymore. It's all messed up. I'm so happy about having my parents and Cowen back in my life, so fucking happy. I wished for this moment every day but now it's here I feel like I'm losing more. And I feel guilty for feeling like this. After everything I've put them through they don't deserve this," I cry into my hands, feeling it harder now I've said the words out loud.

"What do you mean? You feel guilty about your parents or for leaving?"

"Both. I promised Max I wouldn't leave but I've left. Then there's Mum and Dad. I put them through so much, through hell. They're so happy I'm back and all I can do is feel miserable over being here because it means I leave another family. I'm torn in two. But I know I can't have both. And they're my parents and brother. How can I leave them again?"

"I think your mum and dad understand if you want to go back. They just want you to be happy," she tells me, trying to make me better but it just makes me worse because the thought of leaving them kills me just as bad.

"And what if I'm not happy with either? Because no matter what I do I'll still feel broken. How can I put them through that?" I sob. "I don't want them to think I don't love them because I do, I love them so much."

"They know you love them, they love you too," she tells me, bringing me in for a hug. Having her comfort me when I don't deserve it just makes me sob harder into her chest. The sound of a floorboard creaking has me snapping my head up, pulling back from Marybeth and wiping away my tears.

Marybeth and I look to each other with wide eyes before turning to the bedroom door. When I see the door isn't shut properly and is open a few inches, I begin to panic.

"Oh my God," I whisper, horrified. "Did someone hear us talking?"

The thought has my heart beating wildly and I watch as Marybeth gets up, walking quietly but quickly over to the door.

She looks down the hallway, both ways, before turning back to me. "No one's out there."

I sag against my pillows in relief. The last thing I want is to hurt my parents anymore than I already have. I rub my eyes feeling emotionally tired.

"I'll let you get some rest. Do you want me to bring you up some breakfast?"

The thought of food makes my stomach roll. I shake my head, 'no'. "Thank you for asking me, though, and for letting me cry on your shoulder," I smile.

"I'm always here if you ever need to talk to someone," she genuinely offers. She turns to leave but I call her name, stopping her before she leaves.

"Please don't mention our conversation to anyone," I plead.

"I won't, I promise," she assures me and with that, she leaves, shutting the door behind her. I fall back on my bed, closing my eyes and falling back to sleep.

IT'S A WEEK AFTER MY TALK with Marybeth and I still don't feel any different. I thought if I ignored my feelings they'd disappear and everything would be okay but, as the week passed, my feelings only became stronger.

It started the day after mine and Marybeth's chat. I hadn't slept well and needed to get out and get some fresh air.

My walk led me down some familiar streets all the way to Emma's, my best friend's, house. To my utter surprise and complete devastation her mum wasn't as happy to have me back as everyone else. She ended up slamming the door in my face after giving me a few choice words.

I ended up taking the long way back home, the whole way a complete blur. I'd been so lost in thought I didn't even realise how much time had gone by. By the time I got back Mum and Dad were in the kitchen looking frantic and talking a mile a minute on their phones. They took one look at me when I walked in and ceased what they were doing, their bodies relaxing.

After that they sat me down and explained everything about Emma's mum's reaction. Turns out she blames me and Cowen for her daughter's attack, adding to my guilt pile. It's a reason why she wouldn't let me see Emma. She also thinks Cowen had something to do with Emma's sister's death, but he didn't. I didn't need my parents to confirm that to know.

Missing back home became worse after that. I had Joan, the girls, and the lads to talk to, to hang out with. I moaned non-stop about never getting any peace whilst I was there but all I wanted was for one of them to walk into my room.

It didn't happen and with each day I became a shell of myself. I'd cry myself to sleep, miss everyone like crazy and walk around like a robot, trying to find where I fit in with their lives now.

Then yesterday I finally charged my phone, texting the number I had for Emma to see if it was still in service. It wasn't.

So then I emailed her yesterday, hoping she kept her email address, and fortunately for me she had kept the same address. I wrote her a lengthy email, unsure whether it was just her mum who disliked me or Emma too. I wish I had done it sooner. If I had known she was attacked I know for a fact I would have. But back then, with the loss of Cowen, my thoughts never even strayed away from him long enough to think about anyone else. Selfish? Yes. But I was a mess at the time and all I could think of was him and what I'd done. Not even my parents factored into the equation. It just made me feel like a shittier person.

She didn't email me back until late last night, arranging for us to meet up this morning. It's why I've only just gotten in, bypassing my parents on the way to my room, my emotions all over the place.

"I'll warm dinner up later," I shout down the stairs, not waiting to listen to Mum's reply as I hide out in my room.

Falling down face first on to my bed, I sob. I sob for my best friend, for the life I've missed and for missing my life back in Coldenshire.

Emma isn't the girl I remembered. She looked so different, her face gaunt and shrunken. She had lost her luscious curves, her tanned skin was so pale and she was a shell of the girl I once knew. It saddened me to no end knowing what she suffered through. I let her down. Big time. It's something I've been doing a lot lately.

We didn't talk about anything too heavy, but we did talk. At first it was about where I went when I ran away, what the people were like where I went. I told her about Coldenshire and living with Joan and her family. It was hard talking about them so soon. My parents and Cowen had taken the hint that any conversations about them are off limits. Only until I was stronger at least. It just feels wrong moving on like the past year didn't happen, that Max didn't happen. It was hard bringing them up.

We also spoke about her future, what she was planning on doing next. Dodging what happened to Emma was hard but I tried. But then she brought it up herself, making sure I knew she didn't blame me or Cowen and that Darren was to blame for it all.

The second she uttered his name her face drained from what little colour she had. I quickly changed the subject, not wanting to upset her.

We spoke about her plans to move. She wanted to get out of this town, out from under her parents and from everything this town reminds her of. She explained she has her college arranging to transfer her grades to another college a few miles away. I was surprised to find it wasn't that far from Coldenshire and would be the same one Myles is attending. She was just waiting to hear back before she approached her parents.

All of it exhausted me. We cried, laughed, cried, hugged and cried some more. It's the reason I avoided my parents when I came up. They knew where I was because I left a message on the fridge before I left. I swear, having someone to answer to has been the hardest transition. I've spent a year only answering to myself. It's strange having that parental guidance.

The door to my room opens, shaking me from my thoughts. Cowen walks in not bothering to knock as usual.

"Dude, I could have been naked," I tell him dryly, rolling over on my back, resting my head on my pillow.

"I don't care. I miss my friends," he tells me sadly. It seems I'm not the only one missing Max and everyone. Cowen has taken it hard too and he only knew them for a few days. It's sweet really. "And you miss my friends," he nods, lying down beside me on the bed.

"Doesn't matter," I shrug, acting like it doesn't affect me when inside it's ripping me to shreds.

"It doesn't?" he asks, seeming to really want to know and looking a little upset that it doesn't. I don't answer, not knowing how to answer without upsetting someone. He must feel the turmoil going on inside my head because his hand reaches out for mine, holding it tightly as a tear escapes, rolling down the side of my face. "How's Emma?"

"Different," I whisper, sad for my best friend. She has a long way to go before she finally moves on. It's hard to know what it is exactly holding her back. It seemed her parents are a big issue for her. "We talked a lot. She doesn't blame us, not like her mum. She said her mum is just being overprotective."

"I blame me," Cowen admits, a sadness I've not heard from him yet creeping into his tone.

"No! No, Cowen. It's Darren that attacked her, not you. Don't you dare put that blame on your shoulders," I tell him sternly, giving him a warning look. He has enough to deal with.

"But I got drugs."

"Yeah, but did you sell them? Did you force them on anyone? Did you keep selling them when you knew they weren't legit?"

"No. No. Just buy. Not sell. Promise."

"Well, then," I tell him like that's the answer. "She's talking about leaving, wanting to start fresh at a new college," I tell him, hoping it doesn't get back to her mum. She said she hadn't spoken to her about it. She's waiting for the go ahead from the colleges before she brings it up with them. She doesn't want them to talk her out of it.

"Marybeth told me she done a little better now," he says sadly.

"I didn't see her before, when it happened, but I can only imagine how bad it was if today was any indication to go by. She looked so ill. She didn't look like Emma whatsoever. It was sad. Really sad," I admit, squeezing his hand a little tighter.

"She's strong. Always… Always… Always will be," he struggles to get out.

"Yeah," I whisper, knowing my friend really is strong. She's the strongest person I know. Stronger than me. I ran away from my problems, she stayed and fought. We both stay silent, lost in each other's thoughts, when I broach the subject I'm most concerned over. "Are Mum and Dad mad at me?" I ask, thinking how I went out without telling them where I was going or who I was with, just that I was out. Then there's the whole ignoring them when I walked in earlier.

"No. But they have secrets hiding," he whispers conspicuously.

Leaning up on my elbows I look over to him to find he's deadly serious. Why would they be keeping secrets?

"What do you mean? What secrets?" I ask, feeling kind of panicked all of a sudden. I mean, it's not like them to keep secrets from either Cowen or me, but it could be another thing that has changed over the past year. They've always been upfront about everything going on in their lives and have raised us to be the same.

Like the time sex first got brought up when I was with Darren. I went straight to my mum, asking for advice. It's not like she could get mad. She had always said to go to them with anything, no matter what it was and that they'd never get angry with us as long as we told the truth.

I clear my head and eye Cowen when he stays quiet. He rolls his eyes, his expression of one annoyed.

Great! Now I'm annoying my brother. What else can I do wrong?

"Duh! That's why it's called a...a, it's called a secret. And I'm the one supposed to be... to be... dump...no...brain dumb...damaged."

I smack his shoulder, not impressed with his attempt at joking. "But *how* do you know?"

"I heard them talking, whispering. Mum was crying. But she nodded her head," he shrugs. "Oh, but she smiled when she wrote on paper."

Flopping back down on the bed, I begin to conjure up a million and one possibilities of what's going on. They have been acting strange since I returned, always seeming on edge and I have to admit, now Cowen has brought it up, I swear they were whispering the other night before I walked in and interrupted.

My thoughts have me wondering if I'm the reason they're so sad. Am I making them unhappy? Should I leave again? My eyes water with every passing thought, frustrating the hell out of me.

A small knock on the door causes me to jump. I'm so used to Cowen barging in that when the door does bloody knock it scares the shit out of me.

"Lake, sweetie, can I come in? I'd like to talk to you," Mum calls through the door.

"Yeah, come in," I rush out, sitting up in my bed and straightening my wrinkled clothing nervously. Then I realise how ridiculous I'm being and I inwardly roll my eyes.

Cowen sits up too, looking wide eyed at the door like he wasn't expecting Mum to turn up at my door. Mum notices him the second she walks in and gives him a pointed look.

The poor lad has gone awfully pale. I actually feel kind of sorry for him, especially with the annoyed expression Mum is pointing his way.

"I thought you were too sick to eat dinner, mister?"

"I am," he coughs, blatantly faking. "Okayyy," he whines. "I'll go eat dinner."

Getting up from the bed, making as much fuss and noise as possible, Cowen finally stomps his way to the door. While Mum keeps her attention on me I keep my eyes on Cowen, my lips twitching at his juvenile behaviour. He stops once he gets to the door and turns, sticking his tongue out behind Mum's back.

"I'll cut that out," Mum sings, causing me to giggle. I swear the woman has eyes at the back of her head. She's always been like this. No matter what we were doing she'd know like she could sense we were up to no good.

"Dad," Cowen shouts, stepping out of the room. "Mum's going to… She said she's going to cut my tongue out."

There's a moment of silence before Dad's voice booms up the stairs. "You should keep it in your mouth then, boy."

"No! Marybeth likes my tongue…" Cowen starts as he walks away.

Completely grossed out, I cover my ears. "La la la la la la."

"Cowen," Mum gasps turning towards the door.

"Cowen," Marybeth's unamused voice calls from downstairs and Cowen's head snaps back to mine, wide and scared. He's down the hall now but even from my bedroom I can see the regretful look on his expression.

"I shouldn't have said that out loud?" he asks, looking so guilty it's cute.

"Nope," I call back, pronouncing the P with a pop. My cheeks ache, hurting from grinning so wide.

"No shit!" he groans before I watch his shoulders slump, his chin falling against his chest. Mum and I watch as he takes the first step downstairs, both of us amused at his expression. He looks like he's about to face death and not his little, midget girlfriend.

Mum snaps me back to the present when she walks over to the door and shuts it. I gulp, wondering if I'm in trouble. It would explain why my dad isn't joining my mum. He could never tell us no or tell us off. Mum, however, had no problem with discipline and was like a dragon when either of us stepped out of line.

"I'm sorry for sneaking off again," I blurt out. It's the only reason that would explain why she's so upset with me.

She waves me off looking unsure. "You're an adult, Lake. But thank you for putting our minds at rest and leaving the note on the fridge this morning. I'm pretty sure you took ten years off mine and your father's lives the other day," she smiles.

"Okayyy," I say slowly, my mind coming up blank with any other possibilities. She must read the confusion on my expression because she steps forward, sitting on the edge of my bed.

"I want to talk to you about something else, something important. But I need you to hear me out before jumping to conclusions."

"What is it?" I ask, sitting up straighter, my attention focused solely on my mum and what she's about to talk to me about. My heart is going crazy, my stomach fluttering with nerves.

"I don't even know where to start," she admits nervously, wringing her hands in her lap. "We know you don't want to be here..."

I cut her off, my voice sharp. "I do." My eyes widen and the fear of letting them believe I don't want to be here makes me feel sick. I never want them to think that.

"Calm down and listen," she tells me gently, rolling her eyes. "We know you don't want to be here but you also don't want to be away from us. Your father and I got talking and we've decided to let you go..."

I don't hear much else. The constant ringing in my ears doesn't let me register anything else coming from her.

All I can think of is her words.

We're letting you go.

THIRTY

LAKE

THE LAST PLACE ON EARTH I expected to be again was at a strip club, this time not because of a hen party. Men's beady eyes follow me as I make my way to the bar. I can feel their eyes on every inch of my body like a physical touch, making me feel seedy and dirty.

Arriving at the end of the bar, waiting for the chick working behind the bar to notice me, I don't expect to be noticed hidden away. But when the stench of stale beer fills the space surrounding me, causing me to gag a little, I sigh.

"How much for a lap dance, darlin'?"

I turn my head to the slime ball and scrunch my face up in disgust. The man looks like he's been in here a while, *after* partying in a dump for the night. His clothes look a mess: all wrinkled with unknown stains on them. His hair is messy, unkempt, along with his demeanour.

I open my mouth to give him a piece of my mind when a deep, scratchy voice interrupts me from behind.

"She's with me."

Turning around, a genuine smile reaches my face and I dive forward, throwing myself around the huge beast. My arms wrap around his neck and I breathe him in, my excitement doubling at the familiar scent.

"Maverick," I whisper, feeling my throat clog up with emotion.

"Lake," he rumbles, pulling away with a huge grin on his face. "It's about goddamn time, girl."

Maverick and I have exchanged text messages since the day I left. If it wasn't for him or his texts I don't know what I would have done. We've become extremely close and I only wish we had sooner because the guy is one of a kind. He's awesome.

I roll my eyes at him playfully, still grinning. "Marybeth is a slow driver."

"Where are they?" he asks, referring to my brother and Marybeth.

"They've popped out for lunch," I smile and let him lead me out of the club. For a second I forgot where I was and that there were naked women a few feet from me. So as soon as we step into the cool hallway I sag with relief.

As we walk to his office my mind goes back to the day my life changed.

Mum didn't explain herself the first time very well. They weren't letting me go per se, just letting me go for the time being.

You see, it turns out Mum and Dad liked Coldenshire on their visit. They loved how Max and his brothers let Cowen in and that they all seemed genuinely sad to see him go.

It wasn't just about Cowen and his ability to make friends. They enjoyed being there, the places, the opportunities, and the area in general.

But then there was me. They knew how unhappy I was becoming and could see how much missing them was tearing me up inside. I hadn't meant to let my feelings show and believed I was hiding it well. Obviously not. Mum explained that until I had everyone I loved around me they wouldn't truly have their Lake back.

But as much as they were doing it for me and for Cowen, they were also doing it for themselves. Dad would get more work contracts being a self employed carpet fitter in such a huge place. Back home the place was small and he lost money whenever he had to travel out for work. Mum, however, worked at the local doctor's surgery but she said leaving her job wouldn't be anything to cry over. They had been thinking awhile about all of this, even before the accident happened apparently.

It was Joan, though, that brought it all up again. They were having a conversation when Joan asked Mum when they were expected back in Coldenshire.

When it came about that they'd have to leave soon, Joan had mentioned it was a shame they couldn't move to Coldenshire. That she and the rest of the family would enjoy having them around. I'm still unsure if Joan thought I'd be staying or if she knew I'd leave and was trying to persuade *them* to stay. I guess I'll have to ask her when I get five minutes alone with her.

When we got back, Mum and Dad noticed I was withdrawing more and more and by the third day they had a talk about what they were going to do. With the option of moving already up in the air, they both agreed. The only thing that stopped them moving before was because they wanted to be there for when I returned. They didn't want me to come back only to find out that they had moved away without me.

The papers that Cowen saw Mum sign were for our house to be put on the market. And the reason she was crying was because she overheard me and Marybeth talking. Mum and I talked for hours that night, Dad joining us when he realised there wasn't going to be any tears or cat fights. Marybeth and Cowen joined but stayed silent since both had already agreed. So they basically sat there listening to me trying to find any doubts in my parents' minds.

Dad had insisted that it was just a house, that wherever Cowen and I were would be a home. Everything else was just stuff. They wanted us all to be happy and a new start is what we all needed. I even had to talk to Marybeth about it all because, out of us all, it was her moving away from her family. She seemed really excited about the move, reassuring me her parents and brother were only a few hours away.

Which is how I ended up here in V.I.P. I had texted Maverick the news straight away, followed by Joan. They both promised to keep it to themselves as I didn't want to get anyone's hopes up just in case something went wrong. In all honestly, a part of me wanted to keep it quiet so I had time to think of what I was going to say to Max. That time, it didn't help any. I still have no idea how to approach him or what to say, which is another reason why I'm here with Maverick, and not at the house.

Joan has offered Mark's house for us to crash at while Mum and Dad sort everything out back home. They need to pack up, organise all the bills and whatever else they need to do. Luckily, they had already found a house for us to move into, five minutes around the corner from Joan's. They were just waiting for the mortgage to be approved.

"Have you been back to the house?" Maverick asks, a worried look crossing his features, causing my stomach to sink. He hides his reaction pretty quickly, handing me a bottle of water.

I take a seat on the couch in his office, trying my hardest not to look in the direction of his desk. Having dirty images flash through my mind about the night Max took me over Maverick's desk is really not appropriate right now. Mostly it would be embarrassing so let's not go there.

"No, I'm too nervous. No, scratch that, I'm scared as fuck," I admit, taking a swig of my water.

"Have you figured out what you're going to say to him?"

"Nope, I'm just going to wing it," I tell him, chuckling softly.

"I guess all those messages were pointless then," he tells me dryly.

I chuckle for real that time. Poor man. I made him act out the conversation via text messaging and let's just say, it wasn't fun for Maverick. The poor man didn't know whether I was serious or if I was acting out a scenario. I really went crazy on him.

"Yes, you were right. I should just say what comes to my mind."

"Probably not good to mention the dick amputation," he says dryly, covering his own junk with his bottled water.

Okay, so I took my little acting scenarios a little too far. But in all fairness I'm bound to get mad at Max at some point or another and, let's be honest, I'm going to threaten bodily harm after what he did to me.

"He humiliated me in front of everyone," I snap defensively.

He cringes. "I know, but he's sorry and he's hurting too."

My body slumps and I feel saddened at the thought of Max hurting; the same Max who could make a stone laugh.

"Is he at home? That's where I'll go next I suppose. I just wanted to come check in with you first, make sure this is still a good idea," I start, then stand up when the nerves I thought I had banished earlier that day resurface. "What if he's over me or he's moved on? Are you sure he didn't sleep with bimbo one and two? This isn't a good idea. I should call my parents, tell them we can't move here and that there's a plague or something going around. Yeah, I'll do that."

Strong hands grab me at my shoulders, stopping me from wearing the carpet out and from grabbing my phone.

"Stop! You're over thinking this. Stop worrying so much. It's going to work out just fine. And what have I told you? It's Max that should be sorry, not you."

"But I left him," I choke out, my eyes watering. "You said it yourself, everyone has left him one way or another."

"This is different and as far as I can see, he pushed you away and you still came back," he smiles sadly, wiping my tears with the pad of his thumbs.

"What if he hates me? I love him, Maverick, I love him so much and I never, not once, ever believed love like this existed. He infuriates me to no end, makes me madder than all hell, but he also makes me laugh harder than I've ever laughed. He knows how to cheer me up when I'm down, knows exactly what I need even when I don't. And that's just half of it. The way he makes me feel," I sigh dreamily, my mind lost on everything that is Max Carter. "He acts dumb but deep down he's one of the smartest people I know. It's all an act. And under all that tough act exterior he's all heart. I love how he is with Hope and isn't afraid to show it. I've gone through life knowing Cowen is the other half of me, we're twins, but Max, he's the other half of my soul, the other half of my heart. It may sound crazy to some, but not to me, not anymore. Loving him is like an adrenaline rush, it's the best experience of my life. Sometimes, when I really let myself feel what I feel for him, I'm scared I'm going to explode. If he hated me, or didn't return my feelings, where does that leave me? Where does all that build up of love and all that adrenaline go? What will happen to me once all that he makes me feel explodes?"

Realising I just laid myself completely bare in front of Maverick, I duck my head in shame. He probably thinks I'm some crazy chick and is thinking of ways to warn Max away from me. I wouldn't blame him. Trying to explain the tightness inside my chest when I think of Max, it makes me crazy.

"Hey," he says, using his fist to bump my chin up so that I have no other choice but to look at him. "He's a lucky fucking guy, Lake. There's no doubt in my mind that he doesn't love you as much as you love him. He's never been one to let people in and doesn't love easily, but when he does, he loves with his whole heart. I just wish I had someone to love like my brothers do. Because they're all better men for it, but unfortunately, it's something I'll never have."

He says this so seriously, so adamantly, that I'm stunned silent for a second, forgetting what we were originally talking about. "How can you think you'll never have it?" I ask, pushing aside my Max problem for a second.

"Long story," he says, shaking the dark look that flashes in his eyes. The hurt, anger, sorrow and misery disappears just as quickly as it appears, it's heartbreaking.

"Right now you need to go tell him you're back."

"Is anyone else at home with him?" I ask, when I really want to keep pushing the issue over Maverick's love life more. If anyone deserves to be loved and to love, it's him. He's one hell of a catch and has seen and done so much in his life already. He already acts as if he's in his late forties and not in his twenties, the guy really does need to find love.

"Nah, I'll be glad when you get him off the couch. He promised me four days ago he'd clean up his act but all he's done is mope around the house all day in his boxers. I'm getting sick of it. So when you've sorted everything out, can you remind him he promised to interview some tenants for the apartment upstairs for me."

"I will," I chuckle, grabbing my handbag. "Wish me luck," I breathe in.

"You don't need luck," he smiles, punching my arm lightly. "Now go. I have work to do," he says seriously, in mock fury. I laugh, grabbing the door, opening it wide.

"I'll see you later."

"You too, darling," he smiles, sitting down at his desk. "Oh, and take the back door, I don't want you walking through the club when it's open."

"Trust me, I would have found a way to get out of here without stepping foot back in there. Even if I had to climb out of a window," I laugh, waving him off. Walking down the corridor I follow the signs for the exit, ones I vaguely remember seeing from the hen party. The whole place looks different compared to that night, so when I do find the exit I sigh with relief.

My phone rings as I step outside and Mum's name flashes on the screen. A smile lights up my face and a giddy feeling erupts in my stomach like it does every time something small like that happens in my life. It's just another reminder that I have them back.

"Hey, Mum," I greet, walking down the alley way so I'm back at the front entrance of MC5. The town is bustling for five in the evening: people rushing to get last minute stuff before the stores close. I make my way over to the taxi rank, joining the long line.

"Hey, honey, just calling to update you on the progress," she says and I hear the smile in her voice.

"Mum, I left four hours ago," I laugh, cringing when rain begins to splatter. I manage to get my hood up without dropping my phone which I'm grateful for.

"I know, but we just had the best news. The bank called and the mortgage for the new property has been cleared. We'll need you to grab the keys from the estate agent and check the place out and tell us what we'll need like carpets, decorating etc. They close at half five," she tells me and I sigh, disappointed that I'll have to put off seeing Max for a little while longer.

"Which estate agents?" I question, moving out of the line.

She rattles it off and I nearly squeal when I see the agency is only a few stores down from MC5.

"I'm here," I tell Mum.

"That was fast," she comments, seeming impressed.

"I was already in town," I tell her, waiting outside the door until we've finished our conversation. "I went to see Maverick first."

"So, you haven't been back to Joan's yet? You haven't seen *him*?" she asks and I know she's referring to Max. We had a long conversation about him and despite him acting like a complete prick, my mum still loves him. She never once approved of Darren but she whole heartedly gave Max her approval. She was disappointed and shocked at his behaviour at that dinner, but she forgives him.

"No, I was too nervous. I wanted to have five minutes before I threw myself into the wolves," I joke.

"Oh, sweetie, leave the house and go sort it out with Max first. That boy is probably going out of his mind," she scolds me softly. Typical. Trust her to worry about him and not the fact I'm two seconds away from having a nervous breakdown.

"Mum," I groan. "He's already crazy," I tease.

She giggles. Yes, freaking giggles. "Go get him back."

"I'll do this first. It will give me chance to think of something to say," I lie. Really I'm just a big scaredy chicken.

"Okay. Just text us a list of what will need to be done. Your father and I will bring as much stuff as we will need, in the car. The movers will have everything else in the van."

"Okay. Oh, do they know it's me coming?" I ask quickly, glad I grabbed my bag out of the car before leaving MB and Cowen because it has my I.D inside. Still feels weird having that part of my identity back.

"Yeah, I told them you were already down there. We faxed over everything they needed signed already, so it's just you picking up keys."

"Okay, love you."

"Love you more. See you in a few days."

"Bye, Mum," I smile, excited it's all happening.

She disconnects and I open the door, ready to grab the key to the next step in my life. I just hope Max will be as happy as I am.

THIRTY-ONE

MAX

"I'M GOING OUT. CLEAN YOUR fucking shit up before we get back," Myles snaps, grabbing Kayla's hand.

I scratch my balls, ignoring them. They've been on my case for the past two days and I'm sick of it. Literally. I'm literally fucking sick of it.

I've had a hangover since my binge drinking at MC5 four days ago. I didn't even make it outside MC5 before I started puking my guts up. You'd think after all the puking I did I wouldn't have anything left to throw up. Wrong.

Today is the first day I haven't thrown up and I'm relishing in the moment. It's why I'm currently sprawled out on the couch wearing only my boxers, a blanket kicked down at my feet and junk food wrappers littered around me. I've also got a week's worth of cups surrounding me, some with tea in, some with soup. I guess walking into the kitchen was hard enough, I didn't want to add to the strain by carrying a mug along with me too.

"Whatever," I tell him, throwing a pillow at his retreating back. The front door slams and I relax back down on the sofa, turning the volume up on *The Lucky One* and shoving some stale crisps into my mouth.

Don't judge.

When a bloke gets dumped they automatically think we're wired to move on, not wallow or have feelings and shit. They just hand you a beer and tell you to move on, find another pussy.

With chicks, it's different. They get you burning pictures of you together, get you to throw out anything that belongs to your ex and will list a million reasons why you're better off without them and let you have a cry fest. Then they hand you a glass of wine, a box of chocolates and a collection of cheesy romance movies.

I'm not wired that way.

I passed on the wine but I did drink myself stupid on chicken soup. I've eaten my body weight in chocolate and other junk foods, which probably didn't help my queasy stomach. I never had any pictures of me and Lake printed off so I made up some sob story to Kayla and had her go into town and get me some. She did and when I started burning them it ended badly. I should have Googled that shit because I ended up burning a hole in the carpet. Mav and Myles were not impressed at all.

I never had anything that belonged to her, so unfortunately I had to pass on that part of the moving on ritual. Kayla seemed unimpressed but sympathetic when I had her up most of the night crying about Lake, then I'd get angry and then I'd end up crying all over again. It was an emotional experience. One that ended with me getting an earful off Myles and having Kayla, my rock, taken away from me.

Now I'm onto the last stage. The movie fest stage. I decided it was safer to Google it this time, since the burning fiasco with the pictures. I started off heavy, going in strong like a soldier, and watched *The Notebook*.

Somehow Joan sensed I needed her and we cried together as we watched the movie. I passed out not long after the two old people died in each other's arms. The heaviness weighing on my heart became too much and I couldn't cope. The movie was just too much for my heart to handle.

Joan then wrote me a list of recommendations. I've also watched *Titanic*, *Safe Haven*, *Pretty Woman* and *Twilight*. I've still got *Dirty Dancing*, *John Tucker Must Die* and *The Breakup* left to watch. I'm still trying to get the rest of the movies on the list but I'm good with what I've got for now. It's really helping me get through my breakup with Lake. Kind of.

A message alert beeps from my phone and I begrudgingly grab it, looking down at the text message from Myles.

Myles: And take a fucking shower, you stink.

"I don't fucking stink," I grumble, frowning. Bending a little I sniff my pits and gag at the odour lingering there. "Well, shit, I stink."

Getting up, wrappers, DVD cases and the remote fall to the floor in a heap. I don't bother picking them up as I bypass all the shit lying around. I've literally been sleeping on the couch as my bed still smells of Lake. I couldn't stomach the thought of it not smelling like her again, so I left it alone. Joan went to change my sheets and I hit the roof. Thankfully, she hasn't been back in my room since. Not that I would know anyway. I've pretty much ignored anyone who walked through the front door.

Twisting the shower on, I don't bother waiting for it to heat up before I strip myself of my boxers, my new, very expensive boxers and step in. The cold water hitting me is the wakeup call I needed. I can't keep wallowing in my own self pity.

She left and isn't coming back.

Well, not until I get off my lazy backside and tell her I'm sorry. Tell her I fucked up and didn't mean to push her away.

Fuck! Who am I kidding? I can't even build up the courage to even send her a text message, let alone turn up at her doorstep and tell her I'm sorry. Then there's the fact I couldn't ask her to leave her family. It's been a fighting battle in my mind since Maverick told me to make it right. At least, I'm sure that's what he said; that day is still a blur. The only thing that comes to mind when I think of that day is *Cher's, I Got You Babe*.

The only other option is for me to move over by her house which means leaving my family behind. Anyone else I couldn't care less about, but my family... my family is all I've got and I love them. There's never been a time in my life when I've thought about leaving them or moving out of town, no matter how bad life got. We've always stuck together and the thought of being without them and moving hours away turns my stomach.

Some may say I sound like a baby, that one day I'll have to grow my own roots, cut the cord, but when you have a family like mine, they are my roots. We are all equal, always there for each other through the bad and the good. We've never needed space away from each other, even when we argued back and forth. It's always been this way and if I left it would ruin the dynamic of what we have. It's more than just a brother's bond. Plus, they'd miss me. There's only one Max Carter.

The doorbell ringing makes me groan. Cutting my relaxing shower short, I quickly rinse the soap from off my body before stepping out and pulling on a pair of boxers which cling to my wet body. Not bothering with a towel, I run down the stairs, opening the door.

My breath leaves my lungs.

Lake!

It's really fucking Lake. Well, the back of Lake.

I rub my eyes, praying my hangover isn't making me delusional. She was walking away from the house but once she hears my intake of breath, her body spins around, her eyes widening when she sees me.

The heavy pressure that's been weighing down on my chest begins to lighten now that I have her in front of me. She's really here.

She's wearing a leather jacket, blue skinny jeans, with leather boots. She has a small black bag with a gold chain attached to it, along with gold jewellery adding to her look. She looks completely different and something tells me I'm finally seeing the real Lake for the first time. Even her hair is different. Usually she'd leave it down, wild, or throw it up in a bun, but I can tell she's made an effort, straightening her hair, but curling the ends into a loose wave. It looks longer, healthier, along with her appearance. She's wearing makeup, but not much, just some eyeliner I think as her eyes look darker.

"Hey," she whispers, causing me to jump and my body to break out in goosebumps. Fuck! She only said one word and already she has my body reacting to her.

"Hey," I choke out then cough, clearing my throat.

"So," she says quietly, rocking back and forth on her heels. "Nice boxers," she comments, eyeing the new, expensive boxers.

I give her a dry look, not impressed with her sense of humour. "Thanks, seems I've got bowel problems and according to Myles and Mason, I need to be potty trained again."

She giggles, her face relaxing and looking carefree. It doesn't last long and before I know it her expression sobers, turning serious. "Can we talk?"

Furiously, I nod my head. "Yeah, um, come in. Come in," I offer, feeling like a bigger dick for not inviting her in sooner.

We walk into the front room and I watch Lake look around the room with wide eyes, looking disgusted. It's like I'm seeing the room through her eyes and I cringe at the mess.

"Myles," I scoff. "He's disgusting," I mutter, sounding disappointed in my twin brother.

"Myles made this mess?" she asks incredulously.

"Well, yeah. Who did you think made the mess? He's had…. His… um… His goldfish died," I lie, feeling proud that I come up with such a brilliant excuse.

"Oh, I didn't know he had a goldfish," she tells me, her lips twitching.

"Yeah, he doesn't like to show him off. He wasn't gold like normal goldfish and Myles didn't want him to feel like less of a fish."

"Less of a fish?" she asks, her luscious lips twitching.

"Yeah, less of a fish. You know Myles, he doesn't like seeing anyone being bullied," I remind her, rolling my eyes. "The other fish were really mean to him."

"Okayyy," she says slowly and I'm hoping by the small smirk playing on her lips that she believes me.

"Here. Have a seat." I move over to the sofa, cursing when I have to move piles of crap from the sofa. I'm surprised we don't have rats. I'm actually feeling kind of ashamed. Just a little.

She gingerly sits on the sofa, mindful of the mess on the floor and around her. When I notice her hand disappearing down the side of the sofa, my eyes widen and I dive forward, snatching the object she retrieves before she can see it. But it's too late. Her eyes narrow before they light up. Looking up at me with soft eyes, she smiles.

"I guess that picture of me and you is Myles' too?"

I cough, clearing my throat. "Sick prick. I'll have words with him," I grumble, folding the picture up and hiding it away in my back pocket. "He can't go anywhere without having a picture of me."

Out of sight, out of mind.

"Of course," she nods looking clearly amused.

Neither of us speak and the silence is awkward and uncomfortable. We've never had problems before now filling in the silence or having something to talk about. It doesn't feel right.

"How come you're back?" I ask. I've been wondering 'why' since the moment I opened the front door. Is she here to stay or is this some trick so she can ruin my boxers all over again? My heart can't take her leaving, especially since I admitted to myself as well as Mav how deep my feelings for Lake run. And there's the fact I can't afford anymore boxers.

"We're moving here," she tells me, her eyes shining. She looks happy, really happy, and I don't think I've ever seen her look so content, so peaceful and overjoyed before. Her admission registers and I sit forward in the armchair, shocked.

"What? Can you repeat that?"

"We're moving here," she chuckles, a light blush pinking her cheeks.

"Let me get this right, you're moving here, to Coldenshire?"

"Yes, here. Five minutes around the corner to be exact."

"No shit?" I can't wrap my head around it. "Why? How? What about your parents, I don't understand," I rush out, pulling at the ends of my hair. I even pinch my arm just to make sure I'm not dreaming again. When I don't wake up and a red mark appears on my arm, I know this is real. Unless she's playing some sick joke on me, of course.

"Mum and Dad didn't want me to be unhappy. We're all moving here. Cowen, Marybeth and I drove down early so that they could sort out the moving arrangements and so I could come back to make things right with everyone."

"Why would you need to make things right?" I swallow, feeling my chest tighten.

"For leaving when I knew I belonged here," she says surely. That weight in my chest lightens some more and I have to take in a deep breath.

"But I was cruel?" I whisper, ashamed at my behaviour towards her. I acted out of fear and I shouldn't have. I won't lie and tell you the thought of her leaving didn't cross my mind, but as the days passed and her parents made no move to leave, I guess I made myself push it all aside, hoping everything would turn out okay and she wouldn't need to leave.

"Yeah, you were, Max," she whispers, her voice pained.

"I'm sorry, Lake. So fucking sorry. I've replayed that evening over and over in my head and every single time I would change the outcome, change my reaction. I was scared and I acted out of fear when I shouldn't have. It was a dick move to speak to you like that, especially in front of everyone. I love you. I love you so fucking much that it literally scared me stupid that I acted like a complete prick to you. I wouldn't blame you if you never forgive me or if you're here to warn me to stay away from you," I ramble. I'm rambling that much that I didn't even notice Lake stand, looking like a lion after his prey.

"Say it again," she whispers.

"Huh? I don't think I can remember what I just said word for word but I'll have a go," I rush out to reassure her. "I'm sorry…"

"No. Not that. The way you feel," she whispers, stepping closer. Feeling vulnerable sitting down with Lake prowling towards me, I stand up, getting ready for the slap across the cheek that I've been waiting for since she arrived. I deserve a few for my actions.

But then my mind goes over everything I said and my eyes dilate when I realise what she wants me to repeat, what I let slip. Sweating with nerves, I step forward, smirking when I notice Lake's body shudder and watch her eyes fill with desire.

Moving forward a step, so that I'm standing closer to her, our bodies barely touching, but close enough so that when she takes in a heavy breath and her chest swells, her chest brushes across my bare chest. It feels good, and my dick jumps to attention in my boxers.

Leaning down so that my lips are level with hers, I lightly brush a kiss across her lips before moving back a breath. Her eyes close, her breathing heavy and I smirk.

"I love you, Lake Miller," I whisper, putting everything I am into those five words, hoping she can feel how much I mean every single one of them.

Her eyes slowly lift open and the desire, lust and sexual want is written all over her face. She wants me. And by the way her body noticeably trembles when I run my finger down her neck before palming my hand over her heart; I can tell she's holding on by a thread.

"I love you, Lake Miller," I repeat, bending down to run my lips across hers.

Her body moves like lightning and before I know it she's wrapped around me, her legs around my waist and her arms around my neck. Her lips crash to mine and I groan the second I taste her in my mouth. Fuck! I've missed this. Missed *her*.

"Let's just forget it happened," she whispers against my mouth, rubbing her core against my stomach.

My nose crinkles, something Malik was telling me not so long ago coming to my mind. "Do you really mean that you'll forget it, or is this some sort of trick and really you're just waiting to strike?"

She pulls back, sighing. "Yes, I really mean to forget it, okay?"

"I'm puzzled. You used 'okay' in the same sentence and I'm pretty sure when a woman says it's okay, it's seriously *not* okay."

"Jesus, Max. Can we just back to get back to what we were doing?"

"But, we're good?"

"Yeah, whatever," she sighs loudly, not looking impressed at the sudden change of mood.

"Now I know you're still pissed at me. Malik said, Mason told him that when a woman says, 'whatever,' it's really them giving you the middle finger."

"For fuck's sake, Max, since when do you listen to anything your brothers tell you? At one point or another, one of them has done something to you. I can name a few. Mason spiked your drink with laxative, Malik crumbled Viagra in your dinner and I'm not even going to go there with Myles turning you blue. Your pubic hair was still blue a week later," she reminds me, looking pissed.

Christ, I don't win.

"You have a really good point," I point out, mulling it over in my mind.

"I do. Now kiss me and take me to bed before I walk out that door and never talk to you again."

"No need to be mean," I comment before slamming my lips to hers. I squeeze her ass in my hands tightly, loving how good it feels. I stumble towards the stairs, nearly tripping over the leftover takeaway boxes.

Lake pulls away, grinning down at me. "Just out of curiosity, what was Myles' fish called?"

She got me. My mind is too focused on getting in her pants to even think of a name. "Shut up," I smirk before claiming her lips once again.

The door to my room doesn't even close before we're ripping each other's clothes off. Our desperation for each other is making everything feel more erotic. Each touch, each caress, and each taste of her skin makes the sparks between us intensify, blowing my mind as well as Lake's.

The second her orgasm explodes around my dick, I release myself inside her. I've never cum so hard before, it's never been that intense, but to be fair, it makes sense. I've never had sex with someone I've loved before. It's just more proof of how much we belong together. I've slept with so many girls, and a few older women, but none, and I mean, not even one, comes close to how good it feels when I'm with Lake. I reckon just kissing her could get me off.

Breathing heavily, I roll us so we're facing each other. My hand reaches out, moving the hair covering Lake's face and chuckle at her flushed face.

"You're beautiful," I whisper, leaning forward and kissing her nose.

"So are you," she smiles, her cheeks flushed from our activities.

"Pfttt," I scoff. "I'm more of a ruggedly handsome or fit as fuck kind of lad. I am not fucking beautiful."

"On the outside maybe, but on the inside you are truly beautiful," she whispers, her face serious. My breath catches in my throat and I find it hard to respond. I mean, how do you respond to something like that? What's crazier is the fact she's the only person on this earth that truly knows the real me. I hide parts from my brothers, not wanting to come across as a pussy.

Looking at Lake, and I mean really looking at her, it all hits me at once.

She's my saving grace.

"One day, sweet boy, you will let someone inside that big heart of yours, inside your beautiful soul and when they do, they will own you," Nan whispers, her breath coming in short and deep pants.

I laugh. The thought of having a girlfriend, even at the age of eleven years old makes me want to gag. "No, Nan, don't be stupid."

"Not stupid," she smiles, reaching out for my hand. "Only a strong, determined woman will grab your attention long enough for you to really open your eyes and see her, and when that day comes, because it will, she will open your eyes to all the possibilities life has to offer. She will be your saving grace. And when you find her, you'll never want to be without her."

My Nan died a few days later but that conversation always stayed with me. It haunted me. I was always scared deep down that she was right and that I'd get trapped just like my mother did with my dad. If that was what relationships were made of then I wanted no part in it.

"Are you okay?" Lake whispers, her voice scratchy with worry.

"Yeah, babe. I love you, I really do," I tell her honestly, needing her to know.

"I love you too, Max Carter." Her smile is infectious and I can't help grabbing her hips, pulling her body flush against mine.

"You can never leave me again," I warn her, kissing her lightly.

"Won't ever be a problem again."

"I can't live without you. It hurt too much."

"Ditto," she whispers, her eyes watering. I pull her in for another kiss not pulling away until we're both breathless.

"Now what? What happens now?" I ask, unsure of what comes next. After all, this is the first and last relationship I'll ever be in. I don't want to fuck it up by being... Well, by being me.

"Nothing, we just *be*. Be together. Be happy. Be us. But first thing's first," she says seriously. "We need to get Myles back for the blue dye palaver," she chuckles, a mischievous grin tugging at her lips.

"Oh, you're naughty," I chuckle, rolling her onto her back and leaning above her.

"I've learned from the best," she whispers seductively, causing my dick to harden.

"Let's see what else I can teach you," I smirk before leaning down, tasting her lips with mine. "Yep, let's see what else I can teach you. We have a week's worth of classes to catch up with."

"Anything you can do I can do better," she smirks playfully.

I chuckle, a moan slipping from my lips when my cock slides into her wet folds. "Is that so?" I smirk confidently.

EPILOGUE

LAKE

ARRIVING OUTSIDE MAVERICK'S OFFICE, I sigh with disappointment when I see there is still someone waiting. We were meant to be finished interviewing for new tenants yesterday. We would have finished days ago if it wasn't for Max interrogating every possible tenant.

And when I say interrogating, I mean that in the nicest possible way because what he's doing would have the worst criminals crying.

With two coffees I carry on walking but stop short when I see a woman with a small little girl waiting patiently. I grin wide at the cuteness of the little girl. She has brown hair with tight curls. She has a cute button nose with rosy red lips but what has got me smiling is her eyes. They're huge, round and sparkly. They're bright blue, shining with so much innocence, so much love and faith that you can't help but smile at her. She's freaking adorable.

"Hey, would you like some paper and colouring pens?" I ask her gently, remembering the pack I found in Maverick's desk. Apparently the older rugged Carter has a thing for adult colouring books. Go figure.

"My mommy swaid to not twalk to stwangers," she whispers, making sure her mum doesn't hear. Her mum is watching me and has given me a soft smile so I'm not too worried she's going to drag her daughter away from me.

"Shall we ask Mummy then?"

She nods her head before turning to her mum excitedly. "Can weee hav som pwens?"

Her mum smiles at me. "Are you sure it's okay?" Her voice is soft like a lullaby and I know ten minutes in her presence and reading to me, I'd be asleep. Her mum looks much like her daughter. Brown hair, curly, but has some blonde highlights in it, and they both have wide, round, blue eyes with thick, long, black lashes.

"Positive. You're next right?" I ask, picturing the list of potential tenants in my head. I'm pretty sure she's the only woman who's on today's list but Max has been guarding that piece of paper like it belongs to the government.

"Yeah," she smiles, pulling the little girl onto her lap.

"I'll go see if he's finishing up. If he is I'll set up the paper and pens inside."

"Thank you."

I nod my head and get up from my knees, walking into the office without knocking. If he doesn't choose one person soon I'm going to strangle him.

Sitting behind the desk Max sits comfortably, wearing a suit. I have to admit that has been my favourite part because, boy, he looks fucking hot in a suit. He just didn't need to be wearing one for interviews, or at all. But of course, he needed to 'get into character'. His words, not mine.

"You can't just walk in here, babe," he scolds, rolling his eyes with annoyance.

The old chubby bloke with a beer belly hanging over his jeans eyes me like I'm his prey. I shudder, feeling revolted. He's old enough to be my granddad.

"Are you giving him the flat?" I ask, not caring if I'm being rude.

"Just two more questions, babe," he assures me, holding his hand up.

I roll my eyes and make work of getting the pens and paper ready while I listen to him address the old chubby bloke.

"Have you recently or in the past slept with a stripper?" Max asks and my eyes shoot to him. I shouldn't be surprised over his questions. The other day I walked in to him asking if they got angry at walls or doors. Apparently, their security deposit doesn't cover them punching walls and doors.

He also asked one lady if she was in a relationship, what the relationship was like and if she was planning on breaking up with said boyfriend any time soon.

They just keep getting more personal.

"I've had a stripper or two in my day," the chubby man boasts and I have to bite back a disgusted grunt.

"What football team do you support?" Max asks after writing something down on his pad.

"West Ham," the bloke grins, seeming proud. Max frowns, looking up disgusted. *Now* he looks disgusted. Not when the old bloke admitted to sleeping with strippers and looking proud of it.

"Okay, we will get in touch in the next couple of days if you have been chosen. I will say, Mr Billingham, your chances are slim."

"Is it because I don't have a job?"

"No."

"Is it because I asked for free admission to the strip club?"

"Nope."

"Is it because I do the occasional drug?" the chubby bloke asks again, looking confused. Why Max kept questioning him after he admitted to not having a job I'll never know. Maverick doesn't want someone unemployed, not wanting the hassle of chasing up rent.

"Nope. It's because you have shit taste in football," Max admits. "But we may be able to overlook that. We will be in touch."

Mr Billingham nods his head and walks out the door. As soon as it shuts behind him I whirl on Max.

"Because he supports West Ham?" I ask, biting my tongue.

"Babe," is all he replies.

"Nope. You need to pick one. That lady yesterday was nice enough and she worked full time. She also had a hearing aid so she wouldn't complain about noise."

"The walls are soundproof," he deadpans. "And she smelt funny. Didn't want her stinking the place out."

"What about Mr Lei? He seemed nice enough."

"He had shifty eyes, couldn't trust him," he shrugs.

"He was Chinese, Max."

"Can we just interview the next person?" he says.

"Yeah. And you better ask appropriate questions. She has her daughter with her," I warn him. "I like her."

"Okay," he says, waving his hands up at me, but I know him and the way his left eye is twitching... Well, that there is a sign he's freaking lying.

I walk to the door and the woman pokes her head up and smiles at me. Holding her daughter's hand she brings her into the room.

"She can sit over here and draw," I smile, and take the little girl's hand. She sits on the floor next to the coffee table and begins to draw. Once I'm happy she's alright I move back over to the desk, wanting to keep an eye on Max.

"Name?" Max asks stiffly. I groan, looking up to the ceiling. He could at least be polite. He acts more like a copper interviewing a criminal than finding the right tenant.

"Teagan, and the little girl is my daughter, Faith," she answers politely, even with Max's snappy tone. Girl has patience. I would have bitten his head off by now.

Her name too... What a beautiful name. It suits her.

Max opens his mouth but I jump in first, placing my hand on his arm and stopping him from ruining Maverick's chances of actually getting a tenant.

"I'll ask the questions," I smile tightly, giving Max a pointed look. He even has the front to pout like I'm taking his favourite toy away.

"I'm in charge," he states smugly, shuffling the papers before straightening them on the desk. Sighing, I fall back in my chair and wave my hand at him, giving him the go ahead. "So, Teagan, it says here you are twenty-two, is that correct?"

"Yes," Teagan smiles.

"I'm going to ask you a series of questions and I need you to answer honestly. If you fail to do so you're not only wasting my time but yours too."

I roll my eyes, wanting to smack him upside the back of his head. I send Teagan an apologetic smile. Poor woman is starting to look frightened, giving Max wary looks. Well, she's either frightened or worried she's brought her daughter around a crazy person.

"Max, you can't expect her to answer..." I begin, but Max puts his hand in my face, shushing me.

Oh, no, no he didn't just shush me. Turning in my seat I glare him down before addressing Teagan. "I'm so sorry, Teagan, he can get carried away. It's the first time he's been given any sort of responsibility. The last time he was given responsibility was when his brother asked him to watch over the house for a night. He nearly burnt the place down," I deadpan.

"No, I didn't. How was I supposed to know you weren't meant to put tins in the microwave?" Max shouts aghast.

"Mommy?"

Teagan laughs. "Faith, sweetie, it's okay. He's just playing."

"Otway," she smiles.

"Look, Mav put *me* in charge," he tells me again, still looking smug.

"You're not the president," I snap.

His eyes sparkle and I want to slap myself for stroking his ego. "I'd make a great prez, right T?"

"Teagan," she corrects politely.

"Just ask your precious questions, Max. Teagan, I apologise in advance."

She smiles softly in return, not seeming too worried about Max's strange behaviour. If it wasn't for her constant fidgeting I'd never guess she was nervous at all.

"Miss. T, first question is do you work? Can you afford the rent on time each month?" Max asks and from the corner of my eye I notice him pick something up. I shake my head when I look to find him sliding a pair of black glasses up his nose. He doesn't seem to feel my stare or he's choosing to ignore me. He just sits patiently, waiting for Teagan to answer.

"Yes, I work at the local doctor's surgery and at a bakery in town."

"Oh, you a doctor?"

"No," she smiles. "Just a receptionist."

Watching Max struggle to see the paper in front of him, his eyes squinting down at the page, I shake my head. Smirking, and feeling slightly annoyed still, I rip them from his face.

"Hey," he snaps.

"You don't wear glasses," I growl, wondering why I couldn't choose to love someone sane.

"I wanted to look serious," he frowns, looking pissed.

"Just get on with the interview, Mum is going to be here soon."

"Well, I would if you'd stop interrupting and undermining me in front of a potential tenant," he hisses. "How is she going to take me seriously, huh, Lake?" he remarks sarcastically.

"Yeah because wearing glasses and asking ridiculous questions, that's *really* going to get people to take you seriously," I roll my eyes.

"Are we really having our first fight?" he smirks, doing a three sixty with the heated conversation.

I can't help but smile. As much as he frustrates me I can't help but smile back at him.

"Just do your interview," I tell him, hiding my amused smile.

"Do you have a boyfriend?" Max asks.

"No." Her eyes dart between me and Max and I'm pretty certain she's thinking he's trying to pick her up. If only that were the case, he might actually seem sane then for all his random, stupid questions.

Max harrumphs in the back of his throat, acting like he doesn't believe her. "Can I see a picture of an ex?"

"Max?" I gasp, not having seen that question on any of his questionnaire sheets before.

"What?" he asks affronted, acting like it's a legitimate question to be asking when taking on a tenant. "I need to make sure she doesn't date shifty looking men."

"You thought Lee was shifty," I remind him.

"He was bald and had the bushiest eyebrows I've ever seen in my life. I think his hair stopped growing on his head so it could concentrate on his eyebrows," he says looking disgusted. "I'll even bet he has to use de-tangle spray to get a comb through um."

"You're ridiculous," I groan and turn to Teagan. She's watching us silently, looking curious and confused and I honestly don't blame her. If he's going off a new set of questions I pray for her sanity for when she leaves this room.

"No, I don't have an ex," she chokes out, looking uncomfortable, shifting in her chair.

Max raises his eyebrows, turning his head to the little girl drawing quietly in the corner. When she doesn't explain any further, he has the audacity to look disappointed in her.

"Are you on Facebook, Miss. T?"

"It's Teagan and I have an account, yes. But I don't really use it much."

"So are you one of those chicks who stalk people's pages?" he asks accusingly, sitting forward in his chair.

"No, I just like playing the games on there now and again," she shrugs. I'm just glad she hasn't bolted. I've got high hopes for this one and I'm not letting Max run her away.

"Are you a health fanatic?"

"With all due respect, what does that have to do with renting the flat?" she asks politely and I want to high five the chick right there.

Max looks confronted, uncomfortable for a second before putting his game face back on. "Well, let's say we become friends. Friends cook for each other. I don't want to turn up one night and boom, out of nowhere, with no warning, you present me with a salad or, heaven forbid, something veggie," he groans.

"Um.... okayyyy," she says, her eyes scrunched up in confusion.

"Now! This is where we need you to be honest. I'm going to ask you a few personal questions," he starts and both Teagan and I look at him with a 'really' look, but he ignores us, carrying on. "But if you knew the sh- stuff we've dealt with you'd totally understand my reasons for asking," he tells her before leaning in and whispering, "Just so you know, me and my bros have experience in these kind of cases."

"Alright," she says slowly looking at me for help. I shake my head subtly, silently telling her to just let him be. It's easier and safer that way.

"Are you on the run from something or someone?"

Her eyes widen and I'm pretty sure she's going to grab her daughter and flee from the room, but to my surprise, she doesn't.

"No."

"Have any parent issues?" he asks pointedly.

"My parents are both dead," she tells him, sorrow flashing in the depth of her eyes.

"Fuck. I'm sorry... No, wait. Were they good parents?"

"Seriously, Max?" I growl. There's one thing asking the questions he has been asking, but to be downright inappropriate is just asking for trouble. He could be at least a little more sensitive.

"The best," she whispers.

"I am sorry. I just needed to check. We've been shit out of luck when it comes to parents in our group," he explains.

"Hey," I snap, my turn to be affronted.

"Except hers. Hers are pretty great," he tells her, pointing to me. "If your application is accepted, how soon can you move in?"

"Actually we'd be pretty much ready to move in. My landlord is selling the building we're currently living in so we've had to start packing," she explains. That explains why she's put up with Max and his pestering. She needs to put a roof over hers and her daughter's head before they get kicked out.

"Last question before you leave. This is a make or break question too: Batman or Superman?"

"Oh no!" I mutter, my face heating from embarrassment. How is that a reasonable question?

"Superman?" she asks unsure. Max's face stays impassive, not giving anything away.

"I wike Batman," Faith butts in. I hadn't realised she was listening. She'd been so quiet sitting colouring that I forgot she was even here.

Teagan giggles, smiling at her daughter.

"Okay, I meant to say Batman," Teagan corrects. Max isn't listening, his eyes are lit up as he eyes the little girl.

"I like you, kid. Me and you are going to be good friends," he grins.

"I wike fwiends," she tells him, giving him a toothy grin, two little dimples popping out on her cheek.

Max chuckles. "Cool."

"When will we know?" Teagan asks, biting her bottom lip.

"We'll be in touch," Max tells her, standing abruptly and shaking her hand. I give him a look, wondering what he's playing at. He has the perfect candidate standing right in front of him and he's just going to let her walk out of here without an answer.

Shaking my head I walk around the table, giving Teagan a friendly smile. As we get closer to the door I lean in and whisper, "I think you've got this."

"I hope so, but..." she starts before looking at Max over her shoulder. Thankfully he's distracted by Faith handing him a picture.

"He's a nut but he's harmless. He is normal, I promise," I tell her, but honestly, I'm wondering how truthful my words are.

"Okay," she smiles before taking a deep breath. "Faith, baby, come on."

"Bye, Maxy," Faith waves.

"Bye, beautiful princess," he grins, making Faith giggle and run over to her mum.

The door shuts behind them and I whirl on Max. "What was *that* all about?"

"Um, did I miss something?" he asks confused.

"All those questions, Max, you went too far."

"I needed to know they weren't crazy," he scoffs.

"Max, if anyone needs an interview to make sure they're not crazy, it's you," I deadpan.

The door opens and we both turn to find Maverick standing in the doorway. I smile, giving him a friendly wave.

"He chosen anyone yet?" he asks me, not looking at Max once.

"I'm right here," Max deadpans.

"No, he's been... He's been Max. He asked the last person for a picture of her ex," I groan.

"He didn't?" Maverick bites out, his eyes narrowing.

"I can hear, you know?"

"Yep. She's your new tenant too, I decided. I like her and her daughter's cute."

"Okay," Maverick agrees easily.

"Wow! Wow! Wow! Wow! I'm in charge. I get to pick. When did Lake get selected to be tenant picker?" Max growls, glaring at me. I glare back, poking my tongue out at him.

"Come on, Maxy," I tease, Mum is going to be waiting in the car park.

"You can't boss me around, woman," he snaps.

"Just did."

"Need some balls, bro," Maverick chuckles as he follows us down the hall.

My phone beeps in my back pocket and I grab it, smiling when I see my mum's name. "Mum is going to be a few minutes late."

"It's okay, we can wait out in the... What the fuck?" Max snaps and my head whips up confused.

That's when Maverick takes off out of the exit and over the car park. Max follows and that's when my eyes find Teagan pinned up against her car, Faith crying nearby, screaming for her mum.

"Oh no," I gasp and run over, following Max and Mav. Mav is close when the attacker notices him and takes off. Maverick doesn't stop or slow down; he just carries on sprinting after the attacker.

When we reach Teagan and Faith, Teagan looks to be in shock, her hand on her throat and tears running down her face. Her other arm is clutching Faith and my heart breaks at seeing the fear in the poor little girl's eyes.

"Hey, what happened? Are you okay?" Max asks, finally back to himself, his voice laced with concern.

"I...I," Teagan shakes her head. I reach out to soothe her but she flinches. Max is concentrating off in the distance. Maverick is walking back, much slower, and clearly panting.

Bending down I run my hand up and down Faith's arm, hoping it's comforting her.

"Are you okay, Faith?" I ask gently.

"Bwad man hurrtt moommmy," she tells me, her bottom lip trembling.

"I know, honey," I say softly, at a loss on what to say to her.

Footsteps coming closer grab Faith's attention and her head snaps up. Her eyes go round before she launches away from me and her mum and dives for Maverick.

"Youu swaved ma mommyyy," she cries and as if on autopilot, Maverick bends down, lifting the little girl in his arms before straightening.

"It's okay, squirt, she's safe now," he rumbles then looks at Teagan for the first time. It's like his eyes stop, frozen, like they're memorising that moment, every inch of her as he stares unashamedly at Teagan. It's the same for her, neither one looking away. They both look dazed like they're drugged and a smile tugs at my lips.

Max must have the same idea running through his mind because when I turn to see if he's noticed their stare off he's looking at me grinning mischievously.

He winks at me before clearing his throat; both Maverick and Teagan jumping from whatever spell they were both under.

"Mav, meet Teagan, your new tenant," Max grins in a cheerful voice.

The End

SNEAK PEEK
FOUL PLAY

CHAPTER ONE

All my life I've stood out from the rest of my friends. I've always craved that independence all adults seemed to have. Every Monday when I wasn't at school or working, I'd be with my mum, food shopping and paying bills and I loved it.

As soon as I finished school I went straight into work, waitressing at a local restaurant to save up enough money to attend university. With my mum being a single parent she has always worked her ass off, and I guess it brushed off on me because I'm finally where I worked so hard to be.

Blinking away the blinding flash from my camera, I turn it around and look at the picture of me and my best friend grinning away.

I've been waiting for so long for this moment that I'm an emotional mess and wanted to photo document this very moment, so I never forgot it. I did the same not ten minutes ago when we picked the keys up from the estate agent, wanting to send as many pictures of my time here to my mom.

"It doesn't feel real," I whisper excitedly as I gaze up in awe at our building. There is five or six block of flats, but our building is one of the newest built and thanks to Allie's father and his connections we were able to rent one. Everything here is just feeding my excitement, the buildings are bigger, larger than life, brighter and newer and I can't help the squeal that escapes my lips.

"I'm seriously worried about your sanity," Allie, my best friend, now roomie says. We've been best friends ever since I can remember and even though we're polar opposites, we fit. I'm out-going, fun, bubbly, chatty and I love to party. Allie on the other hand is quiet, shy, anti-social, and book nerdy. But she's the bestest friend you could ever wish for. We balance each other out better than most friends or couples do. I get her to live a little, push her out of her comfort zone, and she grounds my free spirit. Don't get me wrong I take school work very seriously, but I also wouldn't lose sleep trying to achieve my goals; life's too short for that.

She also put off college so she could attend the same time as me. We were lucky her dad loves me and understood how much it meant to the both of us to be together through such a huge milestone in our life.

"You'd be more worried if I acted normal," I tease, opening the car door. We both get out and make our way to the back of the car, where we've stacked up all of our luggage.

"Willow, I worry about you period," Allie giggles, pushing her thick, black rimmed glasses up her nose.

"They should have a valet service," I groan, pulling out one of Allie's cases. And I say this with conviction because this must be the case that holds her library. "Why couldn't you buy all this new?" I ask her again.

"They're my books. I wouldn't ask *you* to buy new shoes," she says and to make her point, she takes the case that is specifically labelled shoes. So I love my shoes, what nineteen year-old wouldn't.

"Shall we go see our new home?" I grin, laughing when she nearly tips over backwards grabbing another case.

"Yes. Grab one more bag? I don't want to do more trips than we have to," she moans, and I laugh. I don't mind exercise, but Allie hates any form of it. She has no coordination whatsoever so I understand her hate for it.

Laughing, I heave one more bag out of the boot, chuckling when I nearly fall backwards on my ass too.

"Maybe we shouldn't have squeezed everything in," I mention, still laughing.

"I did tell you," Allie giggles, bumping her hip with mine. Grinning, I begin to roll my two suitcases along with me, ready to see my new home.

Allie grunts halfway up the path making me giggle harder. She looks so out of breath and we haven't even moved far from the car. You'd never believe she was from the richer side of town looking at her right now. She's wearing old, worn, faded jeans, with a Fries over Guys hoody. Her dark brown locks are a complete mess, piled high on her head in a messy bun. All that paired with her thick black rimmed glasses and you get a beautiful disaster. She's also the clumsiest person I've ever known. She proves it when she trips up the bottom step to the flats.

"Who put that there?" She grumbles and I have to stop, clutching my chest as I bend over laughing my ass off at her. "Don't," she warns with no heat. "Why couldn't Alec come and help again?"

"He had to meet his coach," I remind her. Alec and I met six months ago at open evening here at the university. We hit it off straight away and since he lived so close to my old town, we decided to make a go of things.

When a hard tug on my case nearly sends me flying I let out a piercing scream, my heart hammering in my chest.

"What the...," I begin, but I'm cut of when I see *his* handsome face. Letting out a squeal I jump into my best friends arms, wrapping myself around him like a kola bear. Logan and I have been friends since we were babies. Our parents knew each other, but have long lost their friendship for unknown reasons. But Logan and I kept up our friendship, not caring what our parents said. "Oh. My. Gosh. Logan. What are you doing here?" I squeal. He's still as good looking as he was the last time I saw him, which was briefly for a week last summer. His parents are always taking him away on his school breaks, so I've hardly seen him for the past two years. His hair is a little shaggier; his body still slim, but muscular, other than that he still looks the same.

All the girls at school lined up to date him and hated the fact I was so close with him. From the looks of a few passing girls, I can see nothing has changed.

He slides me down his body, his grin permanent on his handsome face and I can't help but grin back, my excitement doubling more than before.

"Hey Will," he greets, his voice deeper than I last heard from him.

"Logan. What are you doing here? I thought you were busy?" I remind him. He'll be on the university football team with Alec and from what Alec and Logan have both said, they had a practice this morning.

"Coach is letting us arrive later so he can fill in all the newbies," he grins, before looking over my shoulder. His grin slips a little, and I playfully slap his shoulder. "Allie," he nods.

Allie doesn't say anything but I can picture her stiff posture, her awkward nod as she greets him back. We all used to be friends, but around the same time our parents fell out, so did Logan and Allie. She's never made me understand her hatred towards him, but she doesn't make me feel like I have to choose between them. I do try and keep them separate, knowing how uncomfortable Allie gets when he's around.

He squeezes me into a tight hug again and I breathe him in. I've missed him so much, I can't help but be happy he's here. Perfect timing too.

Pulling away and taking a step back I notice he's brought a friend along with him. I didn't notice him at first, probably because I was in so much shock about seeing Logan so soon. We planned to meet tomorrow for breakfast, so I'd hyped myself up for then.

I smile at his friend even though his appearance and expression make me feel a little out of sort. It surprises even me because I can talk to anyone and everyone. My mum reminds me all the time that I could make friends in an empty room I'm that social. But something about Logan's friend makes me feel on edge.

Not wanting to be rude, I wave. "Hey, I'm Willow, this is my best friend Allie."

He grunts, giving us a head nod, his eyes scanning Allie with a mix of repulsion and lust, which startles me. I give Logan a questioning look, but he just grins, shrugging his friend's behaviour off. Knowing Logan wouldn't bring around someone to likely hurt us, I don't say anything more.

"Come on, give us your bags," he tells me. Not needing to be told twice I happily let go of the handles of my cases and let him take them from me. I'm about to move and help Allie with her cases when Logan's voice stops me. "Jamie, grab um off 'er man.'

I watch with wide eyes as Jamie - as Logan called him, takes the bags from Allie. Stiffly she makes her way over to me, her eyes wide with a flick of fear flashing in them.

"Shall we go see our new home, roomie?"

"Lead the way, my lady," she giggles and we begin to skip are way to the front entrance. With our fob, we let ourselves into the building, heading to the lift.

The ride to the eighth floor isn't long and before we know it, we're stepping out on our floor. As we reach the door, I have to hold back tears of joy and excitement. So instead of trying to process everything right there, I take my phone out of my back pocket, holding it up, ready to take a selfie.

Logan laughs, taking the phone from me so he can take the photo for us. "Still documenting, I see."

Grinning, I nod at him, smiling for the photo. I've always loved taking photos. It doesn't matter what they're of, I just click away. My favourite pictures are when I capture memorial moments though, ones like right now.

I'd love it as a kid when my mum would flick through photo albums, pointing out memories I'd long forgotten or hadn't been old enough to remember and tell me all about them. I'd stare down at the photo and I'd feel like I was there all over again, old memories resurfacing.

Logan hands me my phone back and I put it back in my pocket, ready for when I need it next.

"Do you have more shit in the car or is this everything?" he asks, but looks doubtful at the four suitcases resting next to the door, knowing us well.

"Yes. There are a few more cases in the back of the car. Allie's dad had most of it sent over with furniture," I smile."Are you going to be a gentlemen and grab them for us?" I wink, teasing him.

"It's why I'm here," he winks, snatching my car keys from my hand.

"Do you want to grab some food after?" I ask, excited to spend some time with him.

"I can't, Will. Need to get to practice," he tells me, an apologetic look flashing in his eyes.

Blinking back my disappointment, I force a smile. "It's okay. We're still on for tomorrow morning, though, right?"

"Yeah, I'm alright for breakfast," he grins. "See you in a sec."

We watch them leave in the lift before turning to each other. "His friend is really creepy," Allie comments straight off.

Laughing, I answer. "I know," I shiver. "Want to go in?"

"Yes," she giggles, clapping her hands. She's just as excited as I am about not being under parental supervision. Her probably more so than me. My mum was trusting and never made me feel suffocated like Allie's parents did with her. As long as I stayed safe, told her where I'd be and what time I'd be back, my mum was happy. I'd talk to her about anything, I still do. Allie's parents on the other hand were always on her back about her grades, her attendance, even going out. She wasn't a social person, but it was her parents who made her that way. They coddled her, gave her a strict curfew on the one day she was only allowed out. Even when she left school her parents only let up some. I was surprised when her dad agreed to let her move so far away.

I'm about to push open the door when the door behind us opens. There's two flats on each floor, on either side of the building, so when I hear the latch to the other side, I'm excited to meet our new neighbours.

Knowing Allie won't introduce herself or me for that matter, I try to calm myself down a little before approaching them. When I'm excited I tend to babble, and people never know how to take me.

Allie and I both turn at the same time, her body freezing the same time mine does. A lad my age or maybe older walks out, his eyes glued down at his phone. He's huge. Like mega freaking huge. He's wearing a jacket, but even that doesn't hide the tattoos peeking out from under his shirt, or the dangerous vibe bouncing off him. He looks broody, and from the way his powerful frame accumulates most of my attention, I'm stunned into silence. How can someone who looks so scary, so menacing, be so gorgeous at the same time? He has a strong cut jaw, dark piercing blue eyes and full lips. His hair is a dirty blonde colour, messy and unkempt and the urge to run my fingers through it is strong.

He truly is handsome and I have a hard time looking way at the rugged beast in front of me. The scruff on his jaw line makes him look even sexier. My breathing picks up the longer I stare at him, worrying me. I've never had a reaction like this to anyone. I've slept with two lads in my life, the second I'm still dating. And although I had chemistry with both, neither made me feel the way this guy does, it's empowering and already I'm addicted.

The door slamming startles me and I shake my head to clear my thoughts of the lad standing in front of me. It takes all my strength to look away but when I do, his friend turns, jumping slightly when he sees Allie and I standing there, side by side staring at them both.

Great! They probably think we're stalkers right now and will put in for a transfer or a restraining order.

"Well, helloooo, beautiful ladies. What can we do for you?" The softer look lad asks, his cheeky grin reaching his eyes.

My eyes flicker to the broody lad once more, and like lightening has struck me, a wave of electricity runs through my body when his eyes capture mine and for a brief, stolen moment it was just me and him. I'm actually struggling to breathe and the fact this other guy wants me to string together a sentence is a horrifying nightmare.

"I, um, I'm Allie, no, I'm Willow," I smile, shaking my head, more to myself than at him. "This is my best friend, Allie. We just moved in," I tell them, motioning to the door behind me.

"Cool beans. We live here," he grins, pointing to the door behind him using the same stiff action as me. "I'm CJ, this moody prick here is Liam, but call him Cole."

"Hey," I wave dumbly at him, my heart picking up once again when I notice him watching me intently. I have to look away quickly, my cheeks heating when I still feel his gaze on me.

No one has ever made me feel so on edge like this before or stunned me to a blubbering mess. I can talk most people under the table. There's never any awkwardness when I'm around to fill in the silence, but right now, I'm wishing Allie would help me out and say something witty or anything really, just to show we're normal.

When CJ looks over to Allie, his eyes flash with something I don't recognise. It's gone almost instantly, but it was definitely there.

"Hey," Allie whispers, and I watch nervously as she pushes her glasses up her nose and tucks in a lose strand of hair behind her ear.

Self-consciously I let out a snort mixed with a giggle as I eye my best friend. She's a nervous and shy person normally, but this is because of CJ. Straight off the bat I can tell she likes this him already. She only ever cares about her appearance when she likes someone, it's her tell. Any other time she doesn't care what she looks like or what people think about her.

When her angry glare snaps to me, I straighten, instantly feeling bad for embarrassing her. Sometimes it's hard to control my reactions to things. Once, I was being told off by the school principle, and I was that intimidated, I started laughing. Not because I found anything funny, but because the situation was so awkward, it was either laugh or cry.

"Well, we...um...we should get going in," I announce, smiling politely, my gaze flickering to Cole once more. He's still staring intently at me with a scowl on his face, like he's trying hard to reach into my soul. The look unnerves me so much I begin shifting on my feet.

"If you ever need anything; sugar, milk, bread, knock on the door downstairs. We never have shit in unless creature of the night here goes shopping," CJ jokes. "I only have to think about doing something domestic and I break out in a rash."

Cole grunts not too pleased with his friend and I can't help but smile. They remind me of Allie and me. They're total opposites but fit.

CJ reminds me of myself, easy-going, fun, and the loud one of the group. His eyes are dark, and from the dim lighting in the hallway, I can't tell if his are hazel or brown. His hair is jet black which compliments his tanned skin tone. It also makes his pearly whites stand out. They're so freaking white; I'm debating whether it's rude to ask him who his dentist is.

"We'll remember that. But the same goes, if you need anything; sugar, milk," I repeat, grinning. "Just knock the door. Allie has a thing about being stocked up on necessities in case of a zombie apocalypse."

"Willow," Allie hisses under her breath.

"Oh crap. No. You can't. Not yet anyway. We haven't had time to do a food shop."

CJ throws his head back laughing. I watch, enjoying the sound and the look on his handsome face. When he gains his composure, his eyes flicker once again to Allie, a light sparking in them which intrigues me more. He doesn't seem to hide it this time either. Turning to gauge Allie's reaction I'm not surprised to find her blushing with her head down.

"Walking Dead marathons round yours then?" CJ smirks, his eyes still on Allie. Her head snaps up to that and I grin. She tries to make me watch the show but with all that blood and gore, my stomach couldn't handle it. Plus, she can't just watch one, she'll watch reruns over and over.

The elevator dings announcing its stop on the floor and we all turn to the opening elevator. Logan and Jamie step out of the lift talking to each other in low voices. When they both look up the atmosphere in the hallway thickens. Tension radiates off all the lads and instinctively my eyes seek out Cole's and I'm confused when I find his eyes narrowed dangerously on Logan.

Apart from Allie, I've yet to meet a person who doesn't like Logan. Yes he had a few girlfriends or fuck buddies turn on him in the past, but I was never a witness to that. And to be fair, most of them expected more from him than he was willing to give. But he was always upfront from the very beginning.

Things go from bad to worse when Logan opens his mouth. "What the fuck are you doing here?" he growls.

What the lovin' vodka.

"Logan," I snap, furious at him for being so rude. "These are our neighbours,

CJ and Liam."

Hoping he hears the clear warning in my voice, I pray he plays nice. I turn to my new neighbours, offering them an apologetic look. Cole seems to be looking at me with a mixture of disappointment and revulsion, while CJ is still got his eyes narrowed on Logan and Jamie. I can understand Jamie, the guy looks freaking shifty, but I don't understand his hostility towards my best friend.

"I know who they are babe," Logan assures me, a bite to his voice.

Babe? Who the ducking hell is he calling babe? It better not be me, that term of endearment grates on my nerves. It's the pet name most lads use for their woman because they can't be assed to just say her name.

"Well then, saves me introducing you doesn't it," I smile widely, pushing two cases inside the door, trying to hide the fact I'm a little peeved off with him.

"You know him?" Cole asks, speaking for the first time. His voice is a deep rumble, the sound sending shiver all through my body. I've never felt anything like it and it catches me off guard. Unconsciously, I squeeze my thighs together, taking in a deep breath.

"Yes," I answer softly, moving to let Allie scurry past to push the other two cases inside the door. Mean time I don't move my gaze away from Coles, staring intently into the deepest blue of eyes I've ever seen. For some reason he doesn't like my answer and I wish I knew why. He dismisses me and I'm not going to lie and say it didn't hurt, because it did, but when he turns his eyes back to Logan, they turn hard, cold even, but what has my back up is the fact Logan is smirking, like he just won some trophy I'm unaware of.

"We'll be seeing you," CJ winks, his eyes holding promise as he takes in Allie, who is currently hiding behind me in the doorway.

When they're gone Logan turns his angry eyes to me, cutting me off before I even have chance to open my mouth.

"Stay away from them, they're bad news."

Not taking his warning as a friendly gesture, but as an order, my back straightens. I hate being told what to do. Not because I'm rebellious, but because I'm a good judge of character and can make my own choices. I know the difference between right and wrong and something in my gut is telling me that CJ and Cole are harmless. Even if one looks like a giant beast that could crush me only using one hand.

"I'll do no such thing. And before you go on, let me remind you that I'm my own person. I get that you're going all big brother on me, wanting to protect me, but I can take care of myself."

His expression softens just a tad, but the hardness and anger is still there, lingering behind his eyes. It worries me some because I've never seen this side of him. He's always been friendly, caring, and loyal, not once since we've been friends have I ever seen him that angry or determined before. It makes me want to ask what the story behind it is, but I never get involved in other people's business. It always gets messy when you insert yourself into someone else problems. Don't get me wrong, I'd do anything for my friends, stick by them, but this is different. There's obviously more going on them a simple group of lads disliking each other.

"Okay, Will. We have to go, but I'll see you in the morning," he smiles, and it doesn't pass my notice that he doesn't apologise.

"Yeah. Alec will be meeting me here around nine," I remind him, not sure if I actually mentioned Alec coming or not. They haven't met yet and I just hope he doesn't act like he did with my neighbours with Alec. Having your best friend and boyfriend hating each other isn't something I need in my life right now.

"Oh yeah," he grunts, a frown appearing for a few seconds before smiling at me. "Can't wait to meet him."

"Good," I grin, glad he's happy about meeting him. I move forward, giving him a friendly hug. No matter what just happened, it still doesn't change the fact I've missed him like crazy. "I've missed you."

"Missed you too, Will," he grins, leaning down to kiss my forehead. I close my eyes smiling, lovin' the fact I've got my friend back.

His mate gives him a subtle nod, his phone in hand. Getting the drift, I smack Logan lightly on the shoulder. "Get going before your coach makes you go back in the morning," I scold him.

"See you in the morning, babe" he winks, then looks over my shoulder. "Bye Allie," he shouts in a too friendly tone. I roll my eyes and push him down the corridor. Once he and his friend are finally out of sight, Allie drags me backwards inside the flat.

"That was the weirdest encounter I've ever witnessed," she admits quietly.

"Ha, mine too," I laugh. "How fit are our neighbours though?" I grin giddily.

"I didn't notice," she says, shrugging it off, but I notice her cheeks turning pink once more. Instead of questioning her over it, I grab her arm excitedly, dragging her into the narrow kitchen ahead of us. It's open up on the left hand side of us, looking out into the front room. There's everything we need, cooker, washer, fridge freezer, sink etc. I open up some cupboards, most empty, some filled with dishes and plates before dragging Allie back out and into the front room. It's spacious and filled with a few boxes I know holds some more of our books. I know I took the mick out of Allie earlier about all her books, but I'm also a huge fan of romance novels. Anything to do with bikers, the mob, or hell, even a hot cowboy, I'm reading that bad boy. Allie on the other hand prefers softer, lighter romance novels, sci-fiction and all that.

"Can't wait to put my books on there," she squeaks, clapping her hands as she eyes the already built bookshelf.

"Such a nerd," I tease.

"Like you're not planning on putting your books on there," she giggles.

"Most of mine are signed paperbacks and just for show. I read on my kindle," I remind her, winking.

"Still don't know how you do that. I can't imagine not being able to turn a page," she sighs.

"You still can, you just press the screen instead of an actual page," I grin.

She shakes her head, and I know there's no use trying to talk her into buying a kindle. I tried to lend her mine once and she complained she couldn't get into the book, it didn't feel right.

We move back down the hall, passing the front door and the entry to the kitchen before stopping in front of the first bedroom on the left.

A bed is already set up, the bed just needing to be made in the far corner. A desk is near the door, with another bookshelf. There's a wardrobe and a chest of drawers but not much else.

"This is my room," Allie grins, turning to me. I grin back and move out, moving to the next door on the left which is a bathroom.

"Wow!" I comment, impressed at the size of the tub. It's also got a shower built inside and I can't wait to test that beauty out. I love baths, but showers? You can't beat a good shower.

Moving out and into the hallway once more, we come to the last door, the door to my room. Opening it, I grin at the same furniture that's in Allie's room, already set up in mine. Her dad really did go all out, refusing to let my mum pay for any of the furniture. He nominated her as the house warming gift buyer, which she did, buying us bed sheets, towels, and an emergency bank account with a low amount of funds. She had it put in mine and Allie's name and under no circumstances can we break into it unless it's for an emergency.

My bed room is slightly bigger than Allie's, but not by much and it's only because mine has a built in wardrobe. Because of my clothes and shoes obsession, Allie made it clear I was to have this room, otherwise I'd only put my stuff in her wardrobe anyway.

"I love it," I gush, and jump up and down on my new bed.

"It's freaking amazing," she giggles, jumping up on my bed with me. Together we jump up and down holding hands, falling into a heap of laughter on the soft mattress.

"Welcome to Whittall University," I grin, feeling like my life is just about to begin.

CHAPTER TWO

A LEC IS RIGHT ON TIME FOR THE first time since I've known him. Usually I have to give him a time an hour earlier to meet because otherwise I'd be waiting around for ages for him to turn up.

It's why I'm in so much of a rush, tripping over boxes and stubbing my toe as I make my way to the front door. I'm actually running late for the first time ever. Had Allie not woke me up, I'd still be asleep.

Allie and I decided to toast our new apartment with a bottle of wine and what was supposed to be one glass, turned into a whole bottle. Which is the reason why I'm currently half an hour behind, kind of hung-over and a little pissed at Alec for choosing today of all days to be on time. It doesn't matter that it was me that mentioned having one more knowing I'm not a big drinker, or the fact it was me that forgot to set her alarm.

Go figure.

Managing to make it to the door whilst hoping on one foot, I fling the door open, not looking up.

"You're early," I tease Alec, trying to cover up my grimace.

"You said nine," a voice that doesn't belong to Alec, but to Logan says.

I look up grinning ear to ear when I see my best friend again. "Hey. Sorry, I thought you were Alec. I told *him* eight. He's always late," I tell him, rolling my eyes playfully.

Logan grunts, looking displeased at my admission. I wave him off and move forward, pulling him into a hug.

Pulling back, Logan's looking down at me with a huge grin on his face. I groan when I realise that I'm wearing my blue moon and stars pyjama's.

"They were the only pair that I could find last night," I defend which makes him laugh. "Let me go change."

"By all means, don't let me stop you," he flirts. This isn't new; this is just in his nature. Playfully rolling my eyes I punch him in the shoulder before rushing down the hall to my room.

I don't waste any time as soon as the door shuts behind me, in getting changed. I've just pulled my top off, braless, when the door to my room flies open. Screaming, I rush over to my bed, grabbing the dirty shirt that I had on yesterday from the end of my bed and cover myself up.

"Logan," I scold, once I'm somewhat descent.

"Sorry," he grins, not looking sorry one bit as his eyes slowly rake my body up and down, seeming pleased with himself.

"What are you doing in here?" I hiss out, embarrassed he just saw me naked.

"Come to see if you wanted me to make a cuppa for ya while I wait," he grins.

"What the fuck?" Alec rumbles, standing in the doorway with a thunderous expression upon his handsome face. His blue eyes narrow on Logan and he looks like he's ready to start a fight.

"It's not what you think," I rush out to assure him, clutching my top tighter to my bare chest.

"And what is it that you think I'm thinking?" he bites out, a tick in his jaw.

"Chill mate. It's my bad. I walked in to see if she wanted a cuppa, I should have knocked first," Logan explains to Alec before turning back to me. "I'll let you get changed."

Alec stands silently, seething, keeping his eyes locked on me. I give Logan a grateful smile and want to slap him when he winks at me before walking out. I'm just happy Alec didn't see him.

When Logan leaves, Alec's jaw tightens before he turns, slamming the door shut, running his fingers roughly through his chestnut hair. He takes a few deep breaths before turning back to me looking unpleased. I don't know what to say. His anger is warranted, but it's not like I'm happy about Logan seeing my tatas either.

"What?" I ask, throwing my top on the bed, not caring about my nudity in front of him. Kneeling on the floor, I rummage through my cases until I come across a fresh pair of underwear and an outfit. I keep it simple, knowing after breakfast Allie and I need to go grab some things from the supermarket and unpack all of our boxes.

Alec stands by the door, watching me change into a simple t-shirt and leggings, brushing my hair and putting on minimal makeup. I'd already showered and brushed my teeth before I heard the door knock, hence the reason I was still wearing my pyjamas. I didn't want to open the door just wearing a towel, so I threw them back on.

"Do I need to be worried?" He asks once I'm finished. It's not the first time he's stressed out over this. No matter how many times I explain that Logan and I are just friends, he doesn't buy it.

"No. I told you, we're just friends," I smile, walking up to him. Wrapping my arms around his neck, I lean up on my tip toes and kiss him good morning, loving the feel of his soft lips. "Hmmmm," I mumble dreamily, a small smile on my face as I pull away.

"I don't like it. I don't like him, but for you I'll try Willow," he says, leaning in to kiss me back. It's all I can ask for really. He's always had a hard time with my close friendship with Logan, always getting annoyed with the million texts he would send. I did explain that Logan was just excited about me starting university this term, because until I came to the open evening, Logan and I only text a few times a week, but then it turned into everyday. But being a typical boy, Alec would just grunt, and make me put my phone on silent.

"Thank you, Al," I smile, genuinely thankful to him for willing to try. I'm also happy to avoid the headache it would come with if they argued constantly. "Let me go see if Allie's ready and we'll go out for breakfast."

He nods, looking back at the bedroom door with a hard jaw. He's thinking about having to go out there and play nice, it's written across his face.

"Don't be long," he warns, kissing me once more before leaving the room.

Grabbing my warm cardigan, I sprits on some perfume before stepping into my boots. Reaching out for my phone that is still on charge, I go in search for my handbag amongst the mess on my floor.

I don't bother knocking on Allie's door when I leave my room. I just walk right in, shocked when I find her sitting in her bed reading a book, still wearing her pyjamas.

"Why aren't you ready?" I squeak, hating the thought of having to wait with Alec and Logan alone while we wait for her to get ready.

She looks up from her book, giving me a dry look before answering. "As much as I love my food, I'm going to have to pass."

"There's no food in," I remind her, looking at her quizzically. She loves her food, so I hope my bait works and she decides to come. She won't go long without something to eat anyway, so I have high hopes.

"Do I have to come?" she moans, sulking.

"Yep," I say, popping the P. "Alec and Logan haven't gotten off to a great start," I wince. "I need you there, please," I plead.

She scoffs, but when she sees me giving her my puppy dog eyes, her shoulders slump, giving in. When she sees me grinning, she scowls unhappily, knowing she just got played.

"Give me ten minutes," she says jumping out of bed. I rush over to her excitedly, jumping into her arms, hugging her.

"Thank you, thank you. Love you roomie," I gush happily, kissing her face.

"Gooo," she giggles, pushing me out of the door.

"I'll drive. That way you can sit up front with me and tell me everything that I've missed back home," Logan declares, wrapping his arm around my shoulders as we walk to the car park. The movement pushes Alec out of the way and I notice him glare at Logan from the corner of my eye. Ready to decline Logan's offer, not wanting Alec to feel pushed out, I'm stopped when Allie asks Alec something about practice, easing the tension between the two. And that is why I love my best friend. She knows Alec well enough to know that anything to do with football takes up all of his attention.

Taking advantage of Allie's diversion, I elbow Logan in the stomach. He grunts in pain, but still manages to give me a dirty looking smirk.

We all jump in the car, Alec not happy about sitting up back with Allie while I'm up front with Logan. We fill the car with conversation about life back home, not that I had much to share.

When we finally arrive at our destination, I may have done a happy dance in my head. The tension in the car was stifling. Now I'm a girl who can ease the most awkwardness of situations, but even I have to admit, the tension in the car was strained, making me feel uncomfortable.

Needing air, I jump out of the car, ready to make my way over to Alec. Logan intervenes before I can reach him, pulling me into his chest with a grin on his face.

"Um," I say, worried about Alec flying off the handle, knowing he has a short fuse. Logan's actions are friendly, but I know it may not seem like that to Alec. I'm not naive.

"Alec? Its okay isn't it if I sit by my girl? I haven't seen her for so long. We've got so much shit to catch up on."

Alec looks at me briefly before staring at Logan. "No, go ahead. Who am I to get in between *friendship?*" he replies dryly.

Entering the cafe we grab one of the empty tables, sitting down. Logan takes a seat next to me whilst Alec sits in front of me, Allie next to him. She doesn't look too pleased about sitting in front of Logan. There is no winning in this situation.

Today is really not happening. Nothing is going right. Wanting to just get on with it, I grab the menu, scanning it.

"I think I'm going to have..." I start, still thinking it over.

"Big breakfast, extra bacon," Alec and Logan chuckle simultaneously.

"Piss off," I laugh, flipping them both off, hating how well they know me.

"Want a coffee or a cup of tea?" Alec grins.

"Coffee. Definitely coffee," I sigh dreamily.

"I'll get it. What about you Allie, what do you want?" Alec asks her and I love that he always includes her, never making her feel like a third wheel.

"I'll have the same as Willow, but no mushrooms," she answers, scrunching her nose up in disgust.

"I'll get these, my treat," Logan steps in.

Surprisingly it's Allie's who's head snaps up first, an incredulous look upon her face.

When Alec opens his mouth, I know it's not going to be pleasant. Not wanting an argument to start I cut in.

"Nope. It's Alec's turn to buy me and Allie brekkie," I chuckle.

"He lost a bet," Allie states smugly.

"Technically it wasn't really a loss. I'd buy you brekkie either way," he chuckles, some tension easing from his body.

"We know," I giggle, reaching over for his hand, taking it in mine.

"I'll come an' order with you," Logan tells him, pushing his chair back a little too quickly.

Once they're out of earshot, Allie turns to me with wide eyes, pushing her glasses up her nose.

"What the hell did I miss this morning? And why is Logan acting like that for?" she asks confused, her eyes looking over her shoulder at the two lads standing at the counter ordering.

"Long story," I sigh, feeling a headache coming. "And Logan seems normal to me. But I can tell there's some tension between the two of them. I don't why though. I'm with Alec, and I'd never look at Logan in an intimate or romantic way," I tell her, which is the truth. Logan may be good looking, but I don't lust after him. I don't have a secret crush, or harbour any feelings for him. I've never seen him as anything but like a big brother.

"I dunno. Logan does seem to be acting stranger than normal and that's saying a lot coming from me because I think he's a weirdo normally."

I roll my eyes. She won't bad mouth him in front of me, she never has. She does steer conversation away from him, and always avoids seeing him. But she's managed to keep her dislike for him from affecting me. Sometimes I do wish I knew what made them fall out. I've always wondered.

"He's probably just looking out for me," I tell her.

"Logan only ever looks out for himself," she mutters.

I don't get a chance to reply to her comment or ask her what she meant because Alec and Logan arrive back at the table, drinks in hand.

"My hero," I gush, smiling widely up at Alec as he hands me my coffee. Immediately I breathe in the coffee, the aroma relaxing me.

"You break my heart," Logan teases good-naturally to which I just roll my eyes before turning back to Alec.

"How is your room?" I ask. He's staying in Kings Hall on the university grounds and I know he wasn't looking forward to sharing a room.

"Ahh, I stayed there my first year here. It's fucking small," Logan comments, sitting back in his seat, blowing on his drink.

"Nah, I like it," Alec answers, his eyes narrowing slightly on Logan.

"Really?" Logan asks, his voice doubtful. "Wait until you get a place of your own, you can have as many chicks over as you want," he smirks, winking at Alec.

"Helloooo," I snap, clicking my fingers in his face, feeling offended.

Alec doesn't look happy either with his comment and answers straight away. "Happy with Willow."

"Oh yeah. Sorry. Who wouldn't be happy with my Will," he grins, looking down at me, hand on my shoulder.

"No offence, but she's not your Will," Alec bites out.

"Okay, I'm actually Allie's, Will. So let's drop it," I plead, trying to keep my tone light, hating this is getting off to a bad start.

"Sorry. I guess I'm not used to sharing her," Logan winces, looking apologetic.

"But she wasn't yours to begin with," Alec snaps, his fist clenching.

The waitress walks over with our tray of food, interrupting the thick tension surrounding the table.

"Thank you," I smile, watching her walk away before turning back to a fuming Alec.

"Calm down, he didn't mean anything by it. Did you Logan?" I make eye contact with Logan, pleading with him silently to make this right.

"Nah, mate. I guess I'm not used to seeing her with anyone."

"That's because you haven't been in her life for the past two years," Alec snaps.

"I've been pretty busy," Logan grits out, displeased with Alec's accusation.

"Will you both pack it in?" I hiss across the table.

"Yeah, but it doesn't give you the right to act like you're the one with my girl," Alec fumes.

"If your that insecure about your relationship then that's on you," Logan says calmly.

The argument is escalating and it's not getting them anywhere but riled up. I've tried to open my mouth to say something a few times, to get them to calm down, but one or the other speaks up, their voices rising and gaining attention of the other customers.

"Fuck you. Fuck you! You've done nothing but try to pull her away from me since you arrived this morning. And what was that, walking into her room whilst she was getting changed? You don't do that fucking shit," Alec growls, the veins in his neck pulsing.

"This is getting out of hand. Alec, Logan has already said he's sorry about earlier and he's just being my friend. You're taking this all the wrong way," I tell him softly, hoping to calm him down.

"You seriously don't see what he's trying to do?" he yells, pushing his chair back roughly, standing up.

"Your blowing this out of proportion," I tell him, my voice pleading, almost begging for him to see how irrational he's being.

He shakes his head down at me, disappointment in his eyes. "Enjoy your breakfast," he snaps giving Logan one last narrowed gaze.

"Alec, don't go," I plead before he leaves, hating that this is happening.

"I can't sit here and watch him be all over you," he says to me sadly, his voice still holding a hard edge.

"Please," I beg again, my eyes burning with unleashed tears as he walks away.

"Let him go," Logan says gently, his hand on my arm, stopping me from chasing after Alec.

"What just happened?" I whisper to the table.

Allie puts her coffee down, her food too untouched and grabs her coat from the back of her chair.

"I'm going to go and let you two catch up. Go easy on Alec though, Willow. You're his girlfriend and he just feels threatened," she tells me softly, her eyes flickering nervously towards Logan.

"It's Logan," I say furiously. "He can't seriously believe something would be going on between the two of us."

I'm actually a little disgusted that he would even imply such a thing. I've told Alec so many times that Logan is like a brother to me, a brother I never had. My mum never remarried after my dad or had a new relationship, so I've always been the only child. Having Logan looking out for me all through school felt like having a big brother, that was the same age.

"Cheers babe," Logan sniffs, his jaw clenched.

"I didn't mean it in a bad way," I tell him. Can I dig a bigger hole for myself?

"Maybe explain it better to Alec and maybe Logan can back off with the touchy feely shit when Alec's around," Allie suggests attentively, seeming uncomfortable bringing it up.

"Jealous, Allie?" Alec sneers. "Maybe you need to get laid?"

"Logan," I snap, not liking what's gotten into him. There's no need to speak to Allie like that, not when she's just trying to help.

"Willow, it's fine. I'm going home to start unpacking. When you get back we'll go shopping," she smiles.

"Okay," I agree, feeling another headache coming. Allie leans down, kissing my cheek before exiting the cafe, leaving me alone with Logan.

"Well that was eventful," Logan mutters.

"Don't," I warn, hoping he's not about to bad mouth Alec or Allie in front of me.

"I'm joking. Maybe we should just stay away from each other. I don't want to be the reason you're unhappy," he says sadly, looking ready to bolt.

"No! Please don't say that. I'm not losing my best friend when I just got him back because my boyfriend doesn't like our friendship. He's going to have to get used to having you around and in my life," I tell him, hating that it's come to this. The two will be playing football together; I don't want to get in the way of that too.

"Okay, but if he doesn't like it and starts getting pushy with you, give me a bell."

"He's not violent," I scoff, smiling at his over-protectiveness.

"You never know. They always say to watch out for the quiet ones," he teases, but there's a seriousness in his voice that I can't ignore.

"Shut up," I laugh, playing it off as his protectiveness over me.

"You excited about starting uni?" he asks, changing the subject, to which I'm grateful for.

I grin. I am more than excited. "Yeah, we start next week. What about you?"

"I'm sad I've only got a year left before I have to leave you again," he pouts. "I want to spend as much time with you as possible."

"I'll always be in your life," I grin, nudging him with my shoulder. I pick up my fork, digging in to my lukewarm breakfast.

"I know," he grins, eating his own food. Swallowing, he turns to me. "When do you find out about the uni paper you were chattin' on about?"

I handed in a course paper, an article on a woman who was kidnapped when she went hiking in the outback's of Australia. That's what got me into the top journalism class the university has to offer, but it's not the paper that will get me into Whittall university newspaper.

"From what the guidance councillor was telling me, I'll have to do another article before they will enter me into working with the university paper. Plus, they'll need to determine if I have a place on their paper."

"That's great though isn't it?" Logan grins around a mouthful of food.

"Yeah. The class only has a limited amount of students. I'm hoping to get a place, but I'll also be job hunting in the meantime."

Logan frowns. "Do you need money? I've got some," he rushes out, but I stop him offering, holding my hand up.

"No! No! I'm fine, I have money. I just want to save enough money over the next year so my mum doesn't have to worry about next year's bills and stuff."

"How is your mum?"

"Good," I smile, hoping he doesn't see the nerves twitch in my eye. My mum doesn't exactly know about Logan still attending the university. She presumed he finished last term and I didn't disagree. I don't think she would have let me attend this uni, or she would have demanded to come with me.

Since mum and Allie's parent's fell out with Logan's, my mum has hated me hanging out with him. She only got off my back about hanging out with him when he left for college, never bringing him up again.

"I'm surprised she let you attend the same college as me," he smirks, knowing my mum's strong dislike for him and his family.

"She's not that bad," I lie, and quickly change the subject. "So, you want to hang out after, come shopping with me and Allie?" I ask.

"How about I come over with a takeaway and a movie tonight?"

"Yeah, okay. Nothing gory though," I remind him, giving him a warning look.

"Wouldn't dream of it babe," he winks. I want to smack this 'babe' shit out of him. I let it lie, not wanting anymore drama and finish my breakfast in silence.

Now all I have to do is make things right with Alec. One thing is for sure, I'm not running to him to apologise, he can come to me. I just hope he's not stubborn enough to let my friendship with Logan come between *our* relationship.

We finish breakfast, talking about places around the university and other random topics. We stay for a while longer, catching up like old times before he drives me back home where we say goodbye.

AUTHOR'S NOTE

I'm praying that I did Max's character justice and that you enjoyed his novel. I can't even tell you how hard it was writing his story.

I had to draw a line between charming and arrogant, funny and cocky and so on when it came to Max. He's not one or the other; he's a character that hovers over the line. He's everything and more. Trying to keep his identity and his characteristics had been so hard throughout the whole book. There were times when he was in a serious situation and I'd have to make sure he was still Max without making him sound like a jerk. I had worked so many nights trying to get this right so I really hope all that hard work paid off for you all.

First off, I wanted to thank all the readers who have supported the Carter brother series from the beginning.

Your support means everything to me.

Your emails, reviews, messages, and posts that I get daily from so many of you have inspired me. You've driven me to become a better writer. It also gave me the confidence boost that I needed. For that, I'll be forever grateful.

To Rachel, my PA, who I regretfully forgot to mention in my last book *sad sighs*, thank you.

We may not have met and we might never get to meet, but I'll never find another friend like you. Even when you post scary doll pictures on my wall I still love you.

Thank you. Thank you for taking the time out of your life to help little old me get release posts sent out. For *making* my beautiful release posts and just generally being there for me when I've needed someone to talk to. But even without the things you do as my PA, you'd still be an amazing person.

Love you woman.

I'm not good at writing these, so I'm just going to finish with a huge thank you to everyone who helps the process of this book getting published. I'm not going to name names because let's face it, I'm bound to forget one.

Thank you, to each and every one of you. Whether you're a blogger, reader, friend, PA, editor, cover designer or a beta reader, this message is to all of you. Thank you.

OTHER TITLES BY LISA HELEN GRAY

If you enjoyed Max's story make sure you check out the other books in the
Carter Brother Series.

Malik ~ Book One (Malik and Harlow's book)
Mason ~ Book Two (Mason and Denny's book)
Myles ~ Book Three (Myles and Kayla's book)
Evan ~ Book 3.5 (Evan and Kennedy's book)
Max ~ Book Four (Max and Lake's book) Now Available
Maverick ~ Book Five ~ Coming late 2016

Forgotten Series
Better Left Forgotten ~ Book One (Cailtyn and Cage's book)
Obsession ~ Book Two (Danni and Nate's book)
Forgiven ~ Book Three (Kelly and Dante's book)

Whithall University
Foul Play ~ Book One (Coming July)
Book Two ~ September 2016

Standalones
If I could I'd wish it all away ~ (Being republished and reedited. Coming July)
Almost Free ~ (2017)

ABOUT LISA

Lisa Helen Gray is Amazon's bestselling author of the Forgotten Series and Carter Brother series.

She loves hanging out, but most of all, curling up with a good book or watching movies. When she's not being a mom, she's been a writer and a blogger.

She loves writing romance novels, ones with a HEA and has a thing for alpha males.

I mean, who doesn't!

Just an ordinary girl surround by extraordinary books

Hey, if you haven't already, make sure you head over to my social pages and give them a like.

Printed in Great Britain
by Amazon